ATLANTIS REDEEMED

THE WARRIORS OF POSEIDON SERIES
BY ALYSSA DAY

Atlantis Rising
High Prince Conlan's Story

Atlantis Awakening
Lord Vengeance's Story

"Shifter's Lady" from *Shifter*
Ethan's Story

"Wild Hearts in Atlantis" from *Wild Thing*
Bastien's Story

Atlantis Unleashed
Lord Justice's Story

Atlantis Unmasked
Alexios's Story

Atlantis Redeemed
Brennan's Story

Don't miss *Atlantis Betrayed*, Christophe's story,

ATLANTIS REDEEMED

A Warriors of Poseidon Novel

ALYSSA DAY

BERKLEY SENSATION, NEW YORK

THE BERKLEY PUBLISHING GROUP
Published by the Penguin Group
Penguin Group (USA) Inc.
375 Hudson Street, New York, New York 10014, USA
Penguin Group (Canada), 90 Eglinton Avenue East, Suite 700, Toronto, Ontario M4P 2Y3, Canada
(a division of Pearson Penguin Canada Inc.)
Penguin Books Ltd., 80 Strand, London WC2R 0RL, England
Penguin Group Ireland, 25 St. Stephen's Green, Dublin 2, Ireland (a division of Penguin Books Ltd.)
Penguin Group (Australia), 250 Camberwell Road, Camberwell, Victoria 3124, Australia
(a division of Pearson Australia Group Pty. Ltd.)
Penguin Books India Pvt. Ltd., 11 Community Centre, Panchsheel Park, New Delhi—110 017, India
Penguin Group (NZ), 67 Apollo Drive, Rosedale, North Shore 0632, New Zealand
(a division of Pearson New Zealand Ltd.)
Penguin Books (South Africa) (Pty.) Ltd., 24 Sturdee Avenue, Rosebank, Johannesburg 2196,
South Africa

Penguin Books Ltd., Registered Offices: 80 Strand, London WC2R 0RL, England

This is a work of fiction. Names, characters, places, and incidents either are the product of the author's imagination or are used fictitiously, and any resemblance to actual persons, living or dead, business establishments, events, or locales is entirely coincidental. The publisher does not have any control over and does not assume any responsibility for author or third-party websites or their content.

ATLANTIS REDEEMED

A Berkley Sensation Book / published by arrangement with the author

ISBN: 978-1-61664-051-4

BERKLEY® SENSATION
Berkley Sensation Books are published by The Berkley Publishing Group,
a division of Penguin Group (USA) Inc.,
375 Hudson Street, New York, New York 10014.
BERKLEY® SENSATION and the "B" design are trademarks of Penguin Group (USA) Inc.

PRINTED IN THE UNITED STATES OF AMERICA

Acknowledgments

To Steve Axelrod, who sometimes just shakes his head and sighs, but sometimes sends me cases of champagne (*New York Times*! Yay, us!), and Lori Antonson and Elsie Turoci, for running the business end of my career so beautifully.

To Suzi Thompson, for her wonderful help with the forums, and to everyone who hangs out there, for the fun conversations.

To the werearmadillos (seriously, don't ask): Cindy Holby, Michelle Cunnah, Barbara Ferrer, Eileen Rendahl, Serena Robar, and Marianne Mancusi, for moral support, celebrations, and a safe place to vent the steam that comes with working in such a crazy business.

To Computer Boy and Princess, who make every single day of my life a whole lot more fun. I was just kidding about wishing I'd had pet rocks instead of kids.

Dear Readers,

Scientific discoveries are often far more fantastical than any fiction we authors can dream up—but sometimes we "discover" a breakthrough first! When I was finishing this book, imagine my surprise when an article in the March 25, 2009, issue of *The Journal of Neuroscience* reported on how brain activity can predict people's choices. Since my whole premise behind the vampire enthrallment of shape-shifters and humans was based on altered brain activity, as Tiernan briefly explained in *Atlantis Unleashed*, it was rather eerie to see my fictional science echoed in reality!

The Society of Neuroscience is an organization devoted to advancing the understanding of the brain and nervous system. However, I am sure that, unlike my fictional IAPN, it is not filled with evil scientists who wish to experiment on live shape-shifters. And apologies to the lovely Mammoth Hot Springs Hotel—I doubt they've ever had vampires crash the party! Thanks to Janet Chapple's excellent book, *Yellowstone Treasures*, for details on the park geography. Any mistakes in my version are fictional license.

I hope you'll love Brennan and Tiernan's story as much as I loved writing it, and as always, thank you from the bottom of my heart for spending some time with me and the Warriors of Poseidon.

Hugs,
Alyssa

The Warrior's Creed

We will wait. And watch. And protect.
And serve as first warning on the eve of humanity's destruction.
Then, and only then, Atlantis will rise.
For we are the Warriors of Poseidon, and the
mark of the Trident we bear serves as witness
to our sacred duty to safeguard mankind.

ATLANTIS
REDEEMED

Prologue

Rome, 202 B.C.

Brennan fell against the stone wall of the tavern, his wild laughter tinged with madness. "Another round for the house!" He fumbled in his pouch for a fistful of silver denarii and tossed them on the woman's tray. Her dark eyes widened until he could see white all the way around her irises.

"But this is far too much," she protested, her gaze darting furtively toward her father, the fat innkeeper in his stained toga that proclaimed him a free citizen of Rome, albeit a dirty one. "He will cheat you, you know," she whispered.

He took the tray out of her hands and dropped it on a table, uncaring that the cups and coins flew in all directions, and pulled her close in a drunken embrace. The generosity of ample breasts, overflowing the low-cut bodice of her stolla, distracted him for a moment from his pursuit of ale. Her right nipple was barely covered by the dingy fabric of her palla, and he experimented with tightening his embrace to see if it would pop all the way out of the blue cloth.

Sadly, his brilliant ploy didn't work. He inhaled a deep breath of the roasted meat and wine scent of the tavern and immediately wished he hadn't, as his head started spinning.

"So, my beauty, is there someplace more private we might go and I will give you a chance to earn even more of that silver?" He grabbed a fistful of her lovely round ass and squeezed, grinning. She was no slave girl, who would have no choice in the matter, but a free woman, his wine-soaked conscience reassured him.

But her face wore an expression of utter confusion. "I'm sorry, I don't know any foreign language," she said, almost cringing, as if he would beat her for her failure. She sidled away from him and scrambled for the scattered coins, slapping the hands of greedy bar patrons trying to help themselves to either coins or free cups of wine.

Brennan blinked, momentarily bewildered, but then he realized he must have been speaking in Atlantean, which had nothing in common with Latin, unfortunately. He had a tendency to fall back on his native tongue in the heat of battle or the lax-brained befuddlement of extreme drunkenness.

He spoke Atlantean a lot these days.

He felt the rumble coming up from his belly and managed to considerately turn his head to avoid belching in her face. "An-another place? Private?" he managed, this time in her language instead of his.

"Oh!" Her face cleared as she understood instantly. He probably was not the first, or even the tenth, of her father's customers to seek out a dark and private place with the buxom wench during the past several days. The thought momentarily sent a shudder of distaste through him, but as he released her and downed the bottom half of his cup, any misgivings vanished in a sea of effervescent intoxication.

Catching his hand, she dragged him through the cheering crowd of revelers, all raising a toast to their benefactor. He bowed sloppily, nearly tripping over the unfamiliar sandals, but the determined woman, almost certainly more enchanted with the contents of his pouch than with him, righted him with a steadying arm and herded him toward a doorway in the back of the tavern.

"Give her a good one, Brennan," one of his most regular drinking buddies, a centurion called Sergius, called. "She likes it if you squeeze her tits while you tup her."

Brennan stumbled again, a disquieting sense of wrongness pervading his sodden mind. Why was he here? He was one of Poseidon's finest, finally called to service in the sea god's chosen elite, and he was rotting out his brains and his gut with second-rate women and third-rate wine.

The wench shoved the wooden door shut behind him and grabbed his cock through the heavy folds of his toga, and his doubts disappeared in a spike of lust.

"Now let's be seeing what coin you have for a poor innocent girl," she cooed, leering at him with pursed lips and narrowed eyes that had not been innocent in years. Then she squeezed his cock again, harder.

He roared out a great whooping noise and grasped her melon-sized tits with both hands. "That's the idea," he said. "Why don't you lift that skirt and let me see what you've got under there?"

As he bent his head to hers, the woman's eyes widened again and then went blank, almost fish-eyed, as they glazed over and then closed. Her head fell back and her plump body went limp, oversetting his already precarious balance so they both went crashing to the filthy floor. Long-ingrained courtesy stirred Brennan to flip them as they went down, so he landed on the bottom of the heap, cushioning her unconscious body from the fall.

"Well. I never had exactly *that* effect on a woman before," he muttered to the amphorae of olive oil grouped around his aching head, as he stared at her in befuddlement.

AND SO YOU STILL HAVE NOT, a voice thundered through the room. Brennan's free hand automatically went to his dagger, but he found only an empty sheath.

YOU THINK TO DRAW YOUR WEAPON AGAINST

ME? the voice continued, and now it sounded somewhat annoyed. Brennan's head tried to clear, but the sheer quantity of wine he'd consumed during the day thwarted any attempt at mental acuity.

"I am a Warrior of Poseidon," he declared, but even to himself he had to admit the claim feeble, considering his present circumstances.

YOU ARE MY WARRIOR, YES, THOUGH I WOULD BE MOCKED AMONGST ALL OF THE OTHER GODS WERE THIS TRUTH TO BECOME KNOWN.

Oh, *miertus.* This was one tsunami of a wine-induced hallucination, if Brennan suddenly thought he was hearing the sea god himself. He struggled with the limp weight of the wench, trying to move her to one side so he could rise and at least face this . . . whatever this was . . . on his feet.

A flash of silvery blue light shot through the dark room, and suddenly the woman was gone—vanished as if she'd never been there. Brennan leapt to his feet and whirled around and around, nearly falling down again as vertigo overtook him.

"What? Where did she—"

THE WOMAN HAD NO PLACE IN OUR DISCUSSION. SHE IS NOW AT HOME IN HER BED, ALONE FOR A CHANGE, came the dry response.

"But why are you here—" Brennan belatedly realized that he was in no way showing appropriate deference to the sea god and dropped heavily to his knees. "My lord, accept my profuse apologies. Do you have need of me?"

WHAT SAD EXAMPLE OF GODHOOD WOULD HAVE NEED OF SUCH AS YOU? the voice thundered. *YOU HAVE TRIED MY PATIENCE WITH YOUR CONSTANT DRUNKEN DEBAUCHERY AND EXCESS. HADES HIMSELF, RULER OF THE NINE HELLS, ASKED ME TO GIFT YOU TO HIM.*

"Hades?" Brennan struggled to follow the sea god's logic. His knees hurt from dropping on the stone floor and his head was thumping from the booming sound of Poseidon's voice. In fact, he was feeling quite sorry for himself and not a little beleaguered by his severe misfortune. "What would Hades want with me?"

PRECISELY. A MATTER OF A SENATOR'S DAUGH-TER, PERHAPS? BUT THE KNOWLEDGE THAT YOU HAVE FALLEN SO FAR, DRIVEN BY YOUR LUSTS AND EMOTIONS, THAT THE GOD OF THE UNDERWORLD WOULD DESIRE YOUR PRESENCE, SADDENS ME GREATLY.

"But—"

SILENCE! BE ADVISED THAT I AM NOT A GOD TO ENDURE SADNESS. EVER. I AM AT AN END OF MY PATIENCE. NOW THAT YOUR EMOTIONS AND HUN-GERS HAVE DRIVEN YOU INTO THE ABYSS, I WILL REMOVE ALL SUCH FROM YOUR LIFE FOR ALL ETER-NITY.

Brennan shifted on the floor, daring to raise his head and search yet again, but the sea god had manifested only his voice. "Not to be impertinent, but when you say eter-nity—"

Lightning and thunder crashed through the room, the percussive force smashing Brennan, facedown, into the oil-and-dirt-soaked stone.

QUESTION ME AGAIN, AND YOU WILL SPEND SEVERAL LIFETIMES CLEANING THAT FILTH WITH YOUR TONGUE.

Brennan nodded, not daring to say another word, as the hot, slow trickle of blood from his battered head spread under the side of his face. Silence. Understood.

I CURSE YOU THUS: FOR ALL ETERNITY, UNTIL SUCH TIME AS YOU MEET YOUR ONE TRUE MATE, YOU WILL FEEL NO EMOTION. NEITHER SADNESS NOR JOY; NEITHER RAGE NOR DELIGHT.

Thunder crashed through the room again, and Brennan belatedly wondered why none from the tavern had come back to investigate the storm taking place in their store-room, before the sea god continued.

WHEN YOU DO MEET HER, YOU WILL EXPERI-ENCE A RESURGENCE OF ALL OF THE EMOTIONS

*YOU HAVE REPRESSED OVER THE YEARS AND CEN-
TURIES AND EVEN MILLENNIA.*

Poseidon laughed, and his laughter contained the sound
and fury of tidal waves that could destroy civilizations.

*IF THAT ALONE IS NOT ENOUGH TO DESTROY
YOU, YOU WILL ALSO BE CURSED TO FORGET YOUR
MATE WHENEVER SHE IS OUT OF YOUR SIGHT. ONLY
WHEN SHE IS DEAD—HER HEART STOPPED AND
HER SOUL FLOWN—WILL YOUR MEMORY OF HER
FULLY RETURN TO YOU, THUS ALLOWING YOU UNTIL
THE END OF YOUR DAYS TO REPENT BRINGING DIS-
HONOR UPON THE NAME OF THE WARRIORS OF PO-
SEIDON.*

Brennan, robbed of any coherent response as the enormity of Poseidon's curse sank in, just lay on the floor, stink-
ing of blood and wine, still too drunk to comprehend the
full extent of what was happening to him. "Bit harsh, don't
you think?" he managed.

*SHE TOOK HER OWN LIFE, FOOL, AND THAT OF
YOUR CHILD SHE CARRIED; A CHILD THE ORACLES
HAD DECREED WOULD BE OF GREAT USE TO ME.*

With a final crack of thunder, the sea god disappeared
with a booming admonition. *REMEMBER.*

The peculiar feeling of heaviness that always accompanied great power disappeared, and Brennan's ears popped
with a sizzling burst of pain as they adjusted to its absence.
Warmth pooled in his ear canals and he wondered what had
burst in his head and whether the healers would be able to
repair what Poseidon himself had wrought, but the self-
indulgent thought immediately vanished, crushed under the
weight of Poseidon's words. Corelia had taken her life?

Denial burned through the alcoholic haze in his brain.
Surely not. He would have heard. Wouldn't he?

A child? *His* child? Pain beyond the imagining of it
ripped through him at the thought, and he clutched his roil-
ing gut and rolled back and forth on the filthy floor. She had
killed herself and taken his child with her? Because of what
he, Brennan, had done? No. *No.*

No. It must not be true. He had offered to wed her and been ridiculed for his trouble. She'd made no mention of a child . . . But a god had said it. Poseidon himself.

As the realization of truth seared through Brennan's consciousness, he threw back his head and roared out his agony, slamming his fists on the stone, over and over. No. What had he done? What—what—

What was happening to him? The pain was vanishing, slipping from his soul as easily as the clothing had fallen from Corelia's body during their trysts. A bland numbness, hideous in its emptiness, settled over his senses. Suffocating him. A brief flash of terror at the alien feeling and then that, too, was gone. A vast nothingness established itself in its place.

Dragging himself up off the ground, nearly insensible to the blood running freely from so many gashes on his arms, face, and body, Brennan sent his thoughts and focus deep, deep inside of himself to discover just how far the void had burrowed into his mind and soul.

He stood there, alone, for minutes or perhaps hours, seeking some fragment of the anguish he'd suffered for Corelia and the babe. Searching for some remnant of his terror at Poseidon's curse.

Nothing. There was nothing. He did not feel pain, and he could not sense the terror. He felt precisely nothing, save for a vast, bleak emptiness in the wasteland of his soul, where—just moments ago—his emotions had resided. He slowly picked up his dagger from where it had fallen into the filth and made his way to the door. He must return to Atlantis and face the punishment for this transgression. He realized that he neither feared nor dreaded the outcome.

Dread, then, was also an emotion. He dispassionately began a mental category of what he had lost, although he was unable to feel the loss itself. The irony was not lost on him, leaving him to believe that irony itself was merely an intellectual construct. Finding his dagger on the floor and shoving it into its sheath, he shouldered his way out of the door and through the tavern, intent on the journey to find seawater and thus the portal. The tavern fell silent as he made his way through it, and even the most foolhardy refrained from calling out to him, as if they could read his shame and dishonor on his face.

But of course they could not, since he could feel neither except as distant realities. To Atlantis, then, although the better, easier course would be to shove his own blade through his heart now. It would be an easy death, though, and more merciful than he deserved for causing the death of an innocent and her child.

His child.

An eternity of punishment could not be long enough for what he had caused.

Chapter 1

Present day: Atlantis, the palace war room

Even those cursed to feel no emotion could experience its paler cousin, curiosity. Brennan had always assumed it was a more intellectual state. He tapped a finger on the photo of the woman staring up at him from the folded newspaper. "This is she?"

Something tugged at him; some flash of, what? Recognition? Admiration? The reporter's face, even in the grainy black-and-white of the newsprint, was beautiful. But it was a quality in the look of her eyes that had captured his attention. Perhaps it was a trick of the light, but it was almost as if he could read the sadness haunting them.

Or perhaps more than two thousands of years without emotion had destroyed his ability to discern it in others. Especially through such an inaccurate prism as that of a newspaper photograph.

High Prince Conlan nodded and resumed his pacing. "That's her. She's our reporter contact, and she has news of who—or what—might be behind the shifter attacks in Yellowstone." Conlan shot a wary glance at his brother Ven, then at Brennan. "She's also the one you, ah, the one—"

"The one you went *miertus* over and had some kind of convulsions about back in Boston," Alexios added dryly.

As members of Conlan's elite guard, the Seven, hand-picked from among the best of the best of the Warriors of Poseidon, Alexios and Brennan had trained and fought together for centuries in the continuing battle to protect humanity from the dark forces that sought to destroy and enslave it. Both were masters at remaining calm and in control under pressure; Brennan through a god's dictate, Alexios through decades of training.

Except, from what Alexios and Christophe had told him, Brennan had failed spectacularly during one crucial mission, going so far as to kill a vampire they'd needed to question. Also, even more unbelievably, he'd then threatened his own friends and fellow warriors—all over a human female.

Tiernan Butler.

He almost could not—*would* not—believe it. If it had been only Christophe who recounted the tale, he most certainly would not have believed it. Christophe's sly sense of humor often caused him to find sport in mocking Brennan's emotionless existence. But Alexios was a different matter. Alexios would never, ever lie to him.

And there was the small matter of the dreams. Flashes of what he now believed to be memories, persistent in spite of the curse. Holding the soft warmth of her body in his arms. Looking down into the bottomless depths of her dark, dark eyes.

"Thus, it must be true," he murmured, coming to the unpleasant conclusion he'd refused previously to accept. Some of his control was finally cracking. After so many years, perhaps even the strongest of steel became brittle. Or—worse—the curse was coming to its fulfillment. Would that be worse or better? He dismissed the question as irrelevant; worse or better, what would be, would be.

Alexios leaned against the battered wooden table that had

seen so many of their planning sessions, and stared off into the distance, studying the ancient tapestries that lined the walls. Or simply trying to avoid meeting Brennan's gaze.

Ven, slouched in an overstuffed chair, one long leg thrown over the side, finally spoke up. "Look, we need to quit dancing around this. We've got to send somebody, preferably a team, to Yellowstone to help Lucas and his wolf shifters defend themselves against the attacks from outside and, even more important, I think, attacks from *inside* the pack. The threat of vampire enthrallment is growing every day. Tiernan is our contact, and she's undercover doing the story on the science conference and the vamp regional leader there, so we need to work with her. So, major problem: can Brennan work with her or not?"

Brennan straightened and inclined his head toward Ven, then put a touch of frost in his voice. "If the vampires are truly able to enthrall shape-shifters now, which they have never been able to do in all the millennia of their existence, this matter is of crucial importance to our mission." He flashed a glance at Alexios and then returned his gaze to Ven, whose relaxed pose could not quite hide the lethal danger of one named the King's Vengeance. "I am perfectly capable, *Your Highness*. I am sure that whatever happened in Boston was a one-time aberration."

Ven rolled his eyes and repeated his familiar threat. "Call me 'Highness' again, and I'll kick your ass. I'm just Conlan's brother, my friend. Leader of the Seven and uncle to one very adorable little baby boy. If we're going to give young Prince Aidan an Atlantis that can rise to the surface, and a surface worth rising to, we need to solve the puzzle behind how these vamps are suddenly able to enthrall shifters when they never could before."

"Tiernan says that whatever they're doing to the humans is different, too," Conlan pointed out. "She and her contacts have proof. Brain scans and the like. This isn't just temporary anymore. The vamps are changing the humans' entire brain-wave patterns to keep them permanently in thrall."

"At this rate, the bloodsuckers will turn all of humanity

into nothing but herds of sheep for their dining pleasure in a matter of years—or maybe even months," Alexios added. "I volunteer to go. Lucas, the alpha of the Yellowstone wolf pack, is an old friend. He even gave me the honor of naming me second pack-father to his new twin boys, and I have yet to see them or bring a birth gift."

Ven grinned. "And I'm sure the lovely Grace will bring along her bow and arrows and keep your ugly butt in line."

Brennan was intrigued to see the dark red flush that rose in Alexios's scarred face, partially hidden by the long waves of golden hair that had once so intrigued the women of Atlantis. Of course, that was before Alexios had returned from one of the darker levels of the nine hells, with his face and his soul scarred beyond—or so they'd feared—any hope of redemption. To be precise, only the left side of his face was scarred, a going-away present of sorts from the vampire goddess Anubisa after two long years of torture.

Grace had brought Alexios back into the light. Brennan wished he had the capacity to feel the joy for his friend that he knew everyone else shared. Alexios's new lady love, who was both human and more, as a descendant of the goddess Diana, was indeed a formidable warrior in her own right.

"Grace doesn't need to put herself in any more danger, especially now," Alexios muttered, a look of grim resignation on his face. "But I may as well spit into the wind as tell her that."

Almost as if on cue, the door opened and Grace walked in, accompanied by Conlan's new bride and infant son, High Princess Riley and Prince Aidan.

Ven started laughing. "Busted! It's like they have radar."

Conlan swiftly crossed to his wife, who handed him the baby. The intense emotion on Conlan and Riley's faces as they gazed at each other and then at the child stirred something dry and barren deep inside Brennan. He filed the sensation away to consider later. A curiosity, no more.

Riley suddenly looked up and cast a startled glance at Brennan. "Brennan? Was that you?"

He bowed. "I beg your pardon, my lady?"

She shook her head, sunshine-gold hair flying. "No . . . It's nothing, I guess," she said, her brows drawing together. "I thought . . . No. Nothing." She laughed. "Being *aknasha* and a new mother certainly is interesting. Not only can I pick up emotions from everyone around me, but I've got an overload of my own to deal with. It makes my mind play tricks on me."

Brennan raised an eyebrow, but she didn't elaborate. He briefly wondered if her emotional empathy had sensed some emotion hidden deep down in his psyche, but he had to discard the idea as impossible. Although there had been that one time when Riley's sister Quinn, an even more powerful *aknasha*, had claimed to feel buried emotion from him . . . But he'd doubted Quinn's claim then, and he doubted it now. Poseidon's curses were not so easily broken. He'd spent many lifetimes coming to that realization.

Grace, a study in lean elegance with her swimmer's body, honey-gold skin, and long, dark hair, crossed the room to Alexios, whose entire face lit up at the sight of her. She leaned into him for a moment, then took a position against the wall next to him and flashed a saucy grin at Conlan and Ven. "So, boys. What's up?"

Alexios looked simultaneously chagrined and amused. "You probably shouldn't call the high prince and his brother 'boys,'" he muttered.

Ven laughed. "Please. She's fine. Great, even. Trust me, it's way better than 'pigheaded fool,' which is what I got from Erin this morning before I'd even gotten out of bed. Seems like my suggestion I go along on her trip to Seattle to visit her friends was 'being overprotective.' It's not like she nearly got killed by a traitor in that witch's coven or anything." His tone was light, but Brennan noticed that Ven's hands clenched into fists at his sides at the memory of Erin's brushes with death.

Riley shook her head at Ven. "You should know better by now. She is a very powerful witch and needs to work with others in her circle to refine her control over the Wild-ing magic. If you want to go along as the man she loves, that's one thing. But as the big, tough guy who can protect the helpless little woman? Not so much."

Ven snorted. "Women." But then his eyes widened, and he jumped up out of his chair. "Maybe I'll just go help her pack. Do we have this mission resolved? Alexios and Grace are heading to Yellowstone to see what they can find out, protect the wolves, so on and so forth?"

"Yes, it is resolved. Alexios and Grace and *I* will go to Yellowstone," Brennan said firmly, leaving no room for them to doubt his resolve. "There is also the matter of the final missing gems from the Trident. We must discover where the tourmaline, aquamarine, and amethyst have been hidden and retrieve them, or Atlantis cannot rise."

"I love the gem names," Riley said. "Poseidon's Pride, the Emperor, and the Siren. Has Alaric figured out which is which yet?"

"Not yet," Conlan said, holding his son to his shoulder and patting the infant's back. A resounding burp sounded in the room, and everyone laughed.

"He takes after his uncle Ven," Conlan said, grinning. Then his expression turned serious and he aimed a measuring stare at Brennan. "Are you sure? We can't afford an incident if you react to the reporter as you did before. I am inclined to trust you, of course, as my father and those before him have trusted you for two millennia. But something is off about your reaction to her."

Brennan, who had never disclosed the full terms of the curse to anyone, not even the kings and princes he'd served, nodded slowly. He was quite aware of the wrongness of his reaction to Tiernan Butler. The sea god's proclamation rang in his mind: only when Brennan met his destined mate would his emotions return to him. But then he would forget her when she was out of his sight.

Destined mate. Destined to reach the soul-meld? But the Atlanteans' most prized tenet was free will. Even lovers who had achieved the rare and precious state of being known as the soul-meld could choose to part, though it stunned

Brennan to think that any would give up such a precious gift.

No matter, though. If the curse were coming to the fruition of its terms, he would need to be very, very careful indeed around Tiernan Butler, although an almost primal need drove him to see her again. To test his hypothesis.

Perhaps, after all these long, long years, to finally feel again. Even if just for a very short time.

He realized everyone was staring at him. "I am aware of the seriousness of the dilemma and will take all precautions," he said. "But the members of the Seven are spread precariously thin these days. Lord Justice has gone to England with Dr. McDermott, Bastien is busy with Kat and the tripartite alliance building with the humans and panther shifters in Miami, and Christophe and Denal—"

"They've gone on a mission for me," Ven interrupted. "Yes, you're right. I never thought to see so many of the Seven gone away on so many different tasks, but the world is changing, and we must keep up with it. Perhaps Conlan should appoint some of you as official ambassadors and select new warriors to become part of his personal guard."

Conlan was shaking his head before Ven even finished his sentence. "No, I won't break up this team. You're right about the need for ambassadorial roles, but—"

"But this is something we can consider at another time, maybe?" Riley asked. "For now, your son and I would like to have dinner with his daddy."

Prince Aidan's tiny mouth opened and he let out a loud wail as if in vehement agreement, and Conlan laughed. "You're right," he said. "For now, Brennan and Alexios will go to Yellowstone, discover what they can, and report back as soon as they learn anything."

"And Grace," Grace added, raising her chin.

"And Grace," Conlan conceded.

Alexios opened his mouth as if to argue, but subsided after Grace shot a narrow-eyed glare his way.

"The world is changing, and this is only a discover-and-report mission. No danger," Grace reminded him. Alexios scowled down at her, but the heat in his eyes belied the ferocity of his expression.

Again, something inside Brennan twisted—just the smallest of twinges, but enough to drive him to conclude the meeting. "Shall we reconvene at the portal in an hour?"

"One hour," Alexios said.

Brennan gestured for everyone to precede him out of the room. Riley glanced back at Brennan over her shoulder as Conlan took the baby and walked ahead, laughing. She hesitated for a moment, biting her lip, but then she offered a brief smile and followed her husband and child as they left the room.

When the last of them had gone through the door, Brennan picked up the folded paper and carefully tore out Tiernan's photograph and put it in his pocket. For recognition purposes, of course. He'd need to recognize her when he saw her.

Or at least that's what he tried to convince himself.

It had nothing at all to do with needing to see her face.

Chapter 2

Yellowstone National Park,
the road to Mammoth Hot Springs Hotel

"I don't like it."

Tiernan, lost again in the memory that had resulted in far too many nights of frustrated arousal and tangled sheets, rolled her eyes as if the man at the other end of the phone could see her. She tightened her fingers on the steering wheel of the midsized piece-of-crap rental and sighed. Driving down unknown roads in the middle of the wilderness—in the dark—was just not the time or place to get into fights with her boss.

"Tiernan, ignoring me is not going to get you what you want this time," he warned, his voice in her earpiece little more than a growl. "There is no way this shindig is going to be just like a party. Security is bound to be on high alert after they find out we hacked into their database."

Tiernan counted to twenty-four beats under her breath, one for each month she'd worked with Rick Lawrence.

"Are you doing the counting thing again? You know I hate it when you do the counting thing."

She sighed again, but figured she'd better answer him before he did something drastic like pull the plug on the whole thing because he sensed danger to her. He'd done it before.

"Rick, I am an investigative reporter. I was an investigative reporter long before you appeared from nowhere and joined the *Boston Herald* as my editor," she said, her voice calm in spite of the fact that this was the tenth time they'd had this discussion, at least. "I do not need babysitting, *or* a big brother, *or* a bodyguard. This is my story, and unless you plan to hire someone to tie me up and stuff me in the trunk, I am going to this party, and I am staying for the conference."

There was a long silence over the increasingly staticky connection. Then he swore softly, a long stream of fairly inventive invective. She smiled grimly at the phrase. *Inventive invective.* Nice. Had a headline kind of ring.

"Look, the new intel says that one of the most dangerous vamps in the country is planning to make an appearance. If we'd known that when we set this up, you damn sure wouldn't be going on your own," he said, his frustration coming clearly through the line.

But nothing was going to stop her now. People were dying, and it was only going to get worse if somebody didn't stand up. Somebody like her. Like the Atlanteans. She hoped.

"All that is necessary for the triumph of evil is that good men and women do nothing," she countered, editing a little as she scanned the road and her surroundings. The moon filtering through the trees looming on either side gave the drive a Stephen King–like quality, and her overactive imagination half expected monsters to jump out at her at any moment.

Bet King was surprised when all those monsters he'd written about for all those years turned out to really exist. Or was he? Maybe he'd always known . . .

"Don't quote Burke to me," Rick snapped, cutting off her mental wanderings. "You're on your way to a weekend that you're hoping will be filled with the worst kind of evil—vamps, possibly enthralled shifters, and sick and

twisted scientists and neurosurgeons who love nothing better than to dissect brains while the brains' owners are still
alive. This is *dangerous*, Tiernan. You are not Lois Lane."

"I don't want to be Lois Lane," she snapped right back at
him, slowing to negotiate a tight turn. "I want to be Super-
man. I want to send the vampires involved in this plot back
to hell, where they came from. I want to be able to sleep at
night without nightmares of how Susannah died, and I want
to be able to face myself in the mirror knowing that I did
something about it."

She lifted a hand to brush the angry tears from her
cheeks.

When Rick finally spoke again, his voice was much
calmer. "I know. I know. I just can't take it if you wind up
like Susannah, or worse. They're not just enthralling shifters, you know."

"I know. That's why we set up this investigation into the
International Association of Preternatural Neuroscience in
the first place. We need to know how they're doing it, so we
can stop it," she said flatly. "Why would any human scientist do such a thing? I mean, I get that the vamps have no
souls. But these are human beings."

"If you use the term loosely," Rick said.

She rounded a curve and recognized her destination,
sighing in relief. "Reporter Lost in Wilderness" didn't have
quite the headline ring to it that she was going for.

"That's the North Entrance station, Rick. I've got to let
you go and put on my ditzy reporter face while I talk to this
guy and pay the entrance fee."

"You're not even blond."

"Funny. I've found that being underestimated gets me
way more info than showing off my brains. Gotta go. Will
call you later."

She tapped the button on her wireless earbud and slowed
to a stop at the gatehouse, flashing a dazzling smile at
the square-jawed ranger who sauntered out to talk to her.
He blinked and then smiled eagerly back at her, all blue
eyes, buzz cut, and Boy Scout sincerity.

"You here for the IAPN conference?" He glanced down at
a clipboard he held, not waiting for her response. "Name?"

"Tracy Baum," she lied smoothly. Her cover credentials
would survive quite a bit of checking. *"Neuroscience Quarterly."*

The ranger made a check mark on his clipboard. "You're
all set, Ms. Baum." A broad smile spread over his face. "You
know, the—"

"Thank you *so* much," she interrupted, putting the car in
gear again as she recognized the sign of a man wanting to
chat. "Much to do, the science news waits for no woman.
Thanks, Officer."

Tiernan settled back in her seat and pulled away from
the guard, heading toward the hotel. If only she'd arrived in
the daytime, she could have appreciated what she'd heard
was an absolutely spectacular view. Electric Peak was reported to be amazing, and the bridge just ahead crossed the
Gardner River, another must-see in the tourist guides.

Not that she was a tourist. Tourists didn't usually try to
discover secrets that could get them killed. She hadn't admitted it on the phone, but Rick had had a good point. Of
course, he usually did—the man was honest to a fault.

If there could even *be* such a thing as honest *to a fault*
when it came to her. Honesty was a gift of grace in a world
filled with deceptions, secrets, and lies. Every one of which
caused her actual physical pain, if her shielding wasn't
strong enough.

But not Rick. He'd insult the heck out of her before he'd
lie. He was definitely a "your story sucks, fix it" kind of
guy. The thought made her laugh a little, as a blaze of lights
came into view.

She'd made it. The Mammoth Hot Springs Hotel. She
pulled into the driveway and edged the car into a space between a ginormous white limo and a flashy red sports car.

"Holy Italian deliciousness," she murmured reverently.
"That's the Lamborghini."

No valets or bellmen were in sight, so she hit speed dial.
Rick answered on the first ring.

"We've got confirmation. I'm looking at the vampmobile. A 2009 Lamborghini Gallardo LP560-4, to be exact." She scanned the driveway for the driver of that very distinctive car, which, as she knew very well, had been made to spec for one very important customer. Its windows were made of black glass, which had been engineered so that not a single ray of sunshine could penetrate.

Rick's voice barked in her ear. "Which means what, Butler?"

"It's the ultimate vamp car. Belongs to Devon, last name unknown, rumored to be the regional head of all things vampire in this part of the country. He likes to wear disguises and dark glasses, so nobody is really sure what he looks like."

"After what your Atlantean buddies have done to the vamp leaders they've encountered recently, it's no wonder he's in hiding," Rick said.

Tiernan's heart did an odd stutter at the mention of the Atlanteans. She'd never told Rick, or anybody else, the full story. That she'd passed out at that awful party in Boston and woken up under the dome of the lost continent itself.

Atlantis.

Brennan. The star, for far too many nights lately, of the most blatantly sexual dreams she'd ever had.

The image of his wild, almost feral, ice-green eyes staring down at her, while his muscular arms held her to his hard, hot body, burned through her memory, making her shiver. That face that belonged on a magazine cover—beautifully sculpted masculine features framed by thick waves of long black hair. He'd been crazed, with power or passion or . . . something. He'd been crazed, and then he'd been gone.

She still wondered about that. About him.

"You still there?"

She blinked. She'd almost forgotten Rick was still on the line. "You're right. Speaking of which, I'd better get out of this car before I look suspicious. Later."

Tiernan grabbed her leather backpack and fake press credentials, put on her slightly ditzy "Tracy Baum" smile, and stepped out of the car. She took a deep breath and raised her mental shields as she straightened up to her full height, keeping the ditzy smile pasted on her face.

The smile was part of her cover. The shields were part of her sanity. The last thing she needed was to be overwhelmed by crashing pain from a hotel full of lying neuroscientists. Her job was simple: all she had to do was work her way through one lying neuroscientist at a time.

All that could matter was the job. The mission. The facts that had to come out—the story that had to come out. The truth, as they said, would set her free.

Pulitzer.

Pulitzer.

Save the damn world *and* earn a Pulitzer.

If she repeated it often enough, like a litany, maybe the truth would be forced out. For Susannah's sake.

As she pulled her single carry-on bag from the backseat, she tried to create a visual focus in her mind. The headline. Front page, above the fold:

SCIENTISTS' EVIL PLOT FOILED:
SHAPE-SHIFTERS AND HUMANS SAVED

But the image of her success kept fading. Wavering. Replaced by a pair of ice-green eyes.

Slamming the car door shut, she wondered where in the hell the valet was. Maybe hiding behind the long hedge that bordered the hotel, sneaking a smoke. Maybe grabbing a quick bite to eat. She shot a considering glance at the vamp-mobile again, and felt the edges of her lips quirk up into a twisted grimace of a smile.

Maybe *becoming* a quick bite to eat.

She never saw the knife until it was taut against her throat.

"Scream and die," a low voice murmured against her ear, and then suddenly she was flying or leaping, moving with a speed and at a height mere humans couldn't attain, over the hedge and into the inky darkness behind it. The lights from the hotel barely shimmered through the tall thickness of the hedge. When their feet hit the ground and her captor released her, Tiernan stumbled, disoriented, and the edge of the blade cut sharply into the side of her neck. She hissed at the biting pain, and the knife wielder yanked the weapon away, swearing viciously under his breath.

"I am sorry to have hurt you, but speed and discretion were needed."

She put her hand to her wounded neck, felt the wetness, knew she'd see the blood if there were any light. "Great. Sure. What's a little bleeding neck wound between friends?"

Maybe sarcasm wasn't the best idea, considering the guy had superspeed and a very sharp knife. But a dangerous combination of fear and anger boiled out of her as defiance. "I'm guessing you're not the valet. So who the hell are you, and what do you want with me?"

He inhaled deeply, so close to her that she felt the rush of his breath when he exhaled. "What I want at the moment has more to do with that bleeding wound and my desire to lick it clean than my actual objective. Perhaps you would agree to a temporary truce so that your anger and my hunger do not force me into sucking on your lovely little neck until I drain you dry."

It wasn't a question, more of a command, and one she wasn't in the slightest bit interested in defying. Bravado had to give way to intelligent self-preservation sometimes, even for crack investigative reporters. His voice was oddly musical, nearly mesmerizing, but not like he was trying to enthrall her. She'd heard that tone before, in other vamps, but this wasn't that. This was his actual voice: deep, confident, and just the tiniest hint of an accent. She thought she'd recognize it if she heard it again.

"Vampire, then?" Her words came out shakier than she'd hoped.

"Those must be the brilliant journalistic instincts I've heard so much about, Tiernan Butler," he said, amusement and something darker underscoring the words.

Fear snaked through her at the sound of her real name,

but she didn't let a hint of it show on her face. "Tiernan who? Look, you've got me confused—"

"Do not insult me," he snapped. "I don't have time to play. You're going to need allies on the inside, but you can trust no one. Expect deception and malice from the least likely sources. Accuse Devon of nothing; he is not yet powerful enough. Those around him will force his hand, and you will die. The greater good outweighs the lives of one unimportant reporter, no matter how lovely she may be."

He fell silent, and Tiernan wondered if she'd just fallen through the rabbit hole. A very dark, confusing rabbit hole, where vampires kidnapped then complimented her.

"Yeah. Malice and deception are my specialties," she snapped. "Um, look, I'm very grateful that you didn't exsanguinate me, but what in the world are you talking about?"

"Redemption must be sought, even if there can never be such for one like me," he said so quietly that she wondered if she'd been meant to hear.

"Redemption." The word tasted bitter in her mouth. "Some acts can never be redeemed."

It was several long seconds before the vampire replied. "Is that aimed at me or at yourself? Either way, does it matter?"

Only a whisper of his breath served to warn her before she felt a strong, cool hand grasp her chin and tilt it to the side, as his mouth settled on her neck. As he licked her neck, then pulled deeply at the wound, she felt an answering pressure low in her body and realized she suddenly knew why the vamp groupies kept going back for more. She raised her fists to shove him away, but he was gone before she could touch him.

"Forgive me," he said, his rough voice nearly a growl. "It has been a long time. Beyond mere hunger, I have reason to believe I will need to be able to find you."

Tiernan blinked, her fury at his attack fizzling in the wake of utter confusion. "Forgive you? Did you just apologize to me?"

"Even monsters can apologize," he said dryly.

"I didn't—"

"You did. And I deserved it, but again, no time for pretty speeches. Be warned and be prepared. I will send you an ally if I can, but even if not, these experiments need to stop. You and the Atlanteans may have to work alone, but know that I'll be working toward you from the other side of this. Remember that not all of the shape-shifters who wear the faces of friends are true."

Tiernan had had just about enough of his cryptic riddles. "Who are you? I've had confidential sources before and never yet revealed a single one. You can trust me, if you really are on my side." Everything in her was telling her that he wasn't lying, but her senses didn't always work with vampires. Truth and falsehood had different meaning to the undead, apparently, so vampire lies didn't always resonate in her soul. Didn't cause her highly calibrated senses to jangle with the discordant sound of dishonesty.

He laughed, but the sound was wrong, somehow, as if he hadn't used his voice for laughter for more years than she'd been alive. "I've trusted human women before. Twice. The first died, and the second paid a terrible price and despises me. Never, ever again."

"But—"

"I have to leave you now. Don't forget," her captor whispered, his voice merely a darker shadow in the night.

"Wait! How do I get out of here?" Tiernan pointed to the impenetrable greenery, but before she could say another word, his hand shot out and wrenched a handful of leaves and branches, and a gaping hole appeared in the hedge.

She whistled. "Well, if you give up the mysterious kidnapper thing, you could try gardener, I suppose."

When he didn't respond, she glanced over her shoulder and wasn't really surprised to see him gone. "Bond, James Vampire Bond," she murmured, before she leaned down and moved sideways through the gap in the hedge, toward the light.

"Miss?" The long-missing valet rushed down the sidewalk toward her. "What happened to you? Are you all right?"

He took her arm and she stood up, scanning the area to see how many people had seen her climbing out of the hedge. But luckily the driveway was momentarily clear. Or maybe it wasn't "luckily" at all. Maybe the vamp had waited for privacy before he let her go. Vampires did have better than average hearing, or so the rumor went.

"Miss? Talk to me. Are you okay? Your neck is bleeding," the man said, pulling her toward the hotel in a fast walk, almost as if he were afraid to be out after dark.

She clapped her hand over the bite mark and managed a smile. "Oh, if you only knew me. Just clumsy, clumsy, clumsy. I fell through those bushes in these terrible shoes. Can you grab my bag for me, please?"

He started to protest, but she narrowed her eyes and lifted her chin. He recognized defeat and moved to lift her case from the sidewalk, where she'd dropped it when she'd been snatched by Captain Mysterious. She took advantage of the moment and grabbed a tissue from the front pocket of her backpack and wiped her neck with it, wincing at the sight of the fresh blood. She wadded it up and stuffed it in the pocket of her jeans as the valet turned around.

"Ready to get checked in and get a good night's sleep?" he asked, pasting a strained smile on his face. "Meetings start tomorrow morning at eight A.M. It looks like it will be an interesting conference."

She handed him her keys and indicated her car, then took a slow, deep breath as she stared at the empty space where the Lamborghini had been parked. "You know, somehow I don't doubt that at all."

Chapter 3

Yellowstone National Park,
southeast section,
official wolf shifter Pack territory

Brennan stepped through the portal from Atlantis and took a deep breath of the crisp air. He had always appreciated the scents of the park, so different from those of the more delicate and flowered trees of Atlantis. The spruce and pine trees scented the air with an aroma that smelled exotic to him, even after so many visits over the centuries. He wished he could fully savor the experience, but there was nothing left to him of pleasure or appreciation. Nothing of joy.

He wondered again, as he had so often before, when he would surrender to the bleakness of his destiny—and end it. Soon, perhaps. But not today. Not until his curiosity about the woman Tiernan had been satisfied.

He turned to face the portal. A cluster of soaring lodge-pole pines stood sentinel on a nearby ridge, casting shadows over the portal as Alexios and Grace crossed through. Grace had one hand on the hilt of the dagger sheathed at her hip and her other hand on her ever-present bow.

"You weren't kidding about wilderness," she said, looking around. "And what the heck is that?" In a single, smooth motion, she pulled her bow off her shoulder and had an arrow ready to let fly at a group of large shadows moving at the base of the trees.

Alexios smiled and, with one finger, gently pushed her arrow down. "That's a bunch of bison, city girl."

Grace lowered her bow and stood staring, her mouth falling open a little. "Bison? I'm standing in the wilderness, surrounded by buffalo?"

"'Surrounded' is not accurate," Brennan pointed out. "They are in a single group, more than thirty feet away from us. If they were behind us, as well, perhaps, but—"

A calm voice cut him off. "Surrounded by wolves is a little more to the point."

The first word had Brennan whirling around, daggers drawn, but as soon as he saw Lucas's familiar face, he relaxed and slid the blades back into their sheaths. The alpha wolf shifter stood a good ten paces away, surrounded by a half dozen of his Pack in their wolf shapes.

Alexios strode forward to meet his old friend, and the two clasped arms. "Well met, Lucas."

"Welcome to my home," Lucas replied, inclining his head. Then his gaze arrowed in on Grace, and a slow smile spread across his face. "This *is* a surprise. How did you get a woman that lovely to have anything to do with you?"

The honey-colored wolf sitting at Lucas's right side bared her teeth and snapped at his leg. Lucas threw back his head and laughed.

"Perhaps your mate does not care for your compliments to another man's woman," Alexios said, bowing deeply to the wolf.

A shimmering glow surrounded the animal for several seconds, and then a woman stood where the wolf had been. Her long wavy hair was the same shade of gold as the wolf's fur. She wore simple clothes—an unremarkable dark shirt over blue jeans—but her beauty glowed like a fine Atlantean gemstone in the moonlit night.

Grace stepped forward, next to Alexios, and elbowed him

in the side. From the "oof" noise he made, Brennan assumed the gesture had not been gentle.

"Remember, we talked about this 'my woman' stuff?" she muttered. Then she looked at Lucas and his mate and inclined her head. "Thank you for the welcome. I'm Grace, and he's still learning."

The female shifter laughed. "I'm Honey, and good luck with that. Starting the day he found out I was pregnant, Lucas tried to treat me like I was a fragile, delicate little thing. Now that the babies are here, he still hasn't let up." She started to take a step forward, but Lucas stopped her with a hand on her arm.

"Maybe we should be sure that this really is Alexios and Brennan before we go any further," Lucas said, his dark brows drawing together.

A wave of understanding washed over Brennan. "The chameleon shifters. Yes, we have heard of that phenomenon. Perhaps you might ask us something that only we would know?"

Lucas was obviously ready for the prompt, because he spoke with no hesitation. "What kind of dance did Christophe tell us he hated?"

Brennan simply stared at the alpha, having absolutely no idea to what he was referring, but Alexios started laughing. "He's no fan of line dancing, if I remember rightly."

The memory of another meeting with Lucas, that one marred by a vicious attack from enthralled wolves, flashed into Brennan's mind, and he curved his lips in a perfunctory smile. Though he could not feel pleasure or amusement, he'd long since learned that it made others more comfortable around him if he at least made an attempt to mimic the appearance of emotion. "I mentioned my fondness for a good waltz, I believe."

Lucas grinned. "Only you, Brennan. Only you would go all nostalgic for a waltz. I bet you and Johann Strauss were buddies."

"I never had the privilege of meeting Johann, the elder.

But I did, on occasion, take a meal with the younger, and offered my sincere admiration at his progress on '*An der schönen blauen Donau.*'"

Honey smiled. "'The Blue Danube'? We played that at our wedding reception for our first waltz."

Brennan glanced at Lucas. "You, too, waltz?"

Lucas put a proprietary arm around his mate and shrugged. "Honey wanted me to waltz, I waltzed. You just wait, Brennan. Someday a woman will bulldoze right over that walled-off heart of yours, and you'll be doing the tango, the waltz, or the freaking Macarena if she asks you."

That was impossible, of course, given the curse, but something dark and dangerous in Brennan's soul twisted at the idea. Tiernan. If she were the one, if only she *could* break through . . . But if and when she did, his returning emotions were cursed to destroy him, or—worse, far worse—her.

Only when she is dead—her heart stopped and her soul flown . . .

The hated words of the curse echoed through his mind, yet again, and the image of Tiernan's face in that newspaper photograph appeared in his memory. If only he could remember the way she'd looked as he'd held her in his arms. He closed his eyes and shook his head to clear it. When he opened his eyes again, an awkward silence had fallen.

"Lucas's feet are really way too big to go in his mouth so often," Honey said gently, stepping forward to put a hand on Brennan's arm.

Brennan found it took quite a great deal of forbearance to refrain from jerking away from her. "I have taken no offense," he said, again forcing that artificial smile. "But perhaps we could adjourn to your home and discuss our strategy for infiltrating the IAPN conference?"

"Right," Lucas said, clearly relieved to be moving on. "We've heard from our contacts. Tracy Baum should be arriving at the hotel soon."

"I thought we were meeting Tiernan?" Grace said, glancing back over her shoulder at the buffalo and then at the wolves surrounding Lucas and Honey. "Also, no offense, but is there a reason your Pack members are staying in wolf form?"

Lucas's eyes narrowed, but his voice remained calm. "Tiernan is operating under an alias. And it is very close to the full moon, so many of my Pack brothers and sisters prefer to run as wolf during this time. Is there a problem?"

Alexios almost casually moved so that he was standing partially between Grace and Lucas. "No problem. She's a city girl, that's all. All this wildlife is making her twitchy for a cappuccino or something."

Grace bristled, but Alexios grinned at her and she laughed, her usual good nature surfacing. "I'm sorry, I certainly didn't mean any offense," she told Lucas and Honey. "But maybe we could go someplace with four walls and electricity or at least a fire? I may be a descendant of Diana, but I'm one with a healthy regard for modern conveniences, and it's much colder than I'd expected."

Honey whistled. "Descendant of Diana, huh? Been a long time since we saw one of those."

Lucas bowed deeply, and Brennan noticed a strange thing. The wolves arrayed around their alpha and his mate all bowed as well, their elegant heads dipping low. The motion was a study in grace in each of them, far more the action of a predator giving honor than that of an animal performing a trick.

Grace bowed to them all in return, but Brennan heard Alexios muttering, "Here we freaking go again."

"The wolf is not Diana's animal," Alexios said, biting off the words. "The panther is. So I don't want to hear any blather about consorts, honorary or otherwise, or I'm so going to kick your ass."

Honey's smile was suddenly sharp and full of teeth. "Trust me, you'd not be the only one doing the ass kicking."

Lucas threw up his hands in protest, shaking his head. "Hey, I don't know what you're talking about. What consort? Also, who even says 'consort' these days?"

"Yeah, you're the one who's going to be getting *your* ass

kicked if you don't stop that," Grace said, poking Alexios in the side, her embarrassment tangible. "It's a long story and certainly one we don't need to bring up again now. Or, you know, *ever.*"

Brennan decided the moment had come to rescue Grace, and perhaps they could dispense with the small talk and move on to the focus of this mission. He stepped forward to state that very premise, but before he could open his mouth to speak, a searing, slashing pain cut through the side of his throat, dropping him to his knees where he stood. "*Pain,*" he managed, gasping out the words. "Fear. Darkness."

A tidal wave of fire and pain raged through his body, twisting him into an impossible contortion until his head slammed down onto the ground so hard it bounced. "He's hurting her. Hurting her. Biting . . . blood . . . no. No!"

Alexios crouched into a squat beside him, grabbing his shoulders and lifting him. "Brennan, what is it? What in the nine hells is going on with you? Hurting who? Who's doing the hurting?"

Brennan tried to answer, but a snarling roar was all he managed as the rage ripped at his insides until he was sure his ribs would explode out through his skin. *Lust.* He could feel the echoes of the vampire's lust as his bite caught at the woman, threatening to pull her under. He caught Alexios by the arm and stared up into his fellow warrior's shocked face.

The world swam red before his eyes, but he finally managed to form coherent words. "He bit her. He bit her, Alexios. He touched her skin with his godsdamned bloodsucking teeth, and now he's going to die."

"Bit who? Brennan, you're not making any sense."

Brennan stared at Alexios, looking right through him as the image of a woman in life-threatening danger seared his mind. "I don't know who. I don't know, I don't know, I don't know," he shouted, dragging himself up off the ground.

Before Alexios could answer, Brennan shoved him out of the way, launched himself into the air, and transformed into mist, shooting through the air in an unerring straight path toward his woman.

Must find the woman. Must find her *now*.

❧

Mammoth Hot Springs Hotel

Tiernan closed the door and leaned back against it. Her room was standard-issue hotel: plaid bedspread on the king bed, phone, lamp, and Internet connection on the desk, and the room service breakfast menu propped up on her pillows. Clean, bright, and bland, but after all, nobody came to Yellowstone for the hotel décor. She crossed the room and sat on the edge of her bed, dropped her bag, and kicked off the stupid shoes, tossing them at the too-small wastebasket over by the desk. One crisis solved: she'd never wear the damn things again.

Now all she had to do was solve the mystery of the vamp who'd bitten her, the vamps who were enthralling shapeshifters, and the scientists who were helping them. With or without Atlantean help, she decided, as she checked her phone for nonexistent messages from what she'd come to think of as the underwater contingent. They weren't much for modern technology.

The single window drew her across the room, and she checked and double-checked that it was locked, even though she was on the third floor. Everything she knew about vampires said that they couldn't enter a home uninvited, but nobody knew for sure what the outer limits of that rule were. Nobody but the vamps, and they weren't talking. Did a hotel room count as a home? She rather doubted it.

Worse, did the blood he'd taken from her allow him special privileges with her—*to* her? Would she become his Renfield?

She rolled her eyes, impatient with her own stupidity. Renfield. *Please.*

She took her toiletries bag to the bathroom and starting unpacking the little bit of makeup she'd brought with her.

Sparkly eye shadow and glossy lips would help the scientists underestimate her. Fluffy reporters were nothing to worry about, after all. She'd already prepared the way through e-mails and phone calls so they thought she was there for a few sound bites on the wonderful medical breakthroughs humans and shape-shifters were making in the spirit of joint cooperation.

Yeah. Right. Maybe that was happening somewhere, but not with this group. They had a deeper, darker purpose, and it was up to her to find out exactly who, what, where, when, and why. She set the gleaming tube of mascara on the counter and made the mistake of looking into the mirror. The smear of blood on her neck highlighted the two small puncture holes, and the black circles under her eyes from weeks of restless nights made her look like she was half-vamp herself.

She wet a washcloth and poured half of the travel-sized bottle of antibacterial gel on it, then gritted her teeth and cleaned her neck. Once the blood was gone, the punctures were barely visible. A little makeup would cover up the evidence, so nobody at the conference would be able to tell she'd served as the equivalent of vampire Cheetos.

A little *snack*.

Bastard.

Something scraped against glass, and she dropped the washcloth. The noise had been so subtle that she might not have heard it if her nerves hadn't shot straight to hyper-alert during the encounter with the vamp.

He was back. He was back, and unfortunately, there were no wooden stakes in the dish with the complimentary soap and shampoo. Calling for backup would only get someone else killed with her; she knew the speed and strength of vampires very, very well. She grabbed the small glass tumbler and filled it with water, then whipped around and faced the window, ready to bluff.

Ready to lie. She was so very good at lying.

"I'm not an easy target now," she called out, pleased that

her voice remained so steady. "This is a glass filled with holy water, and I'm not afraid to use it."

But it wasn't the vampire's face at the window. It wasn't any face at all, but a strange fog that was almost corporeal, almost sentient, the way it moved back and forth across the outside of her window, as if it sought a way to enter.

She knew some vamps could fly, but could they turn into fog? Or was she hallucinating from blood loss?

Tiernan's hand trembled a little, and the water in the glass rippled. "Whatever you are, stay out."

As if it heard her, the fog froze to utter stillness, then receded. In the space of two of her rapid heartbeats, it vanished entirely from the window.

"This is where the stupid person walks over to the window to look out, and the zombie breaks the glass and eats her brains," she muttered, putting the glass down with a little too much force on the counter. "If zombies could float.

"A brilliant investigative reporter, however, calls for help." She pulled her phone out of her pocket and took a step toward the door. But then she dropped the phone from nerveless fingers to the perfectly ordinary carpet in her perfectly ordinary hotel room as the fog, or mist, or whatever the heck it was—*not* perfectly ordinary, oh, no, not at all *ordinary*—streamed into her room through the nonexistent cracks in the seam between the window and the sill.

Her reporter's brain toggled over to its "superobservant" setting, and she took in every detail, shaking her head back and forth, whether in denial or disbelief she had no idea.

The fog coalesced into a sparkling, shimmering shape—a large and broad shape—the shape of a man. The golden light from the lamps reflected off of tiny particles in the water, projecting a cascade of mini-rainbows across every flat surface in a brilliant light show. Then the cloud of mist exploded outward as if triumphantly hailing the man who stepped from it.

The man. The man who, mere seconds before, had been nothing but a cloud. A fog. The man who now stood in the center of her hotel room, breathing hard, staring at her with his ice-green eyes.

Except they weren't as icy as she remembered. No, this man's eyes were pure green fire, and every inch of her skin burned as the heat of his gaze swept her from head to toe and then back, lingering on her neck.

"Brennan?" His name came out in a whisper, but he snapped his head up and stared straight into her eyes when she spoke. A brief whisper of danger sent a chill down her spine, and her senses translated the deadly stillness in his pose as that of a feral animal crouching to leap.

Feral and primitive. Wild and beautiful. His silky black hair fell in waves around a face that would cause the highest-paid TV anchor to weep with jealousy. Pure masculine beauty, with dark brows over those amazing green eyes. The cheekbones and bone structure all the Atlanteans she'd met had shared, as if they alone had posed for the most magnificent of the ancient Greek statues. And his mouth . . . oh, his mouth. How could a simple combination of lips and teeth make her wonder what it would be like to taste him?

As reality crumpled around her, some vestige of control snapped into place and Tiernan managed to force words from her suddenly dust-dry throat. "I'm guessing I missed a pretty spectacular entrance back in Boston when I was hiding behind that couch. I had wondered how you guys busted through that window so high off the ground, but I was more thinking ropes coming down from the roof."

"You are Tiernan?" he demanded, ignoring her nervous chatter. "Tell me. Now."

"Yes, I'm Tiernan. You know me. We—"

She gasped a little and stopped talking as he took a single step toward her, then another, his large, muscled body leaning forward as if he were stalking her. "He dared to touch you," he growled, the words nearly unintelligible. "He put his mouth on you. I will kill him."

She backed away, but the motion seemed to infuriate him even further, because he dove across the several feet separating them as if he really were that wild animal leaping for its prey.

"Brennan, stop! I don't know what this is about, but you need to calm down so we can—" Memories of his crazed wildness the first time he'd seen her flashed into her mind, shutting down her powers of speech as he took the final step and slammed his hands flat against the wall on either side of her head, caging her against his body.

He wasn't going to listen to her. She was in danger. Rick had been right. She should have listened, but no, she had to be tough, and now for the second time in an hour she was facing a predator.

"I'll be damned if I'm going to be prey for a vampire or anybody else," she shouted, shoving at his chest as he leaned farther toward her. It was like shoving a brick wall. A hot, hard brick wall that smelled like salt and sea and man.

He froze in place, then tilted his head to one side, pinning her with a long, considering stare. "Not his prey," he finally said, his deep voice sizzling across her nerve endings.

She caught her breath, but before she could speak he lifted one hand from the wall to touch the side of her face.

"Not *his* prey," he repeated, bending his face down to hers. "Mine."

Chapter 4

She'd been partially hidden; blocked by the door that had stood between them. The door that he would have ripped from its frame with his bare hands. But as Brennan had transformed back from mist into his body, the woman had stepped out into the room and he'd seen her face clearly. The face from the newspaper clipping he yet carried in his pocket. The face from those fragments of nearly forgotten dreams. He saw her face, and the entire world jolted and fell out of orbit. There was no sun. There was only *her.*

Tiernan.

She was so very beautiful. Waves of dark hair framed her face, a perfect frame for her enormous dark brown eyes. The curve of her cheek must have inspired poetry. The curve of her lips must have inspired song.

The curves of her body—well. Those inspired something entirely different. He'd felt his heart pounding in his chest as his body reacted suddenly and fiercely, every inch of him going hard and ready.

She'd stared up at him, defiance and caution mingling in

those dark, dark eyes as she met his gaze. That's all it took. A single glance, and he was done. He was hers.

Then she'd spoken his name, and his calm had shattered. He'd leapt at her, desperate to touch her. To taste her. To take her and make her his and never, ever let her leave him.

She'd said something, shouted something, but only one word penetrated. Prey? Who would dare to make his woman prey? Not prey.

"Mine," he repeated, almost snarling the word, daring her to defy him. Didn't she know? Didn't she understand?

Her eyes widened as if in fear, and something cracked in his heart. How could she be afraid of him? He was hers; had always been hers, would always be hers. The tide of need dragged him under and he lost the thought, trapped in the wanting.

"Would die for you," he managed to say, but then she gasped a little and he could no longer speak. Could no longer think. Had to taste her. Just once. Just the first of thousands, millions of times.

He bent his head and captured her mouth with his own, and the heat of her, the taste of her, the sheer glory of finally holding her blew through him with the force of a percussive blast. He lifted his head and staggered a few steps back, sure that Poseidon himself must have shot a bolt of power at him from the Trident. A shock wave of pain smashed into and through him, and he had little warning before the curse took over and tried to fulfill its directive: his total destruction.

This could not be emotion—was it? No. It was *pain*. More pain than he had ever known. The universe exploded in Brennan's soul as sanity fractured. He yanked his daggers from their sheaths—instinct driving him to defend himself in the only way he knew how—but it was useless. Futile. Weapons couldn't defend against this enemy. He dropped the daggers and fell to the floor, clutching his chest as the tsunami of emotion ripped through him. Shattered two thousands of years of barrenness—drenched the arid wasteland of his soul with pain.

Anguish and unbearable sadness crushed his heart under the implacable weight of it. Thousands of years of loss striking him all at once. Pains never suffered. Deaths never mourned. Never felt. Oh, Poseidon—*feeling*—such a puny word for the pain, the unending agony. Dying would be easier.

Dying would be *preferable*.

"Please, by all the mercy of the gods, just let me die," he groaned, clenching his teeth, grinding them, his jaw aching as he threw his head back, slamming it against the floor, over and over, mindlessly seeking unconsciousness. Relief. Surcease from the pain. He cried out, or at least he thought he did, as grief claimed him, dragging him down under a riptide of agony to feast on his flesh. On his sanity.

On his soul.

A sound caught his attention, somehow, whispering its way through the pain roaring in his ears. He forced his eyes to open and there she was. Tiernan. Crouching down next to him, hesitantly reaching a hand out. He rolled away from her, unable to bear it. Unable to let her touch him. Maybe it was contagious, maybe she would be caught in the black maelstrom of anguish.

No.

Not her. He could never cause *her* pain.

When she touched his arm, he realized that pain and loss were not the only forfeited emotions returning to him. Oh, no. There were others.

Desire. Need. Pure, driving lust.

Hunger.

He wanted her with the power of a fierce ocean storm, with a primal need so dark and desperate that it was as if thousands of years of abstinence had all caught up with him at once, demanding to be sated.

Demanding *her. Now.*

He snapped up into a crouch, catching her wrist in a vise-like grip. Tried to find the words to make her understand. "Tiernan, I have need of you. My body and soul ache for you."

Emotions raced across her expressive face, and he watched her anger battle her fear and conquer it. Good. She should never fear him. Especially not when he needed so badly to touch her creamy skin. Bury his face in the long dark waves of her hair. Remove every bit of her clothing to discover if her skin could possibly be as silky soft on every inch of her body as he expected it to be. If the tips of her breasts would flush and harden at the touch of his fingers. His lips. His tongue.

His cock hardened to the point of physical pain, and some distant part of his mind that still retained the tiniest bit of rationality wondered at the feeling. Hot, pure desire, after centuries—no, millennia—of none.

"Your body and soul can just let go of me and step back, my friend, or I'll kick you right in your Atlantean nuts," she threatened, yanking her arm away from his grasp.

He allowed her to escape, because he realized that yet another emotion was bubbling up inside him in the face of her defiance. *Joy*. It swirled like a waterspout, filling in the parched and corroded corners of his heart and soul with light and music. *Happiness*.

A sound worked its way up through his chest and burst from his throat. Laughter. Rusty, after so long unused, but definitely laughter. Joy sliced through Brennan, sharp as the blades of his daggers, honed on the sharpening stone of absence and abandonment. It was bliss, it was *joy*, it was ecstasy beyond the hopes of the gods themselves. All of the elation he should have experienced over thousands of moments during the course of his emotionally barren existence sprang to life inside him all at once.

Joy, so much joy, thousands of years of experiences that should have brought him delight, but had not. Those lost moments cascaded through him, image after image, speeding up until he was delirious from the panorama of memories that crashed through his mind, filtered through the emotion pounding on every inch of his body; nerve, bone, and sinew.

This, then, was the devious nature of the curse. He would regain his emotions, and they would drive him insane. But he lost the clarity of that realization as she opened her lovely, lovely mouth to speak.

"Brennan," she said again, his name and something else, and her voice was cool water to a parched warrior who'd battled long and hard in the desert wastes of Persia; warmth and softness to one who'd survived weeks hunting vampire warlords in the frozen heights of Siberia. Her voice was joy made into sound, but her words were meaningless.

He *needed* her. Only Tiernan could ride the torrent of emotion with him and help him tame it. She was his, and he was hers, and he had waited for her for all the long years of his life. If only he could climb inside the cool, serene center of her, he would be restored. She had to understand. He had to *make* her understand.

He pushed himself off the floor in a sudden, explosive movement and caught her silken hair in his rough and calloused hands. Warriors' hands. Hands that had no right . . . But the thought disappeared, crushed under the spiking drive of need. He had to make her understand. She was his life and sanity.

She was his everything.

He pulled her to him, ripping at the clothing that formed a barrier between them, desperate to feel her skin, her radiant, translucent, beautiful skin. Closer, closer. She struggled and the pain stabbed at him, joy turning to despair. Would she really try to leave him? Abandon him to a barren existence yet again?

Poseidon's curse roared through his memory. *Cursed to forget her.* No. Never. The idea of it drove him to a panic that clutched him in its sharpened claws and ate at his soul. Thousands of years of enforced solitude shattered around him, and his barren and desperate heart lurched like a hideous creature, squinting, into the light.

"Mine," he snarled. "You will never, ever leave me again." Tearing at the cloth that dared block her from his touch. Burying his face in the warmth between her lovely round breasts, marveling at the contrast of his sun-darkened hand against her creamy skin.

"Lonely," he managed, wondering why the lace covering her from his sight was darkening with wetness, why his mind had gone hot and black. "Help me."

She made a sound, said more words, but though the meaning of the words was lost to him, the meaning of the sound was clear. Pain. Fear.

He was scaring her. Maybe hurting her.

The realization cut through the fog of madness as nothing else could have done. No. He would never hurt her. Oh, by all the gods, what had he done?

What was he still doing?

He threw himself back and away from her, forcing himself to find a semblance of calm. Forcing himself to hear and understand what she was saying.

"Please don't hurt me," she said, her face so white he thought she would surely faint from shock or terror at any moment. "Brennan. Brennan, we're supposed to be allies. What happened? Did the vamps get to you, too?"

She thought he was enthralled? But . . . he needed to tell her. He needed to explain.

"So long," he began, the words nearly choking him. "So long, and the curse. So *lonely.*" A burst of wild laughter surged up from his chest, cutting off whatever he'd been about to say. How to explain an ancient curse to a modern journalist? She'd think him a liar or, worse, insane. He probably was insane.

But he had to try. He slowly stood and backed farther away until he was standing against the window of the small room. "Tiernan. I— Oh, gods, it hurts." He doubled over for an instant, then forced himself upright again. "I cannot . . . cannot begin to apologize enough for my . . . my behavior. I can only beg your forgiveness and hope you will give me the chance to explain."

She jumped to her feet and ran to the door, never stopping until her hand was on the handle. "Are you nuts? After that? I'm going to call the police and . . ."

As her words trailed off, he fought for some measure of rational thought and managed to realize what she must be thinking. "A few moments, please," he whispered, but she seemed to hear him. An eternity passed as she considered his words, but finally she nodded, and he bent over and inhaled long, slow, deep breaths, practicing the calming exercises he had not used since he was a novice warrior. At first he thought it was in vain; that the simple act of drawing breath could not begin to conquer the madness of so many years of returning feelings.

In. Out. In. Out. Finally, tens or hundreds of breaths later, he achieved what he hoped was at least a temporary leash on the raging emotions, and he was able to recall the reason behind their presence.

"If you call the police, our mission here will be ruined," he said quietly. "We cannot afford to draw that kind of attention to ourselves if we wish to discover the truth behind these scientific experiments on shifter and human brains. I can never apologize enough for what happened, but I can attempt to explain."

She hesitated, and then nodded.

A bolt of hope shot through him, threatening to take him to his knees, but he ruthlessly stamped it down. "You are now afraid to remain anywhere near me, however, and with very good reason."

She nodded again, narrowing her beautiful dark eyes but still remaining silent.

"Then perhaps you will do me the very undeserved honor of listening to me for a short time, while I tell you a tale from long ago. All I ask, though it will be almost impossible, is that you try to believe that I am telling you the absolute truth."

She considered that for several long moments in silence, her hand still on the door handle and her body still poised for flight. Finally she apparently came to a decision, because she gave a brief nod. "All right. I'll listen to you. For Susannah. But remember what you said about truth. Trust me, I *will* know the difference."

Darkness shuttered her expression, almost as if the burden of truth somehow pained her. Brennan shook off the fanciful impression and sat down in a chair in the corner farthest from her, so as not to threaten her any more than he already had. He refused to admit, even to himself, that his legs felt as if they would no longer hold him up. Shame swamped him and he was unable to meet her eyes, terrified of the condemnation he'd see in them. That he deserved.

"Let us begin, then, with an unforgivable truth that occurred more than two thousand years ago," he said, steeling himself against the disgust he knew she'd feel for his debauched existence and the deaths he had caused. She was the one—she *must* be the one—and now he would destroy any hope that she would ever have any feelings for him other than fear, revulsion, and condemnation.

After Corelia and the babe, though, he had known he could never deserve a chance at happiness. It had been an eternity since he'd even thought the state possible.

Poseidon had won. Finally and irrevocably. Brennan would tell his story, she would order him from her, and he would welcome death. There could be no going back from this, once it began.

"It was the year you name 202 B.C. I was a young warrior then—" He looked up her, the bitter shame nearly swamping him as she stood, still at the door, clutching the two sides of her ripped shirt together. "Please. If you desire to repair your clothing, I will turn my back."

She laughed, but it was wild and held no humor. "Repair this? That will take more than the mini sewing kit. Turn around, and I'll change."

He did, expecting to hear the sound of the door opening as she made her escape. Instead, after a short pause, he heard the zipper of her bag opening and had to force himself to stomp on the images of her undressing that his mind tried to provide.

"Okay," she said.

He turned around and found her leaning against the wall, one hand again on the door handle. She'd pulled on a dark sweater to replace the shirt he'd torn, which was no longer in sight. Bitter shame burned through him again, but he gritted his teeth against that or any other emotion. She deserved to hear his story without his sniveling self-pity coloring any part of it.

She nodded at him to continue, her dark eyes fixed and staring as if she were nearly in a trance, whether from fear or anger he could not tell.

"Truth, warrior," she murmured. "Sing me the truth of your Atlantean secrets."

Something about her voice sent chills sweeping up his spine. It was different, somehow. Almost hypnotic. Perhaps— but he could not stop to analyze it. No going back, after all. So he sat in the too-small chair in the too-small room and he told her the story of a warrior cursed by his own god.

No going back.

Chapter 5

Tiernan took slow, deep breaths and tried to convince herself she wasn't insane. To stay in the room with this man, who'd assaulted her only minutes earlier—it was stupid and dangerous. But the stakes she was playing for were so high; high enough that she'd been willing to risk her life in order to discover the truth. And the feeling she got from Brennan was not, oddly enough, danger. It was sadness. A vast, unbearable despair. He hadn't even noticed the tears streaming down his face as he'd held her. The lace of her bra was still damp. Her cheeks heated at the memory of his face on her chest.

He'd said he was sorry. He'd mentioned a curse, and it had been the truth. Now she would listen with one hand on the door, ready to escape, in case she didn't like what she heard. She could do that much. She could *risk* that much.

She nodded again, and Brennan began his story. An almost unbelievable story—totally unbelievable to anyone but her—that began in ancient Rome. She studied him carefully as he told her of his "drunken debauchery" all those years ago. Every line of his body echoed his remorse. He sat with his head bowed, shoulders slumped, and hands clasped together and resting between his legs. How he'd failed in his duty, forsaken his honor, and been the worst man ever to walk the planet, according to his story.

Any journalist worth the ink in her printer would have dismissed him as dangerous and deluded, or at least any journalist who couldn't tell truth from lies merely from hearing the words. An unpleasant idea occurred to her and she interrupted him right in the middle of "alone with an innocent maid." Maybe she could no more distinguish truth from Atlanteans than she could from the vampires. She hadn't been in the fabulous ancient city long enough to experience any outright lies, or so she'd thought at the time.

"Hmm. Seems you hesitated a bit over the word 'innocent,'" she pointed out, not mentioning how the word had sounded a warning in her mind.

He hesitated, clearly thrown off. A muscle clenched in his jaw, and she got the impression he was gritting his teeth against another wave of the craziness that had swamped him before. When he'd assaulted her. Adrenaline pumped through her, leaving her nauseous as she edged closer to the door and tightened her grip on the handle.

"I—No, that was my error. She was an innocent lass."

Her senses jangled. Not anywhere nearly as harsh as "nails on chalkboard," but not nearly as mild as "gentle wind chimes" on her personal Tiernan Butler scale, either. She was definitely sensing something; if not lies, then at least deflection.

"They defined innocent as something different way back then?"

A dark flush rose in his cheeks. "I am aware of no difference in definitions. However, her innocence or lack thereof is not relevant to this story."

Another tingle. Still, not enough for corroboration. She needed a baseline. "I need for you to lie to me."

He lifted his head and stared at her, his green eyes widening. "I beg your pardon. I thought you just said that you need me to lie to you."

"That's what I said. I'm a journalist, and I trust my instincts," she said, fudging a little herself. "I need to know if they work on Atlanteans. Tell me a lie, and say it like you really believe it. Like you're trying to make *me* believe it."

"But if you know I'm lying—" he began, his eyebrows drawing together.

"I know, I know. It sounds stupid. But I think at this point you owe me one." She deliberately wrenched the door handle down. "Unless you'd rather I just leave now."

Something dark and deadly shimmered in his gaze before he looked down at the floor again. There was a silence for several seconds, and she thought it signaled his refusal. Then he looked up at her again, and his face had changed. Hardened. The heat in his gaze was almost tangible, and she could feel its weight on her skin.

"You want me to lie to you? As you wish. Listen to this, and listen very closely." He moved his hands to the arms of the chair and grasped them so tightly that his knuckles turned white. "Here is the greatest lie I have ever told: *I don't want you.*"

His big body shuddered and the muscles in his arms flexed as he tightened his grip on the chair, and then he continued, his voice barely more than a rasp, as the heat raced through her at his stark words. "I'm not battling a desperate, soul-searing hunger to touch you, and taste you, and take you. I'm not fighting the results of the curse and two thousands of years of bleak loneliness in order to protect your honor. I'm not ashamed almost unto death that I assaulted you earlier. There is nothing about your beauty or your courage that makes me desperate to carry you away from this place and spend the next several weeks or months or years worshiping your naked body while you tell me every detail about your life."

He stopped suddenly and pinned her in place with the naked yearning in his gaze. "Is that enough of a lie for you, Tiernan Butler?"

She had to catch her breath before she could speak. Her lungs were somehow empty; his words had deprived her of both oxygen and speech. Every nerve ending in her body was jangling, and a new, harsh sound was buzzing in her eardrums. If she had to find a label for this level of lie, it would be chain saw.

Chain saw times one thousand.

He'd been lying, oh yeah. He had definitely been lying at the same time he'd been telling her a very real truth. No man she'd ever known had said anything like that to her. No one had ever wanted her as much as this man—this warrior—wanted her, with an intensity that should have frightened her more than it did. It stunned her and drew her to him, even as it frightened her. Intensity could turn to obsession, fast. She was likely in far more danger than she was willing to admit.

However, her Gift worked on him. She had definitely known when he was lying. She could listen to his story. She could find a way to work with him. She had to—for Susannah. The rest of it, including the odd compulsion she had to go to him, touch him, and forgive him, could be ignored.

She could almost hear Rick's voice in her head, repeating over and over again: *The story is everything.*

She finally took her hand off the door handle and stepped away from the door, ignoring her suddenly wobbly knees. "Maybe I could sit down now," she said, her voice only a little shaky.

She pulled the second of the pair of hotel chairs toward her, still needing distance from him, regardless of whether he was telling the truth or not. He was sorry, yes, but he hadn't said anything about whether or not he'd be able to control whatever had pushed him to attack her in the first place.

As she sank into the chair, her cell phone rang. She glanced at her backpack but then ignored it. Probably Rick. No matter who was calling, it couldn't be as important as this. She fixed a measuring stare on Brennan. "I think that's enough lying. Please tell me the rest of your story. But first I need to ask you one thing, and this time, please tell me the absolute truth."

"Anything," he said, but caution or something else narrowed his green eyes.

"Whatever happened earlier. Can you promise me that it won't happen again? Can you promise me you won't hurt me in any way?" She bit her lip, knowing that everything rested on his answer.

"I pledge this to you, Tiernan Butler. No matter the intensity of the curse as it tries to destroy me, I will do everything within my power to protect you, even should it mean giving my life in order to keep you from harm," he said, each word clear and distinct, spoken with the weight of a solemn vow in that deep, sensual voice of his.

She was shaken by both the words and the utter honesty in which they were offered. He leaned forward, searching her face as if he were willing her to believe him. He needn't have worried. She believed him completely, but of course he couldn't know why. Nobody knew why.

She had no choice but to believe him. She was a walking lie detector.

⌒⌒⌒

Brennan had no hope that she would forgive him, or even stay long enough to hear the rest of his tale. How could she possibly trust him now? After what he'd done to her? He waited, holding on to the flimsy chair as if it could anchor him. Stop him from rushing to her to plead forgiveness. She had no idea that his sanity hung, precariously balanced, on the edge of her decision.

"Go ahead, then," she said, making a circular motion with her hand. "Tell me about this curse."

The blood rushed from his head in a great wave until he felt light-headed with it. She believed him. She would let him explain. That was enough. It had to be enough. The rest was up to him.

"You were at the 'innocent maid' part of the story, if I recall." The hint of a smile twitched at the edges of her lips, and he stared at her mouth, fascinated, focused on how much he would surrender to see her smile, until she cleared her throat. "Brennan?"

"I have never told the story in its entirety to anyone," he said abruptly. "You will be the first, which is only fitting, since you are involved in the curse's fulfillment."

When it was obvious she was going to speak, he shook his head, forestalling the questions that she must have. "It's better if I get this out all at once. Then you can decide if you can bear to have me in your presence."

She frowned but subsided and leaned back in the chair.

"I know you learned a little about us when you were in Atlantis so briefly before. As Prince Conlan and the Lord Vengeance probably told you, we are the Warriors of Poseidon. We all swear fealty to the sea god himself in a ceremony that originated more than eleven thousand years ago. As Poseidon's chosen elite, we are held to the highest standards of duty, honor, and conduct. However, I failed in all three of these," he said, barely able to speak the words. He jumped up to pace around the room, veering away from her when she flinched a little at his approach.

"I was a drunken ruffian. I spent much of my free time, and even time that I should have been training, drinking wine in Rome, carousing with women, and, to put it bluntly, behaving like an ass."

Images from those days flashed in his mind, as vivid as if they had occurred only weeks before. He shoved a hand through his hair and pushed it away from his face and then turned to pace to the other side of the room.

"There was a girl. A woman," he hastily corrected himself. "She was so seductive, and I was more than willing. She was a senator's daughter. I thought—I thought our alliance was simply a pleasurable diversion."

"You had a fling?" Tiernan asked, her expression solemn, although he thought he saw a hint of mischief dancing in her glorious whiskey-dark eyes. The rest of his tale would kill her amusement.

"We were caught," he said flatly. "I offered to marry her. She didn't want me, and in any event, her father said I was unsuitable. There was a scandal and the sea god . . . well. Poseidon was not pleased."

"You took the hit, huh?" Her voice was warm, almost as if she had sympathy for him.

He did not want her sympathy. He could never deserve it.

"He cursed me. He cursed me with such an unforgiving and unending curse that I have spent more than two thousand years of my life unable to feel any emotion." Rage, rage that he could finally feel after so long without it, seared through his blood. "Two thousand *years*," he repeated, and then he bitterly recited the words that had been burned into his memory in that tavern back room:

"*'For all eternity, until such time as you can meet your one true mate, you will feel no emotion. Neither sadness nor joy; neither rage nor delight.*

"*'When you do meet her, you will experience a resurgence of all of the emotions you have repressed over the years and centuries and even millennia.*

"*'If that alone is not enough to destroy you, you will also be cursed to forget your mate whenever she is out of your sight. Only when she is dead—her heart stopped and her soul flown—will your memory of her fully return to you, thus allowing you until the end of your days to repent bringing dishonor upon the name of the Warriors of Poseidon.'*"

He closed his eyes, fists clenched at his sides, in the middle of the room, waiting for her to heap scorn upon him for his failure. Waiting for her to run away from the horrible import of his words.

"Bit harsh, wasn't it?"

His eyes snapped open at the unexpected words. She still sat in the chair, her head tilted to the side, watching him.

"You don't understand. I have not told you the worst of it, for I am a coward." He paused, as another wave of pain sliced through him when he thought of Corelia and the babe. The child who would have been his son or daughter, had it lived.

Had it not died, because of him.

She made an impatient movement. "I understand perfectly well. I understand that you were a hell raiser when you were young, as so many of us are, and I also understand that your sea god is a little bit unbalanced, no offense."

"But I—"

"You did nothing that any frat boy with a keg and a toga party hasn't done," she said, interrupting him again. "Yet somehow you've been punished for more than two thousand years? And I can't believe I'm even saying that. Two thousand years. Just how old are you? Are all Atlanteans as old as you?"

"I killed the mother of my child when she carried him in her belly." The words came out harsh, rasping his throat. Scorching his heart.

The color drained from Tiernan's face. "You . . . what? You—But wait." She drew a long, shuddering breath. "No. That's not true. Or rather, some part of it is not true. I can feel something . . ."

As she fell silent, those enormous dark eyes of hers fixed on him in shock and horror, the pain rose in his chest, cutting off his breath. He bent forward in the chair, catching himself with his hands before he fell out and his face hit the floor. Agony at the loss of his child, bitter remorse over Corelia's death—both vied for control of his sanity.

He began the deep breathing exercises again, forcing himself to climb back into the chair. "It is truth," he said. "Truth enough, anyway."

"Truth enough isn't good enough. Tell me exactly."

He bowed his head and complied, recounting Poseidon's blistering condemnation and accusation. "So you see," he concluded, "she died because of me. My own child died because of me. I have no right to either life or happiness, but I have spent every day since that one fighting to save other women, other children, from death. Searching for something I could never find or deserve."

"Redemption," she whispered. "But, Brennan, she never told you about the baby? You said you offered to marry her."

"She laughed at me when we were discovered and I offered marriage. Said a mere warrior could never be good enough for her. I was a dalliance, at best, and a means to scratch an itch, at worst," he said slowly, experiencing again his furious humiliation, as if it had happened only hours before.

Worse, far worse, humiliation became gut-wrenching pain as he continued. "She never told me about the child. Never a hint. Refused all communication. She had a marriage planned . . . I heard later that her intended husband had learned of her affairs and of the pregnancy from tale-bearing servants. He denounced her publicly, and her so-called friends from her social class abandoned her."

He clenched the wooden arms of the chair so tightly the wood splintered and broke in his hands. Slowly, he released the fractured pieces of wood and watched them fall to the floor, not caring that he'd ripped open the palm of his left hand. Blood dripped, drop by fat, glistening drop, onto the carpet.

"So much blood," he whispered. "She cut her wrists, they said. The human body contains so very much blood, did you know that?" He looked up at Tiernan, desperate that she should understand. "For centuries after, I saw that image in my nightmares. Her life and her blood, drained out on the marble tile. My child's life drained away with it. All my fault."

Chapter 6

"No," she said. "No, it wasn't your fault."

Tiernan knew from her Gift that every word he'd spoken was the truth, or what he believed to be the truth. She also knew that his perception of events was badly skewed; that there was no way any but the smallest portion of blame was his.

"You were wild, like so many young men. Like I would have been, if I hadn't . . . if things had been different. But that woman—Corelia—she was the one who used you, Brennan. She was the one who harmed herself and her own child, because she believed she was too good to marry a mere warrior."

He looked up at her, and she imagined she saw a glimmer of hope through the pain in his eyes. It was too much to take in, though, too much to understand or even try to understand. She didn't know him, couldn't know what he was thinking, but some part of her wanted to help him release so much undeserved guilt and pain. But now wasn't the right time, and she probably wasn't even the right person.

Anyway, he was bleeding on her carpet. That much she could fix. Sympathy and a stronger emotion, one she didn't want to analyze, overcame the lingering wariness she'd felt. She took a deep breath and released the door handle.

"You need to bandage that hand," she said, heading for her backpack. "I have a mini first-aid kit in my bag. Let's get you cleaned up and then we can figure out what to do. Oh, and you're totally paying for that chair, my friend. A reporter's budget only goes so far."

He looked down at his hands and blinked, almost as if he hadn't realized before that moment that he'd hurt himself. "Did you not hear me? What I've done? What I've caused? Order me from your presence and be done with it, if you have any mercy at all," he rasped out, his face starkly white. "I don't know if I can promise to let you go if I remain with you any longer."

Heat swept through her at the reminder of the other things he'd said to her, but she tried to ignore it. *Priorities.* Fix his hands, then worry about the rest of it. She found the kit and withdrew Neosporin and a large adhesive bandage, then glanced at him as she walked to the bathroom to wet a washcloth. "I heard you. I also heard what you didn't say, though. That you tried to do the right thing by her and she wouldn't let you. That she was a selfish woman who committed the worst possible act against herself and her own baby."

A thought occurred to her. "How old were you when this happened, anyway?"

He bowed his head. "I had nineteen years."

She paused, one hand on the faucet. "Nineteen? Are you kidding me? You were a child yourself."

"Age cannot excuse fault."

"No, but if everybody who did something stupid when they were nineteen got cursed, the world would be in for a load of trouble," she snapped, wishing she could get through to him. Wondering why she cared. As she ran water onto the white cloth, she thought of another lost baby, and then she tried to talk past the lump in her throat as she gave him the advice so many others had given her over the past two years. "You need to forgive yourself for something that wasn't even your fault. It's not going to be easy, but you can't get past it if you don't. You can't heal, and you can't move forward, and you'll never be able to live your life."

She paused at the threshold from the bathroom and looked first at Brennan, and then at the door to the hall, weighing the risks and rewards of what she was about to do.

Final answer time, Tiernan. Stay or go.

He looked up at her, the lines in his face deepening as if he could hear her thoughts and expected her to run. She'd never seen so much anguish on anyone's face.

"I will never harm you. I would die first," he said, and again she felt the pure, musical truth of it surrounding her, wrapping her in a sensual haze that belied the stark words. The sheer power of that truth persuaded her.

"I know you believe that. For now, it's enough. We need each other, so let's figure out how to stop these scientists. Together."

"Together," he repeated, and then a smile of such dazzling male beauty spread across his face that she almost reconsidered her decision. He was far too dangerously seductive to be trusted. Or was it herself she didn't trust? Gorgeous, humanity-protecting warriors with tortured pasts were suddenly her thing?

Apparently so. She crossed the room and handed him the washcloth. "Clean that scrape, and then we'll bandage it. We should probably figure out a story for when someone asks—"

He took the cloth from her, and when his fingers touched her hand, an almost electrical shock sizzled through her nerve endings, causing her to gasp a little and yank her hand back. He lifted his head, his eyes narrowing, and again she had that disconcerting sense of a predator catching the scent of his prey.

"I'm not," she said suddenly, wiping her damp hand on her jeans. "Your prey, that is."

"So it would seem. Perhaps I am yours." His deep voice

held an undercurrent of amusement, although his expression was still bleak. He rose to his feet and she caught her breath, realizing all over again just how big he was. How much pure masculine strength was leashed in that tall, muscled body. She was taking a big risk trusting him.

"I will earn your trust," he said, holding out his wounded hand, palm up.

She was instantly suspicious to hear her thoughts reflected back at her. "Can you read my mind?"

"No, but your face is a mirror to your thoughts at times, Tiernan Butler." He studied her, as if trying to memorize her features. "I had not realized you were so very beautiful."

She felt her cheeks heating again and busied herself with the antibacterial ointment and bandage, trying to touch the actual skin of his hand as little as possible. Trying not to notice how his hands were as large and masculine and elegant as the rest of him. He smelled deliciously male, with a hint of salt and sea mixed in, and she inexplicably wanted to wrap herself up in his scent and roll around like a kitten with fresh catnip.

She forced herself to focus on the task, fastened the bandage, and went to wash her hands and discard the wrappings. He followed her across the room and leaned against the doorway, arms folded over his chest, watching every move she made.

"You're all set. Now, what is the plan? I know you've got a cover story in place as some kind of rich benefactor, but Rick didn't—"

The phone rang again, cutting her off mid-sentence at the same time that someone pounded on the door of the room. She stuffed the first-aid items in the top of her open backpack, pulled out her cell phone, saw that it was Rick again, clicked it to voice mail, and headed for the door. Before she could reach it, Brennan was suddenly standing in front of her, a deadly stillness in his posture. He was so fast she hadn't even seen him move.

"We still must discuss who dared to hurt you," he said, skimming her neck with one finger, scorching a trail of heat across her skin. "And then he will die. If I am very lucky, this will be him now."

Brennan jerked the door open, and a man standing on the other side practically fell into the room. He'd clearly been eavesdropping. Tiernan managed to uncurl her lip into a polite smile before he recovered his balance, but he offered up in response only an officious sniff that matched his neatly pressed pin-striped suit. Unfortunately, his balding head flushed a hot red, giving away the mortification that his superior expression couldn't hide. Human, then. Vamps didn't have the blood pressure to do that.

"Ms. Baum? Tracy Baum?" He made a point of looking anywhere but up at Brennan, who had a good foot of height advantage on him. "I'm Mr. Wesley, your liaison to Dr. Litton. He wanted me to be sure and catch up to you right away with your press pass and schedule and answer any questions you might have."

He shoved a dark blue folder at her. Tiernan took it from him and smiled her best ditzy reporter smile, ignoring Brennan's sudden and unmistakable tension at her side. Always good to be nice to the mad scientist's Igor, after all. Brennan was going to have to get used to her in her undercover role if he really intended to stick close.

"Thank you so much, Mr. Wesley. Please call me Tracy. I'm so looking forward to this conference and everything I can learn for my article." She put a hand on his arm and leaned in, as if sharing a confidence. "I'm sure you'll be very helpful."

Behind her, Brennan made a sound low in his throat that almost sounded like . . . a *growl*? She evaluated the odds she could stamp on Brennan's foot without Wesley noticing, then decided to just introduce him instead. "This is—"

"Brennan. Litton is expecting me," Brennan interrupted smoothly. "When do we meet?"

Wesley instantly turned flustered, all but fluttering his hands. "Oh, Mr. Brennan. Dr. Litton is so glad—so honored—uh." He paused, biting his lip. "Thrilled. He's thrilled, we're all thrilled, that you're here to consider further funding of our research. It's really cutting edge. You see, we're—"

"Yes. I will see, won't I?" Somehow, Brennan managed to edge his calm tone with a layer of menace. "I don't just hand out ten-million-dollar grants on the basis of no evidence. So far, what I've seen from my first half million hasn't impressed me."

Tiernan wanted to applaud his technique. He'd be fantastic undercover. Of course, the man actually spent most of his life undercover, come to think about it. It wasn't like he went around announcing he was an Atlantean warrior. She was still waiting for High Prince Conlan's go-ahead to break *that* story.

Wesley wasn't setting off any warning bells in her mind, though. The little he'd told them so far had been the truth. Or at least the truth as he believed it to be, but that was the one constant drawback to her abilities. Litton could have fed his assistant a bunch of crap. People were very, very good at lying to one another—and even to themselves.

"Well, yes. We don't really want to discuss this in the hallway, do we? I just came to give Ms. Baum her materials, and—" Suddenly the man seemed to make the connection he should have wondered about in the first place, and he narrowed his eyes and pursed his lips. "In fact, I am surprised to find you here with a reporter, Mr. Brennan. We certainly . . ." Wesley's voice trailed off and his face turned a peculiar shade of greenish white.

Tiernan glanced at Brennan and had to bite her lip to keep from laughing out loud at the fiercely intimidating glare he was directing at Wesley. The warrior had "arrogant billionaire" down cold.

"Yes. Well." Wesley adjusted his tie, surreptitiously loosening it as he broke into a light sweat. "Dr. Litton will be able to answer all of your questions. I'll be sure to tell him you're here."

"You do that," Brennan said, putting an arm around Tiernan and closing the door in the man's face.

Tiernan shrugged away from Brennan's arm, waited a

few moments, then peeked through the peephole to make sure Wesley was gone. Then she turned to Brennan. "Really, did you need to terrify the poor man?"

"I had a certain reputation to uphold. We have set up my identity as a very eccentric billionaire who is not only arrogant but highly demanding." Stepping closer, he lifted a strand of her hair, then let it slide through his fingers, pinning her in place with the force of his searing green gaze. "He is lucky I did nothing more than intimidate him. When you smiled at him, I wanted to make him bleed."

She caught her breath at the unvarnished truth in his words. "Brennan, you said you would behave."

"Yes, and I will do my best, Tiernan. That does not mean I do not experience the emotions I am now forced to suppress. Interesting irony, is it not?"

A muscle in his jaw jumped, and he pivoted and walked away from her, muttering something under his breath that was definitely not English and definitely not very nice.

"I heard that," she called. "Will you teach me how to swear in Atlantean when this is over?"

He stopped still and then glanced back at her over his shoulder, amusement tilting up one corner of his mouth. "I will teach you anything you want in Atlantean, when this is over."

It was her turn to flush as his intended meaning swept over her, causing certain highly provocative visuals to dance through her brain. But thinking of one extremely buff, unbelievably hot Atlantean warrior naked was not doing anything to move them toward their goal.

"So it's their move," she said briskly. "Now we go to the reception and see what we can find out from drunken scientists with hopefully loose lips?"

He nodded, but before he could respond, Tiernan's phone rang again. She hesitated, then retrieved it and thumbed the screen to "on" just as it clicked over to voice mail. The screen told her she'd missed yet another call from Rick, who wasn't going to be the slightest bit happy about it, but he knew by now that she often went hours or even days without checking in when she was hot on the trail of a story.

"Hot" was certainly the operative word. She shoved her phone in her pocket and studied Brennan as he crossed to her window and looked out into the night. The dark waves of his hair brushed the collar of his shirt, which drew her eye to that lovely expanse of broad, muscled shoulders and back, tapering down to a very nice waist and oh, holy Atlantis, the man even had a tight, perfectly shaped butt. Why were all the gorgeous ones either married or two-thousand-year-old cursed warriors?

She rolled her eyes, both at her black humor and at her easy acceptance of his story. She'd had a long time to get used to unbelievable tales, though, and it didn't hurt that nobody could lie to her. Humanity's reality had changed almost beyond recognition in the past ten years. The world's shock, fear, and disbelief over the existence of shifters, vampires, and who knew what else, had gradually given way to a wary acceptance and then—now—even a dangerous complacency. The monsters counted on that, though. The bad ones. The deadly ones.

Not all of them had wanted to come out and face the light of day and the insane press of media. Many, many of the vampires and shifters had wanted to remain hidden, content to remain the stuff of legend, nightmares, and really bad horror films. But the majority, or at least the most powerful, had won that argument.

Tiernan and her colleagues had discussed the reasoning for years, over endless pitchers of beer, margaritas, cosmopolitans, and mojitos, as drink fads had come and gone. They'd each had their pet theories that had changed over time, but Tiernan had always stuck firm to her original explanation. Vamps were the ultimate game players. Showing themselves to humans and integrating, more or less successfully, had allowed them a much larger arena. Now they weren't fighting just for control of individual territories and the "sheep," as they called the humans who lived there, but for control of countries and kingdoms, insinuating themselves into governments and power centers in industry, finance, and the media. The U.S. had gone the furthest, the fastest: now Congress had a third house, called the Primus, that was all-vampire.

Power on an international level, and why not? It was much easier to take over the world when you could travel to its cities on your own corporate jet, with blacked-out windows and willing donors who doubled as flight attendants or simply came as guests.

Peanuts, pretzels, or O negative?

Now the not-so-lost continent of Atlantis was in the mix, complete with a tyrannical god-ruler who had arbitrarily cursed one of his warriors for a tragedy that wasn't even his fault. Corelia had been the architect of that decision, leaving Brennan no options. He hadn't even known about the baby. To Tiernan, that was the worst punishment of all: to find out that you were a father and find out that you were not, all in the same breath.

An unpleasant thought struck her like a lightning bolt to her stomach: *had* he been? Corelia didn't sound like she'd been the most faithful of women. What if the child hadn't been Brennan's at all? Unfortunately, that led to unanswerable questions: Could a god really know these things? Did Poseidon have some sort of super DNA tester abilities or had he merely been guessing? She groaned at the barrage of questions—ones she could never ask Brennan without hurting him even further.

Brennan had been telling her the truth. He believed he would not harm her; that he would die to protect her. She only had to worry about a recurrence of the strange fit he'd gone into when the curse had struck, and that was easy enough to handle. All she had to do was escape long enough for all of the terms of the curse to apply. "Out of sight, out of mind" took on a whole new meaning. If he couldn't see her, he wouldn't remember her, and she'd be free to get on with her mission.

Alone.

Alone was better, anyway. So there was no reason the

prospect of Brennan forgetting her very existence should cause a hollow feeling in her stomach. She kicked herself out of her mental wanderings as Brennan wheeled around and strode toward her so swiftly that he'd already halted, only inches away from her, before she could think, move, or even breathe. Staring into her eyes, his own narrowed as if daring her to stop him, he put an arm around her waist and pulled her even closer, until her breasts were pressed into the hard heat of his chest. Just when she thought he'd kiss her, he simply rested his face on the top of her head and inhaled deeply, like he was breathing her in. Memorizing her scent.

Every nerve ending she had went from zero to sixty at the feel of his hot, hard body against hers, and she had to struggle against a wicked and entirely abnormal impulse to snuggle even closer. It had been months, no, more than a year, since she'd had any kind of intimate relationship, and her body was crying out that enough was enough of the enforced abstinence, already.

It was more than that, though. The heat sizzling through her limbs was about way more than lack of sex. This was personal—it was about Brennan. The way he looked at her, as if he'd like to strip her bare and take her up against the wall, not to mention the things he'd said to her . . . Well. That had been enough to set the most restrained woman's sexual urges on fire, and she'd never been one for restraint.

He turned his head so she felt his warm breath against her ear, and her traitorous body trembled a little. Her cheeks instantly burned with embarrassment. It was one thing to have the hots for the crazy ancient cursed guy in your hotel room; it was quite another to let him know it.

"I, who have spent so very long being entirely rational, find that any semblance of calm or logic has deserted me, simply from the sight of your innocent touch on that man's arm," he murmured. "I have become a Neanderthal, lacking only a cave to which I might drag you and a club with which to beat off the occasional stray woolly mammoth."

He'd surprised a laugh out of her, in spite of the danger

of the situation. "The sight of billionaire businessman Mr. Brennan in an animal-skin loincloth is just not one I can picture at all," she said, relaxing against him.

He pulled her even closer and pressed a kiss into the curve of her neck, making her shiver in his arms. She put her hands on his chest, realizing in a dim and hazy corner of her mind that this was dangerous. *He* was dangerous. Right now, she so didn't care.

"The sound of your laughter is like a symphony heralding spring to the long, barren winter of my existence," he said, his voice husky. "I cannot think why I am fighting this tidal wave of emotion. Did not my lack of feeling anything at all for so many years constitute sufficient punishment?"

Tiernan felt like she had been captured in a silken web of pure sensuality. The sound of his voice and the feel of his breath sent bursts of heat and driving need pulsing through her body. In spite of the many journalistic awards she'd won for her words, she couldn't seem to find a single one with which to tell him to let her go.

His lips traveled up the side of her neck and then his teeth bit down gently on her earlobe, and she cried out at the sharp bolt of lust that shot through her body, hardening her nipples and causing her thighs to clench together.

"I want you now, Tiernan," he said in that sexy voice that should have been against the law in all seven—okay, eight now—continents. His voice when he spoke the truth was a sonata. Musical, deep, and darkly seductive, the sound of it in her ear was almost enough to make her start yanking at his clothes until she could put her hands and her mouth on hot, male skin.

And *that* scared her enough that she jerked away from him. His arms tensed for a fraction of a second, just enough to let her know that there was no way she would have been able to escape the strength in those steel-banded muscles if he hadn't allowed her to. The thought that he'd let her go both comforted and annoyed her.

"No. No wanting," she said, hating the way her words

came out all soft and husky. "We have a job to do here. We have to get ready for the reception."

She backed away, and he watched her with the intent gaze of a predator stalking its next meal. The thought of lying on the bed, chocolate sauce and whipped cream decorating a few key body parts, flashed through her mind, and her body temperature rose about a thousand degrees.

"What reception?" he said absently as he approached her again, his eyes hot. "Society's rules and rational thought are, in the end, meaningless. I am pleased to discover this after so many centuries of following rules and guidelines of propriety so strictly. There is no reason on earth valid enough to explain why we should not enjoy each other's bodies if you desire me, and your reaction just now gives me some hope."

Tiernan backed up, holding her hands up in front of her. "Oh, I can think of a lot of reasons, Brennan. I need to discover what's going on with these scientists and call my boss back before he fires me, and you need to go back to Atlantis and maybe get checked out. Do you even have shrinks down there?"

"Those are not options that tempt me," he said, stopping only inches in front of her and beginning to unbutton his shirt, one button by one torturous button, baring an exquisite expanse of very masculine chest. "I have spent the last two millennia of my life doing what is right, and rational, and reasonable. Now I have the ability to feel again, for only Poseidon knows how long, and I want to wrap myself in every moment of it. I want to wrap myself in *you*."

"I don't— We don't—" Tiernan suddenly couldn't find a good reason to disagree with him, and her resolve weakened further with every button. After all, they could just have one teensy little hour of wild, sweaty sex, and then get back to work, right?

Sanity popped its ugly head up in her conscience, and she groaned. "No, no, no. I can't just get naked with somebody I barely know. It's really out of my comfort zone, not to mention the curse and who knows what might happen, and why am I even having this conversation?"

He pulled his shirt off in one sudden movement and dropped it to the floor. "I agree. Conversation is unnecessary now. You can speak when you are naked." He reached up and captured a long strand of her hair, brought it to his mouth, and kissed it. "You should remove your shirt so I can kiss your lovely, perfect breasts and taste every inch of your body until you are so hot and wet that you want me inside you as much as I want to be there."

"I—I—" Her mind shut down for a few seconds at the thought of it, her hormones doing a few cartwheels. Then she blew out a breath and tried again.

"Trust me, it wouldn't take long," she muttered, tightening her legs together against the liquid heat she could feel building at his bold words. "But I can't. We can't. I just—No. We don't know each other, and you're under one hell of a curse, and I just—no."

He rasped in a long breath, and then stepped away from her and inclined his head. "Thrice said and done. It is Fae law, not Atlantean, but however desperately my need for you burns inside of me, I will not take you while you have the slightest doubt."

He clenched his hands into fists at his sides and then released them as a shudder raced through his body, and the thought that his reaction was due to suppressed need—for her—almost made Tiernan change her mind. *Almost*. She searched for something to say that could bring the tension in the room down a notch, but before she could come up with anything, her phone rang again. Thank goodness for Rick and his inability to be ignored.

She offered Brennan a tentative smile. "I'd better get that."

He nodded, then bent to retrieve his shirt. As she pulled her phone out of her pocket and opened it, she watched him cover up that glorious chest and didn't even try to pretend that her primary reaction was not relief but regret.

"Tiernan?" Rick's voice barked in her ear, reminding

her that she was supposed to be answering her phone. "Are you there? What the hell is going on there? Have you seen CNN? There was another attack tonight, right there in Yellowstone. The victim's girlfriend is blaming it on wolf shifters, and it looks like it might get ugly for your contact Lucas."

Chapter 7

Brennan concentrated on breathing. Nothing else. Long, deep inhale, and then long, slow exhale. He must find his focus. His center. As Archelaus, one of their mentors in the training academy, had always taught them, every action originated from a place of serenity that formed the core of a warrior's being.

His serene core was blasted to the nine hells right now. He turned slightly to keep Tiernan in his line of sight while she spoke to someone named Rick on her telephone. He had no way to judge the parameters of the curse, or to know if "out of your sight" meant something as simple and brief as turning his back for longer than a moment or two. What if he fell asleep? She would be out of his sight when his eyes were closed in sleep. Was he doomed only to remember this amazing woman for the duration of a single day?

He wanted to howl and rage at the injustice, but there would be no point. He'd known for far too long that gods dealt in caprice, not justice. He had been doomed so long ago by the terms of the curse, and this was simply another, more horribly twisted, level in the torture. He had found her only to know that he would lose her. It was no more or less than he deserved, after what had happened to Corelia and his child.

Even if he could somehow build a future with Tiernan, she was human. She would live only for a brief time, and then when she died, the Tiernan-shaped hole in his soul would never, ever be filled. He almost laughed at the sheer malicious genius behind Poseidon's curse, but stopped himself. He had the strangest certainty that the laughter would come out as a howl.

Tiernan closed her phone and told him what her colleague had said about an attack as she flicked on the television and scrolled through channels looking for park news. She stopped at a channel showing a local news reporter standing in front of their hotel. "That's here," Tiernan said, turning to him. "Maybe—but, no. She's smiling. It's probably a taped segment. Wonder who that is with her."

The reporter smiled her insincere smile into the camera as she wrapped up an interview with a haughty-looking man in front of the entrance to their hotel. "Dr. Litton, thank you for sharing your insights about the IAPN conference. It sounds fascinating. We'll be waiting to hear all about breakthroughs in neuroscience. Now back to the studio."

As the television image changed to one of tiny dancing dogs singing about soap, Tiernan switched off the set. "So that's Litton. Good to know. Nothing about the attack yet; I'm wondering if it was connected with our scientists. Can you call your contacts and see if they know anything?"

She held her phone out to him, but he shook his head. "If you value your technology, do not give it to an Atlantean. Something in the composition of our bodies or our magic wreaks havoc on small electrical fields and destroys them."

She glanced at the lamps and then back at him. "What about large electrical fields?"

"The lamp is not a problem. However, large electrical fields pose a hazard to us, and we, to a lesser extent, to them.

Depending on their strength, they can prevent us from using any of our Atlantean abilities at all, such as the one I'm going to try to communicate with now."

He closed his eyes and called out to Alexios on the common mental pathway all Atlanteans past the age of puberty could access, but he found only silence at first. He took a deep breath, forced down the emotional overload still whirling through his senses, and tried again. Perhaps Alexios had not recognized him.

Alexios? Can you hear me? We have news of an attack and wanted to learn if Lucas and his Pack were safe.

There was another brief silence, and then Alexios's familiar dry tone rang strongly in response.

That was you? Interesting. Oh, and open your door.

Brennan crossed to the door and flung it open again, this time far more pleased to see their visitors. Alexios, Grace, and Lucas stood in the hallway, all of them looking grim. He moved away from the door and stood next to Tiernan while the three entered the small room. When they'd closed the door, Tiernan moved forward as if to shake hands with Alexios, and Brennan's hand shot out, almost without his own volition, stopping her with an iron grip on her arm. Rage, as dark and deadly as it was unreasonable, flashed through his body at a sudden very unwelcome memory, and every muscle in his body tightened to battle readiness.

"You touched her," he said to Alexios, trying to focus through the red haze that moved rapidly to obscure his vision. "She was naked, and you put your godsdamned hands on her body."

He tried for calm, and failed. Tried for serenity, but Tiernan pulled her arm away, trying to escape him, and serenity shattered. He caught her arms and yanked her up to face him, forcing the words out through his clenched teeth. "I am sorry for this, but it appears I must kill him."

Tiernan blinked, her lovely dark eyes enormous in her too-pale face, but then, shockingly, she laughed. "What? You're apologizing to *me*? Seems like you want to apologize to him."

"Damn right," Alexios snapped, both hands suddenly holding daggers.

Brennan hadn't seen Grace move, but her bow was now drawn, the silver-tipped arrow pointed directly at his head. He released Tiernan and pushed her behind him, out of the way of danger.

"Oh, there is going to be a lot of apologizing going on, my friend," Grace snapped, but to Brennan's surprise, she was directing her comment to Alexios. "Do you mind telling me exactly where you had your hands on another woman's naked body?"

Alexios whipped his head back and forth between Grace and Brennan, a helpless expression crossing his face. He opened and closed his mouth a few times and finally managed to reply. "Boston?"

Tiernan made a funny snorting noise, moving up next to Brennan again. "Boston! I was expecting 'only her hip, honey,' or 'just her arm to help her when she passed out,' but he says, 'Boston.'" Her cheeks and mouth quivered strangely and then she dissolved in laughter. "Boston!" she cried out, bending over. "He said Boston."

There was total silence in the room, except for Tiernan's helpless laughter, and then Grace lowered her bow, her mouth quirking into a smile. "He did, didn't he, the big lunkhead?" She started laughing, too. "Boston! Well, now I'm not worried. At least it wasn't, oh, *Cleveland*."

For some reason, that started Tiernan off on a new round of laughter, and the two women laughed so hard their breath began to sputter in broken gasps. Brennan, all urge to murder one of his closest friends in the world having vanished completely, stared at Alexios and Lucas, totally mystified. "Boston? Why is that funny?"

Alexios shot a hard stare at him and then, evidently satisfied that his own death was no longer imminent, sheathed his daggers. "I have no idea," he confessed.

"Women," Lucas said, shrugging. "You guys okay now? Nobody going to kill anybody else?"

Brennan bowed toward Alexios, a deep shame for his

reaction coursing through him. "I cannot hope for you to forgive me for my actions, my friend—"

"Oh, save it," Alexios said, grinning. "I'm going to enjoy seeing you brought low by a woman like the rest of us."

Grace, her bow slung over her shoulder and her peals of laughter dying down, elbowed Alexios in the ribs. "Raised high by a woman, isn't that what you meant to say, darling?"

She grinned up at him, and Alexios pulled her close and pressed a brief kiss to her lips. "Exactly. Now. Before the death threats started, what in the nine hells was going on here? And I think you'd better start with your reaction to Tiernan."

"His reaction to me is none of your damn business," Tiernan said, reaching for Brennan's hand. "Leave him alone. He's been through a lot tonight."

Brennan was stunned into utter stillness when he felt her warm hand clasp his own. Then she did something even more shocking. She stepped forward so she was standing in front of Brennan, as if to protect him.

She wanted to protect *him*. *She* was defending *him*.

His heart, so long unused, fell out of his body and shattered into tiny pieces at her feet. He wanted to weep. He wanted to shout out his joy and triumph to the universe. He did neither, but simply moved to stand at her side, where he hoped to spend the rest of eternity.

"*He's* been through a lot? Look, Butler, he just offered to kill me, in case your memory's not working," Alexios said.

"Yeah, yeah, but it was the curse, so now can we get past the death threat that wasn't, and talk about something important?" Tiernan pointed at Grace and Lucas, then looked at Brennan. "I'm going to say hi to the nice people now. Try not to kill anybody, or I might not come to your rescue this time."

Brennan was speechless, a complicated combination of dismay and amusement warring for control of his emotions. Tiernan was handling him exactly the way he'd seen Grace handle Alexios, and the princes' women handle them, for that matter. Like he was the smoothest, silkiest of Atlantean clay in her hands.

Oh, by all the gods, he was in for a wild ride. If only Poseidon would allow it.

"I'm Tiernan Butler, ace reporter, on the scene for the same reason you are," Tiernan was saying to Grace. "My cover name is Tracy Baum here, so please call me Tracy all the time so you don't accidentally trip and say Tiernan. I'm sorry about the naked thing, by the way. Your guy and a few of his buddies rescued me from a very bad situation with some very nasty vamps and their followers. And when I passed out, I was wrapped up in a *very* big sheet, just so you know."

Grace grinned and shook Tiernan's hand. "In Boston, I'm guessing? I'm Grace Havilland and this is Lucas, the alpha of the Yellowstone wolf pack."

Lucas shook Tiernan's hand, sheer uncomplicated glee lighting up his face. "You have no idea how glad I am to meet the woman who brought the crazy to Brennan."

Brennan inhaled and exhaled long, slow breaths as the volcano of jealous rage tried to climb up his gut again at the sight of the wolf alpha touching Tiernan. She glanced back at him, as if she'd sensed something, and quickly released Lucas's hand and crossed back to Brennan, standing near enough that he could touch her if he wanted.

Wanted. Ah, the cosmic joke of the gods. He wanted to do nothing *other* than touch this woman. Deep breaths. He could do this. Two millennia of reason could not be washed away by a tidal wave of emotion in the space of hours.

"Okay, enough socializing," Lucas said. "The attack in the park? Those weren't my wolves. We didn't recognize them, so they were imports. Witness reports on the scene said that they didn't know where they were or even who they were, from what anyone could tell. They were confused and groggy, like they were on drugs."

"Or like they'd been dosed with drugs," Tiernan said. "That lab must be around here. What if they're releasing test subjects in a kind of twisted experiment?"

"That, or they could have escaped," Grace pointed out.

Brennan nodded. "Either possibility raises serious concerns for the safety of park visitors, not to mention your Pack, Lucas."

Lucas slammed his hand against the wall and bared his teeth in a snarl. "You think we don't know that? My mate and children were less than ten miles away from that attack. What if we're the target? First they take our Pack members, and then they point their murderous thugs in our direction."

Alexios put a steadying hand on his friend's shoulder. "We know. We're here to help you make sure no harm comes to your family."

"What is the plan?" Tiernan asked. "Let's get to it before we're any later to this midnight reception thing than we already are."

"We're staff," Alexios said. "Lucas and I are extra security, and Grace is going in as a backup bartender."

"Seems the regular bartender called in sick," Grace added, her fingers moving restlessly on her bow. "Imagine that."

"She's a member of my Pack, currently taking her children on a holiday away from the park until this situation is resolved," Lucas said grimly. "As Honey should do, if she would only listen to reason."

"Tiernan and Grace should leave, as well," Alexios said, scowling at Grace to forestall the inevitable protest.

"And I will, if things change," Grace said, surprising Brennan, who had not expected the warrior woman to agree to abandon the fight. "You know I will." She touched Alexios's scarred cheek briefly and smiled up at him. "But now I need to hide my weapons in my coat, get to the bar, set up to pour drinks for science geeks, and hope they're anxious to spill their evil secrets to a friendly ear."

"Your ear had better be all that's friendly," Alexios growled.

Grace laughed as she headed for the door. "Right. You want to try that again, naked-woman toucher?"

Then she was gone, the door shutting behind her before Alexios could respond.

"We should be going, too. We're signed on for the midnight to six A.M. shift," Lucas said, glancing at his watch.

"You go. I'll be right there," Alexios said.

After Lucas left the room, Alexios wasted no time getting to the point. "You," he said, pointing at Brennan. "What in the nine hells is going on?"

He turned to Tiernan. "What or who was biting you?"

Before Brennan could react to the fury that seared through his veins at the reminder that someone had hurt his woman—no, not *his* woman, only in his dreams would she ever be his woman—had hurt *Tiernan*, she again seemed to recognize what he needed and took his hand.

"It wasn't as bad as you're making it sound. In fact, I think we have an ally. The problem is that I'm not sure who he was, although I have my suspicions," she began. She quickly told them of her encounter with the cryptic vampire.

"You think it could be this Devon?" Brennan asked, still holding tightly to her hand. Her touch calmed the monstrous rage that threatened to consume him at the thought of her in danger.

"I don't know. Either Devon, or someone who works with or for him. And I have to admit, the car is a slim lead. Maybe it was his chauffeur or maybe the vamp had nothing at all to do with the car. He did fly over that hedge pretty easily. After all, it doesn't really make a lot of sense that the vampire slated to be the big dog over this entire region would suddenly decide to sabotage his own evil plans."

Alexios shrugged, then shot a pointed look at their joined hands. "We can only speculate until we have more evidence. On a more practical note, can you two work together? Clearly your emotions are back, in a big way, Brennan. I very nearly didn't even recognize your call on the mental pathway, it was so tangled up with rage and"—he glanced at Tiernan, then shrugged again, ducking his head—"other things."

"It would be safer for Tiernan if she were to leave this

place," Brennan said slowly, although each word burned him like salt water poured over an open wound.

"Not a chance, buddy," Tiernan snapped, wrenching her hand out of his. "Curse or no curse, you're stuck with me. We'll figure out the parameters of how far apart we can get, for how long, later. Or, actually, probably pretty soon, because I'm going to have to, um, use the ladies' room. But this is my story and I'm staying."

Alexios's eyes widened comically. "I can tell this is going to be interesting. Later. I've got to get to work. Check in with me from the party."

Brennan nodded and stepped forward to clasp Alexios's arm. "I will watch over your woman at the reception. You have my word."

Alexios laughed, but it wasn't a happy sound. "Grace can watch over herself, but thanks for the backup. Watch over your own woman, while you're at it. I have a feeling she might be the best thing to happen to you in a very long time."

Tiernan rolled her eyes. "Watch the 'my woman, your woman' stuff, boys, or it's going to be a very long night."

Alexios just laughed again and left. After Brennan closed the door behind him, he leaned against it and studied Tiernan for so long her cheeks turned pink and she got that delightfully indignant expression on her face again.

"What now?"

"I was just thinking how appealing the prospect of a very long night, spent entirely with you, is to me," he said, allowing every bit of his hunger for her to show in his face and voice. His cock hardened just at the idea of it. Tiernan, naked. He suddenly desperately wanted to remove every stitch of her clothing and memorize every inch of her body.

In patient, loving detail.

She shook her head, and disappointment knifed through him as if his painfully volatile emotions had actually held out hope that she'd offer to strip down and star in his most erotic fantasies.

"What am I going to do with you? No, don't answer that," she said, shaking her head. "Right now, we need to solve a very mundane problem: how can I go to the bathroom without your curse kicking in? Because there is no way you're going to watch me pee."

Chapter 8

Tiernan's face heated up when she realized what she'd just said, but unfortunately she was past the point of niceties in regard to her need for the facilities. It had been a long drive and a lot of caffeine to get there.

She glanced at him, hoping her hair covered most of her almost certainly fire-engine red cheeks. He was either shocked speechless or trying not to laugh at her, either of which was fine. Hey, it was even deserved, but still not solving the problem. "Look," she said. "Surely the curse can't kick in just in the two minutes it will take me behind that door."

His smile disappeared, fast, and the lines in his face deepened as he stared at first her, then the door. "I do not know, and I am unwilling to take the chance, with so little time before we must make an appearance. Are you truly so concerned for your privacy in the face of what is at risk?"

"Well, when you put it that way—" she snapped, but then a thought occurred. "Poseidon didn't know much about modern technology back in the day, did he?"

"I don't understand."

She pulled out her phone and snapped a picture of herself. "Here, hold this and look at my face. I'll be back in two minutes. Less, even."

She slapped the phone in his hand and ran for the bathroom door. "You can talk to me if you need to hear my voice. Look at my picture and talk to me, okay?"

"You look quite distressed in this picture," he said slowly, as she slammed the door and yanked her jeans down, all but hopping on one foot.

"That's one word for it," she muttered. Quickly she took care of business, washed her hands, and pulled the door open with wet hands before even grabbing the towel, not wanting to push her luck. "Here I am again. See how fast that was? You're fine, aren't you?"

He slowly raised his head, and his eyes were emerald fire, burning through her. "I'm not sure," he said slowly. "I do remember you, but the photograph is not sufficient. The edges of your existence began to fade in my mind, even as I gazed at your likeness on this device. I do not believe technology will solve this dilemma between us. A piece of metal and wire is no match for the curse of a god."

She took her phone back, gently prying his shaking fingers away. "So we've reached the limit, but we didn't pass it," she said, keeping her tone light. "That's a relief. Some things a woman just wants to do on her own."

But she realized not just his hands were shaking. His entire body was shuddering, and he reached out for her. She went unhesitatingly into his embrace. He pulled her against him and tightened his arms until she gasped.

"Brennan, I'm having a hard time breathing here," she said, laughing a little.

He loosened his hold a fraction and put a hand under her chin, pulling her head up until their gazes locked. "Then let me breathe for you."

He lowered his head and took her lips in a hard, almost desperate kiss. Heat shot through her with the intensity of a flash fire in the forest; she clutched at his shoulders when her knees threatened to give way. Nothing mattered but that he keep kissing her, keep devouring her mouth with his own. An explosion of pure sensation sizzled through her body, sensitizing every inch of her skin. She wanted to cling to him; climb inside him; ride his hot, hard body until the desperate need was sated.

Suddenly, she realized she was rubbing against his body like a cat, and she pulled away from him, shocked and a little frightened by the depth of her hunger.

"Brennan," she whispered, but he kept kissing her. Her neck, her face, her lips again. She pushed against his chest and managed to speak up a little louder. "Brennan. Stop."

He stopped kissing her but still held her loosely, as he drew in deep, ragged breaths. "I am not sure I will survive a reunion with you after more than a two-minute parting," he finally managed. "I am sorry I keep mauling you like a clumsy youngling."

She shook her head. "I'm not sure exactly why this keeps happening, but it's definitely mutual."

A slow, dangerous smile spread over his face, and her knees threatened to buckle again. The man was pure seduction. "Had I known that emotions would be so incredibly threatening to my control, I am not sure I would have wished for their return. And yet, for the opportunity to hold you in my arms, I would surrender everything I own. Is this how the rest of the world feels all of the time? If so, how do you survive it?"

She tried to answer him, had to swallow past the blockage in her throat, and then finally was able to speak. "No. I mean, yes," she said, her voice husky. "Emotions are threatening my control with you, too, but we have a job to do, and this is so complicated, and—"

"Should we go, then? I must change my clothing to something more formal. I believe a tuxedo is required." He released her, his face again impassive, betraying nothing of what he said he'd been feeling just seconds ago.

Neat trick.

She tried it herself, but was doubtful of her success, since she was still trembling the tiniest bit. "Yes. Except, where are we going?"

"The reclusive billionaire who has donated half a million to the cause, with more to come, surely has a suite reserved for him in this hotel," he said dryly. "Will you determine if this is the case?"

She nodded, not completely trusting her own voice, and turned toward the phone on the desk, smiling to herself when she caught him running a hand roughly through his hair.

Everything he owned to hold her in his arms, he'd said.

She picked up the phone, an entirely different kind of warmth spreading through her body. A warmth that felt almost like home.

Naturally, she couldn't trust it.

The desk clerk picked up on the first ring. "How may I help you, Ms. Baum?"

She told him.

"Of course we have Mr. Brennan's suite ready. Should we send someone to meet him there?"

She took the room number, thanked the clerk, and hung up the phone. "I'm guessing we're getting dressed in your room?"

"Lucas arranged for suitable clothing to be delivered there. You will bring your belongings and come with me?" A hint of desperation sounded underneath the calm, even tones of his voice, and when she nodded, grabbing her backpack, she couldn't miss his relief.

"I believe we have a party to attend," he said. He took her suitcase and opened the door, scanning the hallway before gesturing to her to lead the way.

"A party to attend," she repeated. "Can't wait."

She wondered if she was trying to convince him—or herself.

Brennan scanned his new hotel suite, noting the proximity of windows to the bed. Any attack would come from there;

any intruders would smash through the glass and attack sleeping guests before they had a chance to wake up.

Well enough. He didn't plan on sleeping in that bed.

Tiernan had spent several minutes scanning the room with a small electronic device before telling him the room was free of electronic surveillance. They must be very sure of his compliance, then. He smiled at the thought.

Tiernan blinked. "So that was a scary smile. What are you thinking about?"

"Scientists who overestimate themselves."

She narrowed her eyes, but didn't pursue it. "Well, you can at least turn your back while I get dressed," Tiernan said, tossing her backpack on the bed. "That surely won't be long enough to set off the curse." She sat down on the edge and pulled off her shoes. "Right?"

His mind suddenly stuttered to a stop at the sight of Tiernan sitting on the very bed he'd just dismissed. "What?"

She dropped her second foot on the floor and shot him an exasperated look. "Dressed. You. Me. Turning our backs. Right?"

"Dressed?"

Tiernan sighed. "Okay. What's going on in that scary Atlantean mind of yours?"

He closed his eyes. There was no help for it. The only way to regain his power of speech was *not* to see the woman Poseidon himself had declared Brennan's one true mate sitting on a bed.

His bed.

His woman.

He closed his eyes even tighter and started humming.

"You're freaking me out here, but—wait. Is this your plan? Okay, hold that position for two minutes."

He heard rustling noises, and the images his mind conjured of her removing her clothes were too much for him to bear. He dared to open his eyes just a small bit and was rewarded by an expanse of the smooth silky skin of Tiernan's back as she pulled a froth of sparkly fabric the color of crushed rubies over her head. She smoothed the dress into place and turned around, catching him drinking in the sight of her.

"You were supposed to close your eyes," she said accusingly.

He slowly shook his head. "You are beautiful beyond the dreams of the gods. I will never willingly miss any opportunity to see your body, clothed or bare."

He watched, fascinated, as a rosy flush swept up her cheeks. "It bothers you to hear that you are beautiful?"

"No. Thank you for the compliment. But it bothers me that we're supposed to be doing a job and we're talking about bare bodies." She folded her arms under her far-too-exposed breasts, which were barely covered by the silky fabric. "Get dressed or I'm going by myself."

"You will wear that? Into a room filled with men?" Instantly the unfamiliar rage and jealousy burned through him, and he wanted to put his fist through the wall. Or through someone's face. Anyone who would dare to stare at her breasts or her impossibly long legs in that far-too-clinging dress.

She narrowed her eyes. "I will wear whatever I want. And you have two minutes to get ready, or I'm gone."

Rummaging in her bag again, she pulled out a lipstick and then glanced up at him. "Still standing there? One minute, fifty-five seconds. You'd better believe I'm not kidding about this. Move, already."

He believed her. He moved.

Lucas had arranged for the proper clothing, so he quickly changed into the tuxedo hanging in the closet, not daring to look back and see whether or not she was watching him. She had to help him with the unfamiliar tie, and he practiced breathing exercises while her delicate hands touched his neck. It was the only way he could keep from tossing her lovely ass on that inviting bed and spending the rest of the night learning the topography of every lush curve.

"This is going to be a very long night," he said, trying to hold his breath so as not to be further tortured by the delicate floral scent of her hair.

"You think?" She finished the tie and stood back to admire her handiwork. "So far, my day has been all leisure and bonbons. Shall we go to a party? Vampires, evil scientists, and probably enthralled shape-shifters. How bad could it be?"

He laughed, but it came out sounding grim. "How bad, indeed?"

Her smile faded. "You know, by now I should know better than to say things like that. It's tempting fate."

Brennan just nodded. He knew far more than most about tempting fate, and none of it was good.

A very, very long night.

Chapter 9

Devon smoothed the lapels of his tuxedo jacket as he gazed around the hotel conference room, his expression giving away nothing of the distaste he felt for these self-interested scum. His eyes were covered by the wraparound dark glasses he preferred, which further hid his disgust. Many considered the oversized glasses to be merely affectation. He was glad to let them think it; better that than the truth. A disguise was less effective when known to be one.

The five vampires who had fought for so long and argued so bitterly against any type of collaboration were the very same here to take full advantage now that the consortium was in effect.

Schemers and users. Power-mad and weak both, a most unpleasant combination. Quick to change sides to grovel and flatter the more powerful; quicker to stake you in the back if you fell.

The door opened and the worst of the bunch walked in. Litton. The human. The man might actually be clinically insane. A man who would betray his own kind to the monsters who wanted to enslave them—he was indeed a valuable ally.

And he was also a traitor to be continually watched—and immediately destroyed—at the first hint that he'd turned his traitorous ways against the vampires funding his research.

The obsequious cockroach scuttled up to him, bobbing his head, a grimace of fear mixed with triumph plastered all over his face. Devon clenched his teeth just a little to keep the sneer off his face. "Dr. Litton."

"Mr. Devon, I'm thrilled to be able to inform you that Mr. Brennan is here. Our generous benefactor himself," Litton said, all but rubbing his hands together in a caricature of a mad scientist from a film.

"Brennan. Yes, I know that name." Devon said, remembering the last time he'd seen the man, but keeping his own counsel. "What do we have to show him for his half million?"

"We've got the model lab all set up," Litton said, not quite daring to meet Devon's eyes. "Just as you said."

One of the oldest vampires in the room, in fact one of the oldest vampires still roaming the earth, slammed a fist down on the conference table. This one called himself Mr. Jones, although Devon supposed that when you were that old and that powerful, you could call yourself anything you liked.

"I don't like it," Jones said, his voice a tangle of dark and nasty things.

Humans had been rumored to have gone mad just from the sound of Jones's voice. Litton was unaffected, but for more bowing and scraping, thus strengthening Devon's assumption that the man was already insane.

"Why would we possibly waste time and effort with a human? We are near to our final goal of permanent enthrallment of the sheep and the shifters alike," Jones continued, "thanks to this one and his colleagues. We have no need to perform like trained monkeys."

"I-I'm not a fan of the way you call humans 'sheep,'" Litton dared to say, his voice shaking with either outrage or terror.

"Of course you aren't," Devon said, suddenly tired of the entire game. But he had chosen this path long ago, and one of the disadvantages of his choice was the necessity of working with fools. "Are we ready?"

"We're ready to go forward with the next stage of human trials," Litton protested. "We need more money for that. Lots more money. And Mr. Brennan has ten million dollars earmarked for us. He just wanted to be sure he was getting his money's worth."

"A wise businessman," Devon drawled. "Smarter than your average human, then."

Another of the eldest vampires spoke up. This one controlled much of the Pacific Northwest, now that Barabbas was gone. He styled himself Mr. Smith, either in homage to, or mockery of, Mr. Jones. "Why not just kill him and take his money? I have no taste for the job of humoring humans, and this century brings far too much of it."

"We brought that on ourselves, when we came out and let the sheep know we existed. Far better to have stayed in the shadows, as we have for thousands of years," Jones snarled, his fangs down and glistening with spittle.

Devon looked around the room, at each of them in turn, but skated his gaze past the far corner. Other than Smith and Jones, none of the vampires was willing to speak up and commit themselves to one plan of action or the other.

"We're ready to go forward," Litton repeated. "Can we bring him to the lab tonight?"

Before Devon could reply, a knock sounded at the door, which then opened to show Litton's nervous assistant. "Excuse me, Dr. Litton? Um, sorry to bother you, sir, but we have a little problem."

"I told you not to interrupt me," Litton snapped, gesturing frantically for the man to leave.

Devon thought not. "Come in, please, Mr.—?"

"Wesley, sir. Er, Your Lordship, um, sir," the man babbled, sweat dotting his forehead and the sour smell of fear reeking from his every pore. "It's Wesley."

"Well, Mr. Wesley, what do you have to tell us?"

The man's face contorted as he tried to keep all of the vampires and his employer in sight at the same time. "Uh, well, it's about Mr. Brennan."

"What about Brennan?" Litton said, his voice shrill. "He's here, you told me he was here. Did you give him his welcome packet?"

"Yes, of course, but he wasn't there." Wesley twisted his hands together, his gaze darting nervously around the conference table. "I mean, he was in a room, but it wasn't his room."

Litton rolled his eyes. "Then you take him to his room. What's so urgent about that?"

"We did, I mean, the front desk got him to his room, but it's more who he was with than where he was, if you know what I mean."

Devon sighed. Wesley's nervous grin was beginning to make him want to rip the man's throat out. Not that he was particularly hungry or that Wesley was particularly appealing. It might make the babbling stop, though, and there was great merit in that.

"Who, Wesley?" he said, to forestall any further images of dealing immediate death. "What companion has you so addled?"

"The reporter, sir," Wesley said. "Mr. Brennan was with that reporter, Tracy Baum, and she seemed awfully cozy with him, if you know what I mean."

The rodent-faced man beamed around the room, a leering let's-be-men grin that failed to find its audience among the impatient vampires, who either ignored him or looked at him as one might a particularly aromatic pile of garbage.

"This could be a problem," Jones said. "Why is our reclusive billionaire having dealings with a reporter? Are you sure your research on this man was accurate, Devon?"

Devon leaned back against the wall and folded his arms across his chest. "I am always accurate, Jones. This is why I have achieved all that I have. You would do well to remember that."

"Maybe she's just his girlfriend," Wesley said, his voice cracking mid-sentence. "You know, just a piece of ass for the—"

"That will be enough, Wesley," Devon interrupted. "Unless you want to have drinks with any of my friends?" He waved an arm at the vampires ringing the table and they leaned forward.

"Or be a drink?" Smith said slyly.

Wesley almost knocked Litton down in his haste to escape the room, and Devon allowed himself a grim smile.

"Powerful men can control their women," he said, knowing he would regret the remark later. *She* would be sure of that. "If there were any problem at all, Brennan's previous activities and funding would have been front-page news. He knew full well that his first half million was earmarked for research into enthrallment; that's why he gave it in the first place. So the woman is either his companion or simply a diversion. Either way, I cannot believe she will be a problem."

"I don't like it," Smith said.

"You don't like anything," Devon countered. "I will have them followed at all times. If they step so much as a foot out of line, we will capture them and have them killed. This is a no-lose scenario for us. We have an eccentric human billionaire who wants to fund our research in hope that we will give him the gift of eternal life so that he will continue to be part of the ruling class after we take over. Either he will work with us, or we will enthrall him and he will be our puppet."

"I plan to kill him, eventually, either way," Jones said, stabbing one long fingernail into the polished conference table and carving the letter J into the expensive wood. "I have no liking for these upstart humans."

Devon noticed Litton starting to back toward the door. "Do you concur, Doctor?"

"What? Oh, yes. Completely. We need his money. Must get to the party. See you there." With that, Litton all but ran out of the room after his assistant. When the door closed behind him, Devon sighed.

"Perhaps we could refrain from the 'let's kill the upstart humans' talk around the doctor who controls the research," he said, biting off each word.

"Why do we need Brennan, anyway? We have money," whined one of the younger vamps who hadn't spoken yet.

"Good. You can pay for the damage to that table," Devon said.

Jones sneered.

"More to the point, none of you wanted to risk your own money on these trials," Devon pointed out. "And why should we, when we have willing sheep with money, standing ready to betray their own kind?"

"You should be the next Primator," Smith said. "I have no liking for politics, but you're a natural at the game. If we're going to be in it, we should be in it with someone who can manipulate the rules to our advantage. When the Americans changed their constitution to allow for a third house of Congress controlled entirely by our kind, they opened the door for total domination."

"They all but laid down and bared their necks," Jones spat out, his lips peeled back from his teeth. "It's our duty to accept their sacrifices."

"Perhaps, but one does not become leader of the Primus by murdering humans," Devon said. "The next Primator must be seen as one who can work with them, or he will suffer the same fate as the last two have."

"Or *she*," came a husky voice from the shadows of the far corner. "Perhaps a woman will become Primator this time."

Devon smiled, enjoying the way the champagne silk sheath hugged her curves as she stepped forward into the light. "Of course, Deirdre. If any woman could do it, it would certainly be you, my darling."

She walked around the corner toward him, neither noticing nor acknowledging in any way the lustful and speculative glances from every other vampire in the room. He held out his hand and she took it, her fingers icy cold.

"Shall we dance, my love?" she asked, tilting her head to the side and staring so deeply into his eyes that he almost shivered from the soulless despair in her own.

"Absolutely," he said, bending to kiss her hand. "Gentlemen, we will talk more tomorrow night. Until then."

Not bothering to wait for their agreement, he left the room, still holding Deirdre's hand. The instant the door closed behind them, she snatched it back, and strode rapidly down the hallway.

"Do you think you convinced them?" she said, a safe distance from vampire ears, compulsively wiping her hand on her dress and probably not even realizing she was doing it.

He shrugged. "We'll find out tomorrow. One way or another, this will go forward."

"Litton is a fool."

"Yes, but he's a brilliant fool, and we need him."

She paused in the hallway just before stepping into the edge of light spilled from the ballroom doors. "I don't like fools. They can't be trusted to behave in a consistent manner."

"He'll behave, or we'll kill him. Is that consistent enough for you?"

"Powerful men control their women? Is that really what you believe, vampire?" The ice in her voice was cold enough to freeze the entire world, and yet it only scratched the surface of who she was and what she had endured.

Devon regretted it, but he could not change the past. If only he had that power, there were so many, many actions of his own and others he would undo. Not only vampires had regrets, however. He'd learned that painful lesson recently.

"You know it is not what I believe," he finally answered. "But I have a role to play, as do you."

A dead, humorless smile spread over her pale, pale face. "Then we dance."

Chapter 10

Every muscle in Brennan's body tightened as the first wave of hot, powerful jealousy washed over him. The ballroom was large, but the crowd was pressing in on him, the pounding bass of the music amplifying the pounding in his skull. Hundreds of humans, mostly male, all of them staring at Tiernan, or at least so it appeared to his feverish emotions.

Staring at her. Lusting after her.

They needed to die. Painfully. Slow, bloody deaths.

She tightened her clasp on his hand as if she could sense how near he was to losing all control. "This will only work if you calm down," she said, loudly enough to be heard over the music.

"This would work, as you put it, much better if you were ugly or wore a cloak that covered you from head to toe," he muttered. "I cannot be responsible for my actions if any of these men dare to touch you."

"Who else would be responsible?" she said, laughing at him. The sound of her laughter was like a beacon of light to the darkness of his existence, and it offered him a measure of much-needed calm.

He swept his gaze from the shiny dark waves of her hair down to her smooth shoulders, lingered awhile on the delicious curves of her breasts, barely covered by the red silk of her gown, and then moved on to her womanly hips and long, long legs, until he reached the pointed toes of her silly shoes. "If we have to make a rapid exit, those shoes will be less than useful."

"Shoes can come off. Now, mingle. We need to mingle," she said firmly, gently pulling her hand away. "I'll stay in view, but I need to go be Tracy Baum. A reporter would not hang out in one place with her boyfriend, no matter how good he looks in his tux."

The term amused him. "I am more than two thousand years old, and in all that time, I have never been called anyone's boyfriend."

She flashed a brilliant smile at him. "Stick with me, kid. You'll have a new experience every day."

As she strode forward, somehow not even wobbling on those ridiculously high-heeled shoes, he felt a completely unfamiliar emotion sing through his veins. It felt like nothing he'd ever known, even before Poseidon's curse, and it took him a full minute to realize what it was.

Happiness. By all the gods, it was *happiness*.

In the midst of a roomful of evil-intentioned scientists and surrounded by vampires who would cheerfully drain him if they knew who he really was, his emotions had stupidly, foolishly decided to settle on utter bliss.

He suddenly realized his face felt strange, as though the skin were oddly stretched. He touched his cheek, only to discover that he was smiling. Again. He'd smiled more since he'd met Tiernan than he had in the past two millennia of his existence.

She thought he looked good in his tux.

He stood there, grinning like a fool, until a hand touched his shoulder. He whirled around, hands automatically reaching for the daggers he'd left in the room. It was difficult to conceal daggers in a tuxedo, but he felt naked and exposed without them.

The little man from the television stood there, now clad in a tuxedo, self-importance oozing from every pore. "Mr. Brennan? I'm Dr. Litton. So delighted to finally meet you in person."

Brennan shook the man's hand. "Dr. Litton. Sorry we were late to your party. We wanted a little time to ourselves, of course you understand."

His eyes sought out Tiernan, needing to reassure himself she was still in view. Litton followed his gaze.

"Ah, yes, the reporter. Ms. Baum. I hadn't realized she was with you."

"She is most definitely with me, although I fail to see why that is any of your concern," Brennan said, a knife-edge of menace in his voice.

"Oh, no, no reason." Litton backed up a few steps, holding his hands out in front of him. "I have to give a little speech now, but I'll talk to you soon. I'm very much looking forward to showing you our lab tomorrow."

"I look forward to seeing it. I will be very interested to see what plans you have in mind for my ten million dollars."

Litton's gaze darted back and forth nervously. "Ah, yes. We'll be sure to show you plenty."

Brennan watched the doctor scurry away, and then turned to find Tiernan, his attention drawn to exactly where she stood, as if she were a homing beacon to his soul. She glowed like a gem in her red dress among the throng of black evening wear. One of the men in her group said something and Tiernan threw back her head and laughed. Brennan watched her and was stunned all over again by the power of the longing that overwhelmed him.

To make her his.

For a night, for a year, for eternity.

His.

He started toward her, but stopped when a hideous screeching noise sounded, and then Litton's voice, magnified by the electronic speakers, jangled throughout the room. "Is this thing on?"

Everyone laughed and turned toward the podium, and Tiernan made her way through the crowd toward Brennan. An odd pressure lifted from his chest, and he realized he had been holding his breath, as if he needed her presence even to draw air. She finally arrived, and he pulled her against his side, needing to feel her next to him.

"I just don't like the looks of that man. I know it's stupid, but I've learned to trust my instincts," she murmured near Brennan's ear, an action that made the fit of his pants considerably tighter.

Focus. He must focus. On the mission, not on the curves of her body. She was talking about Litton.

"I agree," he said. "I will be interested to see how your Gift reacts to his speech."

Litton fussed with his tie and the microphone for a bit, and adjusted the stand down to his height. "Can you hear me now?"

After more desultory laughter from the mostly inebriated crowd, Litton continued. "I know it's late and we all need to get some rest for a full day of meetings tomorrow, but I wanted to take a moment to welcome you all to the first annual meeting of the International Association of Preternatural Neuroscience."

A ragged cheer went up from the scientists, who then looked vaguely embarrassed to be caught doing something so common.

"Not a lot of rah rah in neuroscience usually, I'm guessing," Tiernan whispered, a grin quirking up the edges of her lovely lips. Brennan became distracted by thoughts of tasting her mouth, and he lost the next few sentences. Or minutes. When he returned his attention to the scientist, Litton was concluding his remarks.

"—thrilling breakthroughs in science, for today and for all our tomorrows. Thank you."

Everyone cheered and clapped, and Litton's forehead flushed a bright red as he basked in the approval of his peers.

"It's not lies," Tiernan said, her brows drawn together. "He believes that whatever he's up to is going to cause 'thrilling breakthroughs.'"

"For all our tomorrows?" Brennan asked, his voice dry.

"For all of somebody's tomorrows. Probably the power-mad vamps he's working for." She turned her head, subtly scanning the room. "Speaking of which, I think I'm going to go get one of them to ask me to dance. See what I can find out."

Brennan heard a low growling noise and realized it was coming from his own throat. "I cannot allow—"

"Allow?" she asked sweetly. "I'm sorry?"

He swallowed the broken glass that had somehow gotten lodged in his throat and tried again. "It will be difficult for me if you do this."

Compassion softened her face. "I know. The curse. But you have to understand that it's not really me you want, it's just the random nature of the curse making you think so."

"There is nothing random about Poseidon or his curses, I assure you. But I will do my best to carry out my part in this mission."

Suddenly and completely unexpectedly, she put her hands on his shoulders and stood on her toes to kiss him lightly on the lips.

"I know you will. I will, too. Now I'm going to go dance. Why don't you go have a drink?"

"I do not drink when—" He followed the direction of her gaze and saw Grace at the bar, pouring drinks. "I believe I will go have a drink, while you dance with a vampire."

"Get one for me, too, will you? I think I'm going to need it," she said grimly before pasting onto her face the somewhat vacant smile he thought of as her disguise.

Brennan took another long, calming breath before he headed toward the bar. Grace might have news. Important news. Anything to distract him from the thought of Tiernan dancing with a vampire.

~⟶~

Tiernan sauntered through the crowd, offering a smile here and a flirtatious look there, trying not to hear the conversations between individuals because it was distracting. Too much posturing, deception, and outright lying had stretched her nerves so taut that she felt like she might snap, especially on top of the effort it took to maintain an illusion of lighthearted calm for Brennan's sake. She felt the weight of his gaze on her even now, and hoped Grace made whatever drink she gave him a double. She didn't chance a look at him, because he was so gorgeous in that tux that she'd been happy just not to drool on him or fall into his arms like some swooning maiden from one of the various centuries he'd lived through. He was an unbelievably sexy man, and that hint of danger just added to his appeal.

Leashed power in evening clothes.

The conversations filtered through to her as she passed various knots of people standing in twos and threes. It wasn't like she could put her fingers in her ears, no matter how much she might want to avoid hearing the lies, so she gritted her teeth and smiled through the pain of nerves scraped raw.

So many lies.

"—and then he said my paper was the best he'd read in years, and sure to be published."

Lie.

"My wife and I have a very open marriage—"

Lie. Big lie.

"Litton is a genius, but he's a crackpot, if you ask me. I heard—"

Ah. Truth at last. So the good doctor had a reputation even among his peers. Wonder what they'd think of him if they knew he was secretly funded by vampires and working toward the enslavement of humanity?

Stranger and stranger when truth sounded more like the plot to a comic book, but that was life these days. Everybody plotting to take over the damn world; nobody content just to let people live.

People, and their friends, and their friends' babies.

When the second person in a row gave her a strange look, she realized she was letting too much of what she was thinking show on her face, and she paused to pretend to search for something in her purse to gain a little time to compose herself.

A wave of cold lifted the hair on the back of her neck a moment before a deep voice spoke near her ear. "May I assist you with anything?"

The voice sounded so familiar, but when she looked up into the vampire's pale face, half-hidden by oversized wraparound shades, she realized she had no way to know why. Unless, of course, she asked him. Sometimes a direct approach was best, as one of her journalism profs had been fond of reminding them.

"Tracy Baum, *Neuroscience Quarterly*. Did we meet earlier tonight?"

A seductive smile played around the edges of his sculpted lips. She was suddenly glad of his glasses, which protected her from falling into thrall from his eyes. His black hair brushed his shoulders, and he was tall and very well built, filling out his black-on-black tux in a way that had quite a few women nearby checking him out. The vamp who'd grabbed her earlier had been tall and strong, too, but that wasn't enough evidence to convince her that this was he.

"I'm afraid not. I would remember meeting such a lovely woman, Ms. Baum." He bowed. "But I would be happy to correct that oversight. Will you dance?"

It was just what she'd wanted, a dance with a vampire. But still she hesitated. Something about this vampire made her even more wary than usual.

He held out his hand and his smile turned mocking. "Surely you're not afraid of me?"

Even recognizing it for the challenge it was, she couldn't resist. "Of course not. I'd love to dance."

As he took her hand and led her to the dance floor, she glanced back to be sure Brennan was holding on to his calm, and was instantly sorry she'd done so. He was staring at her, his face hard, and even across the expanse of floor and the crowd that separated them, she could almost feel him straining toward her. If she made it through the dance with this vampire, it would be a miracle.

She offered up a silent prayer for miracles.

"You know my name, but you haven't told me yours," she said, smiling up at the distorted reflection of herself in the vampire's glasses.

He pulled her into his arms for the dance, a slow song that bemoaned love lost and loneliness. "My apologies, Ms. Baum. My name is Devon."

"Call me Tracy, please," she said automatically, her mind whirling with possibilities. Curiouser and curiouser. If this were Devon, and he really had been the vamp outside, regardless of what he would or would not admit to . . . well.

This dance suddenly had real possibilities.

Chapter 11

"So," Tiernan said, noting for future reference that vampires felt very, very cold, even through formal wear, "nice car."

Devon laughed. "You like it?"

"What's not to like? The Gallardo LP560-4 is not exactly your mother's Buick." She realized what she'd said and inwardly groaned. "Not that you had a—"

"Mother?"

"Buick. I'm figuring you more for the mother with a carriage, or four slaves that pulled the chariot, perhaps."

He laughed again, but this time it sounded like he was truly amused, not just being polite. Then he pulled her into a twirl and caught her at exactly the right moment. The vampire was quite a good dancer, she was chagrined to admit.

"Not very many women could recognize that car. Are you a car enthusiast or simply a very good reporter?"

She saw no reason to lie. "Both."

"I see. Then I must reward you by telling you that, in fact, my mother owned a single mule, but it was for use in farming only. She walked everywhere she needed to go, which was not very far, since she lived her entire life without venturing from the five-mile radius of her farm." His voice had grown softer as he spoke, making her wish yet again that she could see his eyes. Her truth-telling senses weren't rattling, but she'd never had very good results with vampires, so that wasn't really meaningful. "I would ask that you keep that information to yourself, as the power infrastructure of the vampire ruling class prefers to adhere to the polite fiction that we were all born and raised aristocracy, if not royalty."

"Off the record?"

He smiled down at her and Tiernan stumbled, shock knocking her off her rhythm. There had been real warmth in that smile. He caught her with his strong, cold hands and stopped until she caught her balance.

"Are you well?"

"Yes, fine, sorry. Stupid shoes," she said lightly, holding out one foot for him to see. When he looked down at her foot and leg, and then his gaze slowly traveled back up her body, she had to catch her breath. This man—this vampire—was a deadly predator, who had probably been outwitting humans for centuries, if not longer.

She was maybe just the slightest bit out of her league.

"You are very lovely, Tracy Baum," he said, leaning closer and inhaling deeply. "Your scent is intoxicating, leading me to wonder if your blood might be the same. Perhaps it is time we concluded our dance, unless you would consent to accompany me to my home?"

Thoughts of an inside scoop flashed through her mind, but she hadn't lived as long as she had by climbing into the cage with hungry lions. "Thank you, but no. My date is at the bar, and I really should get back to him."

Devon glanced over in the direction of the bar. "Ah, yes. The reclusive and very rich Mr. Brennan. I am surprised he let you out of his grip for even a moment."

"He doesn't control me, no matter how rich he might be. We're just"—she paused, stumped for a term, and finally settled on the ordinary—"friends."

"Because men, no matter how powerful, no longer control their women, is that right? This conversation echoes another I have had recently, but of course when you have lived as many lives as I have, there is little of originality to be seen, done, or spoken."

She stopped and stepped out of his loose embrace, searching his face. "I'm sorry. That sounds like a terrible way to live. Are you never surprised?"

He lifted a hand and touched her shoulder; it was almost a caress. "I am rarely surprised. Tonight, however, is the exception. I am very surprised by you. Please do say hello to Brennan for me."

Before she could think of a reply, he bowed, turned, and disappeared into the crowd. She stared after him for a minute, but then a pair of already-familiar arms encircled her waist from behind and she closed her eyes and leaned back against the warmth of Brennan's muscular chest.

"That was odd," she said. "There is something so different about that vampire. I really want to investigate him further."

"I believe he feels the same way about you," Brennan said, his voice harsh. "I am sorry, but I could not spend another moment watching you in his arms."

She turned around and gave him a quick hug, sensing how badly he needed the physical contact. "Dance with me. And then we need to talk."

❧

Brennan finally relaxed as Tiernan moved gracefully into his arms. Though he knew the curse to be partially the cause, he could not help a bone-deep relief, as if part of his heart had returned to his body. They moved to the music as one; she easily followed his lead, and they were like partners who had danced through centuries together.

She *fit*. She was perfect for him in every way.

The feeling was impossible and he knew better than to trust it. Love could not come so fast, though attraction and desire flew on swift wings. This was the curse prodding along the pace of what must have already lain dormant in his heart. One of many lessons pounded into the thick skulls of younglings during training was that no god or goddess, no love potion or spell, no sorcerer or even the most powerful witch could compel love. So indeed his feelings for her were genuine and would only grow deeper if he were to spend more time with her. The curse could not have recognized Tiernan as his true mate otherwise.

How, though, could he ever deserve this woman when he—and, equally or more important, she—would always question the legitimacy of his feelings for her? He tightened his hold on her and she leaned her face against his chest, so that the uniquely lovely scent of her hair once again filled his senses.

Lost. He was utterly and completely lost.

Brennan. Brennan! Are you awake in there? Alexios's impatience rang through the mental pathway.

Brennan tilted his head toward the far wall of the dance floor, and Tiernan instantly began moving that way. *I am here. What have you discovered?*

There's a very heavy vamp presence in the guards. Way more than one would expect for guarding a bunch of science geniuses. They're either expecting trouble or they're planning to cause some.

Brennan and Tiernan stopped dancing at the edge of the dance floor and walked toward an empty corner. "Alexios," he said to answer the question in her eyes.

She nodded but said nothing, waiting.

I would guess the heavy guard is planned for me, at the very least. Can't allow the rich benefactor to escape, after all.

Alexios was silent for so long that Brennan thought he'd cut off communication, but then he sent another message.

You'd be exactly right. We've just been shown pictures of you and Tiernan, although they call her Tracy, so at least her cover isn't blown. You'll be honored to know you're both high priority, not to be let out of our sight. Force strongly discouraged, but allowed if you prove difficult.

Brennan's primal warrior's instincts kicked into over-drive, and he only realized he'd clenched his hands into fists around imaginary daggers when Tiernan took one of his hands and gently unpeeled his fingers.

Difficult? I will kill them if they try to touch her, he told Alexios. *I will peel their skin from their bodies and hang their internal organs in the sun to burn. Yes, that could be difficult for them.*

Colorful. I'm in. Talk later. Watch Grace for me.

With that, Alexios cut off the connection, but not before Brennan sensed an impending threat. Alexios and Lucas were facing something big and possibly very, very bad. He needed to get out there and help.

"Alexios is in danger," he murmured in Tiernan's ear. "I need to go to his aid."

"Did he ask for help?"

"No, but—"

"I understand you need to help your friend," she said, so quietly it was nearly subvocal. "But we're being watched very closely, and I'm not sure how you can get out of here without being extremely noticeable." She cut a glance toward the podium under the sweep of her long, dark lashes, and he pulled her into a hug, using the action as cover to glance where she'd indicated.

It was Litton, of course. Staring at them and not bother-ing to hide his scrutiny.

"The good doctor is being just a little too overt for a scientist planning to grovel for money," Tiernan murmured. "Makes me think Plan B is to kill you or try to enthrall you and keep your money, too."

"After all, if they go along with my plans, they get ten million," Brennan said. "If they make me a mind slave, they get it all."

"How much are you supposed to be worth?"

Brennan shrugged, more interested in the delicate curve of her ear than in talk of money. "I don't pay very close at-tention. When our former king insisted we work with human banks and investments, I began to do so. I would imagine I am at an even dozen or so by now."

Tiernan blinked. "A dozen what? Atlantean dollars? Starfish? What do you even use for currency?"

He smiled down at her. "No, we do not use currency in Atlantis. We have no need. My funds are concentrated in American dollars, although I have considerable overseas investments, of course."

She opened her mouth, closed it, and opened it again. "So you're telling me you have twelve million dollars? For real?"

"Of course not."

Tiernan laughed and blew out a big sigh. "Whew. I was really going to have a problem hanging out with you since you're so much older and if you were a millionaire, too. It's not like I'm the sugar-daddy type."

He searched his memory for the term, but could not find it. "I don't know what 'sugar daddy' means, but I do not have twelve million dollars. I have approximately twelve billion dollars. Should we get another drink? I need to get word to Grace."

He started toward the bar, but halted when he realized she was no longer with him. He pivoted on his heel, ready to protect her from any danger, but she was safe. Safe, but standing exactly where he'd left her, with a very odd look on her face. He returned to her side, concerned that she might be ill or—if it were even possible for one with her amazing courage—finally afraid.

"Tiernan?"

"Twelve *billion* dollars? Are you joking?"

He studied her face, trying to decide what the best response would be. As always, he settled for the simplest. "I rarely joke. Without emotions, there has been no way for me to judge the comic potential of most humor."

She blinked. "You rarely joke. Twelve. Billion. Dollars."

A delightful notion struck him, and he laughed out loud. "This is no longer a problem. I can make jokes anytime I want. I can joke with *Ven*."

Tiernan, who had met Ven, raised a single eyebrow. "You might want to start smaller. Ven is more your world-class comedian."

"Shall we go and talk to Grace?"

"Sure, lead away, Mr. Twelve Billion," she said, still in that stunned tone.

Before starting back across the floor, he related what Alexios had told him. "If this gets any more dangerous, you are out of this mission," he said flatly. "No arguments."

Something sparked in her eyes, and the stunned look vanished from her face as if it had never been there. "Wrong. You'd better believe there will be arguments. There is no way I'm going anywhere. If they're worried about us escaping, that means we're on the right track. Now all we have to do is play along, find out what we can, and break the story so the bad guys go to jail."

Brennan shook his head. "Unfortunately, it is never, ever that easy when it comes to vampires."

She grinned. "I know. So you need me. I'm your backup."

With that, she grabbed his hand and headed toward the bar, leaving him no choice but to follow.

"My backup," he repeated, wondering if a nonstop tsunami of emotions could shatter a man's mind—or if Tiernan could do that all by herself.

Alexios picked that moment to communicate with him again.

We've got more trouble. Lucas has to go back to Pack headquarters, there was another attack there, and he's afraid for Honey and the babies. I'm going with him. This is his family in danger, and he might need an extra pair of daggers.

Do you need me? Brennan sent back. For Lucas and his family, he would find a way to escape Litton's watchdogs.

No. You need to stay there and see what in the nine hells is going on. I don't want to leave Grace alone, either. Not to mention Tiernan is human, and she's a target, too. Humans break easily.

Brennan's fury flashed into a towering rage at the thought.

They would have to get past me first.

Meet us at Lucas's HQ after the party, if you can get away. Otherwise, we'll find a way to come to you.

Brennan agreed and shut down the line of communication. Tiernan tugged on his arm and then pulled his face down and kissed his cheek. "Did you see that? Litton's weasel of an assistant just rushed in here looking totally freaked-out. Something is definitely going on."

Litton's face turned red, then white, as they watched the intense conversation he and his assistant were having, and then the scientist rushed out of the room. Wesley began to follow him, then turned and scanned the room, arrowing in on Brennan and Tiernan. He started toward them at a rapid pace and stumbled to a stop.

"Um, Mr. Brennan, I'm sorry to say that the meeting that was set for after this party had to be postponed. We'll, uh, we'll be in touch in the morning. Dr. Litton requests that you stay in the hotel, since there was a report of, er, an animal attack." The man took a deep breath. "Yeah. Animal attack. Safer just to stay here."

"We'll keep that in mind," Brennan said noncommittally.

"Great. Well, um, tomorrow." The man rushed after his employer, almost running in his haste. When he'd vanished through the ballroom doorway, Brennan told Tiernan what Alexios had said.

"I'm sure you don't need me to tell you Wesley was lying through his teeth," she said. "Trouble in mad scientist land, you figure? More experiments going wrong? I sure hope none of Lucas's family or Pack were hurt."

"As do I. For now, we need to tell Grace what is planned, and then we can go to our room and decide what to do next."

"Our room?" Tiernan sighed and then squared her shoulders and flashed a crooked smile his way. "Yes, I guess it has to be. Well, on the bright side, I've never shared a room with a billionaire before. Do you have dollar signs on your pajamas?"

Brennan stared after her, feeling yet again like he was having some difficulty keeping up with this fascinating woman. When she was too far away to hear him, he finally remembered to answer her question.

"I don't wear pajamas."

Chapter 12

Tiernan followed Brennan into his hotel room, after he'd made sure nobody who shouldn't have been was lying in wait. Something about these warrior types; they took their protection seriously. She was rather glad about that after the day she'd had, although Brennan himself was one of the reasons she'd needed protection in the first place. She ran a quick check for bugs again, since they'd been out of the room. Still clean. Either Litton was trusting, stupid, or too arrogant to think their conversation was important.

After she put the scanner back in the bottom of her bag, she turned to Brennan. "We need to talk. Devon may be the vampire who cornered me for the little chat earlier, but I can't be sure. He wouldn't admit it, unfortunately. I didn't want to press, him, either, considering the situation."

Brennan said nothing but just stood there, motionless, his back to her.

"Brennan? Are you communicating with Alexios again with your special Spidey senses?" When he didn't respond, she sighed. "Look, I know full well the gravity of this situation, but I thought that maybe by keeping it light, I was helping you to keep a lid on the emotions. I can't imagine how horrible it must be to get swamped with two thousand years of emotion all at once. I really admire you, to be honest. I think I'd go completely insane if I had to live through feeling everything that has happened to me just in the past twenty-eight years."

He flinched as if she'd struck him, and an icy tendril of concern whispered down her spine. "If the party was too much, the dancing with a vampire and all, and you're going to have another breakdown, please tell me now," she said, edging back toward the door. "Because I've had about all I can take for one day."

He finally turned around, moving very slowly, and raised his head until their gazes met. She gasped and backed up another step, feeling her fight-or-flight mechanism kick into full, adrenaline-charged overdrive.

"Your eyes. They're not green anymore," she whispered.

"What color are they?" He stood perfectly still, as if he knew that she would bolt at the first sign of motion.

She stared into his eyes, which had, impossibly, turned a midnight black. But black with a difference. "They're . . . they're black, with tiny blue-green centers, almost—"

"Almost?"

"Almost like flames. Like tiny, blue-green flames."

He slowly, so slowly, raised one hand and held it out to her. "Tiernan, I need you. I need to hold you, just for a little while. The emotion—it's smashing through me. Pounding through my body and my blood and my bones. Nothing in my life has prepared me to vanquish an enemy that lives inside of me. I can't—I can't hear myself through all the noise."

He drew in a deep, shuddering breath. "You calm the turbulence. Does that make any sense at all?"

She nodded, almost in spite of herself. She knew, intellectually, that she didn't need to get caught up in this Atlantean's problems. Ancient curses, vengeful gods, and sanity-threatening emotion—it was all too fantastical. Too crazy and far, far too much on top of the very real and very dangerous mission she was on now.

She needed him, though. She needed him because he was part of her cover, and Litton and the vamps believed he was important, and . . .

She was lying to herself. She wasn't tempted to hold him for the mission, or for the story, or even for Susannah, in whatever convoluted way that might make sense.

She wanted to hold him for herself.

"Just for a little while?" she repeated, not knowing what answer she wanted to hear: yes, a little while, or no, I will never let you go. It was impossible that she could feel such intense and complicated emotions for this man she knew almost nothing about. Truth, though.

Even to herself. Especially to herself.

She did know him, on some level that had nothing to do with reason or logic or even time itself. "Yes," she whispered. "Yes, for a little while."

He flashed across the room so quickly she never saw him move until he was gathering her into his arms, lifting her up and off the floor. Her shoes thudded to the carpet beneath her feet, and she steadied herself with her hands on his strong shoulders.

"Thank you," he said simply, but there was nothing simple about it at all, as she could tell from the shudder that wracked his powerful body. "I could not bear it. Any of it. Watching them stare at you, the dancing . . . seeing that vampire touch you—" He broke off and bent to touch his forehead to hers, closing his eyes.

She knew what she should do. She should let him go. Let him forget her, and she would carry on by herself. The curse was torturing him. He tightened his arms around her, and her heart told her the truth she'd been fighting. She had no choice. Once he was away from her, he'd forget her and maybe the horrible emotional overload would stop or at least calm down enough for him to stay sane.

He was close to cracking, and nobody deserved that. Especially not this man. This *warrior*, who had done so much for humanity for so long.

She put her hands on his face and looked into his incredibly beautiful black and flame-centered eyes. "Brennan. You have to go. It's too hard, and I can't—I can't watch the pain of all of this drive you out of your mind. I can do this on my own."

He turned his head and pressed a kiss to the center of her palm. "No," he said gently. "I will not leave you. We will work together to discover the truth behind these scientists and their plots, and then I will release you."

"Release me?" She knew she should move away from him, but she didn't want to stop touching him. Leaning into his warmth. Breathing in his spicy male scent.

"You do not need to be drawn into my problems," he said, his eyes and voice both going flat and cold. As she watched, fascinated, the black faded from his irises until they were a pure, pale spring green, and she was forced to wonder how many of his problems centered around her.

～～～

Brennan clenched his hands into fists at his sides and battled the most powerful enemy he'd ever faced: himself. Emotion buffeted him as if he were a storm-tossed ship at sea, and every molecule of his body was screaming at him to take her, *take her*, strip her bare, and make her his.

Discipline. He needed—he must—he would. He would be calm, he would be rational, and most of all, he would be the man she needed and not the man who needed her. Not now. Not yet.

Maybe not ever.

"This Devon may be playing a deep game, toying with us, although I do not discount the possibility that he wanted to dance with you simply because you were the most beautiful woman in the room," he said, steeling himself against the surge of desire that made his cock jump in his pants every time she blushed.

As anticipated, her cheeks took on a particularly appealing rosy hue. "I don't think— Well, thank you. But vampires rarely do anything for simple reasons, especially powerful ones like this Devon." She sat on the edge of the bed and began selecting clothes from her bag, then snapped her fingers. "Wait, I almost forgot. Devon said to say hello to you from him. Have you met him?"

"I have never met any vampire named Devon, although I admit I probably wouldn't have recognized him if I had known him, in that crowd and with those glasses on." Brennan frowned, considering possibilities. "Unfortunately, the first thing that comes to mind is that I may have slain one of his blood pride, and he's out for revenge. That has been very common over the centuries."

She sighed. "It's kind of surreal the way you casually throw out things like 'over the centuries.' When this is all over, can we have a really long talk about all of the wonders you've seen and experienced in your lifetime?"

He froze, realizing the implication in her words, even if she had not intended them. That there would be an "after" for them. That she would want to spend time with him.

That he could nurture the tiniest bit of hope.

"I would love nothing more," he said.

She tilted her head. "That was a lie. Not a big one, but something . . . something was untrue in what you just said."

He considered his words and then, startled, laughed, and that bit of joy opened the floodgates to a darker, hungrier emotion. "You are not an easy woman to be around, are you, Truth Teller? You catch even the palest shades of falsehood in otherwise truthful statements. No, it is not entirely true. But the truth encompasses my desire for you and seemed a bit aggressive for such short acquaintance. There is much more I would love to do with you than talk."

Her eyes darkened, and she drew in a slightly ragged breath, giving him hope that she was not unaffected by him. It was too soon, though, and they had much to do before they explored this passion that flared so brightly between them.

"Let's leave desire to the side for now, okay? Anyway, you just summed up my entire life, Brennan. Nobody ever found me easy to be around, including my own family. Sorry I bother you, too."

He could tell that he had hurt her with his careless words, and the pain of it seared through him, but he was unused to feelings and their aftermath and had no idea how to undo what he had said. He wanted to understand, though, so he could better know her.

"Tell me what it's like. You have a Gift that was long ago lost to Atlanteans. We call those who can hear and feel the resonance of truth and deception 'truth tellers.' They were much revered in our society, or so the ancient tales go, but too often—" He stopped, cursing his stupid tongue.

"Too often what?"

"It is nothing. We should go to find Lucas and Alexios."

"Tell me," she demanded. "Too often they went crazy? Too often everybody hated them? Do you think I don't know that? Do you think it's easy to hear every lie, no matter how small or insignificant? Yes, it's a very helpful talent when I'm investigating a story. But the rest of the time? *Ha.* Society can't survive without polite little deceptions. White lies. 'Yes, you're still as lovely as the day I married you.' 'Great try hitting that ball, little Junior.' 'Sure, I'd love to go to the hockey game with you, honey.'" She put her head in her hands. "I always know. When my date thinks I'm not as cute as his last girlfriend, or my boss thinks my writing is crap, or my dad is having an affair with the babysitter. I always know." When she looked up at him, tears glittered in her lashes and they were like daggers to his heart. "And you know what? I hate every minute of it. I'd give anything to *not* know. Just for a day, or a week, or heck, even an hour. I'd love to *not know*."

"Please forgive me." Brennan dropped to a crouch in front of her and put his hands on either side of her knees on the bed. "I am a thoughtless fool. I will try harder. Please do not cry. I cannot bear it, and I am afraid I will thoroughly unman myself by crying, too."

She smiled a little. "Men can cry, too, in this century."

"Not me. If I start, I am afraid I would cry for at least ten days, or even thrice that. You will be forced to call the front desk and ask for buckets to catch the tears and I will flood the park," he said, deliberately widening his eyes in an expression of exaggerated solemnity, in hopes of making her laugh. "Next the television person will be reporting on bison caught in the flood, being forced to swim for safety."

Tiernan laughed out loud. "Okay, you win. I'll quit feeling sorry for myself, but only for the sake of the buffalo."

He leaned forward and kissed each of her eyelids in turn, tasting the salt of her tears and imprinting her onto his soul like a branding. "You are a courageous and selfless woman, Tiernan Butler. Now let's go find Alexios and figure out our plan."

He stood up, pulling her with him. "We should change clothes before we meet Alexios and the others. I will turn my back, if that will suffice?"

She shook her head. "I need the other room again. I'll be quick." She handed him her phone and dashed off, and he put the phone on the desk and stared intently at her picture while he quickly changed out of the tuxedo. This time, he did not feel her fading in his mind as quickly as before, but the haze still began after only a few short minutes.

"Tiernan? I need to see you," he finally called out, hating his own helplessness.

She flung the door open and stepped out, as beautiful as ever but more covered up in a dark green sweater, jeans, and boots. "I'm here. You know, you really need to petition Poseidon about this."

"I will," he said grimly. "Alaric, our high priest, will surely help me find a way to talk to the sea god. Although I know of no instance, ever, in which Poseidon revoked a curse, once given."

"Well, it can't hurt to try, right? If he says no, you're no worse off than you are now. Maybe . . . maybe I could talk to him for you?"

"You would offer to go before the sea god himself to plead my case?" Brennan felt her sincerity like a body blow, smashing yet another layer of his defenses. She would face Poseidon. For him.

She bit her lip, but nodded. "Hey, no guts, no glory, right? Now, maybe we should focus on the immediate problem?"

"I agree. Now we should figure out a way to get past our unwanted bodyguards and to Lucas's headquarters to discover what exactly is going on there."

"Can you do the mist thing again?" She glanced at the window. "That was pretty impressive, by the way. Nobody would ever catch you traveling that way."

"I could, but I can't carry you that way. Or, to be precise, although I could carry you while in that form, it would be quite startling to everyone watching to see you floating through midair, being carried by an invisible magic carpet."

She bit her lip. "You can't turn me into mist, too, then?"

"No. Only Atlanteans have that ability."

"I have to admit to being a little relieved. I'm not much for having my molecules rearranged. I'm much more McCoy than Spock in that way, if you get my drift."

"Actually, I have no idea what—"

"Sorry. *Star Trek* junkie here. Big fan. Loved the remake." She walked over to the window and peeked out. "It's settled, then. You go by yourself, via the mist deal, and I stay here and get some rest. Maybe order some room service. When you get back—"

It was his turn to interrupt. "I cannot be separated from you, Tiernan. Not that I would leave you alone, with so much danger, in any case. But I cannot leave you or the terms of the curse will be invoked."

She smacked her hand on her forehead. "I know that. I *know* that. It's hard to remember, though, if that makes sense? Like how you keep hitting the light switch in a room every time you walk in even though you know you need to replace the lightbulb?"

Half the time he had no idea what she was talking about, but it in no way detracted from the pure sensual enjoyment of watching her. Watching her mouth move and imagining what she could do to him with those lovely, lush lips . . .

"Brennan?" She waved at him. "You're doing it again?"

"Doing what?"

"Staring at me like I'm on the menu."

"Of course not." But a wave of heat traveled down his body, giving the lie to his words. Considering her Gift, he smiled.

"Perhaps only for dessert."

Chapter 13

In the elevator on the way to the lobby, Tiernan's skin tingled every time Brennan even so much as glanced her way. He was taking the idea of embracing his emotions very seriously, or at least taking the idea of embracing *her* very seriously. He wanted her, and he was going after her. The single-minded pursuit should have turned her off, but it didn't. It had quite the opposite effect. She spent most of her time around him feeling very, very tingly.

"Showtime," she murmured as the L button lit up and the doors began to open. Brennan's seductive half smile transformed into an arrogant glare, and he put a possessive arm around her waist.

"This is part of the act, remember, so don't hold it against me later," he said quietly into her ear.

Seized by a wicked impulse, she dropped her hand to his sexy, firm butt and squeezed. "Same goes." Then she threw back her head and pealed a great rich bout of "gosh, I'm a bimbo" laughter and put some wiggle into her hips as they exited the elevator.

"Are you sure you want to go for a walk in these woods in the dark, Sweetie Pie? I mean, there might be wild animals and scary stuff out there," she said in her best impression of breathless and brainless.

"I'm the only wild animal you need to worry about, now or ever," he said in his deep voice, and though she knew he was playing to their expected audience, something in his tone made her wonder just how much of the possessiveness he was demonstrating really was an act.

The last thing she needed was him thinking he could take over her life. She had a job and a goal to get back to when this mission was done. She was going to expose every single one of the monsters who were behind this horrible plot to enthrall humanity, and she had a feeling Litton and his cronies were only the tip of the iceberg.

Right on cue, a matching pair of no-neck, muscle-bound thugs stepped in front of them as they sauntered toward the exit.

"Sorry, sir, but we're asking guests to remain in the hotel tonight. Just a precaution, you understand," Tweedle Dumb said.

"Yeah. Precautions. Don't want anybody to gobble you up, do ya?" Tweedle Dumber chimed in, leering at her boobs.

Brennan's hand shot out and he gripped Dumber by the throat, lifting him so far up in the air that the man's toes barely scraped the floor. "I am inclined to consider your lascivious actions to be an offense to my lady. What do you say to that?"

Dumber said nothing, which wasn't surprising since Brennan was choking him. The man's face turned a mottled red and he gasped out a few strangled noises while ineffectually trying to pull Brennan's hand away from his neck.

His partner went for a gun under his jacket, and Brennan raised an eyebrow. "Do you really think you want to do that?"

The thug froze, considering his options. Thinking was apparently not in his job description.

Tiernan put a hand on Brennan's arm. "Stop. Let him go. I don't need you to defend my honor, and you're causing quite a scene."

Brennan gave another squeeze, but released the man just as his face turned an interesting shade of deep purple.

"I'll kill you," the man managed to growl between gasping in deep breaths.

"You can try," Brennan returned calmly. "Now, if we're done with this, my date and I are going for a short walk. Detain us further at your own risk, not to mention Dr. Litton might be very unhappy with you if his prize billionaire were to walk out on this whole enterprise."

Dumb and Dumber gaped at each other, clearly at a loss to calculate this new variable. Tiernan didn't wait for them to figure it out, especially when the one with the gun grabbed his radio and toggled it on. She grabbed Brennan by the hand and pulled him toward the glass doors. At first it was like trying to pull a mountain, but finally, the testosterone-driven staring match with the goons apparently over, he followed her. When they were outside, she didn't stop but dropped his hand and strode rapidly down the sidewalk toward the road, having no idea in what direction they were headed but not really caring. He caught up in seconds and shot a sidelong glance at her as she kept hiking along, still moving at top speed.

"Are you angry with me?" he finally ventured.

"Gee, Sherlock, what gave you that idea?" She muttered some of the worst words she knew under her breath. "Just because you endanger the mission and risk blowing our cover all over some stupid guy staring at my boobs? Why would I be *angry*?"

"I should apologize for defending your honor?" Brennan viciously kicked a fallen tree limb out of his way. "Let them act like degenerate scum while I do nothing? And then what? Perhaps lie down and have a fit of the vapors while they put their hands on you?"

She clamped her lips shut to fight the grin threatening to break free, and then stopped and pivoted to face him. "Okay, so many things. First, nobody says 'fit of the vapors.' Try to join this century. Second, overreact much? They were leering. They were thugs, with probably five brain cells to share between them, and they were copping a visual feel. Big deal. I get worse every time I walk past a construction site in Boston."

He folded his arms across that broad chest of his, which made his muscles tighten and strain the fabric of his shirt, and for a moment she lost track of what she'd been saying. The man was flat-out gorgeous. But then she looked up, and the mutinous expression on his face brought her back to the point, fast.

"You know, you look like a two-year-old who needs juice and a nap," she pointed out, but then she came to a startling realization. "In fact, that's probably what a lot of this is about, isn't this? Everybody else learns to control their emotions as a child, but you've had no opportunity to do that. Or whatever you did learn as a child was wiped out in the past couple of thousand years. So you're at the 'I wanna' and 'no, no, no' stage of emotional development."

She threw up her arms and started walking again. "Great. I needed stealth for undercover work and I get Rambo with a definite need for a time-out chair."

He clamped a hand on her arm and pulled her around, none too gently, to face him. "Oh, no. You cannot make proclamations like that and then just walk away from me."

She got right back in his face. Nobody was going to tell her what she could or couldn't do, ancient warrior or not. "Why not?"

"Well, for one thing, you're going the wrong way."

She glanced around, feeling a little foolish. "Oh."

"And for another, I need to kiss you right now," he said, pulling her against her body. "Do you have any complaints about that?"

"I'm sure I'll think of—"

He kissed her, just a quick press of his lips to hers, cutting off whatever she'd been about to say. "You'll think of what?"

Tiernan sighed, then put her arms around his neck. "Nothing. But you're so getting juice and a nap after this, mister."

He laughed and circled her waist with his strong arms. "May I have a cookie with that?"

When she opened her mouth to reply, he took swift advantage with a searing, deep kiss. The forest floor melted away from under her feet. Nothing remained but a swirling tornado of emotion, and she and Brennan stood in the middle, clinging to each other as a drowning sailor clings to a piece of driftwood.

His tongue swept into her mouth and claimed it—claimed *her*—for his own, and he pulled her so tightly against his body that she couldn't miss the hard bulge of his erection pulsing against her exactly where she needed him. She moaned, or maybe he did, and she tunneled her fingers through the silky long waves of his hair and pulled his face even closer to deepen the kiss.

He ravaged her mouth, kissing her with such intensity and skill that she believed her bones were turning to liquid silver in his arms. She was helpless to do anything but cling to him and tighten her hold, devouring him as if the kiss itself were the only thing keeping her from shattering into pieces and flying off into the storm of passion.

She pulled back a little, trying to catch her breath and regain a little balance, but he kissed his way down the side of her neck and then oh-so-gently kissed the exact spot where the vampire had bitten her earlier.

"What are you doing?" she whispered, as he gently cupped her breast with one large, elegant hand.

"I am torturing myself," he said, breathing hard, "since there is no way I will allow myself to take you against the side of one of these trees, even though everything in me screams to do nothing else. I am having fantasies of lifting this sweater and covering your lush, ripe breasts with my hands and covering your lush, ripe nipples with my mouth. Then I want to kneel before you and peel these jeans down to your ankles and lick the sweetness from your lush, ripe body until you come in my mouth."

She was breathing pretty hard herself by the time he was done painting that visual picture. "That's a lot of lush and ripe," she whispered.

"I need you, Tiernan. Two thousand years of need," he growled. He lifted her completely off the ground, and she instinctively wrapped her legs around his waist as he carried her over to one of the trees he'd just mentioned, more than a dozen yards away from the road and deep in the night shadows cast by the other trees. Even the moonlight didn't penetrate to where they stood. "Let me do this. Just for a few short minutes. Let me give you pleasure."

He stopped when they reached the tree, and ever so gently, he pressed her back against the cold bark. "Please, please, please," he mumbled against her mouth before taking her lips in another searing, passionate kiss.

Exquisite waves of ecstasy sizzled through her body just from the touch of his mouth on hers, and she knew she should remember all the reasons why this was a bad idea, but all she could think of was *yes*, and—after all—*two thousand years of need*, and so she said it.

"How can a girl resist that? Yes, yes, yes," she whispered, urgent, needing his hands on her. Needing his mouth on her.

He roared out a sound of triumph or possession or maybe it was just an Atlantean lovemaking thing, but she didn't care because seconds later he was lifting her sweater and pushing her bra cups to the side, and before the first chill could even spark goose bumps on her skin, his hot mouth covered one nipple and his hot hand covered the other. He made a humming sound against her breast and it tingled, but before she could react he put his lips around her nipple and sucked so hard she cried out.

"Brennan, Brennan, oh, God, yes." She tightened her fingers in his hair, and he took it for the encouragement it was, apparently, because he began rhythmically sucking that nipple and flicking it with periodic swipes of his tongue. She squirmed against him, the hot, liquid desire pooling between her thighs, opening and readying her for him. She wanted, she needed, and oh, yes, he pushed the big, hard bulge of his erection against her and began pressing against her in the same rhythm that his mouth used on her.

A flash fire of sensation raced through her veins, and she was so close to coming, just from his mouth on her breast. So close, oh, how could she be so aroused so fast, and then he bit down gently on her nipple and his fingers pinched her other nipple, hard, at the same time, and she cried out.

The heat, oh, the heat, the sheer driving, pounding force of her need was climbing through her and demanding more and more. More of the incredible sensation.

More of *him*.

Tiernan was nearly crazed with the wanting, it was so powerful. Never, ever had she felt anything even close to this before. Desperate, she pulled at his head until he released her nipple with a wet, sucking pop that she felt all the way down to her toes.

He looked up at her and his eyes were glowing emerald flames. "Tell me," he demanded. "Tell me what you want."

"I want you," was all she could manage. "I want you now, I need you, oh, please oh, please."

He carefully released her, until her feet were on the ground again, and she had to lean back against the tree to hold herself up since her wobbly knees were not cooperating. Then he stared at her, his gaze sweeping from her flushed face and swollen lips to her breasts that were still bare, her hard nipples so swollen that every breath of the cold wind touching them built her arousal even further. He gently pulled her sweater down.

"So you don't get a chill," he said tenderly, and she was bewildered, trying to make sense of his words. Was he stopping?

"What? What? But I thought we—"

"Oh, we definitely are," he said, grinning wolfishly, and even in the dark she could see the gleam of his teeth. He dropped to his knees on the leaves at her feet and in seconds had stripped her jeans and panties down to her ankles. Before she could take a breath, or think, or move, he caught her hips in his hands and put his mouth on her.

At the first touch of his hot, clever, skillful tongue on her clitoris, she cried out again, and then she couldn't scream, couldn't even catch her breath as he licked her and sucked her and swirled his tongue around her until she was almost crying with pleasure.

"Please, please, please, please," she begged, repeating the word until it was meaningless sound, just a wordless plea, and then it didn't matter, she couldn't talk, because he put his fingers inside her and drove them in and out, in and out, and began sucking with the same rhythm and pressure he'd used on her nipple. Mere seconds later, the pressure and pleasure and passion rocketed through her body and exploded out the top of her head and she screamed again, calling out his name, as the most powerful orgasm she'd ever had in her life took her up and over and into the universe.

She lost consciousness or at least went fuzzy for a few seconds, and when she blinked her way back, he was cradling her in his arms, gently kissing her forehead. She flushed when she realized her pants were hanging down around her ankles, and her bra was still unfastened under her sweater.

"I—" She had to stop for a calming breath. "I have no words for how amazing that was. But I need to get dressed."

He laughed. "I am very happy to have pleased you so well," he said, and there was plenty of smug male satisfaction in his voice.

She had to grin. After all, he deserved to feel satisfied. Wow. "The scent of wilderness is going to be an aphrodisiac to me for the rest of my life," she said, laughing a little herself.

He kissed her again and bent to retrieve her pants and underwear before she could do it, stopping midway to kiss her stomach. When he'd pulled her pants halfway up, he paused and swiped his tongue across her in a last long, savoring lick. She gasped and clutched the tree behind her as the burst of sensation flashed through her sensitized skin yet again.

"I needed one final taste of you to sustain me until the moment I can do this again, more properly and thoroughly," he said, smiling up at her.

"If you're any more thorough, I'll pass out."

He laughed again and then pulled her jeans up over her hips, leaving the fastening to her. Since she was looking down, she noticed the huge bulge in his pants, which was even more pronounced than it had been earlier, and a trace of guilt surfaced.

"You didn't, um . . . We didn't do anything for you," she whispered, feeling her cheeks flaming.

"Now isn't the time, but trust me when I say you can have no idea of how much you did for me." His voice was incredibly deep and husky, and it resonated through her, making her shiver in anticipation of what exactly "more properly and thoroughly" might involve.

She finished arranging her clothes and glanced up at him, fascinated by the way his eyes were glowing with magic, or power, or maybe Atlanteans got glowy eyes when they were turned on. "Maybe later, we could get to know each other more? See where this might take us when we're not hiding from evil scientists and power-hungry vamps?"

He pulled her close for a quick hug, then froze, his body against her going ramrod straight.

"Brennan—"

"Shh," he whispered in her ear. "I believe we're about to have company, and it's nobody good."

Chapter 14

Brennan heard the leaves rustling, but it was their only warning before the vamps were on top of them, flowing out of the trees like dark ribbons of liquid night. There were only three, but they were armed with daggers, which was unusual for vamps. Generally they counted wholly on their preternatural strength and their fangs.

This wasn't a good development.

"Stay behind me," he ordered Tiernan, who responded with her usual meek submission.

"Like hell." She bent and grabbed a small fallen tree branch and snapped it in half. "Two stakes for the price of one, what do you think about that, boys?"

The vampires arranged themselves in a three-point semi-circle around them, and one of them bowed deeply before speaking. "You mistake our intent, Miss Baum. We're part of the security force for the conference, and we merely wish to be sure you make it safely back to the hotel. There were vicious animal attacks near here tonight."

"We're wounded that you would so quickly assume we intend you any harm," said another, fake innocence oozing from his oily tone. "Just because we're vampires doesn't make us bad people. You, as a reporter, should know that."

"It's not the vampire part that bothers us," Brennan said. "It's the security guard part. We are not at all in the mood for a second unpleasant encounter with overzealous security."

"Exactly," Tiernan added, flashing a big smile. "Some of my best friends are vampires."

The vamp farthest away from them made a strange gurgling sound, and it took a moment for Brennan to realize that it was laughter. "Some of our best friends are humans, little snack."

"Just a guess, but I don't think calling a human 'little snack' is usually going to win you points, buddy," Tiernan said, pointing one of her newly made stakes at him. "You wouldn't like it if I called you 'bloodsucker,' would you?"

The vamp who'd bowed to them earlier hissed in a breath. "You know, this is not going as smoothly as I'd hoped, and now I'm bored. Either come with us now or we will take action you will not enjoy, I promise you."

Brennan unsheathed his daggers and snarled at them, dark urges to stab and cut and kill swarming through him. "There isn't much about you that I enjoy so far, so I don't see that we'd be any worse off. We're not going anywhere with you."

"Perhaps not willingly," the vampire countered. He slashed his hand in a signal to his friends and all three of them started forward.

Brennan was ready for them. He shoved Tiernan behind him so that her back was against the tree, a more defensible position. Then, daggers whirling, he faced the three. "These have silver tips. Is that an injury you are prepared to suffer for whatever they're paying you?"

The leader hissed but froze in place. Silver wounds did not heal easily for vampires and could even be fatal. Not something your average human billionaire businessman might be expected to know, but Brennan wasn't too concerned about protecting his cover story at that particular moment.

"We heard about the animal attacks," Tiernan said. "We promise to come back soon. We just wanted a little alone time." She laughed, and it was light and flirtatious—almost a giggle. Brennan clenched his jaw tight to keep his mouth from falling open.

Tiernan? *Giggling?*

Damn, but she was good at this undercover work.

The vampire leader shot another glance at Brennan and his daggers, but whatever orders he was following evidently didn't give him room for independent decision making. "We may bleed, but your woman will suffer threefold for every blow you land on one of us."

"I look forward to playing with her a little," one of the others said, and then he laughed, a long, shrill cackle of unholy glee. "Devon didn't say we couldn't play with them."

"Devon?" Tiernan's voice was sharp. "He knows you're doing this?"

The leader made an ugly hooting noise. "Knows? We follow his orders, little snack."

Before he'd even quit speaking, the vamp launched himself at Brennan, leaping twenty feet through the air, nails lengthening to outstretched claws and fangs glistening in the ribbons of moonlight that shone through the trees.

Brennan met him in midair.

Daggers clashed and steel rang, but Brennan's towering rage gave him the strength of ten warriors, and he parried the vamp's attacks and whirled around, one dagger extended in a death blow. Even before the vamp's head thudded onto the ground, the neck still smoldering from the orichalcum blade, Brennan turned and shot four razor-sharp *shuriken* in a smooth underhanded motion at the second vamp. The throwing stars served their purpose brilliantly, decapitating the second vamp as neatly as his daggers had done to the first.

He whipped around to the tree where he'd left Tiernan, just in time to hear her scream. The third vamp was closing in on her, laughing and dancing from foot to foot, mocking her and making lewd suggestions as to what he was planning to do to her cold, dead corpse.

Tiernan, from the tone of her remarks, was not a fan of this.

Brennan's newly found emotions swept through him with the force of a hurricane. Part of him was overcome with pride to see his woman holding off a vampire with only two sticks. Another, far larger, part of him was burning with a fierce rage so powerful that it seemed as if the earth itself must be scorched from the heat of his fury.

Then the vamp shot out a claw-tipped hand and scratched a furrow on the side of Tiernan's face before she could block him, and the balance tipped far, far over into insanity.

Brennan rode the fury, harnessed it and pulled magic, water, and power out of the soil and the trees and the very air itself. He roared out a challenge—a grim promise. "By Poseidon and Atlantis, you will die for daring to touch her."

He called to the water and transformed it into perfect, shining spears that rained icy death onto the vampire. Each glittering spear arrowed into the vamp's neck, one after another, with unerring accuracy. None a whisper off, none posing the slightest danger to Tiernan, and none missing its mark.

In a split second, the vampire was down, dissolving into a nasty pool of slime on the forest floor, only the ice spears standing to mark the spot where they'd pinned him to the ground.

But Brennan had gone far, far past the point of reason. He was drowning in the rage—no longer a man, or a warrior, but a being of anger, fury, and madness. He yanked Tiernan into his arms—his woman, only and forever *his* woman, how had they dared to try to touch her—and held her so tightly that she could never, ever get away from him. She struggled a little, and he threw back his head and screamed his defiance into the night, a wordless howl of pain and feral wrath.

Into the silence, broken only by the echoes of his rage, a familiar voice called out a quiet challenge.

"Brennan," Alexios said. "You need to put the nice human down, or I'm going to have to kick your ass for you."

Brennan dropped Tiernan to her feet and whirled around to face the new threat, recognizing but not recognizing his friend through the red, shimmering haze of berserker fury that smashed through his mind. His skull pounded with the driving need to hurt, to kill, to tear and maim.

To protect.

To protect *Tiernan*. His only purpose as the rest of his mind fractured.

"Tiernan?" he said, his voice hoarse and broken. "Tiernan is safe?"

Alexios nodded, but didn't take his hands off his daggers. "Tiernan is safe, my friend. She's right behind you."

"I'm right here, Brennan," she said, the sound of her voice like a balm to his ragged soul. "Turn around and look at me. Please."

He turned, and she put her hands on either side of his face and looked up into his eyes. "I'm here. I'm safe. You saved me from those vampires. You killed them all."

"Killed them?" he croaked. "Safe?"

"Come back to me, Brennan." She put her arms around his waist and leaned forward into him, sharing her warmth with his cold, cold heart. "Come back."

Brennan pulled her closer and stood like that, unmoving, for several seconds, holding her as tightly as he dared, content simply to breathe in her scent and bask in her warmth.

Alexios cleared his throat. "I think we probably need to talk."

Brennan cautiously opened his eyes, and blew out a sigh of relief when his vision was clear. The berserker haze was gone. The miraculous healing power of holding Tiernan in his arms had restored him to some measure of calm.

"Are you able to let me go now?" Tiernan asked, an expression of utter trust on her face, and he pressed a brief, hard kiss to her lips and released her from his arms, but kept her hand clasped firmly in his own.

As he turned to face Alexios, he had a sobering realization. Everything that he was—everything that he would be from now until the end of eternity—depended entirely on this woman and her trust and happiness. If he'd seen the slightest bit of doubt in her eyes, it would have broken him.

"This isn't what it looked like at all, then, is it?" Alexios said, studying Brennan and Tiernan as he sheathed his daggers. "You were attacked, not attacking her?"

Brennan felt an actual physical pain slice through him at the words. "You could doubt me after so many centuries?"

Alexios shook his head. "I could never doubt *you*, my friend. But you're under the effects of a very powerful curse right now and we don't know what that's doing to you. If you thought Tiernan was trying to leave you . . ."

The vise grip that squeezed Brennan's chest at the thought was enough to underscore Alexios's words. "No, you are correct, unfortunately," he admitted.

"I'm not going anywhere," Tiernan said, glaring at Alexios. "And Brennan doesn't need this from you after he had to face two human thugs in the hotel and three murderous vamp guards out here."

Alexios scanned the area. "If there were three, there could be more. I don't suppose they happened to tell you what they were up to?"

"They did, actually. They wanted Brennan and me to go back to the hotel, but when we didn't immediately go along with the plan, they decided that they'd force us."

Brennan tensed all over again, remembering the dead vamps' threats against Tiernan. "They weren't overly concerned with keeping us uninjured, either. I fear that something has changed in the overall strategy."

A trilling birdcall sounded through the darkness and Alexios smiled. "We're here," he called, and moments later Grace stepped through the trees, her bow drawn and an arrow at the ready. She nodded at Tiernan and Brennan and lowered her bow.

"When I was leaving, I overheard some of the guards saying that three of the vamps haven't reported in, so they're going to send out a search party for you two," she said. "This would be a good time to get out of Dodge."

Brennan stared at her, confused, but Tiernan supplied the translation. "She means we need to get out of here, fast. Reinforcements are on the way."

"I can't call the portal except at a body of seawater," Alexios said. "I'm not that strong with the magic, and it rarely answers me. Damn capricious thing."

"Nor can I, generally, but I will certainly try now," Brennan said grimly. He squeezed Tiernan's hand and then released it. Holding both arms up to the sky, he closed his eyes and called to the portal. "If ever you heeded my call, please let it be now. We have need of you for transport to the shining isle."

At first, there was nothing, but they all waited, breath held, in hopeful anticipation. After a full minute had passed, Brennan sighed, his shoulders slumping. "It's no use," he began, but Tiernan grabbed his hand again.

"I think you're wrong about that," she whispered, nodding her head toward his left.

As they all watched, a silvery glimmer of light formed in the shape of a long, straight line and then stretched and widened in three dimensions until a glowing ovoid sphere floated steadily about a foot off the ground, its shape tall and wide enough to admit them, one at a time.

"It worked," Brennan said, filled with an awe so poignant his throat ached with it. "The portal knew I needed to protect Tiernan, and it answered my call."

"Love conquers all," Grace said, patting her stomach in an odd manner, and Alexios started laughing and then led the way through the portal.

"Next stop, Atlantis?" Tiernan asked, with only the tiniest quiver in her voice.

"Next stop, Atlantis, my brave warrior woman."

Still holding her hand, Brennan stepped through the portal, bringing the woman who would change everything to the place where nothing ever seemed to change. Oh, by all the gods, this might prove to be a wild ride, but she was safe, and she was his one true mate, as ordained by Poseidon himself.

Nothing else mattered.

Chapter 15

Dr. Litton's lab,
underneath Yellowstone National Park

Devon stared around the main laboratory, silently taking inventory of the destruction. Hundreds of thousands of dollars' worth of equipment—smashed. Shattered beyond hope of repair. Months of work—ruined. He stepped over the dead body in its bloodstained lab coat and walked over to the primary experiment chair. It was a wreck. Cables and cords yanked out of their sockets, some still sparking dangerously. The chair itself knocked loose from its base.

Litton stormed into the room, then skidded to a stop as he took in the extent of the damage. It almost amused Devon to watch all blood drain out of the scientist's face, until his pallor rivaled that of any vampire.

Almost.

"How did this happen?" Litton said, still gaping. "Who is responsible for this?"

Devon kicked a bloody chunk of what looked like shifter fur out of his way. "The obvious answer is that you are, Dr. Litton. This is your lab."

Litton's face crumpled and his mouth worked, but all he managed to do was make incoherent squawking sounds.

"If that translates to 'why, yes, Devon, I am at fault and will be glad to explain how I let a multimillion-dollar experimental lab be destroyed *the day my new benefactor comes to town to see it*, I would love to hear more."

Devon stalked across the room to the bank of computer stations where the techs recorded data, as he knew from the single time he'd been able to stomach watching. Paths and choices, he reminded himself. He only needed to stay focused and the real prize would soon be his.

Litton was reduced to sputtering now, but still nothing that made any sense was coming out of his mouth, and Devon quickly grew tired of waiting for him to regain his powers of speech.

"Guards," he called out. "Clean up this mess. We need it to be in perfect shape by tomorrow afternoon."

Three of the shifters and two vampire guards rushed into the room and immediately began working. One of the shifters pointed to the dead scientist.

"What do we do with him, sir?"

Devon shrugged. "Whatever you want, as long as there isn't as much as a sticky spot on the floor tomorrow to show that he was ever here."

One of the vamps eyed Devon cautiously before speaking up. "Sir, I'm sure you've thought of this, but is there a record he was working with Litton? If there are any questions about his disappearance, we don't want him connected to the project."

"Good point. We'll take care of that. Thank you." Devon made a mental note to remember the face of this vampire with such excellent strategic thinking skills. It would be very useful for later.

Another of Litton's scientists, a human, wandered in from the doorway that led back to the holding area. The man was covered in blood and seemed to be in a profound state of shock, judging by the blank stare and stumbling gait. His name tag was dangling from his ripped lab coat, so Devon had to tilt his head to read it.

"Dr. Orson, what happened here?"

It took Orson a while to focus, but he finally managed to train his gaze somewhere near Devon's shoulder. The man's eyes were rolling around in their sockets, though, and the effect was quite unpleasant.

Devon steeled himself to objectivity; Orson was a man who had chosen to experiment on his own kind. He was one of the worst kind of sheep and deserved no pity.

"The shifters," Orson mumbled. "The shifters can't all take it. There were two of them at one time, you know, we had the new chair, and they both broke free and attacked."

Devon turned to Litton, who was still wringing his hands in a corner, staring at the wreckage of his pride and joy. "What is he babbling about? What new chair?"

"What? Oh, the chair," Litton said, waving a hand at it. Unfortunately, it was as badly damaged as the primary chair. "We just connected the second chair yesterday so we could run two test subjects through at once. Too many of the shifters' brains rejected the treatment. Something about their brain patterns is so different from human brain patterns that we couldn't quite overcome it."

"What happened when you couldn't overcome it?" Devon demanded, pretty sure he already knew the answer, but wanting to hear it confirmed.

"This happened," Litton shouted, waving his arms at the destruction. "They go nuts, become wildly aggressive and violent, and we have to put them down."

"Put them down?" Devon repeated. "You have to *put them down*?"

Even Litton, the king of self-absorption, must have noticed the deadly menace in Devon's voice, because his head snapped up, and after one look at Devon's face, the scientist backed rapidly around to the other side of the destroyed chair.

"What else could we do? They were horribly dangerous. Not just to us, but to each other and to themselves. They even cannibalize each other." Litton shuddered, his lip curling back from his crooked teeth. "Sometimes it happens here, but sometimes, like this week, they seem fine and under control, and we release them to perform some task and they blow up. Sort of a delayed reaction to the mind control."

"So much blood. All over the place, blood and blood and blood," Orson added, still stumbling around. "So much blood. Going to take a shower now."

Devon and Litton watched him in silence as he wandered back out of the lab, smacking his head on the doorway as he walked through it.

"You'd better get him some medical treatment," Devon ordered one of the guards.

The man nodded and rushed off after Orson, and Devon returned his attention to Litton.

"So, this brilliant success," Devon said, making perfectly sure that Litton heard the harsh sarcasm in his voice, "this made you think it was a good idea to experiment on two shifters at once?"

Litton made those odd scrunching motions with his mouth again, and Devon wanted to weep that he'd been reduced to working with such a blind, pathetic fool. He wondered, yet again, how far he was willing to take this path. Did the end truly justify the means, or was that merely a convenient excuse for morally ambiguous madmen?

"We had plenty of guards," Litton finally said weakly. "I don't understand—"

"I know you don't understand, you egomaniacal idiot," Devon shouted, cutting the damn fool off. "You don't understand anything about shifter packs or prides or any other units of family, but you dare to experiment on them?"

Litton puffed, drawing himself up to his full height, but he still had to look up to meet Devon's gaze. "I beg your pardon, but I happen to be the neuroscientist here, and I—"

"Know nothing. You know nothing," Devon said quietly, realizing shouting wasn't accomplishing anything, however much better it might make him feel. "If two shifters are from the same pack, for example two wolves from the Yellowstone Pack, then being in close proximity to each other strengthens them far beyond any resistance they might have on their own."

Litton scoffed. "Moral support means nothing against science."

"I'm not talking about moral support. I'm talking about power. Real power. Magic." Devon shot a pointed look down at what remained of the experimental chair. "The kind of magic that allows them to shift in the first place causes an actual change in their brain patterns, you incompetent fool. Did you think that human brain patterns stay the same when the humans shift into animal form?"

Litton hooked a finger in his collar and nervously yanked it away from his neck. "Ah, we were working on that, but—"

"But you got your asses handed to you on a platter. By shifters. Where are they, by the way?"

"Where are who?"

It took everything in him to keep from smashing the doctor's head into his own computer bank. "The shifters, Dr. Litton. Where are the shifters who caused all this?"

"They're dead, sir." The helpful vamp spoke up again. "They killed each other before we could stop them."

"Right," Devon drawled. "I'm sure stopping them was such a priority."

A flash of hate skittered over the vamp's eyes, but he simply nodded and got on with the cleanup.

Litton, however, wasn't smart enough to let it be. "They're not humans at all," he said. "The shifters. They're freaks of nature. Mutations. Most people think they should be destroyed, but we want to study them so we can learn how to control them. Harness them for the good of others. We should be rewarded for this humanitarian service, not forced to hide in the dark."

Devon studied the man. Was Litton brave or stupid? Strangely enough, he was never quite able to come to an answer on that. "Interesting you'd say 'freak of nature' to a vampire. Especially when you—a human—betray your own kind."

"I don't—"

"Experiment on humans? No? You forget, Doctor, that I've seen your tapes of the various test subjects." They had sickened him, not that anybody but Deirdre had ever seen his weakness.

"Scientific experimentation is the purest form of scientific pursuit," Litton snapped. "When the International Association of Preternatural Neuroscientists meets in Ireland in a few months, I should have very interesting data to present."

"Will you?" Devon slowly turned his head from side to side, studying the room once more. "Or will you be out on your ass now that you have let your lab be destroyed? We need Brennan and his money. Why would he give it to us now, when it's clear we've wasted what he already donated? You may have killed this project before it really had a chance to begin. Congratulations, Dr. Litton. You're still the same royal screwup you were at USC. Only now, you don't have tenure."

Litton slammed a hand down on the nearest computer and then jumped back when sparks showered from its damaged monitor. "You're not in charge as much as you think you are. When the others get here tomorrow, they'll listen to me."

"Oh, I'm sure they will listen," Devon said, baring his fangs. "I'm not at all convinced, however, that they're going to like what they hear."

He'd had all he could take. It was time to go before he added Litton's corpse to the tally of mess that needed to be cleaned up. He turned and headed for the door.

"I want this spotless and ready for demonstration by tomorrow afternoon," he called out to Litton, not bothering to look back. "Or you may find your brain is the next one to go under the probes."

Litton huddled in the corner of his office after triple-checking that his door was firmly closed and locked. He held the phone in trembling hands, pressing it close to his ear so no sound escaped.

"I know. But he threatened me, and—"

The vampire on the other end of the line muttered dire threats against Devon, and Litton smiled a tiny, private smile. Excellent.

"You need to get here tomorrow and run this meeting. I think—"

A burst of hideously cacophonous sound skittered out of the phone and crawled down Litton's spine. "I'm sorry," he all but babbled. "I'm sorry, no, I wasn't giving you orders, of course. I'll see you tomorrow night. Thank you. Good-bye."

He slammed the phone down and wiped his hands on his pant legs.

"They'll see, won't they?" he asked the empty room. "They'll all see."

He started laughing, and he laughed and laughed, seeing the destroyed room, his dead colleague, and Orson's shocked, glazed eyes all front and center in his far-too-vivid memory.

"We'll just see who is giving orders in the end, blood-suckers," he said, again out loud, even though he knew how crazy he sounded. And then he laughed and he laughed, and he couldn't quit laughing for such a long time that it didn't even sound like laughter anymore.

Not like laughter at all.

Chapter 16

Atlantis

Brennan had always believed that his lungs expanded more fully with the rich air of Atlantis than they ever did when he was above. Yet now, with Tiernan in his arms, he finally knew what it was to exist wholly within each individual breath.

Entirely in the present, living only for the now. This moment of utter perfection, home in Atlantis with all hope of future happiness embodied by the woman he held so tightly.

Joy threatened to knock his legs out from under him; fear that he would lose her iced his heart. How could emotion carry such powerful yet equally opposing forces?

"We have to go back," Tiernan said, pulling out of his arms. "We're so close. We have to go back and discover what they're up to. I can't lose this. Not now, when I've worked so hard for so long."

"Not a chance in the nine hells," he said flatly. "I forbid it."

They stood in the palace garden with Alexios and Grace,

the sweet fragrance of the flowers surrounding them an eerie contradiction to the danger they'd just escaped.

She planted her hands on her hips and glared at him. "Are we back to that again? You have no right to forbid or allow me to do anything. If you don't want to go back, that's fine, but I'm definitely going back to that conference as soon as you can magic me out of here."

Grace sank down on an ornate wrought-iron bench, sighing as if she were exhausted or in pain. "It's dangerous, Tiernan. They're sure to know something is up now after three of their goons disappeared. Vampire goons, even. Luckily, dead vamps dissolve, so there are no bodies lying around to give them a clue."

Brennan was surprised to hear Grace agreeing with him. She was a warrior through and through. She was holding her hand over her abdomen again, though.

"Are you ill? Or injured?"

She looked up at him, startled, and then followed his gaze down. A peculiar expression passed over her face, and Brennan turned, only to see an echo of that odd look on Alexios's face.

"How far along are you?" Tiernan asked, smiling.

Grace bit her lip, then shrugged. "It was bound to come out sooner or later," she said, smiling up at Alexios, who was now standing behind her, massaging her shoulders.

It took Brennan another couple of seconds to catch up, but then an enormous smile spread over his face. "With child? You are with child?"

Alexios nodded, pride and happiness fairly bursting from him. "We are. We haven't told anyone, yet, but—"

"But we're glad you're the first to know," Grace said. "We were hoping you'd stand in as one of her godparents."

Brennan threw back his head and whooped, then leapt over the bench, threw his arms around Alexios, and pounded him on the back. Alexios returned the gesture with a quick, fierce embrace.

"My friend," Brennan said, finally understanding the

depth of feeling behind that word. "May life bring nothing but joy to you, your woman, and your child."

They clasped arms, and Brennan saw the mixture of happiness and concern in Alexios's eyes.

"You feel it, don't you?" Alexios asked. "You finally feel."

Brennan nodded, a simple motion of his head. His heart was too full to allow words to escape. He avoided the issue with the simple solution of rounding the bench to kneel before Grace.

"Welcome, my sister," he said, taking her hand in his. "I thank you for the joy you have brought to Alexios."

Grace smiled at him, her eyes sparkling with unshed tears. "It's wonderful to see you able to feel happy for us, Brennan." She put a hand on his arm. "We'll figure this out, okay? The curse stuff? I am not a descendant of Diana for nothing. One dedicated to a god should be able to help out another, right?"

Tiernan made a small sound behind him, and Brennan glanced back and up at her to see that she was also fighting tears. He stood up and took her hands in his. "Why are you crying, *mi amara*?"

"I'm not crying," she said, blinking rapidly. "Something in my eyes."

She shoved her hands in her pockets. "Congratulations on the baby news," she told Grace. "That's wonderful, and I completely understand why you don't want to risk putting yourself in danger. But I've got to go back, dangerous or not, don't you see that?"

Grace sighed. "I see it. I'd do the same thing in your position, and I don't even know your reasons, but I'm guessing they're pretty important to you."

Tiernan nodded. "More important than I can explain, especially now. It's late, and I'm exhausted. You definitely need to get your rest, for the baby. So maybe you could show me to a guest room?" She pointedly addressed the question to Alexios, and a savage heat flashed through Brennan.

"I will take you to my room, and you will sleep in my bed," he growled. "Do not ask another for assistance."

Before she could respond, probably to flay him with her tongue, judging from the look of the sparks flashing dangerously in those dark eyes, he firmly grasped her arm and started walking toward the palace door, all but dragging her behind him.

"Brennan," Alexios called out. "Be advised that you will pay for treating her like this. I'm telling you this from experience."

He heard Grace laugh, or thought he did, but Tiernan's low, furious cursing drowned out everything else.

"I am surprised that you even know this vocabulary," he muttered, shoving open the doors and pulling her across the entryway without pausing.

"If you don't slow down and quit dragging me along like this, you're going to find out all sorts of things I know, like how to ram my knee into your—"

He cut her off by the simplest method he knew: he stopped and swept her up into his arms and then kept going, striding toward his rooms in the palace, a fierce determination burning through him.

She didn't struggle, but the glare she pinned him with could have melted Atlantean sea glass. "You don't know me at all if you think you can get away with this."

He stopped in front of the door to his rooms, threw it open, still carrying her, then slammed it shut with his foot. Crossing the room in a few short strides, he tossed her on the bed and then pounced on her, covering her body with his own before she could move.

"I don't know you?" He bared his teeth in something that wasn't at all a smile. "I can still taste the sweet honey of your body on my tongue, *mi amara*."

He nudged her legs open with his knee and settled his weight onto the sweet, lush curves of her body, clenching his teeth together to keep from moaning with the primal need to strip her bare and take her.

She gasped at the feel of his hard, heavy cock when he pressed it between her thighs and her eyes went wild and unfocused.

"Do you feel that? That is how much I know you and want you and need you."

He took her mouth in a kiss that was just short of savage, the red haze of fury behind his eyes fading only when she responded to him—when she kissed him back.

The kiss went on forever; for an eternity. It was about possession more than pleasure, but which one of them was possessing the other he did not know. Maybe each of them was both possessor and claimed.

Finally he forced himself to pull away, when it was clear that if he touched her for one second longer, he'd tear her clothes from her and take her—make her his by force—like the animal he would never, ever allow himself to become. He threw himself away from her and rolled up to sit on the edge of the bed, his heart pounding in his chest and his breath coming in harsh, rasping heaves.

"You cannot put yourself in danger, Tiernan. You cannot go back into that situation with the scientists who could do vicious, inhuman things to your brain. You are the most courageous woman I have ever known, but I will not let you do this. It's madness, and it's suicide."

She was silent so long he began to fear she would never speak to him again, and then finally she rolled over and put a tentative hand on his back. "I have to do it, Brennan. This is my mission, or my warrior's duty, or however you want to think of it. I have to do it, and I wish you'd help me, but I understand if you don't want to risk it."

He laughed, and the laughter felt as though it were acid, ripped from his chest by an angry god. "Not want to? I would follow you through each level of the nine hells, for only the gift of a smile. If you must do this, I will be by your side all the way. But if you care for me at all, let me fulfill your mission, while you stay here safely in Atlantis."

She jumped up out of the bed and walked around until

she could see his face. "Brennan? Even if I didn't owe this to Susannah, I wouldn't let you do it alone. Remember the curse? If I let you go—even if I wanted to let you go alone, which I don't—you'll forget me, and then what? Go through all this with the emotions again when you next see me? How could you bear it?"

His hand shot out and captured her wrist, and he slowly pulled her toward him, until he could lean forward and press his face into the softness of her belly. After a couple of seconds, she put her hands in his hair and caressed his head in a gentle, soothing motion that made him want to remain in exactly that position for the next year or so of his life.

But wishes were not seahorses, or sea nymphs would indeed ride, as the saying went. So he raised his head and stared up into her drowning gaze.

"I will give you up," he said, each word a stake through his own heart, as though he, too, were a vampire. "I will never bother you again, or have anything to do with you, if you will promise to stay safe."

A shadow of something he could not define crossed behind her eyes, and she pulled away from him yet again. "Would that be so easy to do? Give me up?" Her voice was a challenge and, though he thought she herself didn't realize it, a plea.

"I have never done anything in two thousand years that has been even a fraction as difficult," he said quietly. "I would prefer death by torture to the mere idea of allowing you to walk into danger. What good are these emotions anyway, that slice my soul to ribbons at the thought of losing you?"

He abruptly stood, weary of the futile discussion, and gestured toward the doorway to his bathroom. "We should shower. And rest."

She attempted a smile, but it did not reach her eyes. "Sleep now, leave all questions of death, torture, and death-defying activities until the morning?"

"Exactly."

"I can do that." She headed toward the bathroom, but not

before he'd realized one crucial fact: to fulfill the terms of the curse, he would be forced to watch her bathe.

To fulfill the terms of his own honor, he'd be forced to restrain himself from touching her.

The concept of *torture* suddenly gained raw and jagged edges.

Chapter 17

Tiernan realized the difficulty as soon as she stumbled to a halt in front of the glass wall of Brennan's enormous shower. The bathroom itself was so gorgeous it belonged in a decorating magazine; all gold-veined white marble and thick, sparkling glass. Was there an *Atlantean Home Journal*?

She smiled a little as the exhaustion-induced stupid rambling went on in her tumbling thoughts for a bit. Thinking about how incredibly beautiful the palace was in every way was a simple defense mechanism.

It kept her from thinking about how beautiful Brennan was.

Even now, as he silently pointed to the marble tub with its gold-and-silver faucets, raising a single eyebrow, something about his large, powerful presence made the oversized room seem just a little bit smaller. Just a little bit more intimate.

Both of them could fit in that tub . . .

"No," she said quickly, both to herself and to his unspoken question. "The shower is good enough. I'd fall asleep and drown in a tub right now."

A flash of something predatory crossed his face, but it was gone almost before she saw it, and he simply nodded and did something with a complex system of weights and levers in the shower. A rainfall of water immediately misted into being, water coming from all directions, showering forth from hidden spouts. She could feel the warmth and steam even from where she stood, a few feet from the opening.

"I cannot leave," he said, his voice low and hesitant. "The curse . . ."

She nodded, too tired to argue about it. He'd seen her naked in the woods, after all. A warm flush climbed up her neck and face at the memory. He'd done far more than see her.

"If you'd just turn around," she finally said. "Until I get in there. I'd appreciate it."

He turned immediately, but something in the tense way he held his shoulders told her plainer than any words could how very difficult all this was for him. She'd felt the sheer, primal force of his fierce arousal, both in the forest, earlier, and on the bed just moments before. But he'd held back, both times.

He'd held back. She hadn't. She'd been sort of a shameless hussy.

She grinned at the outdated phrase and the notion of it fitting her, of all people, as she made quick work of stripping out of her clothes and quickly stepping into the shower. She resisted the automatic moan of pure, hedonistic delight when the wonderfully powerful spray hit her body from all directions.

All directions. Her eyes widened when she turned a little to lift her hair off of her neck and one stream of water happened to strike very sensitive flesh. Oh, boy, this shower could be a lonely single girl's best friend. Her gaze immediately went to Brennan, because it wasn't a pulsating shower jet she wanted between her legs.

It was him. All of him. Every hard, hot inch that she'd felt between her thighs when he'd captured her on that giant, soft, made-for-wild-passionate-nights bed. A hot blush rose from her breasts and swept up her neck and face to her hairline, and she silently offered a thank-you that he wasn't watching her right then.

But when he turned around to see her because of the curse, and caught her staring at him like a lust-struck idiot . . . She hurriedly reached for the intriguing glass bottles on the shelf. Shampoo and soap. That's what she needed.

That's all she needed.

Brennan tried his best, he really did; he'd be prepared to argue before the highest Atlantean court his case that he'd given it his best efforts to keep from looking at her as long as he could. However, when the sound of bath oils being uncorked came to his ears, at the same time that the edges of his grasp of Tiernan's reality grew hazy in his mind, he was forced to turn around and catch a single glimpse of her.

It was almost a hardship, really. His conscience scoffed.

His breath dried in his mouth and all of the air in the room vanished, replaced with longing, need, and desire. She was turned slightly away from him, so that she didn't see him watching her, and as he stood, entranced, she raised her arms to wash her lovely dark hair. He inhaled sharply as the iridescent mass of bubbles formed and then sluiced away in the multiple streams of the shower, leaving her hair and body glistening, covered with drops of water.

He'd never been jealous of drops of water before.

He wanted to lick each one of them off her body, one at a time.

His body was shaking with need, and his cock strained against his pants so hard it hurt him. He was aroused beyond anything he'd ever known, just from the sight of the curve of her back and hip, down to her firm, round ass. He caught a glimpse of the silken shadow between her legs as she turned, and he was suddenly urgently, fiercely sure that he'd never wanted anything in his life as much as he wanted to go to her, stripping his own clothes off as he went, and plunge his cock into her so deeply that she'd cry out his name.

Instead, he turned around. Turned away.

All heroic sacrifices did not involve weapons and battle and death. Some were about a beautiful human woman standing in a shower.

Several minutes later, during which he'd taken only two quick glances when he felt the curse snaking around the edges of his mind, she finally called his name.

"Brennan? I'm done and wrapped up in these wonderful towels. I don't know how to turn off the shower, or if you wanted to—"

"Oh, by the gods, how I want to," he growled, then he turned and pounced on her, yanked her off her feet, and kissed her, fast, furious, almost bruising. "But I won't." He released her and, tearing at his clothes, stepped into the shower, throwing shirt and pants and boots against the far wall with, at least in the case of the boots, satisfying thunks.

She sighed loudly, and he heard it even over the roar of the shower and the pounding of so much blood in his skull. "I'm too tired right now, or we'd have a little chat. Do you have spare clothes?"

He pointed to the cabinet under his sink, then squeezed his eyes shut, so he wasn't tempted to see her bend over. The towel was long, but, still . . .

"I have several sets of sparring clothes under there. They'll be too big, but they're soft enough to sleep in."

"Thank you."

When he was forced to open his eyes to see her, for fear of the results of the curse, she was dressed in a soft gray sparring outfit, and the sight of her wearing his clothes sent a spear of fierce possession thundering through him.

She was his, and he would keep her safe, even if it had to be in spite of herself.

He had no choice.

"I'll just lean here, okay?" she called out, leaning back against the wall and closing her eyes. Every line of her body drooped with exhaustion and he hurried his bathing so he could put her to bed.

His bed.

She would be in his bed, and he would have to somehow, by all the gods, refrain from touching her.

He caught the groan before it escaped, and with a quick glance at her, still resting against the wall, he turned so that his back was to her, in case she should look up. With a fierce, practiced stroke, he pumped his cock once, then twice, in a painfully necessary attempt to take some of the edge off his need before he had to share a bed with her.

Even as seed spurted from his body and was instantly washed away by the force of the shower stream, he knew it was futile. No mere physical release would ever keep him from wanting her.

He was hers, and he was cursed, and any future they might have together was doomed. He made a sound of pure despair, deep in his throat, and shut down the shower.

Maybe sleep would make it better. He didn't see how it could make it any worse.

Chapter 18

Tiernan stared at Brennan, who was lying on the other side of the bed from her, as relaxed and at ease as, oh, a slab of marble—if marble could radiate misery. She was feeling a little tense herself, after the glimpses she'd snuck of his naked body in that shower. The man was pure, muscled, hard-bodied, delicious goodness, which was entirely unfair.

"Worse," he muttered, his eyes clenched shut. "Oh, gods, of course it will be worse. I can't see you when I sleep."

"You can't see me now."

He opened one eye and glared at her.

"Your fierce glare does not scare me, oh, black-eyed one," she said, grinning in spite of her exhaustion. "You're pretty used to barking orders and people falling in line, aren't you?"

His other eye popped open. Now both of them glared at her, in all their long-lashed, color-changing gorgeousness. "I am not. I am accustomed to working with bullheaded warriors with more guts than brains. I wonder why I am surprised by anything about you, now that you mention it," he said, his voice nearly a growl. "You could be related to Christophe. Or Ven, for that matter."

She laughed out loud as the purity of his truth rang through her veins like champagne filtered through her blood. "Wow. That was purely true, not even a shade of deception about it. Do your friends know you think so highly of them? Bullheaded with more guts than brains, I believe you said?"

"Believe me, I have said this to them in far more colorful language," he said dryly, and she started laughing again, an edge of wildness in it.

He narrowed his eyes at the sound and then he sighed, his face relaxing, and held out his hand. "You are tired beyond the endurance levels of your body and mind. Please rest."

Slowly, cautiously, she reached over and twined her fingers in his. At the touch of his warm, strong hand, realization dawned. "Oh, Brennan, I didn't think," she whispered. "When we're asleep, of course you won't be able to see me. Do you think— I mean, will the curse—"

His expression grew even more grim. "I have no way to know the answer to that, but my expectation is that, yes, closing my eyes in sleep will activate the curse and I will forget you."

Pain sliced through her at his words, emphasizing the truth she'd been trying to hide, even from herself. "I don't want you to forget me," she whispered. "I know this isn't about me, and this is so hard for you, and our mission is far more important than my stupid feelings, but, oh, Brennan."

She stopped and scrubbed tears from her eyes before they could slide down her cheeks to the silken pillowcase. "I don't want you to forget me."

He froze, going so still that for a moment she thought he hadn't heard her, and then his hand tightened on hers and he pulled her slowly, inexorably, across the wide expanse of bed until she was nestled against his side. His chest was bare, so her face rested on smooth, warm skin that covered rock-hard muscle, but he'd pulled on a pair of the soft sparring pants, probably for her sake.

She wished he hadn't.

"I could never forget you completely," he murmured against her hair. "No matter the curse, no matter how powerful the god who commanded it. You are the lost part of my soul, Tiernan Butler, and I only wish for years and years and years to prove it to you."

She stiffened a little in his arms, and he pulled her a little closer into the heat of his body, but she shook her head. "I don't want your feelings to be the result of a god's curse. I want to have time to get to know you, to explore these feelings between us. If you forget me every time you go to sleep, it's going to be very tough. Maybe impossible."

He raised a hand and stroked her hair back from her forehead, then kissed her there. "You said feelings between us, did you not?"

"Yes, but—"

"Did a god curse you to care about me?"

She knew where he was going, but answered him honestly. "No, of course not."

"And yet you admit you have feelings for me, even a little?"

"More than a little," she admitted. "It's kind of crazy, but there it is."

"Kindly grant me the right to the same feelings, then, leaving out whatever a god may have encouraged," he said, his voice gone deep and husky, resonating in very private places in her body.

"I want you to kiss me, Brennan, but we don't seem to be able to stop at kissing, and I'm so tired, and so afraid of the curse kicking in when we're asleep, and so worried that everything I've worked for is falling apart around my ears."

"Just let me hold you. I'll stay awake as long as I can, which will be no hardship with you in my arms," he said, a slow, dangerous smile spreading across his face.

"Huh. Lucky you," she muttered darkly, wondering if

she had the energy to go for a very cold shower. "Also, that was a lie."

He laughed and leaned over to kiss her nose. "Yes, it was a lie, my beautiful truth teller. Holding you is, in fact, very *hard*."

She laughed in spite of herself. "Very, very hard?"

He caught her hand and pressed it against his erection and then released it so quickly that she was caught off guard, with her hand hovering uncertainly above his very impressive and, definitely, very hard penis.

"It's a constant state since I met you," he confessed, looking pained at the admission.

A little niggle of guilt scratched at her. After all, in the forest it had been all about her. Shouldn't she reciprocate?

"Talk to me," he commanded, surprising her yet again. "Tell me about growing up with your Gift. Just for a little while, until you fall asleep." He turned to her, his pain and worry naked on his face. "Please?"

That *please* got to her in a way that commands never would have.

"It was hard," she began, then laughed a little at the unintentional use of the word. "No, let's go with 'difficult,' okay?"

"Difficult. I can see how that would be so. Were there never any compensations?" He twined his fingers through hers and rested their joined hands on his hard abdomen.

"Never? No, I can't say never," she said, forcing herself to sift through long-buried memories. "I saved a boy from being falsely accused of stealing a teacher's purse once. His family was really poor so everyone thought he'd taken it for the money. He was telling the truth, and I asked a few questions of a few of the other students, pretty impressed with my mad Nancy Drew skills, and found out that the principal's son actually stole it. Acting out to get attention from Daddy, who was kind of a jerk, I think."

"Were you pleased? To be able to help?"

Her smile faded as the rest of the memory surfaced. "I

was. For a while. The boy who'd been falsely accused even gave me my first kiss."

Brennan growled, the sound and vibration of it startling beneath their joined hands. "I don't need to hear about you kissing anyone else."

She laughed. "We were twelve. This is not exactly a threat to your manhood, so calm down, wild thing."

"I can't imagine you twelve. Or maybe I can. Your daughter will look exactly like you, one day."

She turned to look up at him, startled by something in his voice, only to find that his eyes were glowing that hot green again. "My daughter?" she said faintly.

"I felt it premature to say 'our' daughter."

She heard the smile in his voice and grinned a little. "You think? Well, anyway, the boy I'd rescued wanted to know how I knew, and I thought I could trust him with the truth about me."

Brennan's muscles tightened as his body went stiff again. "Did he betray your trust?"

"Not exactly. It was more that . . . he thought I was *cool*. You know? He was a twelve-year-old boy and suddenly he had a walking, talking lie detector. He wanted to experiment, and for a while, I was glad enough to play along."

"Just to have someone to play with. A friend," Brennan ventured.

She sighed. "I guess so. Close enough. But I couldn't do it for long. I was a freak, a curiosity to him more than a friend." A tiny pang of sadness struck, and she realized to her surprise that it still hurt.

After all these years.

What would it do to her if she lost Brennan?

In a swift motion, he rolled over so that he was facing her, both of them on their sides, and he still cradled her in his arms. "I am your friend. No matter what else, I will always be so."

The simple truth of it took her breath away, as did the

heat in his now-black eyes, with their centers of blue-green flame.

"I . . . thank you. I am your friend, too," she whispered.

"Later? When you were older? Adults spend much of each day engaged in deception. How painful is that for you?"

His clear perception of what life had been like with her Gift offered a calm that soothed her, and she relaxed against him a little.

"It was—it is—easier to be alone. Alone so often that sometimes I forget what it means to be anything else." The painful admission caused her eyes to burn, but she refused to let the tears fall. Not here. Not with him.

She'd cried enough tears in her life.

"Shh, *mi amara*, shh. Please. You don't need to tell me any of this when it brings you such pain." He stroked her hair and her back, making shushing noises, murmuring gentle words in a musical language that must have been Atlantean. "Hush, please, my beautiful one. You don't need to share any of this with me."

But she found, to her surprise, that she wanted to share it. Wanted to unburden herself of some of the years of pain. "It was hard when I was a kid, but the teenage years, wow. Talk about torture."

She rolled over onto her back and stared up at the ceiling, remembering high school. Johnny. Kim. Prom.

"My boyfriend in high school didn't lie to me. At least that's what I thought. He never gave me the slightest reason for suspicion. Nothing he told me ever pinged my truth senses. Even when he was never available to go out on Friday nights."

She rolled her eyes. "He was studying. Or visiting his sick grandmother. Can you believe I was so stupid?"

Brennan propped his head up on his hand. "He was lying to you?"

"He was lying to me. He was dating my best friend at the same time he was dating me. Except she knew about it, because he acted like my boyfriend at school. She was acting really odd, but she said she was stressed-out about college applications, and she was careful never to actually lie to me."

She laughed and shot a cynical glance at Brennan. "Of course, I never came out and asked her, 'Are you sleeping with my boyfriend?' either."

"This man," Brennan began, then stopped to take a deep breath. "This boy. You were . . . intimate with him, too?"

Alerted by something in his tone, Tiernan whipped her head around to stare into his eyes, which had gone icy green again. "No, and even if I had been, you can't possibly be jealous of a seventeen-year-old boy."

"Jealousy is not it, exactly, but he hurt you, and I find myself wanting to beat some sense into him," he growled. "He is not seventeen today."

"He was my first in another way. He was the first person to lie to me that I couldn't feel it, but he wasn't the last. They're rare, but they're out there. I think it's maybe the same kind of person who could pass a lie detector. Socio-paths or narcissists; people who really don't care about the results of their lies, so they don't register with me."

"You can tell when I lie," Brennan said, a purely mascu-line smile on his face. "I care very much."

She smiled, but her eyes drooped shut and she had to fight to keep them open. "I know you do. My parents, they didn't last. Their marriage. Too many lies between them, too many deceptions. I don't usually trust anybody, but somehow—" Her mouth cracked open in a giant yawn and she leaned her head on his shoulder, snuggling close to his solid, warm strength. "Somehow I know I can trust you."

"You have given me a gift beyond price, Tiernan Butler," he murmured. "I would rather have your trust than all the sunken treasure in the ocean."

"Easy for you to say, Mr. Billionaire," she said, laugh-ing. "Who needs sunken treasure when you could buy and sell Boston a couple of times over?"

He tucked the silken covers around her shoulders and lightly kissed her lips, sending a shiver of pure, sensual need through her that almost—*almost*—cut through her exhaustion. "Rest now, and we will discuss treasure and buying Boston in the morning."

She stopped fighting the waves of tiredness and sank into the softness of his bed, the strength and warmth of his arms, and the magic of Atlantis. She was falling asleep in Atlantis, with a warrior straight out of the pages of a lovely fairy tale.

"Rest, *mi amara*. I'll stay awake and guard your dreams," he said, and she sank down, down, into a cloud of peace and calm. Tomorrow she could return to worry. The last thing she saw was an edge of light as morning broke through the window. They'd stayed up all night, and ushered in the dawn.

"The first of many, I hope," she whispered, and then the darkness took her.

Chapter 19

Brennan awoke to the very rare and yet highly appreciated sensation of a warm armful of woman curled up against him. He waited awhile before opening his eyes, searching his memory to see if he could pinpoint just how and when the night before he'd broken his own rule about bringing women to his rooms in the palace.

He'd learned long, long ago the consequences of slipping from a very straight and narrow path, after all.

When nothing—nobody—came to mind, he mentally cursed the vast quantity of Atlantean ale he must have consumed and then gritted his teeth against the arduous task that faced him. He needed to get her out of his rooms with the minimum of post-coital drama. It was unfortunate Christophe was not nearby to offer advice; the man was a master at managing irate women.

The woman stirred against him and then her soft, unexpectedly musical voice confirmed that she was awake. "Brennan?"

She knew his name, then. Too bad he could not reciprocate that knowledge.

He'd postponed as long as he could; honor demanded courtesy, at the very least. He opened his eyes and found himself looking directly into the most vividly beautiful eyes he'd ever seen. Not brown exactly but the darkest amber shade of ancient gems, with tiny flickers of honey-gold near the pupils.

"You fell asleep?" she asked, and there was something unexpected in her voice. Not curiosity or lazy satisfaction or even petulant demand.

No. It was anxiety—or even fear.

"Perhaps I was well sated, my lady," he said, smiling in spite of himself at her beauty. He had chosen well, even in his obviously drunken state. And yet—

She bolted upright and he realized what had been niggling at him. She was fully dressed, in what looked like a set of his sparring clothes. He glanced down at himself and realized he, too, wore a pair of the soft trousers.

Her eyes widened until he could see white all the way around her irises. "Did you just say well sated? Wait—and call me your *lady*?"

He sat up as well, feeling at a distinct disadvantage, and examined her again, as if repeated viewing could bring her name or circumstances to mind. Her tousled dark hair shone in the morning light from the window, and her soft curves were very apparent, even under the loose fit of his sparring top.

"Brennan? Did you forget me? The curse—did you fall asleep and forget?" She grabbed his arm and the contact sizzled heat lightning through him like a summer storm at sea. His body arched backward from the jolt and his head slammed into the carved wooden headboard of the bed.

"Brennan!" She jumped back and away from him and scrambled off the bed. "It's me. Tiernan. Please tell me you remember, and you're not going to have another attack."

"Attack? What attack? Did I hurt you?" A horrible . . .

memory? premonition? was itching at the back of his brain. Had he hurt this woman?

The pain merely from the idea of it smashed into him with the force of a body blow. He could not have hurt her. Not such a woman.

But how did he know what kind of woman she was?

She stared at him, and fear battled determination on her very expressive face. Finally, coming to a decision, she climbed back on the bed and put her hands on each side of his face. "Brennan, it's me. Tiernan Butler. I know you've forgotten me, because you're cursed to forget your true mate whenever she's out of your sight, and you seem to think that she's me, but you have to remember. I need you. We need to finish this mission, and I don't know how I'll do it without you. Please, please remember."

"The curse," he whispered. "How did you know the terms of the curse?"

She closed her eyes, grimacing in despair, and then her eyelids snapped back open. "You're no Sleeping Beauty, but this is all I've got," she said, and it was his only warning before she leaned forward and kissed him.

She kissed him—oh, gods, it was her, it was Tiernan, and she was kissing him—and the world shattered around him.

Emotion, piercingly vivid, burned through him. Fire and ice and lightning bolts shot through him as if aimed from Poseidon's trident itself. She kissed him, and his soul gathered its fractured pieces and remade itself in her image.

Tiernan's image.

Emotions flooded through him in a torrent, a perfect storm, and the waves of emotion carried flotsam of a most unexpected kind: his memories. Memories of her, of them, of the past day and a half—by all the gods, so short a time?

His hands tangled in her hair and he pulled her closer and kissed her back. A kiss of gratitude for saving him, for finding him, for redeeming him from a life of bleak loneliness and despair.

She finally pulled away, breathless, and smiled tremulously. "You'd better remember me, buddy. Because if you kiss every strange woman you find in your bed like that, you and I are going to have a long talk."

"You, Tiernan Butler, are the only strange woman I will ever kiss again," he said, serious as a vow, and he did not understand why she laughed.

"Oh, Brennan, do you really remember me? The curse didn't take over?"

"It did. But perhaps sleep does not affect a permanent forgetting?" He pulled her into his arms, onto his lap, unable to bear even a moment more of separation from her. He was shaking, his body shuddering with his fear that he might have lost her forever.

"I need you. Now," he said, barely able to force out the words between his gritted teeth. "If I cannot be inside your body, I may not survive this emotion."

She stared into his eyes for so long he was sure she would deny him, but then she smiled and, in one swift motion, pulled her shirt over her head and tossed it to the side. "I need you, too. So what are you going to do about it?"

~~~~~~

Tiernan couldn't believe she'd done it. Thrown her shirt and her caution aside; probably her common sense, too. But relief and passion and something far stronger than both pushed her toward this. Toward him.

He tried to be a gentleman about it, she could tell, but it was hard for him since he was staring at her breasts like heaven had opened up and dumped a load of angel dust in his lap.

She grinned at him. "Men. You're all the same. Human or Atlantean, you're all helpless in the face of naked boobs."

He dragged his gaze up to her face, and his eyes had an expression of such savage intent in them that she shivered, suddenly just the smallest bit afraid.

"You understand what you are offering me," he said, his

voice barely above a growl. "There is no going back from this. You will be my woman in every way."

She shivered again and started to cross her arms over her breasts, but he caught her hands in his, still staring deeply into her eyes.

"I wasn't planning to sign a contract," she said, attempting a chuckle. "I just wanted—"

"Mine," he repeated. "I'm going to claim you now. This is your last chance to change your mind."

She lifted her chin. "I could say the same for you. I'm not changing my mind, but I'm getting kind of cold, so if you're done talking . . ."

He pounced. There was no other word for it, no finesse, no smooth seduction. He pounced on her, and in seconds she was on her back, her pants, too, stripped off her body and tossed aside, and he was staring down at her with such exquisitely blissed-out happiness on his face that she laughed out loud.

He blinked, as if drawn out of a trance by the sound, and then a dangerously seductive smile spread across his face. "I love the sound of your laughter, Tiernan Butler."

"I love the sight of that sexy smile of yours, Brennan of Atlantis," she replied. "Now, can we quit talking and maybe you can kiss me?"

"I will kiss every inch of your body, and take hours in the doing, but now I find I cannot wait." He took her mouth, captured it, captured *her*, and, catching her wrists in his hands, pulled them up and over her head. He kissed her mouth and her neck and bit down on the sensitive curve of her neck, and heat sizzled through her, a delicious fullness and tingling invading her limbs and making her writhe underneath him, seeking more.

"More, more," she demanded. "Now."

He shouted out a laugh, and then his hands were on her and it was she making the noise, moaning as his fingers touched her, spreading her, testing her.

"You are so wet for me," he said, his voice rough with

need, and she wanted to bite him. Put her mouth all over him and taste him, but most of all she needed—she *needed*.

He stood up and yanked his own pants down and his erection was enormous, jutting out in front of him, and he didn't stop, didn't hesitate, but leapt back onto the bed, on top of her, clearly intent on only one goal. He spread her thighs with his big hands and entered her with one powerful thrust, as deep as he could go, until she cried out from the pressure and fullness and the ecstasy of having what she wanted so badly, what she needed so much, exactly where she needed him.

"Mine," he said, withdrawing and thrusting into her again and again. Long, powerful strokes. Claiming strokes, dominance and possession in every movement of his body. "Mine, and mine, forever and ever."

She wrapped her legs around him, digging her heels into the hard muscles of his thighs, and he lapsed into Atlantean again, murmuring endearments or offering promises, and oh, oh, she'd never felt anything so wonderful. The truth of whatever he was saying rang in her head, a symphony of bells, so no matter that she didn't understand the language, she heard and understood his truth.

"More," she cried out, delirious with need, poised on the edge of some marvelous fulfillment. "More and more, and don't forget you're mine, too," she cried out, and then she was gone, flying up and over into the stars themselves, or through the dome into the ocean over Atlantis, flying free fall into ecstasy and release.

Her orgasm must have triggered his, because he drove into her, one final time, deeper and farther than ever before, and then his big body shuddered over her as he poured himself into her.

She had a moment for sanity and common sense to return, and thoughts of pregnancy, before all of that vanished under an onslaught of pure sensation and unbearably beautiful light and color. She was falling, but somehow falling . . . up? Sideways? No.

Into. She was falling into Brennan's soul, and it scared her to death.

~~~~~~

Brennan roared out his pleasure, a vast and unimaginable sweet, sweet madness, as release took him and his seed poured into her. His, only his, always his. She must acknowledge it, must agree, or he'd lose his grip on sanity. He must tell her, make her understand.

"Tiernan," he said, but he managed only that word, her name, before it took him. The soul-meld. He stepped out into the abyss and willingly, so willingly, dove into her soul.

Her childhood, so alone, so different. She was so frail and thin, never eating enough, not hungry, afraid to come out of her room too often, afraid to hear the lies her parents told each other over and over again.

Her friendships, ruined, one after another, from casual lies or careless deceit. Deliberate cruelties that stabbed all the deeper for being so unexpected, until she couldn't trust, couldn't love, couldn't let anyone in. Not ever.

The pain of it nearly crushed him, burying him under an onslaught of emotion for which he was spectacularly unprepared. She'd been so alone, for so long, a mere span of years compared to his own, but a lifetime was a lifetime and she'd been isolated for as much of hers as he'd been in his.

"Never again," he swore. "You will never be alone again."

She shivered in his arms, and he realized she was still crushed underneath him, bearing his full weight. He rolled over, feeling an instant sense of loss when his cock slipped from the warmth of her body.

"I'm sorry, *mi amara*," he said, stroking her hair away from her face. "I was lost to reason for a moment—"

She raised her head and her eyes were wild, almost mad, as if she were lost in the wilderness of insanity. The soul-meld should never have caused that.

"Tiernan?"

She didn't answer him, and he grasped her shoulders and shook her a little, terrified by the utter blankness of her face, a chilling counterpoint to the crazed look in her eyes.

"Tiernan. Answer me," he demanded. "Come back to me now, *mi amara*. I need you."

"Don't call me that," she said, and the edge of madness had migrated to her voice. "*Mi amara*. I know what it means. Don't call me that. I am not your beloved, and I never, ever can be."

His hands slipped away from her as she threw herself off the side of the bed and crouched down, yanking the sheet off the bed to cover herself. Pain sliced through him to think he had caused that look of utter terror on her face.

"Tiernan, what has happened? What did I do? Did I hurt you? I am a fool," he said bitterly. "I should have been more gentle, I should have waited—"

"You were gentle," she interrupted, her face softening for an instant, even as she backed away from the bed. Away from him. "You . . . It was wonderful. But we can never, ever be together like that again."

He'd had swords slice into his gut and cause him less pain than those few words. He doubled over from the body blow, shaking his head in denial. "No. No, you can't mean that. Why would you— What have I done? What—"

A terrible thought occurred to him. "What did you see? In my soul? Is it so blackened and beyond hope of redemption as to earn me this rejection?"

She paused, then resumed her steps, backing away from him. From any hope of a future. "I can't, Brennan." Tears streamed steadily down her face, but there wasn't a hint of indecision in her eyes. "I can't."

Anguish was choking him, killing him, and he only hoped it would be a fast death. It was far, far too late to be a merciful one.

A knock sounded at the door, and Tiernan rushed toward

it even as he shouted at whoever it was to go away. He had no need of witnesses. Not now.

Tiernan cast one last anguished glance at him, then pulled open the door, either uncaring that she was nude but for the sheet, or else so desperate to escape him that she would display herself to all and sundry.

He heard the housekeeper's voice, muffled as if she were speaking from the bottom of the deepest chasm in the ocean floor. Words. Meaningless words. Tiernan had rejected him, so what else could have value?

He almost didn't hear Tiernan close the door, but then she was standing in front of him, holding, ridiculously enough, a tray of coffee, juice, and pastries.

She put the tray down on a table and simply stood, staring down at him, twisting her hands together. The hands that had so recently been touching his body. Holding him.

"I still need you, Brennan," she said, giving him a glimmer of hope, but crushing it with her next words. "I can't finish this mission without you."

A layer of polar ice settled around him, shielding his reborn emotions from any further devastation, almost as if an ice god had seen his pain and pitied him. He raised his gaze to meet hers and the ice gave him a desperately needed calm.

"I shall assist you in this mission, and then you need never see me again," he said, only mildly interested to note that the ice had slipped from his soul to settle in his voice, as well. "We should prepare to brief the prince and then return to Yellowstone, should we not?"

Tears still streamed from her eyes, but her face hardened and she nodded once, sharply, and turned away from him, whispering something under her breath that he knew she had not wanted him to hear. Unfortunately for both of them, his hearing was superb, so every heartbreaking word imprinted itself on his heart.

"I didn't think it would be so easy for you to let me go," she'd said, and though her back was to him, he could tell from the way her shoulders shook that she was crying. He wanted to go to her, but the ice was there to comfort him.

To stop him from yet again risking her rebuff.

After all, ice was a form of water, and he was Atlantean. Ice should come to his call; answer his need. And so it did.

She cried, and he turned away.

Chapter 20

Tiernan silently followed Brennan down the corridor to the room where she'd met with the princes—Conlan and Ven—the one other time she'd been to Atlantis. They had to report, he'd said. She hoped he planned to be the one doing the reporting, because she was caught in a bizarre haze of shock and regret that seemed to have put her brain on pause.

The soul-meld, he'd called it. The name fit perfectly that sensation she'd had of very nearly losing herself inside of his memories. More than memories, really. The experiences that had made him who he was, over so many centuries that her all-too-human mind could barely comprehend the passage of time. It had been like flash-forward photography in a surrealistic film; colors and images and experiences had barraged her, swamped her, until she'd felt actual, physical pain.

But the pain was nothing. She'd been hurt worse playing in the newspaper softball league. It was the *future* that had devastated her. The image of what Brennan's future would be if they continued to care about each other. Brennan would suffer the most, and his hold on reality would shrink and diminish until he was lost in the madness of the curse.

She'd seen it in front of her as if she'd already lived it: Brennan, waking up over and over and over, day after day after day, with a strange woman in his bed. Growing to love her but never remembering it for longer than the space of a day. In her visions of him, trapped inside his soul, he'd become nothing but a man-shaped whirlwind of rage and confusion. Even pushing her away, eventually. Rejecting her in order to save them both from yet another repeat of the "Who's Tiernan?" game.

That was bad enough, but she'd almost have been willing to take her chances with that. Risk a desperate future in hopes she could change it. He was worth the risk.

But their baby—oh, no. She would never risk that final scene becoming reality. She'd seen herself, resting in the same bed where they'd made love so wildly, holding a tiny, bundled baby in her arms. She'd looked tired but she was glowing with joy, and the baby had been so small. It had to have been a vision of herself just after giving birth.

Her heart had turned over with so much love at the sight of her potential son or daughter, but then Brennan had entered the vision, bursting through the door from the hallway. He'd been flushed with excitement, and the Tiernan in the vision had smiled and held the baby up for him to see.

Brennan had stopped dead, nearly skidding to a halt, and stared at Tiernan and the baby in his bed, his mouth slowly dropping open in shock. Then, finally, after such a very long time, he'd spoken.

"Who are you, madam, and why are you and that child in my bed?"

That had been all it took. She'd wrenched herself away from the vision Brennan and the real Brennan, although it took tremendous force of will to escape the waking nightmare. The soul-meld.

She would risk a lot for a man like Brennan, but she would never, ever risk their child.

He glanced back at her, that horrible icy sheen coating the dark green of his eyes, almost as if he'd picked up on her thoughts. Before she could think of anything at all to say, he turned away from her and sped up his pace. Trying to get away from her, probably. For a man who'd made such extravagant claims of devotion, he'd been easy enough to deny.

That's not fair and you know it, her conscience accused her. *You told him never. That you could never, ever be with him. What would you have had him do? Abduct you?*

Yes. Maybe.

No.

She would do anything—anything—to keep that hideous vision from coming true. Even staying away from the one man who'd ever made her feel safe, even just for a little while. They'd succeed on this mission, and then they'd part. Brennan could figure his future out without her.

And if she could ever figure out a way, she was going to kick Poseidon's ass for him.

Brennan made a sharp turn and knocked on a door on the right side of the corridor. It wasn't a particularly elegant or ornate door, but it did look sturdy. So did the two warriors standing guard outside.

Tiernan raised an eyebrow. "Guards? Inside the palace? Inside Atlantis?" Her journalist's nose was smelling news, but she didn't like the implications at all. If the princes thought they needed guards here, then the threat of violence must be high. Brennan's mouth flattened, but he said nothing, and the guards remained silent, too. Maybe they had to; maybe there was some kind of silence required while on guard duty, like in London.

The threat, then. Would they call it treason? Or sedition? She was uncomfortably reminded that she knew next to nothing about monarchies, beyond what she'd read in Margaret George or Philippa Gregory novels. History had never been her thing.

She was more a current-events girl.

Woo, boy, was she going to help put some current events

on the map. The thought of it—the challenge—helped lift her out of the dark pit of gloom she'd sunken into after the visions in the soul-meld. She was Tiernan freaking Butler, and she would figure it out on her own.

She always did.

Alone again. She tried very hard to ignore the pain that kept wrenching her chest at the thought of it.

The door swung open and she sighed with relief. Better to worry about treason now, and a lifetime of loneliness later.

It was Conlan himself who had opened the door, something she wouldn't have expected from the high prince of Atlantis, but then again, it wasn't the first time he'd surprised her.

"Tiernan, be welcome," he said now, all black hair and great cheekbones; tall, dark, and princely. Nearly as gorgeous as Brennan, definitely imposing in his physical presence. Like Brennan.

Surely she'd get over comparing every man she met to Brennan sometime soon. Right?

Brennan did that mysterious single-eyebrow lift again, but not even a hint of warmth cut through the ice in his expression. "Tiernan?"

"I'm coming," she muttered to him, wondering how or even if she should explain what had happened to her during the vision. "Hold your seahorses."

Conlan laughed and bowed to her. "Oh, Tiernan Butler. You are indeed very welcome to Atlantis."

They followed Conlan into the room, and Tiernan's stomach let loose with a very unladylike growl of happiness to see the spread of lunch laid out on the long wooden table. She was starving, suddenly, in spite of the circumstances. Or maybe because of them.

"Lunch looks great," she said, forcing a cheerful tone to her voice. She smiled at the room in general, encompassing High Prince Conlan and his wife, Riley. Her smile only dimmed a little when she caught sight of the high priest, Alaric, in the far corner, doing his usual brooding, menacing thing. For some reason she didn't want to explore too deeply, the theme music from *Phantom of the Opera* always started playing in her head when she saw Alaric.

Riley grinned at her. "Welcome back. Want to see the somewhat drooly center of my existence?" The princess held up a small baby and Tiernan stumbled to a stop, the memory of the baby in her vision—of herself holding up the baby in such a similar way—freezing her in her tracks. Something deep inside Tiernan cried out, but she kept the pleasant smile on her face. All that undercover work was finally paying off in terms of her acting skills. She'd be up for an Oscar any day now, at this rate.

Riley's smile faded, though, and her eyes widened. "You—you and Brennan—"

Brennan, who was leaning against the wall, stood up and bowed to Riley. "I am here, my lady."

The "my lady" threw Tiernan off, and her guard slipped, just a little. Riley suddenly cried out.

"What happened?" she said, her voice shaking. "Between the two of you? So strong—but so wrong, so very, very wrong."

"I would prefer that you refrain from using your *aknasha* powers on me, with all respect, Your Highness," Brennan said, a muscle in his jaw jumping. Clearly he was controlling his anger out of respect for the princess. "Emotional empathy is not—"

"Not applicable to you, yes, I know," said Riley. "Never before, at least, although there was that one time with Quinn." Her face had gone as white as those fluffy towels in Brennan's shower, Tiernan noted with interest and dismay.

"But now . . ." Riley's voice trailed off and then she handed the baby to Conlan and crossed to Brennan. "You're running flat out on sheer adrenaline and pain," she murmured, lightly touching his arm.

Brennan's jaw tightened, but he held still under her touch, which, out of pure contrariness, made Tiernan want to rip the woman's hand off and stuff it down her skinny throat.

Riley's head whipped around, and she pinned Tiernan in place with the weight of her penetrating stare. "You, too? You and Brennan? But how is this possible?"

Conlan, cradling his child in one arm, put the other around his wife. "Maybe you could tell the rest of us what's going on here?"

The color drained out of Riley's face until she turned white and stumbled toward the comfortable chair she'd been sitting in a few minutes earlier. "I think they need to explain it," she said, waving a hand in the general direction of Brennan and Tiernan. "Because the thing where Brennan hasn't had any emotion for centuries?" Riley whistled, a long, slow sound. "That's so over."

Alaric stepped forward, gliding through the room so elegantly and effortlessly that Tiernan almost wanted to check him for a pulse, in case he really was a soulless vampire.

The thought of Alaric's reaction if she did made her grin a little bit, but she stepped back and gave him a wide berth as he headed straight for Brennan.

"The curse?" the priest demanded, getting right up in Brennan's face. "Did the curse finally come to fruition and you have not informed me of it?"

Brennan's icy stare would have intimidated most people enough that they'd back off, but either Alaric was brave or he was stupid, because he poked Brennan in the chest. "Too busy playing with your human?" he said, sneering. "Did I not command you to tell me the instant you felt any—"

The rest of them didn't find out what Alaric had been about to say, because Brennan hauled off and punched him in the stomach. Hard. Alaric flew backward from the force of it and ended up tripping over a cushioned chair and sprawling into it. Then he just sat there, shock and murder fighting for control over his expression, his eyes glowing hotter and hotter with power.

"I should kill you for that," Alaric finally said, and it was all the more terrifying because of the utterly calm way he said it.

"You can try," Brennan replied, baring his teeth. "I would

welcome the chance to kick your pompous, overbearing ass after all these centuries, youngling, so be prepared to bring your best."

"Youngling?" Alaric's eyes were popping out of his head, and it wasn't a good look for him. "Did you call me a youngling?"

"I was one of Poseidon's elite when you were still suck-ling your mother's tit, *youngling*," Brennan taunted. "Show some respect for your elders."

Tiernan and Riley both gasped at the same time and shared a glance of utter shock.

"So," Conlan said mildly. "I see that Brennan has his emotions back."

"Oh, I will show you some respect, warrior," Alaric snarled, flying up out of the chair. *Literally* flying. He sprang at Brennan, but Tiernan had been ready for him, and she ran to put herself between the two of them, realizing even as she did it that it was one of the stupidest things she'd ever done in her life.

"Stop!" She held up her hands, knowing she couldn't in a million years hold off Alaric. He stopped in midair, though, at her command, almost as though she had some kind of magical power. She blinked at him, then down at her hands.

"Um, did I just do that?"

A low rumbling started behind her, sort of like a freight train picking up speed, and it took her a couple of seconds to realize it was Brennan, swearing a blue streak from the sound of it, in ancient Atlantean.

"You are an idiot," he yelled at her. Well, he'd been yell-ing at her for a while by then, but those were the first words in English.

"I was just trying to protect you, you lunkhead," she shouted back. "He wanted to kill you and no wonder. You can't just go around punching people like that."

She was so furious that her mind didn't know what to do with her anger, so her body took over and did the stupidest thing possible.

She punched Brennan.

Right in the stomach, which only hurt her hand on the steel bars he evidently called muscles. He didn't even flinch, just looked down at her, every line and angle of his face hardening in utter fury.

"You could have been killed," he said, still shouting, even though she was standing right in front of him.

"Better that than have you forget me and our baby, over and over, for the rest of my life," she shouted right back in his face, without thinking, without considering, without any care for how it would sound. All she knew was that the words came boiling up from deep inside and wouldn't be stopped.

Everything else, however, stopped. All sound, all talking, even all breathing seemed to go silent around the two of them. The silence made Tiernan painfully aware of their audience.

Suddenly, shockingly, Alaric started laughing. He punched Brennan in the arm, but it was a friendly, guy sort of punch, and there was no sign of the violence he'd intended only minutes before. "Oh, this is priceless. The baby? She's pregnant, too? And Alexios and Grace haven't had a chance to make their big announcement?"

The priest started laughing again. "Atlantis is turning into a giant nursery. This is how the humans will finally defeat us. They're turning our most prized warriors, one by one, into diaper-changing weaklings."

Brennan's eyes widened and he got a panicked look on his face, but before he or Tiernan could say anything, Alaric shook his head and vanished. Just *poof* and gone. No mist, no special effects—he was just gone.

Tiernan whirled around, searching for him, but he was nowhere to be seen. "Did he just—"

"He does that," Riley said. "It's one of his many annoying habits. Deep down he's a good guy."

"Really, really deep, I'm guessing," Tiernan muttered.

"So, you're pregnant? Um, not to be analytical, but didn't you and Brennan just meet each other again yesterday?"

Riley tried to be subtle about the way she was checking out Tiernan's flat stomach.

"No, I'm not pregnant. It was a vision, that's all. Of the future. A future that's not going to happen now, okay?"

"I think maybe you have a few things to tell us," Conlan said, his voice still mild, but it wasn't a request, and they all knew it. It was definitely a royal command.

Brennan ignored his prince, though. He had eyes only for Tiernan, and the ice that had chilled them was gone. Melted. Now his green gaze was burning right through her and he was looking at her like he wanted nothing more than to strip her bare right there and then and take her up against the wall.

She swallowed and then took a deep, shaky breath and looked at Conlan. At Riley. Anywhere but at Brennan. "Once upon a time, a god cursed a warrior," she began, not quite knowing how to go on past that.

Everyone was silent for so long she started to panic, but then help came from an unexpected source.

"The curse was also a blessing, had the warrior but known it," Brennan said.

Her shoulders slumped with relief, but before she could think of the next line, Brennan grabbed her by the shoulders, lifted her up off her feet, and kissed her in a hard, passionate, take-no-prisoners kind of kiss. The kind of kiss that told her and everyone else in the room that he was damn well going to get her naked later and she was going to love every minute of it.

After he released her, and her knees stopped wobbling, she just stood there, stunned, for a bit. "Well," she finally managed. "Maybe we'll be able to figure something out."

Brennan's smile was more wolflike than Lucas's had ever been, and he clasped her hand firmly before he turned to face Conlan again.

"Let me tell you about a very old curse, and the woman with the power to save me from it," Brennan said.

Riley took Aidan back from Conlan and walked over to the table, still covered with as-yet-untouched food. "Let's eat while you talk," she said. "I have a feeling this is going to be a long story."

"All the best stories are," Tiernan said, finally daring to feel like they could figure this out. "I have a story to tell you, too, about a fox shifter named Susannah, the scientists who killed her, and how Brennan is going to help me stop them."

"He is?" Conlan asked, aiming a long, measuring stare at her.

"Yes," Brennan said, still holding her hand. "I am."

Chapter 21

It took an hour, but Brennan finally finished telling them every bit of it. The full nature of the curse, much of what had happened in Yellowstone, and his reaction to Tiernan. He'd left out certain parts of the tale that were nobody's business but his own, but he'd noticed the way Tiernan watched him. She knew what he was leaving out and certainly could guess at why. In fact, she'd done some creative editing of her own as Brennan, believing himself honor-bound to do so, began to confess to his attack on Tiernan in the hotel room.

"Everything got a little crazy then," she'd said, interrupting him. "Then when Litton's flunky, Wesley, showed up . . ."

Without missing a beat, she'd filled in the gaps of his story, her keen journalistic observations contributing quite a lot that he'd missed. But never, not once, had she returned to that particular part of the story, and she cut him off a couple of times when he edged close to the subject.

"You do not have to protect me," he'd snapped at one point.

She'd planted her hands on those luscious hips and stared him down. "Tell that to Alaric," she'd sweetly suggested, and rage burned through him again at the thought that Alaric could have hurt her.

Rage and something deeper. More possessive. She had hurled herself in harm's way—in *Alaric's* way—for him. Even after telling him they had no future together.

It was clear proof that she cared for him, too. Now he only had to find out what had happened during the soul-meld and somehow fix it. Break the curse. Persuade Poseidon to allow him to keep her, forever. To take her as his wife.

"You can't go back," Conlan said. "To Yellowstone, I mean, although of course I don't see how you can go back to the time before Tiernan broke the curse either, but let's leave the metaphysical discussion for later."

Riley nodded, though she looked troubled. "You can't even be sure you'd learn anything of value, Tiernan. They're going to lie to you, at the very least. More likely they'll just try to kill you."

Tiernan glanced at Brennan, a question in her eyes, and he nodded. It was time to tell all of it. "Tiernan is a truth teller," he said. "She possesses the lost Atlantean Gift of divining falsehood whenever it's spoken."

"Almost whenever it's spoken," she corrected him. "Sociopaths, pure narcissists, and vampires don't register with my . . . talent."

"Atlantis has always put truth tellers immediately to death," Conlan said, and suddenly he loomed over her, his eyes shuttered and the threat of her immediate murder in every line of his face. "I see no reason why that tradition should not continue."

Brennan instantly threw himself between Tiernan and Conlan, his hands going for the daggers he'd left in his rooms. To kill a prince was treason, punishable by death. He'd willingly pay that price.

"Conlan," Riley said, rising from her chair. "No!"

Tiernan caught her breath, but then she laughed and put

her hand on Brennan's arm. An instant wave of peace swept through him, taking his rage with it. "It's the tuba. You're the tuba when you lie, Prince Conlan."

The menacing expression vanished from Conlan's face as though it had never been there, replaced by one of quizzical interest. "Tuba?"

"Lies resonate with me on a sort of sound-wave frequency, if that makes any sense. Some lies are like fingernails on a chalkboard, or a petulant rooster screeching at dawn. Your lie sounded like the tuba, but played very badly by a beginning student." She grinned. "Sorry if that was insulting, Your Highness."

Conlan grinned right back at her. "It's only insulting if you ever call me 'Your Highness' again."

Brennan tried to keep up, but the adrenaline shooting through his body was muddling his mind. "It was a test?"

"It was a test," Conlan confirmed. "I'd heard stories that the ancient truth tellers used a musical analogy to describe their Gift. I find it interesting that the old ways still ring true."

"Ring true? No pun intended?" Tiernan laughed and squeezed Brennan's arm. "It's okay to stand down now, but thank you for protecting me."

Riley blew out a breath. It was not a happy sound. "We shall talk, my darling husband," she told Conlan. The baby started to cry, either alert to the tension in the room or waking from his nap.

"I think Prince Aidan has had enough of war-room talk," Brennan said.

"I hope he never has to face war-room talk on his own," Riley said, a cloud passing over her face as she cuddled her fussy son close.

"As do I, my love," Conlan said. "Perhaps you should take him somewhere more pleasant and I'll tell you everything when we're done here."

Riley lifted her face for her husband's kiss, and Brennan turned away. Beside him, Tiernan squeezed his arm again.

After Riley had said her good-byes and departed, the

three of them that remained in the room stared at one another, somewhat at a loss.

"I'm going back," Tiernan said. "If you try to hold me here against my will—"

"I'm going with her," Brennan said, and she rewarded him with a brilliant smile.

"I'm not trying to stop you," Conlan said, throwing himself down into a chair. "I'm going to suggest that we have a plan, though."

"Like what?" Brennan wanted to pace the room, but forced himself to sit, pulling Tiernan down to sit next to him. "Conlan, they are torturing shifters, and humans. If they succeed in determining how to permanently enthrall either group, we will have lost this war before a single battle is joined. Whatever plan we develop, we must make sure that we waste no time."

"Here is a plan, warrior," Alaric said, suddenly back in the room and sitting in a chair across from Brennan. "If you ever hit me again, you'll discover what torture really is."

"I think I've had enough of you threatening Brennan," Tiernan said, glaring at the priest. "Cut it out. Also, that poofing in and out is just annoying; has anyone ever told you that?"

Every nerve in Brennan's body went on alert as he prepared for whatever terrible retribution Alaric might try to take, but he was completely unprepared for what the priest actually did: he smiled.

"You know, I like you, Truth Teller," Alaric said.

"My verdict is still out on you, Priest," she countered, but then her eyes widened and she smiled back at him. "That was truth. You do like me."

"Or else I'm a sociopath," he said, the power in his eyes flaring hot for a moment.

"Sometimes we *have* wondered," Brennan told him.

Conlan tapped the table. "Enough. Let's figure out what to do next."

"There's a chance our cover isn't blown," Tiernan said,

going straight on the offense. "Brennan is set up to be an eccentric rich guy. What eccentric rich guy doesn't take it in his head to do something out of the ordinary sometimes? So we went off the grounds. We can pretend we were, ah, we were . . ."

Brennan rescued her when he realized the rosy blush rising in her cheeks was all about what they actually had been doing, both the night before and this morning. His cock twitched at the memory and he had to do some quick, serious mental maneuvering to calm his newly raging libido. Just the thought of her flawless skin was enough to turn him into the youngling he'd accused Alaric of being. He hadn't had to fight a cock stand in an inappropriate place in more than two thousand years.

"One thing is definite," Alaric said. "We cannot allow these vampires to enthrall either group. Certainly not in light of the prophecy. We will need them all as allies. Even the Fae, I fear."

It was the first Brennan had heard of a prophecy that needed allies. "What prophecy?"

Conlan and Alaric exchanged a look that—just for a second—left Brennan feeling uncomfortably like an outsider.

"It's not important right now," Alaric said dismissively.

"That is a lie," Tiernan shot back. "A big lie. Huge. Want to try again?"

Conlan tilted his head, but his considering gaze was aimed at Brennan, not Tiernan. "How much do you trust her? She is a reporter, after all."

"With my life," he said without hesitation. "That is, after all, what she already holds in her hands, through means of the curse."

"So you have no choice," Alaric said.

"I want no other choice."

Tiernan waved her hands around. "I'm right here, boys. Right here, in the room. Talk to the nice reporter, and not around her."

Conlan and Alaric exchanged another glance, but then Alaric, surprisingly enough, answered, "It's the Ragnarok. It's coming all over again."

"The Gotterdammerung?" Brennan blurted out. "You truly believe this?"

"The Doom of the Gods?" Tiernan said, her brows drawn together. "He's not lying," she told Brennan. "But why is Poseidon's priest worried about Norse mythology?" She shot a sly look at Alaric. "Confused, much?"

Conlan answered her. "Simply because primitive peoples tried to order their world and their gods by regional pantheons does not mean the world or the heavens ever actually worked that way. Did you never wonder why an Egyptian death goddess leads the vampires?"

"Anubisa?" Tiernan said the name with the loathing befitting the abomination who had killed and consumed thousands over many lifetimes. "Egyptian?"

"She claims to be daughter-wife to Anubis," Brennan said, revulsion snaking up his spine at the thought. "More important, though, when and where did this new prophecy originate?"

"We have learned much that was previously undiscovered since Keely started working with her. Her object-reader Gift has helped us find objects hidden in plain sight, even within the walls of the palace," Alaric said. "This scroll was found hidden in the base of a statue of Poseidon in the library. Heavy magic protected it, and Keely was knocked unconscious merely from touching the outside of the statue."

"I am sure Lord Justice was very happy about that," Brennan said, wondering how many warriors had ended up in the healing chambers because of Justice's rabidly protective nature. Then again . . . He stole a look at Tiernan's profile. He'd have done the same himself.

"Not only must we return the remaining gems to the Trident for Atlantis to rise, but we now must facilitate the eventual intermarriage of all races with Atlanteans," Conlan said. "The prophecy is short and quite to the point: *The*

Doom of the Gods is on the horizon. Only a child born of all races, ruling Atlantis into the future, will prevent it."

"Sounds like Keely is helping you guys out quite a bit," Tiernan pointed out. "I hope you're paying her a lot."

"I would give her the crown jewels themselves, were they mine to give, for the nature of her revelations about Nereus and Zelia," Alaric muttered.

Tiernan raised an eyebrow, and Brennan gave her the short version. "Priests were evidently able to marry and have families in ancient times, so apparently the vow of celibacy is a new development. Alaric finds this to be—"

"Useful knowledge?" she interrupted. "Fabulous? Holy crap, happy day, crazy good? The future's looking bright for you, my friend."

Alaric narrowed his eyes at Tiernan's remarks. "The future will be bright or dark, with or without me."

"You will not abandon the priesthood for Quinn," Conlan said firmly. "Not now when your people need you. When we need you."

Alaric turned anguished eyes to his prince. "Really? You, of all men, would try to use that argument against me? After you were fully willing to abdicate the throne itself for Riley?"

Tiernan cleared her throat. "Maybe we can argue the fate of all Atlantis and the world later? Right now we need to get back to that hotel or we may as well give it up as a lost cause. We can come up with a cover story that may just barely keep us out of trouble, but not if we delay any longer."

Conlan frowned. "Brennan, this decision I leave to you. Can you handle this mission with the curse and your un-bound emotions hanging over you like the Sword of Damocles itself?"

"I can handle anything," Brennan said quietly. "So long as I am with her."

Conlan sighed and shook his head. "You know, that's how it starts. Alaric has a point about the diaper changing."

Brennan inclined his head. "Yes. You will remember I was with you when you first spent time with Riley."

"I'm not pregnant," Tiernan said, the flood of indignation in her voice reducing it to a squeak. "It was—"

"Something we can discuss later," Brennan said firmly. "For now, we're going back to Yellowstone to stop these vampires and their scientist flunkies."

As if on cue, they all stood up from the table, and Conlan bowed to Brennan and Tiernan. "Keep me informed. I'll rally the warriors and send in reinforcements, but for now you're on your own."

"No, he's not. I'm his backup," Tiernan said.

"All of humanity and the entire shifter community are depending on you, small one?" Alaric said, rolling his eyes.

Tiernan whipped a small canister out of her backpack and held it up. "Hey. I've got pepper spray, and I'm not afraid to use it."

Alaric was still laughing seconds later when she whirled around and brought a sharpened wooden stake in a rapid strike to stop only inches away from his throat.

"People underestimate me," she said. "I use it."

"People fear me," Brennan said. "I use that."

Alaric looked back and forth between the two of them, that gleam of amusement still in his eyes. He finally smiled, and the stake in Tiernan's hand glowed a hot green and she yelped and dropped it.

"I don't care what people think about me," Alaric said. "But come with me, Brennan. I have something that might help."

Chapter 22

Mammoth Hot Springs Hotel

Brennan's warrior senses shot to high alert when Lucas's Pack driver pulled the limousine into the hotel driveway. "We're on," he told Tiernan, who'd been clenching and unclenching her hands for the entirety of the short drive.

"Thank you," Tiernan said to the driver. "Please thank Lucas for meeting us and providing us with the car, too."

The driver nodded, and Brennan suddenly realized the man hadn't spoken a single word since they'd climbed into the ridiculous vehicle. He'd put his hand on the door handle, when the driver surprised him by finally speaking up.

"They were my friends. The ones that those scientists took and messed up their minds? They were my friends. Make sure you get these bastards and call us when you need help," he said, more than a little of the wolf in his voice.

"We will. You have my word," Brennan said.

The driver met Brennan's gaze in the rearview mirror and then nodded again. "You're friend to Lucas, so your word is good enough for me."

Tiernan put a hand on the driver's shoulder for a moment, and then the door opened and the hotel bellhop leaned down. "Checking in, folks?"

Brennan exited the vehicle and extended a hand to Tiernan to assist her in climbing out, but he didn't let go of her hand once she had.

"No, we're just coming back from a little overnight jaunt," she said cheerfully. "All rested and ready to go. How's the conference going?"

"Everything is running very well, ma'am." The bellhop accepted Brennan's tip and rushed ahead of them to open the door.

Once they entered the lobby, the first person they saw was Dr. Litton, hurrying toward them.

"They must have had a lookout for us," Tiernan murmured.

"Undoubtedly."

"Mr. Brennan," Litton called out as he crossed the lobby toward them. "We've been looking for you. Where have you been?" He pointedly ignored Tiernan.

Tiernan, of course, wasn't about to stand idly by for that. She flashed him a charming smile. "Oh, hello, Dr. Litton. We went out for a drive in the moonlight and wound up staying out all night. It was so romantic, don't you think, honey?"

It took Brennan a couple of seconds to realize she was talking to him with that last, and another couple of seconds to banish his stupid smile from being called "honey."

"It was an excellent journey," he agreed. "We were so caught up in the . . . *scenery* . . . that we wound up touring the entire area."

Litton's narrow-eyed gaze darted between Brennan and Tiernan as if he were trying to decide if they were telling the truth or not.

Brennan, telling himself it was for their cover, casually pulled Tiernan into his arms and kissed her so thoroughly that he nearly forgot they were standing in the middle of a very public place. When he finally released her, something flashed in the corner of his brain—a glimpse of nearly forgotten memory, elusive as moonlight on choppy waves. The barest glimpse of her curves, shining wet in the shower the night before.

He *did* remember her. He would *always* remember her. He'd worry about the *how* later.

Litton cleared his throat quite loudly. "Well. Yes. How lovely for you. But science waits for no one, and we have quite a lot to cover. If you'll come with me, we have transportation ready to show you something I'm sure you'll find very much worth your time."

Brennan raised an eyebrow. "Ten million dollars' worth of my time?"

Litton's pasty face turned a little bit paler, but he nodded. "Definitely. You will be very, very pleased. Shall we?"

The doctor gestured that they should precede him out the door, and Brennan glanced down at Tiernan once their backs were to Litton. She shook her head in a tiny gesture, barely noticeable, but clear enough for him to know that she'd caught the truth.

Litton was lying. He didn't expect Brennan to be pleased at all.

As they walked back through the doors they'd just entered, a pair of shiny black vehicles rolled up, gleaming in the afternoon sun. They were enormous, not long like the limousine, but square and high like army tanks. More ridiculous consumption of fuel. Didn't these humans realize they were the custodians of the planet?

"Hummers," Tiernan murmured. "Compensation for small penises."

He couldn't keep the laugh from escaping. "You continually surprise me," he told her.

She smiled a mysterious female smile. "Good."

Litton joined them and pointed to the first of the two vehicles. "We can travel in this one, Mr. Brennan, and Ms. Baum can ride with our second group."

Tiernan's hand tightened convulsively on Brennan's, and he stared down at Litton. "She goes with me."

Litton made a few sputtering noises of protest, but Brennan ignored them completely and crossed to the vehicle, helping Tiernan climb up into the seat.

"Thank you," she whispered into his ear.

He climbed up next to her and pulled the door shut, leaving Litton to climb into the front seat next to the driver, who was yet another goon. This one was thickly muscled with a bald head and tattoos on his neck, but he obviously wasn't a vampire, given the time of day. Shifter, maybe?

Before he could ask, Tiernan did it for him.

"Yeah," the guy replied, after looking at Litton. "I'm with the local Pack here in the park."

Tiernan touched the back of Brennan's hand and made a back-and-forth motion with her fingertip, telling him that the shifter was lying about being in Lucas's Pack. Interesting. What motivation could he have to do that? They had no knowledge that Brennan knew Lucas, did they?

A darker thought occurred. What if this were one of Litton's enthralled shifters—an experiment? What if he went crazy with whatever had infected the others? Brennan regretted allowing Tiernan to enter the vehicle first; now she sat directly behind the driver, in his reach if he twisted around. Shifters were quick, even in close quarters, as he'd had many occasions to observe over the centuries.

Brennan would just have to be quicker. He touched the pocket of his jeans, reassuring himself that the small bottle Alaric had given him was still there. His secret weapon, if they were . . . detained.

As the shifter put the vehicle into gear and drove away from the hotel, Litton started a stream of general commentary on the local sights, what had happened thus far in the conference, and so on. A nervous talker. Brennan hated nervous talkers.

Tiernan leaned across him to gaze out his window, and the warm weight of her body against his nearly made him groan. Memories of their lovemaking that morning were not conducive to keeping him sharp and alert in the presence of potential and proven enemies.

"Look at how beautiful it is here," she said, pointing to the shimmer of water through the trees. "Let's take some time after the conference and explore it, okay?"

She turned her head to smile up at him, and her lips were only a breath away from his, so it was only natural that he'd lean forward and close that space. As fleeting as a forgotten wish, yet even such a brief touch from her lips still had the power to spark liquid gold inside the dark crevasses of his soul.

Brennan had to grin: oh, how Ven would mock him if he'd heard *that* thought.

"I'll take that evil grin as a yes," Tiernan said, straightening up and moving back into her side of the seat. "I've heard the waterfalls here are spectacular."

Litton, who'd been droning on about waterfalls earlier, made a snorting noise, settled into his seat, shoulders hunched, and quit talking altogether. As much as Brennan appreciated the silence, he knew he should be doing something to advance their cover story. He leaned forward a little.

"Tell me more about the lab, Dr. Litton. I understand it is in a very secure location?"

Litton twisted around in his seat. "Definitely secure. We wouldn't want your money to be in any danger, would we, now?" He laughed at his own wit, and Brennan frowned. There was an edge of madness there, to be sure. Not that most true geniuses didn't have that streak of incipient madness, and Litton was nothing if not a genius. His research and discoveries in mapping the brain and ways to manipulate brain chemistry and function were nothing short of miraculous.

That's why they were all here, after all. Just the crazy scientist, the brainless reporter, and the not-very-perceptive billionaire.

Tiernan shot him a look, and he realized he'd tightened his grip on her hand so much that he was probably hurting her. He instantly released her.

"I'm sorry, *mi*—Tracy," he said quietly.

"No worries. Good as new." She wiggled her fingers to show him.

"We're almost there," Litton said. "It's about twenty minutes outside the gate. We're going to give you a special demonstration of our capabilities and experiments to date, and also present our plans for the future. With the help of your funding, we anticipate great strides in the very near future." The man was all but preening. "Great strides," he repeated.

"Well, you are the genius," Tiernan said, a bland smile on her face.

Litton shot her a suspicious glare, but she kept the smile on her face, no matter that she believed the man to be a contemptuous rodent. Brennan was impressed.

"Yes," Litton said, turning back around to face forward again. "I am."

Tiernan rolled her eyes, and the driver made a choking noise that he turned into a cough. Brennan glanced up and met the man's gaze in the rearview mirror. The shifter was fighting a grin, so he'd clearly seen Tiernan's reaction. Brennan smiled, too, inviting the driver to share the joke.

Never hurt to enlist allies. The shifter might not actively help them, but it's harder to shoot a man when you've shared a joke with him. Ven had taught them all that. Although Christophe was fond of telling Ven that it was his jokes that might get *him* shot. Brennan smiled at the memory, and at his ability to find joy in something so ordinary as the bantering between his fellow warriors.

They sat in silence for the rest of the trip, and Brennan memorized their directions and notable landmarks so he could find the place again. After the promised twenty minutes, the driver turned the car off onto a tree-lined road that narrowed for a few miles until it was no more than a single lane. If they met any cars coming the opposite way, someone would need to pull clear off the road into the grass and weeds.

They took a sharp turn a little too fast, and Tiernan fell

against Brennan. He took advantage of the moment by putting his arm around her—any excuse to touch her. The look in her eyes when she glanced up at him made him want to touch her in many ways. Naked ways.

"We're here," Litton announced.

Brennan put thoughts of Tiernan, naked, to the side for more careful consideration later, and studied the enormous, blocky, white-painted building.

"It's a warehouse?" Tiernan asked.

"We bought the warehouse and made major renovations to the inside," Litton said. "We needed a large space that we could retrofit to our own precise specifications."

"Of course," Brennan said. "Easier when the basic structure is in place." As if he really were a businessman and had done such things many times. He felt the warmth of Tiernan's approval even before he saw it in her eyes.

The shifter pulled right up to the front door and parked the car, then jumped out to open the door for Tiernan. She had no polite way to refuse, so Brennan had to endure several seconds when she was in easy reach of the driver. If the shifter really had been experimented on and chose this moment to succumb to the madness, Brennan wouldn't be able to reach her in time to save her. Brennan had far too much experience with the damage an enraged shifter could do with his claws and teeth to be anything but tense until she safely reached his side.

"Welcome to the Litton Neuro-Research Institute," the scientist said with a flourish, opening the large metal door. "Prepare to be amazed."

"Oh, I am, Dr. Litton," Brennan told him as they entered the building. "I definitely am."

Chapter 23

Tiernan had been nervous enough about the drive down the back road to Out-in-the-Boonies, but the metal detector at the doorway ratcheted her anxiety level to an eight or nine. Brennan surely had his daggers with him, and that was going to go over badly. Really badly.

The shifter had lied about being part of Lucas's Pack, so he was definitely one of Litton's thugs, but that was no surprise. Litton was too paranoid to have anybody but people he could control around him, she'd bet. She'd met the type before, and they hadn't even been mad scientists.

Brennan never even paused. He sauntered through the metal detector like he was a celebrity on a red carpet. The machine didn't make a peep.

After all her worry about Brennan, the machine buzzed loudly when she walked through, and she flinched. The very bored-looking attendant perked up, probably at the opportunity for trouble. He shot up out of his seat, his hand hovering near the pocket of his jacket. "Weapon?"

Tiernan smiled. "Cell phone." She put the phone in the

little tray and walked through again, this time with no buzzing. Litton, who had been practically dancing from foot to foot the whole time, led them down a short hallway and into a large conference room.

"We'll be in here for the presentation, and then I'll take you on a tour of the lab," he told Brennan.

"I'd prefer a more casual approach," Brennan said. "Why don't we walk around the lab now and save the formal presentation for later or even tomorrow? I like to see my dollars at work, so to speak."

Litton didn't like that idea at all. His face turned an unhealthy purple color and he started spluttering. "Oh, no, no, that won't do at all. You know scientists, Mr. Brennan, a bunch of people more set in their ways you're unlikely to find soon. We have to let them follow the plan or they'll get confused and unhappy. Unhappy scientists don't do good work."

"We're so lucky you're not like that, Dr. Litton," Tiernan said sweetly, finding it hard not to laugh when he scuttled out of there, muttering something about coffee and back in fifteen minutes.

Brennan crossed the space separating them until he was standing so close to her that his breath ruffled her hair when he spoke. "You shouldn't tease the evil scientist."

She shivered a little from the sensation of his warm breath traveling down her neck. "I know, but he annoys me so much. Even if I didn't hate him for everything he does and everything he stands for, I'd still want to kick him in the nuts just on general principles."

The deep timbre of Brennan's laughter sent another shiver down her spine and she moved a prudent distance away, pretending to be fascinated by the tray of coffee cups. Then she remembered what she'd wanted to ask him and returned so she could speak quietly and avoid any eavesdroppers or bugs.

It wasn't paranoid if there was a good chance it might be true.

"How did you make it past that metal detector?" she murmured, scratching her nose to cover her mouth in case they were on video surveillance. Although maybe that was a bit over the top. What was the likelihood that they had lip readers on staff?

"The only—"

She cut him off by pulling his head down and kissing him, then pretending to nuzzle his ear. "The room might be bugged. Maybe whisper in my ear?"

He put his arms around her and pulled her very close to his hard body. "Finally, a mission I approve of one thousand percent," he said. He returned her kiss, taking full advantage of the situation to thoroughly claim her mouth. She was dizzy by the time he stopped.

"The only weapons that can survive transforming into mist with us are those made of a native Atlantean ore, orichalcum. It has the added benefit of not triggering metal detection, even masking other metals that are combined with it," he murmured near her ear. She was pleased that his voice was ragged; this insane attraction between them was definitely two-sided.

"Even the silver?"

"Silver?" His eyebrows drew together. "What silver?"

"You told those vampires your blades were tipped with silver."

His face relaxed into a lazy grin. "Ah, Truth Teller, it surprises me that you ask me this."

She blinked. "You lied?"

"Call it more of a bluff."

It was her turn to laugh. She had been so worried about more important things, like *not dying*, that it had never occurred to her to listen for bluffs.

"You're devious, Brennan."

"You're beautiful, Tiernan," he whispered, and then he kissed her again, but only briefly, and she heard the voices heading down the hall toward them right after he raised his head.

"Here we go," she said. "Showtime."

Brennan let Tiernan turn to face the door but kept his arm wrapped around her waist, telling himself it was because she needed the comfort of his touch. She would have called him on that lie immediately. His fear for her safety was spiking adrenaline and pure, primal aggression through his body so powerfully that he had to work hard to control himself. It wouldn't be good for either Tiernan or their mission if he were the one to commit the first overt act of hostility.

Litton burst through the door, reminding Brennan again of nothing as much as a hairless rodent, leading to an odd and utterly random curiosity about whether or not were-rodents existed. Seemed unlikely.

Several men and women in lab coats followed Litton through the room. Litton gestured toward the large conference table and everyone took a seat, except for one man who hurried over to the equipment on a desk near the front.

"Welcome to the place where the magic happens," Litton said, sweeping his arms out.

"Bit grandiose, isn't he?" Tiernan said under her breath.

Brennan's rage calmed down several notches at the amusement in her voice. His mate was not afraid; that fact went a long way to dampen the fury threatening to swamp him.

"Please take a seat," the man at the equipment said.

Brennan and Tiernan took the two open seats at the end of the conference table. They were farthest from the door. Brennan forced himself to draw in slow, deep breaths to fight the animal instinct of being cornered.

The predator in him didn't like it one bit, no matter that none of the humans between Tiernan and the door seemed likely to put up a fight. Lab coats could conceal a great many things, weapons among them.

Even Brennan could not always outrace a bullet.

Litton nodded, and one of the scientists, a female, distributed dark blue folders to each person at the table. She hesitated when she got to Tiernan, biting her lip, and she shot Litton a look, but he just nodded again and she put the final blue folder in front of Tiernan and then rushed back to her own seat.

"You will find in front of you documents that detail a great many of our more important findings in the area of neurophysiological control," Litton said.

As Brennan and Tiernan opened their folders, an image flashed on the screen at the front of the room. A group of large, obviously strong men were working on a skyscraper. They were all happy and smiling for the camera.

None of them was human.

"Those are all shifters," Tiernan said. "You can tell from the way they're hanging off the side of that building, or those two who are carrying huge steel beams with one hand. Only shifters would have that kind of strength and agility. But why—"

"Correct, Ms. Baum," Litton said, as if rewarding a prize pupil. "They are all shifters. But not just any shifters. These are all men who, just one month before this picture was taken, were hopeless derelicts. Leeches upon society. They'd taken the worst of the shifter existence—violence, dominance, bloodlust—and warped it even further, until they were roaming as a gang in Chicago. Brutalizing innocents and terrifying even the police force."

He stopped and grasped the lapels of his lab coat, looked around the room, and smiled his smug, self-satisfied smile. "We made them productive members of society in *just three days*."

"I thought you said one month?" Brennan said.

Litton was clearly prepared for the question. "Well, it took them three-and-a-half weeks to learn construction."

Everyone in the room, but for Brennan and Tiernan, laughed, but it had the tired sound of being well rehearsed. Brennan looked down at the papers in front of him and scanned the people in the room out of the corner of his eye. Most of them had telltale signs of exhaustion and anxiety. Pale and deeply drawn faces, nervous quirks such as tapping the arms of their chairs or the table, fidgeting, lip-biting. It didn't take a shifter to read this body language. A select few, however, were leaning forward, all eagerness. They were the zealots, then.

Something was very, very wrong here.

"I made a fascinating discovery about the brain," Litton continued, clearly in his element being the center of attention. "The activity in the caudate nucleus can not only predict people's preferences, but it can and does reinforce decisions already made."

"The caudate nucleus is part of the striatum, isn't it?" Tiernan asked, clearly surprising Litton.

"So lovely to see you're not just a pretty face," he said, beaming.

Brennan noticed the female scientists in the room—and some of the men—wince at the comment. Potential allies? But they all looked too defeated to strike out against Litton, and certainly they wouldn't be able to stand up to vampires.

Tiernan, however, ignored the remark entirely, focusing intently on Litton.

"Yes, the caudate nucleus is part of the striatum, which is involved in generating movement." Litton made a motion, and the image on the screen changed to a diagram of the brain. The caudate nucleus looked rather like an Atlantean sugar bean and was situated on the right side of the image.

Tiernan whistled. "That's a pretty major discovery. Can you activate the caudate nucleus?"

Litton smiled. It was a singularly unpleasant smile. "Not only can we activate it, Ms. Baum, but we can control it and, by so doing, control the desires and resultant actions of the person whose brain has been activated."

Tiernan slumped back in her seat, shaking her head. She turned to Brennan. "That's not only major, that's control-the-world major," she said in an undertone. "And if he's telling us this, he has no intention of letting us out of here, ever. He would not only be shut down so fast by the scientific community that your head would spin, but this is criminal prosecution time."

"Anything you'd like to share with the group?" Litton said, sneering at them.

"Very impressive," Brennan said, clenching his hands into fists on his thighs but presenting a calm face to the room. "Looks like you're putting my money to very good use, Doctor. How long does this control last?"

Litton's smug smile faltered, and he broke eye contact. "As long as we want it to last, of course."

Brennan didn't need to see Tiernan's tiny head shake to know that Litton had just lied, but the confirmation convinced him that he needed to get Tiernan out of there, and fast.

"Is your head still aching?" he asked Tiernan, who glanced up, surprised.

He took her hand in his. "We should get you some medicine and have you lie down for a while before we continue this."

"Oh, no, I'm fine," she said firmly, pulling her hand from his, the light of battle in her eyes. "This is fascinating, Dr. Litton, please continue."

"We have a bit of video you'll be very interested in, Mr. Brennan. This will show you what we've done so far, what we're planning to do next, and where we hope to ultimately arrive with our research and practical trials."

From the first image of video footage, Brennan knew it was going to be bad, but even he, hardened by millennia of battle, had not anticipated the sheer depth of evil—all committed in the name of scientific research.

Litton's voice, sounding somewhat tinny, narrated the footage, describing the testing and failures that led to eventual success in the human trials. The video focused on two subjects, one male and one female, and the results were fairly innocuous at first. The subjects were shown submitting to a procedure whereby they were fastened into a chair and various electrodes were attached to their body. A metal helmet bristling with knobs and antennae, looking like something out of the science fiction movies Ven and Riley enjoyed so much, was fastened over their heads, and the scientists administered what looked like a series of electric shocks.

Tiernan, beside him, was clutching the arms of her chair so tightly that her knuckles were as white as her face. "Is that—is that the procedure to activate?"

Litton nodded, his attention fixed avidly on the screen. "Yes. Depending on the level of natural resistance, which varies from subject to subject, we may have to repeat the procedure multiple times."

The test subject on-screen, the female, screamed and arched her body and then fell back against the chair. Brennan saw the tears trickling down from the corners of her eyes, and he wanted to smash something.

Smash someone.

And his prime candidate had the nerve to chuckle.

"Sometimes they feel a little discomfort," Litton said, still chuckling. "But they forget it when we're through."

"You can affect memory, too?" Brennan said, instantly imagining the worst.

"Not exactly. Something about the procedure does cause a bit of an amnesia effect, but that only seems to relate to events around the actual procedure itself. It's the trauma of the procedure, we believe."

"Gee, you think?" Tiernan snapped.

Litton frowned. "All great scientific achievement and progress must come with some sacrifice, Ms. Baum."

"What did you sacrifice, Dr. Litton?" she shot back.

"I gave up a high-ranking faculty position at a very well-respected university to found this institute," he snapped. Then he gathered his dignity. "I'm sorry, Mr. Brennan. Usually it's hard for laypeople to understand the hard work and dedication that goes into this sort of scientific endeavor. Since you've been so heavily involved in research before, I'm sure *you* understand."

"Of course," Brennan replied. He took Tiernan's hand in his own, under the table, and squeezed it in warning. So far they didn't have any real proof of what was going on. Her rapid breathing rate was signaling Brennan that they didn't have much time before she exploded, though.

"Please continue," he told Litton.

The video continued to mild scenes of the humans accomplishing simple tasks and performing feats with physical dexterity that they hadn't had before the procedures. They watched the subjects juggle, walk on a thin balance beam, and climb a rock wall.

"We activated the woman to believe she was a concert violinist," Litton said, as the images on-screen switched to show her in a room, playing the violin with an expression of dreamy bliss on her face.

"It's beautiful, but . . . wrong," Tiernan whispered.

It was true. The woman's music was technically proficient but oddly soulless, much like the look in her eyes when the camera zoomed in for a close-up.

"Think of how much this talent enhanced her life. Absolutely beautiful. That's Bach, I believe," Litton said. "Imagine the music we could bring to the world."

"Where is she now?" Tiernan asked. "Playing the concert circuit?"

For the first time, Litton looked uncomfortable. "No. She, ah, she had certain difficulties."

"What does that mean, exactly—difficulties?" Brennan asked.

At first, he thought Litton wouldn't answer. The scientist clamped his lips together and glared at them. But then he gave a little shrug. "She became obsessed. Wouldn't eat, wouldn't sleep, or even stop to drink water. Never put down the violin, not even for a minute, and became extremely violent when we tried to take it away from her."

"Where is she now?" Tiernan repeated, enunciating each word.

Litton glared at her, and Brennan's fury spiked into his skull, starting up a pounding that almost drowned out the scientist's response.

"She's dead," Litton spat out. "She played the violin, okay? While she starved and became more and more dehydrated. She played herself to death."

Brennan looked at each of the men and women at the table for a reaction to the news they all surely must have already known. Some were ashamed and ducked their heads, pained expressions on their faces. Others were callously indifferent or even bored. A few were smiling, as if it were all a great joke.

He hoped those last were the ones who tried to get in his way when they left.

Tiernan's hand, still resting underneath his on his leg, tightened until her fingers were digging into his skin. She was near to the breaking point, and he needed to get her out of there whether she wanted to go or not.

Litton, apparently completely unaware of the effect his video was having on them, turned back toward the screen, and the image changed again.

"Ah, now we get to the interesting studies," Litton said. "The shifters. We've had mixed results with them because of the variances in brain structure from humans."

"Shifters are human," Brennan said. "Surely you know that?"

Litton spun around and stared at Brennan. "They're animals. Mutants. Very little human about them. They make good lab rats, but that's about it."

Tiernan's breath changed, and she made a low sound of anguish deep in her throat. "They're human, you—you—"

Litton ignored her and turned back to the screen, where a woman wearing a hospital gown and cap, shown from the back, was being helped across a room. She was stumbling, obviously ill or injured. "Watch this and I'm sure you'll change your mind on that. This is fox shifter subject 12A, originally located in Boston. She was one of the subjects most resistant to the activation, of any we've ever found, and we were forced to repeat the procedure on multiple occasions, over more than a week. Finally, however, she succumbed. Unfortunately, her brain rejected the activation when she was out in the world again on a practice run, and I believe she was killed by police."

He said this in a completely calm and indifferent voice, as if he were discussing the weather.

"Boston," Tiernan repeated. "Did you say Boston?"

Brennan's anxiety for Tiernan soared to all new levels. He never should have allowed her to come here. Litton was completely, dangerously insane.

The men on the video moved out of the camera angle and the woman's face was visible for the first time. Tiernan gasped and dug her fingers into Brennan's leg.

"That's Susannah," she whispered. "That's Susannah. This is all the proof we need, we need to get that video and get the hell out of here."

On the screen, a scientist—Brennan looked at him closely and then at one of the men down at the other end of the room; yes it was him—put the helmet on Susannah. Before he'd even fully fastened the wires to her body, she began to scream.

Tiernan shot up out of her chair so fast that she knocked it over. "Oh, you evil son of a bitch. You are going to pay for hurting her."

Brennan shot up to stand next to her, pulling his daggers out of their concealed sheaths as he did. "I believe that is my cue."

Chapter 24

"We're calling the police," Tiernan said. "You're all going to jail for a very long time."

Most of the scientists jumped up and started running for the door in varying levels of panic, except for Litton and the ones Brennan had marked as zealots. Litton smiled that nasty little smile of his and signaled the man over by the computers. "Security. Now."

"This is a new definition of undercover," Brennan told Tiernan as she yanked her cell phone out of her pocket. "I'd thought we would gather the evidence, leave this place, and then contact the authorities."

"Stash me someplace safe, you mean."

"Ideally, yes."

She started pressing numbers on her phone. "I don't need safe. I need justice."

"What you need is to put that phone down. Now." Litton's voice slashed across the room like the crack of a whip. "Or I will have my security team shoot first you, and then Mr. Brennan, in the head."

The scientists blocking the door parted like water, and four thugs with guns entered the room, all of them pointing their weapons at Brennan and Tiernan.

"Right now, I need for you to shut up and sit down and watch the rest of our film, Mr. Brennan. You surely want to know what we're going to do with all of that lovely money of yours after we take control of your mind, don't you?"

"Was this the plan all along?" Brennan asked, calculating the odds that he could destroy all four of the thugs before one of them shot Tiernan.

"You didn't think we'd show you all of this and then let you go, did you?" Litton laughed. "I must admit, I never took you for a fool."

"Funny," Tiernan said, handing over her phone to one of the scientists. "I always took you for a murdering bastard."

Waves of fury were radiating from her skin, and Brennan wondered how nobody else in the room could feel it. She was running so hot that it seemed impossible that the paint on the walls was not blistering.

Or maybe he felt it only because of the soul-meld, which meant if anything were to hurt her . . . He'd seen berserker rage only once in all of his years, and the path of carnage and destruction had been hideous beyond belief.

If they hurt Tiernan, they'd see worse.

As the rage climbed higher and higher, pounding through his veins, Brennan's power climbed, building and building until his body ached with the attempt to control it. Power sought release, and power this wild was going to blow the roof off if he didn't control it. He glanced almost reflexively up at the roof.

Maybe that wouldn't be such a bad thing.

"Please sit down, Mr. Brennan," Dr. Litton said with exaggerated politeness. "We have more to see."

"We don't want to see it, you sadistic monster," Tiernan cried out. "If it's the last thing I do, I'm going to see you pay for that."

Litton laughed, long and hard. "Oh, my dear Ms. Baum,"

he finally said, wiping his eyes. "The lovely cliché of it all. The last thing you will do is probably going to involve your naked body and one or more of my guards. They like to try out the new subjects, and I see no reason not to let them."

A red haze swamped Brennan's mind, short-circuiting reason and logic. The need to kill, fierce and urgent, took over and filled him, searing through body and mind and soul, until nothing was left but the rage.

"You will not hurt her," he said, snarling the words.

"We have the guns, Mr. Brennan. Your knives are not much use, are they? I would be interested to know how you got those past the metal detectors, though," Litton said. He beckoned his guards. "Take them to their accommodations, please. Oh, and leave the knives on the table."

Brennan had no choice. The guards were trained professionals, and two of them always stayed well out of his range. They'd shoot Tiernan if he fought back. He'd have to watch for a chance when they left the room.

As they filed out the door, sandwiched among the four thugs, the images on the screen painted a violent threat of what their immediate future might hold. Susannah, still tied down to the chair, was screaming. Only this time, she was doing it in the shape of a fox.

One of the thugs shoved Tiernan and she tripped, twisting her ankle, and cried out. Brennan's tenuous hold on his temper shattered. He lowered his head, pretending to look at the floor, so they wouldn't see the magic glowing in his eyes, and he called power on a scale beyond anything he'd attempted before. He wanted water in destructive force.

He called the thunder.

The first percussive boom shook the walls of the building, and the crack of an accompanying lightning strike struck hard in its wake. Brennan pushed harder, and hail pounded down on the roof, its rapid drumming echoing through the room.

"What the hell?" one of the guards said, instinctively looking up when another lightning strike, more powerful than the first, smashed into the building and the electricity in the room blew out.

"Down," Brennan shouted, hoping Tiernan would listen to him, but not willing to trust that she would. He launched himself at the two guards in front of him and snapped the first one's neck before the man ever saw him coming. Brennan whirled around and sent a vicious kick into the second guard's throat, not quite snapping his neck but taking him down.

The backup generators for the building came on, and a row of lights, dimmer than those that had been in the room before, switched on, and Brennan went for his daggers. He leapt over the downed guard and headed for the table, only to find that one of his blades was missing. He hurled the one he found into the third guard's throat and spun around, searching the room for Tiernan, who would have been on the floor under the table, if she'd listened to his command.

She was standing over the body of one of the scientists, holding Brennan's dagger, and the blade dripped blood. She raised her head and stared right across the chaos of the room at Brennan, horror and disbelief warring on her very expressive features. "I killed him," she said, and somehow he heard her over all the noise and shouting and screaming. "I killed him."

A gunshot tore through the noise and everything stopped. The final guard stood two feet behind Tiernan, and he'd fired the shot straight up in the air, ripping a chunk out of the ceiling.

"Everybody down on the floor and shut the fuck up," the guard roared. "Anybody still standing in five seconds is going to get shot."

Brennan didn't move, and Tiernan didn't seem to have even heard the guard, but everyone else but Litton hit the floor. Tiernan just stood, silent, possibly going into shock, staring down at the dead scientist. Tiernan dropped the dagger and flinched at the sound it made when it hit the ground.

Litton stalked across the floor toward her, and Brennan

tensed to hurl himself at the scientist, but the guard leveled his gun directly at Tiernan's head. There was no way he could miss from less than two feet away.

"You try it, buddy, and her brains hit the wall," the guard said calmly. There was training in that calm; the man was cool and controlled when everyone else was frantic. He'd kill Tiernan before Brennan could even get close.

Brennan slowly put his hands on top of his head and released his hold on the power. A stray lightning strike might rattle the man enough to make his finger twitch on that trigger. The drumming of the hail on the roof slowed and then stopped.

"Kick her knife over here," the guard commanded. "I won't underestimate you again, rich boy."

Brennan stepped closer to Tiernan and kicked the dagger across the floor. It skidded to a stop next to the guard's boots.

Litton looked down at the dead scientist, the one from the video, and then he drew his arm back and slapped Tiernan's face. Hard. Her head snapped back with the force of it, and Brennan felt her pain and shock. Brennan's control, near to breaking, frayed even further. Only the gun trained on Tiernan's head kept him from ripping Litton's head off his neck.

"I needed him, you bitch," Litton snarled, his face nearly purple with rage. "He was worth twenty of you. *Journalists*. Bunch of leeches upon society."

He raised his hand again, but then shook his head. "No. You're not worth it. I have a far better plan for you, Tracy Baum. You're going to go in the chair. Tonight. I need a guinea pig to see if it functions properly since we repaired the damage. There's a chance it will turn the next subject's entire frontal lobe to pudding." He laughed that nasty laugh again. "Who better than you to try it out?"

"You will die slowly if you touch her, Litton," Brennan said, and the guard narrowed his eyes, measuring his opponent, then took a firmer grip on his gun.

Litton just waved a hand in the air. "Shut up. I don't

need to hear your mouth, I just need your signature on all those lovely wire transfers we're going to do later. My worries about funding are now over, aren't they?"

"This is your last warning, Litton," Brennan said, his voice gone dead and icy. "I will let you live if you release her now."

Litton pointed at the guard. "You. If he talks again, shoot him. No, wait. If he talks again, shoot *her*. Just in the leg. Something that will hurt but not kill her. Maybe her foot."

The guard nodded, stone-faced, so Brennan couldn't tell if Litton's casual cruelty disgusted the man or if it was simply another day in the life of a mercenary. It didn't matter anyway. He held a gun on Tiernan. He would die, too. The power climbed up Brennan's spine to his skull, until he thought his bones would shatter from the sheer force of it.

Kill them, destroy them, death to any who threaten my mate, the power said, and for the first time in his lifetime it was sentient and had a voice, and it was the voice of utter destruction to these monsters who dared to harm Tiernan. It took every ounce of control Brennan possessed to keep from attacking, but the sight of that gun, aimed at Tiernan, served as a very efficient leash.

Litton kicked one of the men on the floor in the ribs. "Get up, you idiot. Go get more security people. We need help getting them downstairs. Also call Devon and tell him we need a cleanup crew here. One of his people should be able to get rid of this mess."

The man scrambled up and ran for the door. As if Litton's words had released Brennan's olfactory senses, the rich, coppery smell of blood suddenly seemed to permeate the room. Instead of making him nauseous, it fed the berserker rage, and the predator inside of him woke up and smiled. He would bring death, and soon, to these men who dared to threaten his mate.

The meaning of Litton's words suddenly broke through the haze of killing fury clouding Brennan's mind. Devon, he'd said. So the vampire was behind all this. Brennan needed to transmit the information to Alexios, whom Alaric had said would be returning to Lucas's Pack headquarters this evening. The thought of their conversation reminded him of his need to conceal the vial Alaric had given him. Brennan briefly tried to establish a mental pathway, but Tiernan made a horrible noise and his concentration fractured.

"Brennan, I killed him," she moaned, and the utter despair in her voice terrified him. Someone who despaired would not fight back, and they were going to need to fight back, very soon, or Litton would have her in that mind-destroying chair.

Over my dead body, he swore to himself.

Tiernan's eyes widened, and she doubled over, making a terrible noise that came more from her gut than her throat. Litton yelled at her to stand up, but the guard took two steps back and away from her, the gun still trained on her head, as if he knew what was coming next, as did Brennan.

She cried out and then vomited, gagging until there was nothing else to heave up. Litton scrambled back and away to avoid it.

"Get her out of here as soon as the others get here," Litton ordered the guard. "I'll meet you at the holding pens."

Before Brennan could say something—anything—that might stop him or even slow him down, Litton was gone, and a half dozen more guards, these heavily armed, were swarming into the room.

These men were well trained, too, no common thugs. They worked as a team, herding Brennan and Tiernan down a long corridor and then through a doorway to a set of stairs leading down. And down, and down, and down. Brennan calculated they must have been at least four stories underground by the time they came to the bottom of the stairs and the men prodded them through the doorway into another hall.

Brennan's guards kept him separate from Tiernan, and both of them now had guns pointed at their heads. The electricity down here had not been affected by the lightning strike, apparently, since harsh fluorescent lighting flooded the corridor. He got a glimpse of Tiernan as they moved down the hall, and her face was dead white, almost a greenish gray under the lights. Shock had set in and she looked like she might pass out any minute.

He needed to find a way out, and he needed to find it quick. He hadn't liked the sound of "holding pens" or the gleefully evil way Litton had said it. The guard behind him shoved Brennan between the shoulder blades with the barrel of his gun and cursed at him to hurry up. Brennan glanced back over his shoulder and bared his teeth at the man just for the pleasure of watching him flinch.

"Better watch this one," the guard called out to his comrades. "He passed rational and took the crazy highway a couple of stops ago."

Brennan started laughing, but kept moving forward as directed. The crazy highway. They had no idea.

When they arrived, it was as bad as Brennan had feared. They were cages, nothing more. Tiernan moaned again, and Brennan wanted to slash and burn and kill for her. The need to protect her sliced through him like one of his own daggers, now left lying useless on the floor above.

"Brennan," she called out. "Do you see it?"

"Shut up," one of the guards snarled at her, shoving her into the bars of the cage. Brennan roared out a threat in Atlantean that ripped up from his soul and forced its way out from between his clenched teeth.

"Shut up, you," the guard behind him snarled, before smashing his gun into the side of Brennan's head so hard it knocked him down to the floor.

"The wiring, Brennan. Look at the wiring," Tiernan said, ignoring the guard who threatened her again. "It's the equivalent of an electric fence. Didn't you say—"

She cried out—one of the guards must have struck her—and Brennan, driven beyond endurance, lunged up from the floor, only to meet the butt of another guard's gun on its way down to slam into his face. The world went hazy and he fought for consciousness. If he passed out now, he'd wake up not knowing Tiernan, with both of them trapped here. His one and only goal was to stay awake, stay alive, rescue his mate.

No matter how many had to die for him to do it.

Chapter 25

Yellowstone National Park, Pack Headquarters

Alexios paced back and forth in the spacious living area of Lucas's HQ, stopping every few minutes to shut his eyes and try to establish a mental pathway to Brennan.

"Nothing. Gods damn it, nothing. It's wrong, somehow. Not silence or an emptiness, which would happen if he were out of range, but more an odd static and a—" He broke off. He trusted Lucas completely, but there were several other Pack members in the large wood-and-brick room, and he didn't want to give away what he'd felt from Brennan. There were too many variables, too many chances that one of them might be compromised.

It had happened before. The very night before, in fact.

Lucas gave him a narrow-eyed stare and then nodded almost imperceptibly. "Let's set up a perimeter watch," he ordered his second. "I want everybody out there, keeping us safe."

The shifter jumped up, not quite meeting Lucas's eyes. Alexios did not fully understand Pack politics and hierarchy and believed none but shifters really could, but he knew enough about dominance and shifters to realize that Lucas was one of the most powerful alphas he'd ever encountered, on the level, power-wise, of Ethan of the Florida panther shifters.

Thinking of Ethan led his tumbling thoughts to Marie, sister of Bastien, one of his closest friends and a very powerful warrior. He still couldn't believe Bastien's sister, Marie, leader of the Temple of the Nereids, had fallen in love with Ethan during such a brief trip to Florida. They were trying to work it out, but as Grace had said once, Ethan and Marie gave a whole new meaning to the long-distance in the term "long-distance relationship." Atlantis-to-Miami trips took quite a bit of planning. For Ethan to travel to Atlantis was, as yet, forbidden.

"Deep thoughts?" Lucas said, and Alexios looked up from his mental ramblings to realize the room had emptied out and they were alone.

"It's something bad, Lucas," Alexios said, suddenly whirling around to smash his fists down on the pile of wood near the fireplace. He watched, almost unseeing, as the pile collapsed with a crash and logs rolled across the floor.

"Honey will love that," Lucas said dryly. He crossed to a side table and poured them both glasses of a clear brown liquid, then handed one to Alexios. "What is it?"

Alexios took a deep sniff of fine Scotch whiskey, then drained his glass in two gulps. He wiped his mouth with the back of his hand, and Lucas snatched the glass out of his hand, pointedly looking down at the logs. "I like these glasses," he said, holding up the bottle and raising an eyebrow.

Alexios shook his head. "No more. I need a clear head. Brennan isn't gone, exactly, but he isn't there, either. When I open a pathway, I get a flooding sensation of rage and violence, almost animalistic in nature."

Lucas's face went hard. "Don't give me that bigoted bullshit. It's not the animals who kill each other for no reason."

"I didn't mean that, and you know it. It was more fury

and unreasoning pain, like an animal caught in a trap. Does that make more sense?"

Lucas drained his own glass and put it down on the table, considering. "Would pain alone block the pathway?"

"No. That's the problem. Something else, some kind of magical or psychic interference or—" His gaze went to the lamps, and another connection formed. "Electricity. If he's somehow bound with electricity or held in one of their science labs, which we have to assume is filled with electrical equipment—" The obvious conclusion hit him with the force of a tsunami. "Oh, by all the gods, Lucas. What if they're messing with Brennan's brain? If their science conflicts with Poseidon's curse, it may destroy Brennan in the process."

"Stop. Stop thinking that way, it achieves nothing," Lucas said. "First of all, they haven't been missing that long, right? So it's unlikely that the scientists have had time to experiment on anybody. Plus they think he's Mr. Moneybags. They'll want to play nice with him, at least until they can figure out how to get their murdering hands on that money."

"If they haven't broken through his cover story," Alexios said grimly. "We don't know what they know or what resources they have. You of all people know that."

Two more of Lucas's wolves had gone insane during the night, one slaughtering his wife in their bed and then killing himself with knives. He'd gotten quite a lot of carving done before he finally died of the blood loss, apparently. Lucas, who had seen a great deal of violence in his life, had gone a little pale around the edges when telling Alexios about it. The second to succumb to the madness, convinced he was a were-hawk, had climbed very high up in one of the tallest trees near Pack headquarters and tried to fly. Even wolf shifters couldn't survive some things. The man was dead, every bone in his body shattered.

Lucas's face hardened. "When I get my hands on this Litton—"

"If it really is Litton. We don't have proof yet," Alexios

reminded him. "That's why Tiernan convinced Brennan that they had to go back. We all knew it was dangerous, we just thought they had a little bit of time before the noose tightened, since the scientists clearly believed Brennan to be who he claimed to be. Litton is desperate for funding."

"He can't get any from normal sources, since he's doing the mad science. No ethical companies, hospitals, or government organizations would fund him."

Alexios shot him a look. "The unethical ones are still a pretty deep pool. Especially with all the radical shifter hate groups springing up in the past few years."

"But he went for Brennan's bait. My best computer guy set up that billionaire businessman cover story," Lucas insisted. "It would take CIA-level access and knowledge to hack past it. I still think the cover story held."

Alexios crossed to the window and stared out into deepening shadows of dusk. "Then maybe that didn't matter anymore. If you can control the mind of a billionaire, you can have all of his money. Why take a mere ten million when you can have everything?"

"We'll find them," Lucas told him. "Now that Honey took the children and all the young and elderly away, we're left with only our best fighting force, and no worries about family to distract us. We'll find them."

"We'll find them, all right," Alexios vowed, his hands on the hilts of his daggers. "If we have to take every damn scientist in that entire conference hostage, we'll find them."

Chapter 26

Litton's labs, deep underground

Brennan slammed his body against the bars, and again the electricity zapped him so hard that it knocked him to the floor. This time, probably the dozenth, he stayed down a little longer. He was beginning to weaken and tire; an animal trapped in a cage, his much-prized logic and control gone.

Tiernan. The rage and terror built and built inside him, overwhelming him, driving him to escape, to protect her, and he was killing himself trying. But his frenzied mind had gone feral—insisting he had no other choice. He gathered himself for another charge.

"Brennan."

Just a single word, just his name, but it had the power to calm something; to soothe the edges of the madness long enough for him to look up and find her. They'd put her in the cage right next to him, and most of the guards still stood around the room, calling out taunts to Brennan and vile remarks to Tiernan.

She ignored all of it, an oasis of purity in the midst of the cruelty and violence. She ignored the guards and the cell and everything but Brennan, focusing her gaze on him so intently that he could almost feel the weight of it, tangible, upon his skin.

"Brennan, you have to calm down," she said, trying to smile a little, perhaps to offer reassurance. *She* was trying to comfort *him*, when he had let her be captured. Allowed her to be harmed.

When they escaped, he would spend the rest of his life making it up to her.

"I need you to be calm. For me. I'm freaking out here, and you're not helping," she said softly.

Shame swamped him. He must find his control, for her even more than for himself. He closed his eyes, searching for his serene center, but it was impossible. His newly found emotions were churning like a tempest at sea. He could manage a semblance of tranquillity—the thinnest of veneers—but no true calm. Not until he had her safe in Atlantis, preferably locked in his rooms, for the next hundred years at least.

"Brennan?"

He opened his eyes. She was so pale; her eyes dark and haunted. She needed him, she'd said. He'd be damned if he'd let her down.

"That man," she began, her voice soft and trembling. "I—I killed him."

He moved a little closer to the bars between them, a small movement so as not to attract the guards' attention. "I know. He was a monster. I saw him hurt your friend in that video. He deserved to die."

She flinched a little. "Is it so simple in your world? You just pick who deserves to die? No trial? No remorse? It's not like that for me."

He remained silent, not knowing how to comfort her. Emotion was too new to him—a foreign language in which he could not navigate nuance. Wielding words like blunt weapons would cause more harm than help now.

"And yet I killed him, you're thinking," she said. "But it

wasn't like that. I—I picked up that dagger to defend my-self when one of the guards came at me, and then you were there fighting them, and the lights were off, and I heard his voice and swung around. I was going to hit him, and, well, I guess I did hit him, but the knife was in my hand and . . ."

Her voice trailed off and she covered her face with her hands. He could tell she was sobbing, because each shaking movement of her shoulders fractured another piece off the edges of his heart. He needed to hold her, and there wasn't a damn thing he could do about it. The electric charge on the bars would kill a human with any prolonged contact. It had almost knocked him out, and he had an Atlantean war-rior's strength and endurance. He tried to find his calm cen-ter again, to analyze their options, but the only thing he came up with was, again, the obvious: they were in very deep trouble.

"We're kind of screwed, aren't we?" she said, unknow-ingly echoing his thoughts as she wiped her eyes with her sleeve.

"No. We are not. Remember that Alexios will be on his way to find us very soon." He put far more confidence in his voice than he felt. Alaric had told them that any type of massive electrical force would interfere with their abilities. Brennan studied the wiring connected to the bars and con-ceded that the entire setup certainly qualified as *massive*.

Oh, yes. They were definitely screwed.

"That was a lie. You don't believe Alexios is on his way at all, do you? I think we should—" Her eyes widened as she jerked her head up to stare at something over Brennan's left shoulder.

"How about you let me do the thinking," came the surly, accented voice from behind him. "These morons guarding you should let me do the thinking, too."

Brennan slowly turned and positioned himself so that he could see the new player but still keep Tiernan in his line of sight. The man was built like one of Yellowstone's bison. Thick, broad, all muscle and no neck. He wasn't quite as tall as Brennan but twice as wide, probably not an ounce of fat on him. He also was far from stupid; keen intelligence shone from his unusual gray eyes as he assessed the situation.

"I hear you've been making a run at the bars, over and over," he said to Brennan. "Want to tell me how you're not dead yet?"

Brennan said nothing, just swept a dismissive glance over the man.

"Right. Well, you're not a shifter, and you're not a vampire, and you're sure as hell not Fae, so I'm wondering what other kind of wee beastie we've caught in our net."

British. Or somewhere in the British Isles. Brennan hadn't heard "wee beastie" in several hundred years.

"A rich beastie," one of the goons called out, and the rest of them started laughing.

"Shut up, or I'll shut you up," the newcomer said, but without heat. He was still studying Brennan, who had the uncomfortable feeling that the man was trying to mind-probe him. Some definite psychic power there.

"Stay out of my brain," he growled.

The man laughed. "You'll wish it was me in your brain after Litton gets done with you. Crazy bugger is a menace. It really ought to be him locked up in here like an animal, but he's the one that signs the checks."

"Is money all you care about?" Tiernan called out. "You're willing to torture your fellow human beings for that monster—and all for *money*?"

The guards started laughing, but the British one did not. He simply trained that dead, measuring stare on Tiernan. "I'll do a lot of things for money. Nothing else matters, does it? And if you think your boyfriend here is human, well, I'd guess you're going to have a very interesting honeymoon."

"Yeah, Smitty, if they live to have a honeymoon. Odds are bad," one of the guards called out, to the loud amusement of his colleagues.

Smitty, if that's who he was, aimed that dead stare at the loudmouth, who quit laughing immediately.

So. This was the one of whom to beware. Brennan carefully noted everything about him. The time of reckoning would come, and soon. Smitty must be first in line to die. He was the biggest threat.

Smitty walked around the outside of the cages until he reached Tiernan's cell. "Begging your pardon, ma'am, but take your clothes off."

"What?" Tiernan moved away so fast that she nearly backed into the bars. Brennan called out a warning and she stopped, only a breath away from a massive jolt of electricity.

"You'd survive it," Smitty told her. "Once."

Brennan found that he was cursing; a steady, virulent stream of ancient Atlantean that should have singed the flesh off the man's bones. He switched to English. "Touch her and die. I will hunt you down, peel the skin from your body, and eat the beating heart from your chest if you touch so much as one hair on her head."

Smitty's head jerked up at the icy menace in Brennan's voice, and he, too, seemed to mark Brennan as the one true threat in the room. "I don't respond to threats, and I don't hurt women," he said flatly. "But these morons almost certainly didn't check you two for weapons, and I'm not going to wake up dead because your fancy piece there slipped a switchblade in my carotid artery, the way she did to that idiot upstairs."

"Carotid artery?" Tiernan repeated, and her face drained of all residual color until she resembled a ghost or, worse, a vampire.

Smitty grinned, displaying large, crooked teeth. "It's the artery—"

"I know what it is," Tiernan shrieked, an edge of madness in her voice. "I didn't do it, though. I didn't . . . I didn't mean it." She abruptly sat on the floor, pulled her knees up to her chest, and dropped her head down on them. "I'd like this day to be over now," she whispered, but Smitty heard her.

"Right. You can get some sleep in a few minutes, but first I want those clothes," Smitty said, producing a large and deadly looking gun from somewhere. "Do it now, or I'll shoot your boyfriend in the leg." He cast a dispassionate glance over at Brennan. "You're next, cupcake, so you may as well strip down now."

Brennan's rage consumed him, and he hurled himself at the bars, desperate to get at Smitty. The jolt from the high voltage seared through him, knocking him back several feet.

"Brennan. Brennan!" Tiernan was standing up now, pulling her shirt over her head. "Stop. It doesn't matter. None of this matters. We just need to get through it."

He stood there, his body shuddering with the force of the electrical shock and the fury, fighting to control himself, but when he raised his head, gasping for breath, he met Tiernan's gaze and the connection between them locked into place with an almost audible snap. He'd seen inside her soul, and he knew what she needed now.

She needed him to be in control—for her. There was no way in the nine hells he'd let her down.

The fury cooled to ice, and he nodded. "Yes. None of this matters." He yanked off his own shirt and then stripped out of his jeans as Tiernan did the same. The sight of her, trembling in her undergarments, triggered his rage again but he simply funneled it into the ice, to be carefully preserved for later. For when he fought his way free and killed them all.

The guards outside the cells were hooting and making lewd remarks, but most of them shut up when Brennan slowly turned his head and trained his gaze on them. Marking them. One by one.

Smitty held his hand through the bars, and Tiernan, stumbling, took her clothes to him. He took them and shook them, then patted them down for weapons.

"If you'd turn around, miss," he said, still emotionless. "I think you can keep your knickers if I can see all the way around that you're not concealing anything in them."

She hesitated, then held her hands out to her side and turned in a single revolution until she faced Smitty again.

"That's fine, then. Thank you," Smitty said. He handed Tiernan her clothes back and she yanked them away from him and moved farther back in the cell before scrambling into them.

Smitty turned to Brennan, saying nothing, and held out his hand. Brennan weighed the odds of Tiernan's survival if he grabbed the man's arm and pulled him tight against the electric bars until the high voltage fried the thug.

"Don't even think about it, mate," Smitty said, glancing from Brennan to the bars. "All those guns are trained on the two of you, and she dies first."

Of course the man knew what Brennan had been thinking. It's what Smitty would have considered had the roles been reversed, Brennan realized. His estimation of the man as a threat—which was already high—grew. He tossed his clothes at Smitty, then lowered his head and coughed, holding his hand over his mouth. When he straightened, Smitty was feeling along the seams of Brennan's jeans.

"Let me see your hands, and turn around," Smitty said.

Brennan glared but did as he said, spreading his fingers wide so Smitty could see that he concealed nothing. "You have my daggers, and nothing else would get past your metal detectors," he snarled from between clenched teeth.

"You look like the sort who could appropriate what he needed," Smitty told him. "You'll have to tell me how you got those daggers past my screener, though."

Brennan laughed. "Sure. Just let me out of here, and we'll have a long conversation about all sorts of things."

Smitty's grin was a dead thing, like his eyes. "Right. You keep on hoping."

He tossed Brennan's clothes back to him. "Now, if I were the bastard you think I am, I'd keep your clothes, and take your girl's lovely underthings, too, and let my men here enjoy the view."

"You're a real hero," Tiernan said bitterly, and Smitty turned to her and laughed.

"Ah, the little bird has a bite, does she? No matter. After what the doc has in store for you, I think you'll be chirping a different tune. Maybe even want to get to know me a little better." Smitty swept a long, appraising look up and down Tiernan's body, and the rage threatened to burn through the ice in Brennan's mind, but his control won out.

By a thread.

Smitty grinned at Brennan, then tossed him a mock salute. After that, he herded all but two of the guards from the room, ordering others to set up shifts in the monitoring room. Tiernan had been right about the video surveillance, then. Brennan decided he'd wait until Smitty left the room to try to find the cameras. The man was too sharp.

"Until later, mate," Smitty said, and then he sauntered out of the room.

Brennan toyed with the idea of trying to call water in the shape of ice spears, but the constant buzz of electricity reminded him of how futile the attempt would be. He'd have his chance. He'd simply have to be patient.

"Brennan," Tiernan said, moving closer to the bars separating them. Her face was still pale, pale white, as if fear had drained the blood from her head. "Whatever you're thinking, don't do it. I'm afraid that if you hit those bars again, it might incapacitate you, and—I know this is selfish—but I'm afraid to be here alone, if they knock you out. Especially since"—her voice, which had already been quiet, dropped even further until he could barely hear her—"when you wake up, you won't know me."

She stared up at him, and her eyes were enormous in her pale face. "I can't do this without you. I can't."

Brennan took a deep breath. "You will never, ever have to do anything without me, ever again," he swore.

"Now what?" She looked over at the guards, who were mostly ignoring them and arguing about some bet they'd made on sports, from the sound of it.

"Now," Brennan said, "we make a plan."

Chapter 27

Tunnels, deep underneath
Yellowstone National Park

Devon might have thought he currently stood in the worst situation in his long existence, had he not previously faced down insane ancient vampires and—only once, but that had been far and away enough—the vampire goddess herself.

This, however, was running in the top five.

If all of them made it out alive, it would be the first vampire conclave he'd ever attended where that was the case. Even the notion of vampires, who were notoriously unable to play well with others, forming alliances was ridiculous.

He spotted Jones over where the powerful vampire was holding court on one side of the long, bare room. Jones was the one who had discovered these tunnels more than a century ago and expanded them with the help of a large workforce of slave labor who later did double duty as food. Now only the bones of the dead workers knew the location of the vampires' meeting halls, and as everyone knew, dead men told no tales.

Unless the dead men were vampires. Then the tales were

not only told, they were embellished, or exchanged for outright lies.

He needed Tiernan Butler. Although, perhaps not. Her
Gift apparently did not extend to vampires or psychopaths.
Since many vampires were psychopaths, he idly wondered
if that made their lies more impenetrable to her or if the two
conditions canceled each other out. He'd have to ask her.

If he lived to ask anyone anything, ever again.

Smith drained the goblet of very fine brandy he'd been
sipping and slammed it down on the table. "Who was that
on the phone?"

Devon glanced down at the cell phone he'd just discon-
nected, then back at Smith. "It was Dr. Litton, our favorite
evil genius. He has captured Brennan."

"The rich human?"

"Precisely." Devon frowned. "I'd specifically told him to
hold off and play along, but he claims that the man insti-
gated violence."

"I wonder how Litton manipulated him into doing that,"
Jones said, sneering. "He is one of the most unpleasant of
the sheep I've ever had the bad fortune to encounter, but he
is a clever little bastard."

"Does it matter?" Smith asked. "We have our money
now, don't we? Isn't Brennan some kind of billionaire?"

Devon shrugged. "Perhaps. But how pathetic are we that
we hide in tunnels and depend on humans for our finances?
Which among us is qualified to be a leader if we cannot
fund our own plans?"

He knew that of every vampire in that room, he alone was
rich enough to take on any and all political challenge. Everybody else knew it, too.

Jones spat on the floor. "We know you have money,
Devon, you don't need to drop these heavy-handed hints.
But why spend our money when we can so easily control
the sheep?" He dropped an arm around his current blood
slave, a dim-witted bottled blonde who was the heiress to
some kind of soap products fortune.

Jones had always chosen his food wisely, but in spite of the string of rich women he'd enthralled over the years, he never managed to hold on to much of the wealth.

Why bother to save money when you could simply enslave another rich woman?

Devon struggled to keep his expression calm and not show the disgust he felt. "The question at hand is which of us will run for the office of Primator? The concern, of course, is that if the office lies vacant too long, the humans will begin to wonder if there is any need for a Primator at all. And if no Primator, then why a Primus? They muddled along with only two houses of Congress for more than two hundred years, after all."

Smith nodded. "Some of the humans are already making noises that we are too violent and unstable to be in Congress. Plus they're holding town hall meetings across the country, and there is very strong sentiment among those who dare speak up against us."

"The humans are less afraid to speak up since the rebels have been so successful on their many incursions against us," Devon said.

Jones hissed, his eyes glowing a vivid red. "We must squash these rebels once and for all. They are doing all they can to smash holes in our carefully constructed image of ourselves as law-abiding citizens."

"If they can get us kicked out of Congress, the laws protecting our rights are going to be repealed next," Devon said, widening his eyes as if this were the first time it had occurred to him.

"And the damn shifters will be in line to fill in the gaps. After all, they have powerful lobbies selling the idea that they're humans, just with a simple difference. A virus that makes them shift shape occasionally. They're not *dead* like we are," Jones said.

Devon swirled the blood in his goblet, then put the glass down on the table. Cold blood held no appeal for him. "If we control the shifters, all power is in our hands. The rebels will have no chance against an alliance of vampire and shifter."

Jones slammed his fist on the table. "Not an alliance. We don't ally with animals. We must control the shifters through this enthrallment procedure we've put so much time and money into. Only then can we count on total power."

Devon inclined his head. "Of course. Why do you think I am spearheading this effort? I merely was pointing out that the effort must look like an alliance to the outside world, or a panic would ensue. Ultimately, we are no match for missiles fired from air force jets or bombs dropped on our strongholds. Human technology has come a long way from stakes, burning torches, and pitchforks."

A couple of the older vampires in the room shuddered, probably at centuries-old memories of angry mobs of villagers holding just those weapons.

"What about Atlantis?" Jones suddenly asked.

Devon went still. "Atlantis?"

"There are too many rumors of vigilante warriors claiming to be Atlantean for us to ignore it," Jones insisted. "Certainly they were involved in that raid on the Primus."

Devon laughed politely. "Did they bring the boogeyman with them? Or possibly the tooth fairy?"

Jones snarled at him, baring his fangs. "Mock me if you will, but I know what I've heard, and only a fool ignores a very real threat."

"When I hear of a very real threat, I'll certainly pay attention. For now, can we put aside the idea of underwater fish men from the lost continent that Plato probably made up in the first place and get back to our plans?"

"I've had enough of talking about it," Smith said. "I say we vote. Right here and right now. Devon for Primator. None of the rest of us has the political connections or the money."

"That will change when we have this Brennan's money in our control," Jones challenged.

Devon shrugged, feigning a casualness he did not feel. "I don't want the job, but I'm willing to take it if you want me. Remember, though, that any vote is subject to one major contingency."

Some of them looked puzzled, and others looked scared, but only one of them had the courage to speak the name.

"Anubisa," Deirdre said, strolling over to Devon out of the corner from where she'd been studying the room. "Our not-so-benevolent goddess. Are you willing to be front and center on her to-do list, my love?"

Devon bowed over her hand and kissed it. "Anything for you, my darling."

She threw back her head and laughed, and the sound of it shivered ice down his spine. "Let's vote, then. All for Devon for Primator?"

Every hand in the room went up, save for Jones's; he only glared at Devon.

"If you want the job, please take it," Devon said, bowing gracefully.

Jones shook his head. "You know I don't. I just don't want you to have it, either. You're a slippery son of a bitch, and I can smell something wrong about you. I just don't know exactly what it is, yet." He studied Devon for another minute, but then shook his head. "When I find out, I'm going to enjoy ripping your heart out of your chest."

Devon smiled. "I look forward to the challenge."

Deirdre folded her arms over her chest and looked at Jones. "Vote. Enough with the drama. Yea or nay for Devon for Primator."

Jones slowly raised his hand, and then turned his thumb up.

Devon didn't let any of them see the relief that nearly weakened his knees, but he did bow to the room in response to the scattered applause.

"Congratulations, Primator," Deirdre said, casting a mocking glance at Devon. "Will we now get a sheep in every pot?"

"I thought it was chicken?"

"I don't like chicken," she said, shuddering delicately. "All those nasty feathers."

"Shall we go meet our new benefactor?" Devon held out

his hand and Deirdre lightly put hers in his. He'd pay, later, when they were alone, for putting her in this positon. Making her touch him.

"In a while," she said, showing her fangs. "All this talk of chickens and sheep has made me . . . hungry."

"Dr. Litton is waiting for us," Devon reminded her.

"Let him wait." She took his hand and made a show of dragging him toward the door, intent on eating something. Probably him. He plastered a fake leer on his face and confided as much to the vamps he passed on the way out, inviting the laugh.

Before they exited, he looked back at Smith and Jones. "We'll meet at the lab tomorrow night."

Smith nodded, but Jones just stared at him from hooded eyes.

When they hit the hallway, Deirdre continued to drag him along for quite a bit before she ducked into a side hall and jumped away from him, shuddering with disgust and frantically wiping her hands on her pants.

To remove any trace of the feel of him, undoubtedly. He ignored the familiar pain and pretended not to notice.

She finally stopped the compulsive wiping and looked up at him. "What's the plan?"

"We can't talk here. They could walk out any minute."

"We'll hear them," she said impatiently. "I'm watching the corridor, too. The plan?"

He listened for any sound of pursuit, but when he heard nothing, he shrugged and told her. "Their cover was blown or, if not, it doesn't matter. They've been captured. They've probably got allies coming, if they've had a way to contact anybody. We need to make plans, fast," Devon told her. "In my rooms, not here."

When they turned to leave the hallway, Jones was standing right past the corner, flanked by a half dozen of the vampires from his blood pride. Devon noticed right away that they were all wearing heavy leather gloves, and he knew, instantly, that this was going to be bad.

"Did you think one as powerful as myself couldn't mask the sound of approach?" Jones stared at Devon as if he really expected an answer.

"I didn't think you were powerful enough to wipe your own ass without assistance," Devon said, shrugging. "Surprise."

Jones snarled and his eyes glowed a fierce scarlet, but Devon had miscalculated. He hadn't provoked Jones into a personal attack. Jones made a hand gesture instead, and his minions came for Devon and Deirdre, who was making a steady growling noise, low in her throat, behind him.

Devon had been right. They had silver chains. It was bad.

Chapter 28

Litton's holding pens

Tiernan knew if she couldn't find a way to help Brennan calm down, he would lose it and kill himself battering his poor, abused body against those electric bars.

The room was a steel-and-concrete box, and the ceiling sloped oddly, making her think the structure wasn't much more than a cave or tunnel, as opposed to the foundation of an actual building. She'd heard rumors of a system of tunnels under Yellowstone, but it was usually in the same papers that ran with sightings of Big Foot, or celebrity alien babies, so she'd never paid much attention.

"Brennan, he was telling the truth. Smitty. When he said he doesn't hurt women, I mean, but the rest, too. Maybe we can use that," she whispered, keeping an eye on the guards.

"It won't matter, if he has his way," Brennan growled, his eyes glowing hot green. "You'll be enthralled and he won't need to hurt you."

She flinched at the idea, but then blinked. She suddenly understood why he'd spent so much time shielding his eyes or looking down at the ground. "Your eyes. Is that why he said you aren't human?"

Brennan's eyes faded to an ordinary, non-glowing green. "No. I can hide the power at will. He suspected something since I could withstand multiple contacts with those electric cell bars."

"We should be okay until morning, don't you think?" She glanced at the guards. "They don't seem interested in bothering us, at least for now, thank goodness."

"Smitty warned them off. He has an interesting value structure, for a mercenary killer." Brennan's gaze was never still, as he scanned every inch of the room. "You should try to get some rest," he said abruptly.

She almost laughed. "Like I'm going to be able to sleep now? Trapped in the mad scientist's evil lair? I've fallen down the rabbit hole, but instead of Wonderland, I'm in the middle of one of those really bad horror films." She pulled her knees up against her chest and rested her head on her folded arms. "If a killer tomato shows up, I'm out of here."

Brennan stared at her and then shook his head. "I have no idea what you're talking about."

"Probably better that way," she said, closing her eyes. A shiver suddenly raced through her body and she curled herself up even tighter. The concrete floor was cold and the room was freezing. She just hadn't had time to notice it before.

A moment later, something soft and warm landed on her head. She smelled Brennan and knew it was his shirt before she even opened her eyes. Pulling it close, she allowed herself a brief respite of imagining that the warmth of the fabric was the comfort of being back in Brennan's arms. Then she forced herself to let go—both of his shirt and of fantasies of what she could never have.

She held it out to him, trying not to stare at his muscular, bare chest. "I can't take this. You'll freeze."

He shook his head and shoved the long waves of his black hair away from his face. "My body temperature runs hot. I have no need of that and it might help you."

Memories of just how hot his body temperature was flashed into her mind, and her cheeks warmed up quite a bit. He smiled that slow, seductive smile of his, and she was afraid that he knew exactly what she'd been thinking about.

"Tell me about Susannah," he said, surprising her. "If you can bear to talk about her."

She thought about it before responding, but realized she really did want to talk about her friend. She never had before, except for the basics, to Rick and a few others. She'd had a friend who was a shifter. Who'd been killed in a confrontation with police.

Tiernan had never really told anyone about Susannah. She discovered that she wanted to share her friend with this man whom she might actually have been able to love, under different circumstances.

"She loved coffee, which was a great quality in a roommate. All day long, not just in the morning," she said, smiling at the memory. "All of those fancy, flavored kinds, you know. Irish cream and gingerbread spice. She'd surprise me on the weekend with breakfast in bed, sometimes, always trying to get me to try a new kind of coffee."

"She sounds like a wonderful friend," he said. "I cannot imagine Alexios bringing me breakfast in bed."

She laughed a little at the idea, but her smile faded as reality crushed in on her. She was trapped in a cell that she might never escape with her mind intact. She'd—she'd—

"I killed that man," she whispered, the image of his bloody body vivid in the forefront of her mind. "How can I live with that?"

She stared at Brennan, searching his face for answers. "How do *you* live with it?"

"You live with it because you have no choice. He was attacking you, and you were defending yourself. You did not intend to kill him, even though you had just seen him torturing your friend." He held out a hand, as if to reach for hers, but then lowered it before it touched the bars. "Tiernan, you have no blame in this."

"I know you believe that, but I definitely have blame," she said bitterly. "I dragged you into this through my arrogance that my crack undercover reporting would get us in, get the story, and get us out. All the blame goes on me."

Brennan's face hardened and, if possible, grew even grimmer. "And I am a warrior with centuries of experience in dangerous situations. Is not mine the greater fault?"

"But—"

"No. Enough of fault, please. Tell me more of Susannah. You said she brought you breakfast in bed. Was she a good cook?"

She pulled his shirt more tightly around her shoulders, sinking into its warmth and his clean, seawater scent for a moment before she answered. "I know what you're trying to do. You're trying to distract me."

"Is it working?"

"A little," she confessed. "The mind has an amazing capacity for denial, doesn't it? If I think about Susannah, I don't have to think about what might happen to me tomorrow."

"Tomorrow Alexios will arrive with Lucas and reinforcements, and we will be safe," he said, his eyes glowing hot again. "Tonight you will tell me about Susannah and then rest."

So she did. Susannah, who'd had an odd quirk of her own: she never lied. She was, in fact, a psychology major, studying lies and human behavior. Everyone else had seen her as rude and abrasive; total honesty was nearly impossible to live with in polite society. But it had been a wonderful quality in a friend and roommate for Tiernan. So peaceful to be around someone who never jangled her nerves with the discordant clamor of lies.

Tiernan had even liked Susannah's boyfriend. He was a nice guy. Easygoing. The only lies he'd ever told, at least around Tiernan, were of the "your hair looks great with that new cut" variety.

It had been a glorious, golden time. "Peace," she said, "is vastly underrated. Silence, too. For nearly four entire years, I spent most of my time, other than class or working, with Susannah, and toward the end of that time, with both of them. So much silence and peace and—even better—the musical beauty of utter truth."

"You had no other friends?"

She shook her head. "I didn't need any other friends. I tried, but I always had to escape when they'd start lying. I couldn't bear it anymore, you know? I'd been so spoiled by Susannah. She had a few other friends, which was great, since I enjoy time to myself, sometimes, so I'd hang out in our apartment when she went out."

"But something happened," he said, and it wasn't a question.

"Something happened. Yeah, that's one way to put it." She clenched her hands together, hoping to stop them from shaking. "Something happened, and then she died."

❧～～☙

Brennan needed to comfort his woman. He would have given his sword arm for the ability to break through the bars and lift Tiernan into his embrace, then vanish through the portal to Atlantis before the guards could raise a finger, let alone one of those damned guns. But the portal wasn't answering his call, he couldn't reach Alexios, and he was alone, completely powerless, trapped in a concrete cage far underground and far, far away from the haven of the Seven Isles.

If—no, not if. *When* he got her out of here, he was going to tie her down to keep her from taking any more risks. Just the thought of what she must have done before she met him was enough to turn his heart over in his chest. She was fearless and stubborn—a bad combination in a warrior, but at least a warrior had weapons training and the skills to get himself out of corners. A journalist . . .

He stopped, forced to admit the flaw in his logic. He was a warrior of great renown, and what good had training and skills done him? He was just as trapped as she.

"She was a shifter, as you saw upstairs before all hell broke loose," Tiernan said abruptly. "A fox shifter. But guess what? I lived with her for four years, and the first time I ever saw her in fox shape was on that video. The first time I even knew what she was?" She turned an anguished face to him. "The night she died."

"She never told you?"

"She hid it. I don't know how she managed, because she never lied to me, but she did. I never suspected a thing." Tiernan laughed a little, but it was a bitter laugh with little humor in it. "I never asked her, 'Hey, do you turn furry at the full moon and run around eating rabbits?' after all, but, still, you'd think one of those times she was out all night I would have caught something off about her story when she came home."

"It's not a normal thing to wonder about one's friend," Brennan said gently. "You should not blame yourself for not suspecting."

"It wasn't a normal thing until about eleven years ago. But now everything is normal. Friends who are shape-shifters. Police officers who are vampires. Vampires in Congress, for God's sake. Don't you think Thomas Jefferson and the Founding Fathers are rolling in their graves?" She narrowed her eyes. "Did you know Thomas Jefferson?"

He smiled, but shook his head. "No. I did, however, meet Sacajawea once. You remind me of her. The same fearless, adventurous, questioning nature. She would have liked you."

Tiernan's eyes widened, but he could tell she liked the idea. It pleased him to distract her, even for an instant, from the pain of her story and her fear about their current situation.

"That's the oddest, yet maybe the best, compliment I've ever gotten," she finally said.

He remembered something she'd said to him. "Stick with me, kid. You'll have a new experience every day."

Recognition dawned in her eyes, and she smiled. It was just a tiny smile, and it faded instantly, but it had been real. Real enough to let him know that she was strong and resilient and could survive this, just for a while longer. Long enough for Alexios to find them.

He refused to think about how, exactly, Alexios would find them when Brennan could not reach out on the mental pathway. Somehow, Alexios and Alaric would find a way. No matter if they didn't, either. All he needed was the slightest opening.

"That's the look," Tiernan said, lowering her voice even more as two new guards came in to relieve the pair on duty. "Your predator face. Oddly enough, it makes me feel safe."

They fell silent then, closing their eyes and pretending to rest, as the new guards spent some time near the bars, taunting them. It was easy enough to ignore them. They were nothing. Litton was the one in charge. Of the thugs, only Smitty had the power and the brains. None of the others had anything to say that Brennan felt it necessary to hear.

Brennan watched Tiernan through barely open eyes, afraid to close them for too long. Afraid that even a few minutes without her in view would trigger the curse. She was pretending to doze, but every line of her body was tense and held in readiness to defend against an attack. She had courage, his woman.

His mate.

He would never let her be harmed.

Time passed, perhaps half of an hour, and the guards grew bored with their games and retreated to the comfortable chairs over by the far wall, where they pulled out drinks and snacks and began a discussion of sports and women. Or women playing sports. They mentioned something called roller derby, but Brennan had no reference for the term.

It was irrelevant anyway. All that mattered was that they leave Tiernan alone, so perhaps she could get some actual rest. Her shoulders were slumped down and she seemed to be relaxed, so perhaps she truly had fallen asleep. He was glad of it. She needed rest.

She opened her eye, proving him wrong. "Susannah wasn't just a fox shifter. I mean, that wasn't all she'd been hiding from me. She was pregnant, too."

He took a second to get his bearings in the story that she'd taken up as though they'd never been interrupted. "Pregnant? This is hard to hide, even for humans, yes?"

She smiled a little. "Yes. Or, at least it's hard to hide after a certain point. She was still in her first trimester, and her belly was almost perfectly flat. I never would have guessed for quite a while, with the loose dresses she liked to wear anyway. It's not like we walked around the apartment naked, having slumber parties, right?"

Brennan lifted his head from his folded arms. "Could you perhaps elaborate on that last?"

She tilted her head. "What part? Oh, trimesters? It's—"

"No. The naked slumber parties, please." He flashed his best fake leer, and she laughed, just like he'd hoped she would.

"Been watching too many *Atlantean Girls Gone Wild* videos in your lonely old age?"

He nodded, heaving a deep sigh. "Alas, I am severely deprived of wild girls in any form or manner."

"How do you do it? How do you make jokes when we're . . . when things are so dire?" Her voice was steady, but her eyes were pleading.

"I do it because things *are* dire," he told her. "When the situation is at its most bleak, you discover your inner resolve. Laugh in the face of danger, life is darkest just before the dawn, and all of those horrible clichés that are no less true for being overused."

He cast a surreptitious glance at the guards and then eased the tiny vial Alaric had given him out of his pocket. "Also, I do it simply because I can. I have never been able to make jokes in two thousand years. You cannot imagine the tonic effect the simple sound of your laughter has on my wounded soul."

"Was that a joke, too? Your wounded soul?" She stared at him, all humor gone from her beautiful face. "Your speech patterns are so different. Sometimes you sound almost modern, and then you'll toss in one of those 'two thousand years' comments or 'wounded soul' and I'm thrown off."

"I cannot help that. Imagine if you had lived the first decade of your life in France, the next decade in Spain, and the next in Germany. Your French would have German and Spanish words mixed in, don't you think?"

She nodded. "I've heard you speaking another language. Is that Atlantean?"

He shot a look at the guards, but they were laughing about something and paying their prisoners no attention. "Yes, but let's keep that between us."

"Conlan told me as much, when I swore my oath of secrecy the first time I visited." Her gaze dropped to his hands, and her voice dropped to a whisper. "What is that?"

He slowly pulled the stopper free and shifted position, pretending to yawn and stretch, then he coughed. While his hand covered his face, he squeezed two drops of the potion onto his tongue. It immediately burned its way down his throat like liquid fire.

Whatever was in it, it certainly felt like it was working.

He shifted position again, stoppering the vial and hiding it back in his pocket. Hopefully they would not force him to strip again. He'd been lucky the first time, hiding the vial in his mouth when he'd tossed Smitty his clothes, but he doubted he'd get something past the mercenary a second time. Unfortunately, there had been intelligence in those cold, dead eyes.

Tiernan was still staring at him, but her eyes were narrowing and he could tell she was about to demand answers, so he forestalled her with a dollop of information and another question. "Alaric gave me a little pick-me-up to keep me from falling asleep. I can't afford to take the chance, after what happened this morning. Tell me more about Susannah. Was she happy to be with child?"

"Will it be enough?" she whispered, ignoring his clumsy attempt to change the subject. "Will it work?"

"I don't know, but I feel a surge of energy even as we speak," he said, and it was true. A wave of tingling heat was washing over him, shimmering sparkles through his vision until Tiernan appeared to have been dipped in silver gilt.

The image made his cock jump in his pants, which made him groan at the exceedingly inappropriate timing for his libido to make an appearance. Desire apparently did not care to give way to danger or even sheer impossibility.

"Brennan? What are you thinking?"

"Trust me, you do not want to know," he said, then turned the conversation back to somewhat safer topics. "Alaric gave me the potion, so it is almost blasphemy to think it would not do exactly what he ordered it to do."

"Do you really want to hear more about Susannah?"

"Only if you want to tell me."

Tiernan took a deep breath. "The main thing left to tell is that she's dead, and I killed her."

Chapter 29

Tiernan remembered that evening as clearly as if it had happened only the week before. Forcing the words past the lump in her throat was entirely another matter. The shock on Brennan's face for the few seconds before he'd schooled his expression back to his normal impassivity goaded her on, though. He needed to know.

She needed to tell it. Finally, *finally* tell it.

"I was working on a story. This story, in fact. The rumors of enthralled shifters had just started working their way around, and I had a source, and, well, I was hot on the trail. Staying up all night, fresh out of college, chasing down leads. The high—I can't begin to tell you what it's like. Believing you're a champion for the greater good—" She stopped, mid-sentence, realizing what she was saying, and to whom.

Brennan's lips were turned up at the edges. "I think I might have an idea," he said.

"Of course you do. Well, then, you *get* it in a way few people outside of journalism, or I guess police work or medicine, can. It's a calling. A need to help, to be part of something bigger than yourself. To right society's wrongs." She stopped and rolled her eyes. "Whatever. I'm babbling. But I was in the zone, on that high, and it was big. I could tell it was huge, and there was a Boston link. I had proof that a local scientist was involved in a conspiracy to abduct shifters and experiment on them."

Brennan leaned forward, his hands clenched into fists on his thighs. "You ran willingly into the middle of this?"

"More than willingly. It was my story. I was the lead, I wouldn't even share, for fear of being scooped. That night, I was supposed to meet a bear shifter who'd lost a friend to the abduction ring and had some information for me."

"A bear," he said, biting off the words. "A bear shifter, one of the most dangerous kinds of shifters."

She nodded, watching him carefully in case he made a move to slam his head into the bars again. His muscles had all gone tense and hard, like he'd be happy to thunk *her* head into the bars. She understood the cause, because she'd seen inside his soul. He had a protective streak a mile wide.

Except when it came to her. With her, it was as wide as the ocean itself.

It scared her even as it sent a thrill through her. Nobody had cared enough to want to protect her for a long time, except maybe for Rick, and even with him, the story always came first.

"Anyway, moving on," she said, "Susannah picked that night to tell me about the baby. I was thrilled for her and she was so happy and her boyfriend was so happy, and I guess she decided to just put everything on the table, so she told me she was a shifter. A fox shifter."

Brennan nodded. "This made you unhappy?"

"Not that she was a shifter. I thought that was kind of cool, had a million questions for her. But my mind couldn't get past the fact that she'd hidden it from me, for all those years. She'd known she was a shifter since she was thirteen years old—and for four of those years, she'd hidden it from me. Her best friend." She shoved a hand through her hair, frustrated, wanting him to understand. "We'd lived together, and all that time she never trusted me enough to share her deepest secret with me."

"It hurt you."

"It nearly broke me," she admitted. "I had a childish temper tantrum, to be honest. Yelled at her that she wasn't my friend, how could I trust her when she clearly didn't trust me, that kind of thing. I hadn't slept much in weeks, on the track of that story, and everything just exploded in my skull."

"You left for the meeting?" Brennan asked, his clear green gaze holding sympathy and something deeper. Shared pain. Of course. Corelia and the baby.

She nodded. "I did. The last thing I ever said to this woman who was closer to me than any sister could have been was that maybe I should just move out and leave them to be one big, happy family." She felt the hot, bitter tears slide down her face but didn't bother to wipe them away.

"She died thinking I hated her."

"No," Brennan said. "She died knowing you loved her. Friends and family argue and fight, but it means nothing. It's human nature. Love isn't perfectly patient or kind or sunny. Love is volatile and tempestuous and forgiving." He leaned forward. "She forgave you, Tiernan, probably before you ever made it out of the house. The woman you describe would have done no less."

A boulder the size of one of Yellowstone's bison suddenly lifted off of Tiernan's heart, because he was right. Susannah had never held a grudge, even when Tiernan ate the last yogurt or forgot to give her a phone message or screwed up in the hundreds of different ways a truth teller, overwhelmed by the demands of living in society, could screw up.

She belatedly realized she was using Brennan's term for her, and wondered if accepting his identification of her talent meant accepting that it truly was what he said. A Gift, instead of a curse.

But she hadn't told Brennan the rest of the story. Maybe he, too, would look at her with the same disgust she'd felt for herself since Susannah's death.

"I didn't tell her. I didn't warn her about the kidnapping ring, even though she'd just told me she was a shifter," she said quietly. "I ran out, angry, to go to my meeting, and *I didn't tell her.*"

The tears blurred her vision now, and she had to wipe them away with the corner of Brennan's sleeve.

"By the time I got back to the apartment a few hours later, ready to apologize for being such an ass, she was gone. I never saw her again."

"They captured her," Brennan said, the lines on his face deepening.

"They captured her. The next time I saw her was three weeks later on TV when she was in a fight with half of the Boston Paranormal Special Operations unit. She was so strong, Brennan—she threw one of them clear over a car. They—" She had to pause, to catch her breath from the pain cutting off her air supply.

He waited, giving her time, not pressuring her.

Finally she could breathe again and she met his gaze. "They shot her to death. Right there in the road. They said in a press conference that she was the one who had brutally killed a local politician, but I knew it was impossible. Until I linked the two, the mind control story I was working on and her abduction.

"If I'd told her—warned her . . ." The pain took her, and she buried her face in her hands, fighting to stay quiet and not attract the guards' attention.

"If you'd told her, she would have been careful, but she was young and in love, and they were and are a well-organized team of trained killers," Brennan said. "They would have taken her anyway. This is not your fault, Tiernan. Nobody but Litton and the monsters he works with and for are responsible for this. You did not kill her."

His words fell on her withered soul like a benediction, and warmth and light followed in their wake, breathing hope into the dark places in her heart that she'd feared could never be redeemed.

"I didn't kill her," she said slowly, forging another link in the chain that connected them. "Just like you didn't kill Corelia and her child."

His head shot up and a haunted expression darkened his eyes. "That's different."

"No, it's not. So either you admit that you don't bear the blame for Corelia, or you leave me alone with my guilt for Susannah," she fired off, desperate for him to find the same absolution he was offering her.

Wonder dawned, first in his eyes, and then his entire expression changed. Lightened. Almost as if a burden exactly like hers, or maybe one weighted down so much more, by two thousand years of gravity, was beginning to lift.

"You are more than I could ever deserve, Tiernan Butler," he said, his voice low and husky. "I will see you safely out of this hell if it is the last thing I ever accomplish in this life. You are mine, my revelation and my redemption, and I will never let you go."

The intensity in his voice shook her to the center of her being, but the memory of the vision she'd had in the soul-meld was still with her, still vivid. The baby he didn't—couldn't—recognize.

Maybe, just maybe, visions could be changed.

"I still want to have a chat with Poseidon," she said, but a yawn escaped in the middle of the sentence. Exhaustion and hunger were finally catching up with her.

"Rest now," he said. "I will watch over you, and we will discuss Poseidon when we escape from this trap in the morning."

She wanted to say that there was no way she could sleep on a concrete floor in a cell, with murdering thugs and evil scientists all planning horrible things for them, but her drooping eyelids proved she was wrong. So she nodded and curled up in the tightest ball she could manage, as close to the bars as she could safely be while staying out of range of accidently striking them in her sleep. Just before she drifted off, an idea flashed in her mind and wouldn't let go. She raised her head and looked at Brennan.

"Why don't you tell Poseidon that you're sorry? After all this time, surely he'd accept your apology, right? Even gods should be able to forgive."

He stared at her, his mouth opening, then closing, but he said nothing for the longest time. "Tell him I'm sorry," he said, as if the words themselves were a revelation. "You are a miracle, *mi amara*. You truly are."

She smiled a little and gave in to the waves of tiredness pulling at her. "*Mi amara* yourself, buddy. I know what that means, remember. And if you get me out of this, you can call me anything you want."

~~~~~~

Brennan managed to ingest two more drops of the potion, dismissing any slight concern of overdose. All that mattered was that he stayed awake to protect Tiernan.

To remember Tiernan.

The heat of manufactured energy rushed through his body again, sizzling through blood and bone. His skin itched and burned, and even his hair follicles tingled. It was unpleasant, but not to the point of pain; physically he was fine. Emotionally, however, was far different.

Emotionally, he was strained beyond endurance. Anger seared into rage, and fear for Tiernan's safety descended into pure terror. He stared at her, curled up in a huddled ball on the floor, and self-disgust for how he had failed her became utter loathing. He sat there, his body shuddering with the force of it, but he could have fought it. Could have beaten it. Except for yet another emotion.

Desire. Desire crescendoed into raging lust. His hands clenched with the need to touch her. Take her. Plunge his cock into the heat of her body and pleasure her over and over and over.

"Ah, look, the big strong guy is shaking. Think he's crying for his mommy?"

Brennan jerked his head up to see the two guards standing near the bars of his cell. He bared his teeth at them in a snarl, but they laughed. They *laughed*, and he knew he would kill them.

They spent several minutes at the bars, taunting and jeering, but thankfully Tiernan didn't wake up. When one of them made a crude suggestion of what they might do with Tiernan, Brennan lost all control and hurled himself at the bars. As before, the electricity slammed him back, but this time it nearly knocked him unconscious. The stimulant in the potion evidently stimulated everything—emotion, sensation, and even thought—because Brennan found his mind racing at the speed of a bolt of lightning, examining, analyzing.

Solving.

He would be still. He would not react. Another jolt of that electricity might kill him, and Tiernan needed him. He sat, stone-faced, and ignored the verbal abuse from the guards until, bored, they turned away and retreated to their chairs and their food.

He would endure, and then he would destroy, and Tiernan would be safe. Tiernan would be safe. He repeated it in his mind, over and over, and it became his mantra. Several hours later, when Litton arrived, Brennan was still repeating his vow.

Tiernan would be safe.

Litton walked up to the cell, standing a prudent distance from the bars. Apparently he'd heard about Brennan's repeated attempts to crash through them. A few seconds later, Smitty walked in, followed by several of his thugs, all armed with pistols.

"It's time to wake up, Ms. Baum," Dr. Litton said in a grating, singsong voice. "We're going to experiment on your lovely brain now."

Chapter 30

Brennan shot up off the floor, the berserker rage flooding his brain again. Must protect Tiernan, who was sitting up, groggy and blinking sleepily.

Smitty studied him like he was a rat in a cage. Maybe he was, but they would not harm his woman.

"You touch her, and you will pay," Brennan snarled. "I will hunt you down, no matter how long it takes, and I will torture you for years before I let you die."

Litton paled and danced back a few steps, but Smitty just smiled and gestured to the thugs and their guns. "Mouth making promises your circumstances can't keep? You're locked in a cage, and we've got guns. Try anything, and we shoot her first."

Tiernan scrambled to her feet and backed up. "Please. Dr. Litton. We're on your side, remember? I'm sorry I got carried away before, it's just that Susannah was my friend, but we agree with what you're doing and we can help. Brennan has money and I have contacts in the news and—"

"Shut up," Litton said. "You gave yourself away. Do you

think I'm stupid, to be deceived by a pretty story or a pretty face now?"

"You should relax, miss," Smitty said, not unkindly. "It hurts less if you don't fight."

Either Smitty's calm or Tiernan's fear evidently gave Litton courage. "I've changed my mind," he said, a cruel smile on his face. "Brennan goes first. We activate him, and not only will he sign over his fortune, but we can dispense with all this chest-beating nonsense."

Brennan dropped his hands to his side, in order to appear as nonthreatening as possible. "Yes. Take me. I will go quietly, just let her go."

Litton threw back his head and laughed. "Nobody is going anywhere. A journalist on the loose with this story? Right. I may as well shoot myself in the head now."

"Don't let us stop you," Tiernan said, and Brennan wanted to applaud.

"We're going ahead with this. Now. Get him out of here and strapped into the chair," Litton ordered Smitty.

Smitty didn't move. "Is Devon okay with this? I thought he wanted you to wait for him. I don't have any plans to run afoul of the top vamp in the region, you understand. I like having my full quota of blood."

Litton rounded on him, his eyes bulging. "You do what I say, do you hear me? We don't have to listen to Devon anymore, that pretender. Jones is in charge now, and he called me not twenty minutes ago and told me to go ahead. You answer to me, you overpriced bodyguard, so do what I tell you or get out."

Smitty stood calmly through Litton's tirade, even when the scientist started yelling at him. When Litton finally stopped, Smitty simply nodded. "You're the boss."

"Yes, I am. Don't forget it," Litton said smugly.

Brennan couldn't believe that the scientist, supposedly a genius, could be so completely unaware of reality. Smitty was no tame thug. The man could reach out and snap Litton's neck in an instant. Clearly, Smitty had a reason for being here beyond payment.

Or else the payment was really, really good.

Brennan had money, too. He could work with that kind of motivation if he got another chance to speak to Smitty alone.

He glanced at Tiernan, trying to communicate with his body language and facial expression that she would be safe. She was staring at him with such hopeless defeat that the pain of it knocked him back a step.

"Tiernan, it will be all right. I'll be back soon, and remember what I told you last night. Have faith in them. Have faith in me." He stared into her eyes, memorizing every detail.

"Brennan, if they take you away . . ." She stopped and glanced at Litton and Smitty. "You know what will happen. I'll—I'll do my best to remind you. To help you remember, okay? Don't worry." She offered him a shaky smile of reassurance, and again he was knocked off balance.

She wasn't afraid for herself. She was afraid for him.

"This is very touching, but I'm afraid it's time to go," Smitty said. He nodded to the guards over by the control monitors. "Turn it off."

They did something, and suddenly the constant buzz of electricity shut down. It was so abrupt that Brennan almost missed his chance. He froze for a moment, but then blasted an emergency call through the mental pathway so loudly that Alexios would surely hear it—unless he'd gone back to Atlantis.

Come now. They have Tiernan and they're going to try to manipulate our brains. Come now. He tried to give a visual of their location, but by then Smitty was advancing into the cage, holding out a small metal device.

"Let's not try anything, shall we?" Smitty said. "You'll notice that my chums have their guns trained on your lady friend, and they're all trigger-happy. It's so hard to get good help these days."

Brennan tensed, every fiber of his being wanting to pounce, to kill, to rip Smitty's arms off and use them to beat Litton to death, but Tiernan made a small noise and he turned to see that four of them were all lined up around her cage, pointing their guns at her head and chest.

There was no way they could miss at that range.

He nodded. "Yes, I will go willingly." He put his hands on top of his head and clasped them together in the universal posture of a prisoner, but then he pinned Smitty with a look that held every bit of his intent. "I will hold you responsible if any of them hurt so much as a single hair on her head."

Smitty slitted his eyes nearly shut and grunted noncommittally. It was the best he was going to get, so Brennan walked slowly out of the cell. Litton scurried out of the way, careful to stay several paces away from Brennan. So. The man had at least some wisdom.

Before he left the room, he stopped and looked back at Tiernan. "Trust me," he said.

"I do," she replied, tears streaming down her face. "With my life."

Brennan nodded, vowing to Poseidon himself that he would honor that trust. Then he followed Litton out of the room.

They led him only a short way down the corridor to another room, this one enormous, all white walls and gleaming metal, with the astringent smell of chemicals permeating the air. Litton rushed over to a huge chair that dominated the room, all but dancing around it like a pagan preparing for a human sacrifice.

Brennan knew who the sacrifice was going to be. He knew an instant of pure, icy terror, and adrenaline shot through his veins, kicking his fight-or-flight instincts to a frenzied peak. Smitty narrowed his eyes and raised his gun, but Brennan had no fear of the weapon. He had no fear for himself. Every ounce of that terror was for Tiernan, left alone in that cell.

If he died, she would be alone, and she would suffer for it. Therefore, he must live, no matter what they did to him.

He must survive it.

They strapped him into the chair, and he didn't struggle.

Didn't fight. He sat passively, restraining the rage and the need to kill them all. But he couldn't completely hide the berserker inside him. Anyone who bothered to look in his eyes saw it and involuntarily stepped back from the intensity of the hatred staring out at them.

Everyone but Smitty. He just nodded, recognizing a fellow predator, and continued strapping Brennan down to the chair.

Litton approached to put the metal helmet on him, and an instant sense of claustrophobia clawed at Brennan, in a way that the hours in a cell had not. He strained at the leather bonds holding him to the chair, suddenly mindless, knowing only that he had to escape, had to find a way, couldn't let them get to his brain.

One of the guards made the mistake of coming just that fraction of an inch too close, and Brennan reared back and smashed his head into the man's face. He shouted in triumph at the crunching noise and the guard's scream, then whipped his head around to where Smitty stood on the other side of the chair.

"Can't say I blame you, mate, but can't have that," Smitty said. Then he lifted his hand and touched the metal box to Brennan and a powerful, painful jolt of electricity seared through his body, arching him off the chair and locking his clenched jaw in place so hard his skull ached from it.

When the buzzing and the pain stopped, Brennan found himself wavering at the edge of consciousness, unable to move or fight. Unable to protect Tiernan, his mind thundered at him. *Failed, failed, failed.*

Then Litton laughed and came closer and closer, holding up that godsdamned helmet. "It will be all better soon, Mr. Brennan," he crooned, as if talking to a child. "All better—for me."

With that, he slammed the helmet down on Brennan's head and began attaching electrodes. Brennan tried to struggle again, but his muscles didn't want to obey his brain's commands, and after a few seconds, Smitty reminded him of why he must not struggle.

"They've still got those guns pointed at your woman. Do you really want to give us a reason?" Smitty's dead eyes held something for an instant—maybe a flash of empathy—but then it vanished. "You know I'll give the order."

Brennan fell back against the chair, and he didn't move again until they turned on the machine and the electricity shooting into his skull from the helmet sliced his brain into pieces.

He couldn't help it. He started to scream.

Chapter 31

The first lightning bolt seared through his mind and Brennan's consciousness shattered, pulled in so many different directions he couldn't breathe. Couldn't find a balance. A kaleidoscope of visions fractured through his mind: Atlantis, Tiernan, Alexios, Tiernan, Conlan and Riley, the baby, Tiernan.

Always back to Tiernan. He knew he had to hold on to her image, to her memory. Must keep her fresh in his mind, no matter what.

"Turn it up," somebody said, a gleefully evil voice, and he knew the voice, knew the man. It was Litton. Dr. Litton. He was fiercely glad to have found the name, but then the lightning struck again and it vanished.

Someone was shouting or screaming, somewhere close, but it wasn't until he tried to swallow that Brennan realized it was him. He was screaming. He was in so much pain that it would surely split his skull in two at any moment.

A face appeared in his field of vision and the pain ceased,

blessed relief, and then the face spoke, and it was a strange voice, a voice he instinctively hated.

"I'm your friend, Mr. Brennan. I'm here to help you," said the voice, but the face was wrong, the face was Litton, and Brennan lunged at him, forgetting the restraints.

"Not enough," the face said, sly and pretending a regret that it did not feel. That Litton did not feel, Brennan reminded himself; he couldn't lose touch with reality. It was not just a disembodied face talking to him, but that monster Litton, and they still had Tiernan, and he must endure.

Must endure.

The lightning spiked again, screaming through his brain, and he tried to hold on to the faces, to the memories, of his family and his friends. Of . . . the woman. The woman—he saw her face. Her lovely dark eyes and her creamy skin. Her dark silky hair that he longed to wrap around his fingers again, as he once had—Tiernan. He found her name in the fragments of his mind and offered a prayer to Poseidon—no, not Poseidon.

Why would he pray to Poseidon? Poseidon's curse— something about Poseidon's curse—

The lightning struck again. And again, and again, and again.

Each time it stopped, the face came back. The face talked to him. Told him it was his friend.

Each time he denied it.

Finally the face grew enraged. Screamed in Brennan's face. Told the lightning to go to its highest level.

Someone, another voice, said things. Red zone. Danger. Other words that should have had meaning, but the only meaning left was the lightning. The woman. What woman? Had the lightning killed the woman?

The face came back. It was oddly purple and its eyes were bulging. "Remember this. I am your friend, and you will do what I tell you. Can you remember that?"

Brennan could remember nothing, not even the woman. The woman? But a long-dormant memory from a very long time ago came to him and he nodded. "Yes," he said, but his voice was rusted and ruined and he didn't know if the face heard the words. "I can remember."

The face smiled. And then the lightning came again and shattered the entire world until it faded to black.

⌒〜───⌒

Brennan opened his eyes, to find that he was lying in a chair. He remembered the chair. The lightning came to the chair. His mind was a muddle of confused impressions and conflicting impulses, torn between the imperative of his oath to Poseidon and the longing to believe the face. No, not the face. Litton. Dr. Litton. Brennan's friend.

He turned his head and saw Litton, sitting in a chair near a bank of computers, talking to another man. The second man was familiar. Dangerous. Smith. No, Smitty. Smitty. The one to beware.

Too late for that. Sanity slowly, painfully returned, even though his mind remained a fractured nightmare. He knew who he was, and where he was.

He knew he had to play along.

Litton turned and saw that he was awake. He and Smitty got up and crossed the room to stare down at Brennan, who realized he was still restrained in the chair.

"Do you know who you are?" Litton asked.

"Brennan," he croaked. "Water."

Litton nodded and one of his flunkies brought water with a straw and allowed Brennan a few sips before taking it away.

"Do you know who I am?" Litton's gaze sharpened, and he held his breath.

Brennan stared at him for a few long moments, wanting to make it believable. "Litton," he finally rasped out. "Dr. Litton. My friend."

Litton's face transformed and he actually clapped his hands. "I knew it. I knew he would succumb, Smitty!" He clapped Smitty on the back and only Brennan saw the murderous glint that flashed for a second in the mercenary's eyes.

"Really? I don't exactly trust it," Smitty said, staring down at Brennan. "Seems a bit too convenient."

Litton snorted. "Convenient? You fool, you know nothing about science. No human has ever needed this much before. He took as much as the strongest shifters we've had in here. Whatever mutant anomaly he happens to have in his brain, we've overcome it. He's ours."

The man reached out and actually caressed the side of Brennan's face, and it took everything in two thousand years of discipline to keep him from biting a chunk out of Litton's hand.

"Aren't you, Mr. Brennan? My friend?" Litton said, again in that crooning voice that made the bile rise in Brennan's gut.

The effects of the machine had caused him to be so nauseous that he wanted to vomit. He smiled instead. "Yes. My friend," he said, his voice a little stronger. "Sleep now?"

"Yes. You should sleep now. We have your quarters all prepared for you." Litton nodded at Smitty, who ordered a guard to unfasten Brennan's restraints.

They helped him up, but Brennan noticed Smitty and another guard stayed well back, out of his reach, even though they were again pointing their guns at him. They had to help him walk at first, but he managed to stumble his way back across the corridor.

When they entered the same room where he'd stayed all night, he realized they were putting him back in the cell. "Cell?" he said, balking at the doorway. "Not a room? Need a bed."

"We've moved a cot in there, and a bathroom," Litton said smoothly, and Brennan turned to look. Sure enough, a cot, complete with blankets and a pillow stood on one side of the cell. A guard held the cell door open, while another opened a door in the back of the cell that he hadn't noticed the night before, probably because it was simply part of the wall. It must have had a hidden mechanism with which to open it. He could see past them to the small bathroom contained within the room.

A small noise, like that a wounded animal might make, caught his attention and he turned his head to look. A woman stood, trembling violently, in the cell next to his, her door still locked. She stared at him, and he felt the tiniest hint of recognition in his mind. Did he know her?

Whoever she was, she was pretty. She might even have been beautiful if her face hadn't been so pale and tearstained and her eyes so red. She must be afraid . . .

She must be . . .

But the wisp of memory floated back out of his mind, and he had nothing to offer her of reassurance or hope. Not even he, a trained Atlantean warrior, was able to escape this nightmare. What hope had she?

"Brennan?" she said, her voice shaking with some violent emotion. "Are you okay? Do you . . . do you know me?"

A flash of something crossed his mind. A name? A feeling? But then it vanished and all he was left with was utter weariness. He shook his head. "I'm sorry. I'm very tired."

Litton grabbed his arm and stared up at him, then shot a look at the woman. "That's Tracy Baum. You came with her. There's no reason your long-term memory should be affected," he said, staring into Brennan's eyes. Suddenly he recoiled.

"His eyes. Look at his eyes," Litton said.

Smitty came around to the front of Brennan and stared into his eyes, then slowly backed up and trained his gun, in a double-handed stance, on him. "They're glowing," he said flatly. "Maybe now we'll find out just what kind of wee beastie we've got."

"He's not human?" Litton backed up in a rush. "But— but he's not a shifter."

Smitty shot a look of thinly veiled disgust Litton's way. "There's a lot more out in the big, bad world than just shifters and vampires, you know."

Brennan wanted to ask the man how he knew, or what he knew, but suddenly black was spiraling in from the edges of his vision and he stumbled again, nearly falling. "Am tired, friend," he told Litton.

"Get him in the cell," Smitty ordered, and two of the guards rushed up to help Brennan in. They shoved him onto the cot, and he tried to remain upright but he fell over onto his side.

The woman rushed to the bars dividing their cells, and she was crying harder. Her pain caused a terrible, answering ache in his chest, and he did not know why.

"I'm Tiernan, Brennan. You have to remember me. You have to remember."

Tiernan? Something sparked, a tiny flame deep in the blackness trying to claim his consciousness, but it was quickly extinguished by the exhaustion and residual pain. Every muscle in his body ached as if he'd been smashed by a tidal wave.

"What did she say?" Litton said. "Tiernan? What is that? We know who you are, Ms. Baum. *Tracy* Baum. What is that word, Tiernan? Is it a code?"

The woman started laughing, the tears still pouring down her face. Brennan struggled to stay awake, sure that whatever she had to say was somehow important to him, but she collapsed down to her knees on the hard, hard floor.

"Yeah, it's code," she finally said. "It's code for we're totally screwed."

Brennan wanted to help her. She looked so very sad and terrified as they opened the cell and went for her. He knew his mission. He must protect humanity. He was a warrior of Poseidon, and Conlan had sent him to . . . sent him to . . .

But there was nothing. His mission was gone and his mind was blank, and even as he struggled, the dark took him yet again. As he fell down into the darkness, he heard the woman scream.

Chapter 32

Atlantis, three days later

Alexios paced the war room, ignoring Grace's hand signals that he should calm down or sit down or, knowing Grace, go bang his head against the wall to let off some steam. If he didn't move, he was going to explode.

"We've searched everywhere. After Brennan nearly blew out my brain cells with that mental blast, there was nothing. Just that weird buzzing again. I need Alaric, Conlan. I'm not powerful enough to do this without him, and Brennan is in serious trouble or he'd be answering me."

"Are you sure?" Conlan drummed his fingers on the table. "The curse broke and his emotions . . . Maybe he wants some time alone with Tiernan?"

"In the middle of a mission? Are you nuts?" Alexios stopped, remembering he was talking to his high prince. "I'm sorry, Conlan, but I'm really worried here. I need you or I need Alaric or, preferably, both of you."

Conlan stood up in an explosive movement and suddenly hurled his cup across the room, where it shattered on the wall. He whipped around to face Alexios, and his eyes were wild. "Do you think I don't know that? That I'm not worried, too? Brennan is one of mine, Alexios, just like you and Bastien and Denal, Justice and Ven, and hells, even Christophe. The responsibility for each and every one of you lies squarely on my shoulders."

Alexios shoved his hair out of his face, heedless of his scars. Conlan had seen them before. "He was mine to protect, but I got there too late. We've searched everywhere for him and for Tiernan, but nothing. Nobody saw anything, nobody knows anything. Nothing."

"Where is Litton?" Grace asked. "Or that turd Wesley?"

"Nobody has seen either of them," Alexios said. "Lucas's computer guy is tracking down Wesley's home address. Litton dropped off the grid when he founded this company. He seems to live there, too."

Conlan nodded, closing his eyes. A full minute later, he looked at Alexios, who had to squint against the power shining from the prince's eyes.

"He's on his way," Conlan said. "Alaric. He's bringing some of the local rebels with him. They seem to think it's going to be a fight, that there is some kind of underground fortress. Quinn will meet you at Lucas's headquarters."

"Quinn knows Lucas?"

"Quinn knows everybody," Grace informed them. "How do you think she got to be the leader of all rebel groups in North America?"

"And you?" Alexios asked Conlan.

"I," Conlan said grimly, "apparently am called to a command appearance before the High Court of the Fae."

"Seelie Court?" Alexios asked.

"I wouldn't even consider going if it were Unseelie Court," Conlan snapped. "Not with Riley and Aidan—no. Just no."

"This, however, is an offer you can't refuse," Grace muttered. "Trust me, I know way more than I want about the Fae."

Alexios shared a look with her as they both remembered the last time they'd encountered Rhys na Garanwyn, high prince, High Court, Seelie Fae. He'd pulled a Rip Van Winkle on them, as she called it, and they'd briefly been afraid that he'd stolen years of their lives. Instead, he'd stolen something they still hadn't been able to identify, from a very unpleasant vampire, and then left Grace and Alexios to face the consequences.

Honor had a very different definition to the Fae than it did to the Warriors of Poseidon. They couldn't lie, but they never told the truth. They laughed at the very idea of loyalty. No, Alexios had no desire to see any Fae, ever again. If Rhys had put out a royal request to meet, though, it was tantamount to a declaration of war between Atlantis and the Fae if Conlan refused.

"When do we meet Quinn and Alaric?" Alexios said, heading for the door, Grace right behind him. There was another fight he was going to face: telling her that she could not risk herself and the baby in a fight, even to rescue Brennan.

"The sooner, the better," Conlan said. "And Alexios?"

He stopped, one hand on the door. "Yes?"

"Bring them home."

Alexios could only nod, humbled by the pain on Conlan's face. "I swear it," he said.

Chapter 33

Brennan walked into a wall. Again. He kept smashing his face into hard surfaces. After the first few times he'd run into the cell bars, they'd shut down the electrical current, because they were afraid he'd inadvertently kill himself.

He didn't want to kill himself. He didn't want to keep running into walls. Something in his brain was directing his body in ways over which he had no control. He was a puppet to whatever they'd done to his caudate nucleus—yes, he remembered the scientific name for that small pea-shaped structure in his brain that was causing all of his trouble.

He didn't want to kill himself, but he didn't particularly want to live, either. He was indifferent to anything, except for the lightning. Over and over, for hours or days or weeks, he didn't know which, they'd put him in that chair and called the lightning.

He, Brennan, had once been able to call the lightning. It was a fleeting memory, or more probably only a fantasy. There was nothing left but such fleeting memories.

Those and the lightning.

He heard a sound, but took a moment to place it, then dully turned his head to see if she was still there. He'd forgotten her, again. His world had narrowed to the lightning and the woman, and it struck him as somehow desperately wrong that he kept forgetting even the woman.

She was in the other cell, and he did not know her name, but when she looked at him and called his, a tendril of knowledge tried to unfurl, deep, deep in his soul. About her. About who she was.

Who she was to him.

But then the haze would settle over his mind again, because the lightning left no room for memories. Only for obedience, and he could not give it that. Everything else, but not that. Not yet. Maybe not ever. He had sworn an oath to a god, and no machine could override that, no matter how much it scrambled his brains.

They didn't take the woman to the lightning as often. She was human, not . . . what he was. Not Atlantean. Not a warrior. He looked at the bars again and reached out to touch one, feeling only cold metal and not the surge of electricity. Thinking there was something he should know about the bars, and something he should be doing.

He couldn't remember, though. His mind was empty of so much, and even his emotions, which for some reason he knew should be important to him, had been dulled.

The woman, too, had lost hope. For the first hours, or days, she had called out to him. Called his name. Talked to him constantly; told him stories of himself and of her. Of the two of them, together. Her name was Tracy, or maybe Tiernan. She knew him, and he knew her, she claimed.

She was wrong. He only knew the lightning. He feared it less now. Almost welcomed it. Everything else was dull and gray, and he kept hoping now that the lightning would take him to the waters of the ancestors. He was ready to end the cycle of cell and chair and cell and chair.

Except, he was not. Not quite yet. He couldn't give up. He didn't know exactly why, only that he should be helping the woman. He was a Warrior of Poseidon. It was his duty and his calling.

The men opened the cell, but not his, so it was not the lightning. It was late; he knew that somehow even though the cells had no windows. The guards on duty at night were worse than the others. Rougher. Louder.

They entered the woman's cell, and Brennan sensed danger. Danger to her. A primal instinct to protect seared through his mind and the fog slowly cleared. Memories flooded his mind, and his heart, and his soul, dragging pain and shame and horror in their wake. Dredging up the memories. The first clarity he'd known in such a long time burned the rest of the haze from his mind, and he remembered. For the first time in days, he *remembered*.

"Hey, pretty lady, we just want a little bit of fun," one of them said, shoving the woman—*Tiernan*—into the arms of the other. "We're bored here every night, all alone. Why don't you be nicer to us?"

She didn't even scream. She'd given up all hope of rescue or help, even from him, Brennan realized.

One of the thugs reached out and ripped the sleeve of her shirt away, and Brennan threw his head back and roared out a challenge. The guards jumped away from Tiernan and whirled around to stare wide-eyed at Brennan.

"What the hell? He's been damn near comatose for three days," one of them said, reaching for his gun.

"Maybe he's going crazy like those shifters," the other one said, yanking Tiernan in front of him to use as a shield.

"It's my turn," Brennan said, clarity returning in a searing rush, and he called the power. Everything that he was and ever had been answered his call, jumping to his use to protect his destined mate. She had been right here all of this time, enduring unimaginable suffering. Giving up hope.

They would pay. They would die.

"Settle down," the coward who had Tiernan said, his voice rising. "Stop doing that glowing thing with your eyes. Stop it or I hurt her."

Brennan formed the water into spears of ice in his mind before he ever forced them to materialize. When they did, they were already in motion, slicing through the air at the speed of sound. The guards were dead, both impaled through the middle of their foreheads, before they ever hit the ground.

Tiernan stared at him, stunned, unable to believe what she saw. "Brennan? Are you—are you back?"

"I'm back, and I owe you a thousand apologies, but we must leave. Now. The keys?"

She bit her lip, but didn't waste time arguing, just bent to search the guards' pockets, coming up with the keys. She quickly opened his cell, but backed away from him, her eyes wary, when he would have gathered her in his arms.

"Fair enough," he said, knowing he deserved nothing more from her, after he had failed her so badly. "Now we escape."

"It can't be as easy as that," she said, but she handed him the keys readily enough and watched as he put one of the dead guards on each of their cots, then covered them in blankets.

"It's less than nothing as a ruse, but maybe it will buy us a minute or two," Brennan said, locking the cell doors.

She ran over to the bank of computers. "There are monitors here, of the corridors and the lab." A grimace crossed her face. "That damn chair. I'd like to come back here with dynamite and blow that thing out of existence."

"We will," he promised her. "We will come back and make sure Litton never, ever harms anyone again."

"We can head down this corridor, it might be an exit." She pointed to the one in the opposite direction from the lab. "I doubt there are guards everywhere, this late at night. After all, they believe we're safely locked in our cages."

She clenched her fists on the console, and her ripped sleeve hung free of her shoulder. "They will never get me in that cage again. I'd rather they just shoot me."

"Never again," Brennan agreed. "Now we run, before

Litton gets back with more of his thugs. Or Smitty, which would be worse."

She nodded, then touched his face so briefly he barely felt it. "Oh, Brennan. I thought you were lost."

"Never," he swore. "You will never, ever lose me."

She nodded, but there was still no belief in her eyes. "Now we run," she said, and headed for the door.

Chapter 34

The central salon of Mr. Jones, deep underneath Yellowstone National Park

Litton, at that very moment, was wishing to be somewhere, anywhere, else. These vampires were monsters, torturing one another indiscriminately. What kind of creature did that for no reason other than some perverse pleasure?

Although, if he had to watch anyone being tortured, it wasn't that much of a hardship when it was Devon and that snotty bitch female vampire who went everywhere with him.

The pair of them hung by their arms from silver chains. Litton could tell the chains were silver by the way smoke curled up from the vamps' skin. That must be incredibly painful. He'd wondered in the past if vampires could even feel pain, since they were, of course, dead, but from the look of Devon and Deirdre, they definitely could.

It was Litton's first time in Jones's quarters, and he tried not to stare around him like an ignorant yokel on a trip to the big city. Velvet and silk hangings covered the walls of what was, basically, a cave. Paintings stood up against walls, or on shelves, everywhere. Litton was no art connoisseur, but some of those looked real. As in originals, should-be-in-museums, worth-millions-of-dollars real.

Why did they need Brennan's money so bad when these guys had this kind of wealth?

"Vampires keep what is theirs, human," a voice hissed in his ear. Litton jumped almost a foot in the air, and the vampire who'd spoken, Mr. Smith, laughed, displaying very sharp fangs.

Jones dropped the pincers he'd been using on Devon's ear and whirled around so fast that Litton almost didn't see him move at all. "Why are you here?" he snarled at Smith.

Litton backed away, getting clear of the path between the two.

"I'm here for him," Smith said, inclining his head toward Devon, who raised his head and looked up.

Litton gasped at the vampire's appearance. Devon's skin was shrunken to the bones of his skull, and he looked as though he'd aged more than a hundred years in a few days. Litton couldn't believe he was even conscious or still alive. Well, alive in his undead way. He'd been tortured, and not just with pincers, either. Gashes and bruises and blood covered his face, body, and what was left of the rags of his clothes. But he was still alive, and conscious, and directing a stare of such burning hate at Jones that Litton wondered the vampire didn't spontaneously combust.

Deirdre had not fared so well. She hung limply in her chains, either unconscious or dead, the front of her dress ripped and her chest and belly covered with similar bruising, wounds, and blood.

Devon licked his lips, then met Smith's gaze. "Release me so I can kill him and his territory is yours."

Smith nodded. "Good enough for me." He raised a hand and a swarm of vampires flew through the doorway into the room, all attacking Jones en masse. Litton scrambled under a table and pulled a tapestry around and in front of him, praying that they would forget he was there. He sat, huddled in on himself, shaking with terror, trying not to think what so many vampires would do to a human they found in their midst when they were in the middle of a blood frenzy like these obviously were.

Jones put up a hell of a fight, for being so outnumbered, but once one of the vamps ripped the silver chains off of Devon, it was all over. Emaciated and weak from hunger and torture—it made no difference. Devon went after Jones, and the next thing Litton saw was Jones's head rolling down the middle of the floor toward him, stopping only when it hit his feet.

"Oh, God, oh, God, oh, God," he stammered, knowing it was the end for him.

Devon, who had immediately ripped the chains off Deirdre and now stood cradling her in his arms, stared across the room at Litton. "You were here to report, Dr. Litton. So report."

Litton blinked, afraid to answer. Afraid to breathe. Also afraid he'd pissed in his pants. He froze, not moving or speaking.

Smith's face appeared as he bent down, grabbed Litton's ankle, and yanked him out of his hiding place.

"I said, report," Devon repeated, and there was something in his tone that told Litton he would not repeat himself again.

Litton scrambled to his feet, cursing all vampires in his mind, and himself for ever getting involved with them. "Brennan is ours, sir. He took so long, and Smitty thinks he's some kind of creature, not quite human, but the scans say human, and anyway, three days of treatments at max was long enough. He's docile enough, and he'll sign anything we want. We can begin transferring his funds to the institute's accounts."

Devon nodded. "Good. Make sure he is unharmed. No more treatments until I can evaluate him. We may want to use him as the public face of our research, along with yourself, of course, and if he's a drooling idiot, it would defeat our purposes."

Litton nodded and bobbed his head, practically bowing, anything to get out of there alive.

"Mr. Smith, would you be kind enough to ensure Dr. Litton makes it back to his lab safely?" Devon shifted his grip on Deirdre, but did not put her down. "I worry that a hungry vampire might . . . detain him."

Smith laughed. "How do you know I won't detain him?"

Devon's smile was less than reassuring to Litton, who already hated him. "All in good time, Mr. Smith. All will come to those who stand by my side."

Smith cast a cool, assessing glance around the room and then down at Jones's head, still lying on the floor but slowly dissolving into slime. Litton felt his belly lurch at the sight of it.

"I like to back the winning horse," Smith said.

"Don't we all?" Devon replied. "Now go."

They went.

Chapter 35

Yellowstone National Park, Pack Headquarters

Alaric materialized from the mist in the shadows under a tree, hidden from the sunrise. He wanted—no, needed—a moment of peace before they saw him. A moment to prepare himself to see her again.

Quinn.

After so many long years of celibacy, of Alaric sacrificing his needs to those of his people, the human archaeologist and object reader Keely had discovered a bitter truth: Poseidon had never decreed celibacy for his priests. Not even his high priests, of whom so much was demanded.

No, the call for chastity had instead been the desperate attempt by a group of elders to prevent Atlantis from being destroyed. So far, that was all they knew. Not how or why. They knew the when, approximately eight thousand years ago. Nereus had been high priest and Zelia had been his wife.

Wife.

The word knocked the air from Alaric's lungs. He immediately thought of Quinn's reaction to such a term, and couldn't stop the smile from spreading across his face. Rebel leader, yes. Warrior, certainly. Brilliant strategist, without question.

But wife?

The leaves near him rustled slightly and he tensed, knowing that enthralled shifters roamed the woods. He called power and stood ready. However, it was not an enthralled wolf shifter that leapt out of the trees to land lightly, in spite of its enormous size, in front of him. It was Jack.

Humor gleamed in the tiger's slanted eyes, and he made a deep, rumbling sound that a fool might have mistaken for a purr. The fool would have lost a hand shortly thereafter.

Alaric inclined his head. "Jack. Always . . . interesting to see you."

The tiger bared its teeth, but Alaric merely raised an eyebrow.

"Now, boys, play nice," she said, appearing from the woods on the opposite side from where Jack had been. Alaric turned to look at her, and the rest of the world disappeared.

"Hello, Quinn. It has been too long." He was proud of himself for managing the calm tone. He was even more proud of himself for not snatching her up and abducting her to somewhere no one would ever, ever find them.

Someplace with no demands on either of them. No responsibilities.

A place, then, that existed only in fantasy.

"Hello, Alaric," she said, and the husky sound of her voice resonated in every nerve ending in his body. His power flared hot and bright, and he wanted to call a waterfall, a thunderstorm, a tsunami, and lay them all at her feet.

Jack snarled and swiped a paw against a young tree, taking half of its bark off.

"I think Lucas will not appreciate that," Quinn told him. "Will you please wait in the headquarters for us?"

Jack snarled again, but Quinn just aimed that steady, weighing gaze at him, the one nobody ever wanted to have find them wanting. No wonder she was such a good leader. Men and women would die for her.

Had died for her.

She carried them all in her soul.

Jack turned around, swishing his tail hard so that it smacked into Alaric's legs, and then bounded off toward Lucas's giant log-cabin headquarters. As he crossed the clearing between the trees and the house, he shifted shape between one bound and the next, so that the tiger seamlessly became the man, fully clothed, in the space of seconds.

"He's very good at that," Alaric observed, hearing the inane stupidity of his words even as he spoke them.

But Quinn only nodded. "He dislikes you," she said, in her blunt way. She confronted most problems head-on. "He thinks I'm pining away for you, and he thinks I should be his mate."

Alaric went deadly still. "What do you think?" he asked, when he was able to speak.

She shrugged. "He's right, and he's wrong. I am pining away for you, and I'm not his mate. His human soul cares about me, but his cat is indifferent. Friendly enough, but definitely not in a mating way. The dual-natured must find the mate that both halves of their soul desire for true happiness."

"Do you believe in that?" he asked her. "True happiness?"

She looked into his eyes, and he fell into hers, drowning in the deep, liquid dark. "I used to," she said. "Once, long ago."

"Your sister Riley is happy with Conlan," he challenged her. "Soon they will rule Atlantis together, with their son beside them."

A shadow of pain crossed her face. "I still haven't met my nephew. Tell me about him. Aidan. Is he well?"

He nodded. "He is a healthy, well-formed boy with a fierce spirit. He is definitely his parents' son."

She smiled. "I was hoping for that. For her. She deserves to be happy. But with Atlantis on the verge of war, how happy can the ruling family be?"

He frowned. "War. You think it will come to that?"

"What else? We are on the verge of world domination, if these scientists succeed in their experiments. The entire planet will become a feeding ground for vampires if somebody doesn't stop it."

He touched her face, and a bolt of pure desire raced through him, just from the feel of her cheek under his fingers. "Why does it always have to be you?"

She leaned into his touch, shivering like a frightened doe. But this was Quinn, and if she'd ever been truly frightened, he'd never seen it. Shivering with pleasure at his touch, perhaps. The idea warmed him, but she had not answered his question.

"Why you?" he repeated, knowing the answer, not wanting to hear it, but compelled to ask.

She closed her eyes and turned her face, then pressed the gentlest of kisses on his palm. "Who else?" she whispered. "Answer me that, Alaric. If not me, if not you, then who else? Do we stand by while our world is destroyed?"

"You could return to Atlantis with me. The vampires will never reach us there," he said, knowing it was futile. Knowing it wasn't even something he would want for her, and it could never be what he would do. Trapped, knowing they sat idly by while the world ended.

Never.

She knew it, too, because she moved away a little, but she smiled. "And Alaric fiddled while Rome burned," she said. "Somehow I can't see it."

"Wishes have voices sometimes."

"Do they?" She stared off into the distance, and he wondered what she saw there in the dark corners of her mind. "Mine do not. They have gone silent and still."

"The dictate of celibacy," Alaric blurted out. "It was a lie."

She slowly raised her head, sudden passion mixed with hope burning in her eyes so brightly he wanted to cry out. But then her eyes dimmed, and she turned away. "Even so. My reasons are unchanged. We have no time to discuss this now, while your friend is in danger."

She started walking away, following Jack's path, but Alaric couldn't bear it. He caught her arm and pulled her back. "And after? Will you at least hear me out?"

She stared at him for a very long time, but then she nodded. "After. Now we have to go. I have an idea of which direction they went."

Chapter 36

Tiernan and Brennan ran. Past the rooms that looked like more labs, more holding cells, and guard quarters. They ran, and they were lucky. They didn't see anybody. They didn't see an exit, either, so they kept running, although they were slow and clumsy from captivity and trying hard to be quiet, which slowed them up even more.

They came to a branching intersection and skidded to a stop.

"Sure. All that expensive equipment and nobody could afford an exit sign," Tiernan said bitterly. "Which way?"

He shook his head. "I can only guess."

"Let's go right. We've taken enough left turns on this mission," she said.

They took the right-hand turn and ran, and when the corridor snaked left, they followed it, only to run into two very surprised people heading toward them.

Strike that. Litton and a very scary-looking vampire.

Brennan raised his hands into the air, but a buzzing sound came from behind them with no warning, and the next thing Tiernan knew, Brennan was down on the floor, straining against the electricity of the Taser charge.

"You didn't think you could escape, did you?" Litton said, sneering.

"This is the human with the resistance?" The vampire stared down at Brennan. "Easy enough to subdue." He kicked Brennan in the head.

Tiernan screamed. "No, damn you!" She dropped to Brennan's side, ripped her torn sleeve off completely, and wrapped her hand in it to pull the Taser leads from his skin. Then she lifted his head into her lap. He was bleeding, but he was still breathing. She stared up at the vampire and silently swore she'd stake him in his nonexistent heart before she died, if she had to spend the rest of her life trying.

"Now it's your turn," Litton said, and she flinched, but he obviously didn't mean her turn to get kicked in the head.

They dragged her off and strapped her back down in that damn chair. She fought them until one of the guards came into the room.

"Dr. Litton, we thought you should know that Mr. Brennan is dead," he said, and Tiernan's mind couldn't process it. No. It couldn't be the truth, but the guard was not lying; she would know with this guard. His lies had always sounded to her like sandpaper rubbing on steel, and there wasn't a hint of that now.

That couldn't be her heart, tearing apart inside her chest. And yet it was. She gave up, and let out the cry. It came from so far deep inside her that even the vampire took a step back, flinching at the sound.

"Please," she whispered to the vampire. "I would prefer the kick now."

The vampire stared down at her, puzzled, but then Litton fastened the helmet on her head, and nothing else mattered but the pain and the light. Her brain shattered and reformed, as it had so many times before, but this time there was a difference. This time she had entirely given up hope.

She quit fighting it, but her Gift resisted in spite of her conscious mind, and when Litton kept returning, over and over, and telling her he was her friend, her Gift forced her to tell him that it was a lie.

Litton was not her friend. He never would be. He had killed the one man she'd ever wanted to spend her life with; the one man whose courage and kindness had given her hope for the future.

He finally shrieked with frustration or rage and ordered them to ramp it up to the red zone, and she laughed. The red zone might mean freedom, now that she had seen there truly was nothing left to live for. Susannah was gone. Tiernan would never live as a slave to this monster, and although her heart and mind and soul flinched away from the thought, Brennan was dead—Brennan, dead in this horrible place after two thousand years protecting humanity.

She faced death with little regret, except that she would never be able to break the story, bring this evil to the light of day. Brennan was gone, so there was no point to hoping for a future for herself.

She heard Litton's voice: "If she can't be enthralled, she may as well be dead."

She laughed. She'd won. She was free. The red haze of agony lightened and turned to a pure and indescribably beautiful white light, and suddenly everything else and everyone else fell away and a single figure stood there, limned by the light, carrying a bundle in her arms.

"Welcome," Susannah said, smiling, holding her baby. "I've missed you so much."

Tiernan smiled and stepped forward into the light.

Chapter 37

Devon's eyes snapped open from the brief rest. He needed more, the long, healing day sleep, but there was no time and, underground, he could survive without it. He immediately warmed several bottles of blood; he and Deirdre needed the sustenance. He hated to wake her, but she would be terrified if she woke alone.

"Deirdre," he said. She shot straight up off the long bench where he'd put her when they made it to his rooms and flew at him, her eyes blind with fear.

He caught her and soothed her, repeating her name over and over until she came out of it and calmed down. She drank four bottles of blood in huge gulps, not stopping until she'd drained them all. Then she wiped her mouth and stared at him, still silent.

"I have to go after them," he said. "I need to get to Brennan. You should stay here, where it's safe. The others will see me as weak now, after Jones, and I'll have to battle at least one, if not several of them."

"I'm going with you," she said, showing her fangs.

"It's not safe."

"I have never been safe," she said flatly, and the argument was finished. She was going with him.

Chapter 38

Alaric scanned the room. Lucas and twenty of his shifters, Jack, Alexios, Quinn, and about a dozen of her rebels all stood ready to assist. It would have to be enough.

"We have an idea of how to get in, but we're not entirely sure," Quinn said. "We're going to need to search."

"I know the direction Brennan's last mental blast came from," Alexios said. "We can use that to triangulate."

Alaric nodded. "I have been trying to reach him since I arrived, but the static you mentioned is too strong. It is almost certainly electrical interference, on an enormous scale. A laboratory full of equipment would not be enough, I don't believe, so I'm somewhat confused."

Quinn shoved a hand through her choppy dark hair. "It could be Tasers. Or an electrified cell. Or you may have to face the possibility—"

"No," Alexios said firmly. "No. The only possibility we face is the one where we find them, alive and mostly unharmed. If you believe different, feel free to get out."

"Alexios," Alaric snarled, but Quinn held up a hand, shaking her head.

"I'm sorry, Alexios," she said. "I've seen too much death lately, and I'm becoming hardened to it. We'll find them alive."

"No time like the present," Lucas said. "It's a plus to catch vamps in the daytime, even if they are underground. They'll be weaker."

They headed out the door, coordinating directions among them. Quinn stepped into the lead vehicle with Lucas and Alexios, and Alaric leapt into the air. He would fly as mist and keep an eye on her.

Just in case.

Chapter 39

Brennan struggled to his feet. He had to get to . . . the woman. He had to save her—he couldn't fail her again.

He *wouldn't* fail her again, although he couldn't remember her name. It was right there, teasing the edge of his mind, but not quite available. Not quite real. It didn't matter, though. Wasn't relevant.

He had to focus, to ignore his body's weakness and fight them. They hadn't even bothered to lock his cell door yet, since he'd been collapsed on the floor and they thought he was unconscious. The two men guarding him had both gone to the door and were talking to someone else in the hall.

Fools. He'd kill them both before they realized he was awake. Kill them and rescue the woman, and then find another way to escape, if he had to kill a thousand vampires and these thugs, too. The men had guns. Brennan knew how to use a gun. Ven had taught him, in spite of his reluctance. Now he was fiercely, triumphantly, glad of it.

He took two steps, cleared the cell door, and had almost reached the thugs, who still didn't notice him, when the world—or simply thousands of years of lost emotion—crashed down on his head, smashing him to the floor. Memories flooded into him, through him:

Tiernan, collapsing in his arms in Boston. His emotions soaring back, swirling around him like playful waves.

Tiernan, in the hotel room. In the forest. In Atlantis.

Tiernan, Tiernan, Tiernan, whose courage and unshaken belief in him had been enough to help him survive the ever-increasing torture of the chair and the helmet.

He *remembered* her. He wanted to shout and dance with joy, but the guards turned around and saw him, and anyway, the joy turned to despair, because it was too late.

Too. Late.

Because the words of the curse were tolling bells of death in his mind:

YOU WILL ALSO BE CURSED TO FORGET YOUR MATE WHENEVER SHE IS OUT OF YOUR SIGHT. ONLY WHEN SHE IS DEAD—HER HEART STOPPED AND HER SOUL FLOWN—WILL YOUR MEMORY OF HER FULLY RETURN TO YOU, THUS ALLOWING YOU UNTIL THE END OF YOUR DAYS TO REPENT BRINGING DISHONOR UPON THE NAME OF THE WARRIORS OF POSEIDON.

He remembered her. *Fully*, as Poseidon had decreed. That could only mean one thing. He threw back his head and howled, so loud and so long that he almost didn't hear the guard rush up to the ones standing at the door. Pain ripped through his gut, tearing him apart, eviscerating him.

"Isn't Brennan dead? I told the woman that he was dead, like the scientist told me to, and she quit fighting. They killed her," the man said, hoarse with fear or excitement. "The woman. Tracy Baum. They jacked up the juice too high, and she's dead."

Brennan wanted to die. He was ready to beg for death, so that he could follow her into the next life. *Soon, Tiernan*, he vowed.

First, he would kill them all.

The berserker rage flamed up inside him, but this time,

instead of trying to control it, he fed the fire. The sensory overload triggered another memory, and he rolled over onto all fours, hunched into himself, and slipped Alaric's vial out of his pocket. He'd forgotten it, when he'd forgotten her.

Now he would remember, and he would make sure that no one who'd had any part in harming her would ever forget. He drained the tiny bottle, feeling the energy shoot through his body like bottled starlight—if starlight were mixed with rocket fuel and magic.

"Now," he snarled, leaping to his feet. "Now you will all pay."

He called the power, and his body itself became a lightning rod for the energy and the starlight and the sheer, destructive force of a Warrior of Poseidon who had nothing left to live for.

They'd killed his woman. They would feel his wrath.

He threw water at them in the form of a tsunami, or at least that's what he intended, but instead a lightning bolt shot out from his fingers and smashed through the room, zigzagging through the space, leaving nothing but devastation in its wake. It exploded the steel bars of the cells, crushing them into an insane sculpture of twisted metal, and smashed the men into piles of broken bone and flesh on the floor.

The electricity in the room sparked wildly, trying to ground itself, but he didn't allow it to dissipate; he took it into himself and felt the power surge through him. When every cell in his body was lit up like a supernova, he headed through the door toward the lab.

Litton was going to die first.

Chapter 40

Brennan ran through the hallway with lightning at his fingertips and murder in his eyes. Nothing mattered—nothing would ever have meaning again—beyond the single imperative: kill them.

Kill them all.

He burst through the door to the lab and saw her pale, still body, death's unfeeling messenger having come and gone and taken its toll. The small, cold corner of his heart that had held out hope—in spite of the guard, in spite of the curse—shriveled and died in his chest.

Four came at him: two in the white coats of science, one with his gun already in hand, and one with fangs bared. Brennan never slowed down. He blasted them with the dark power; the lightning they'd called into his brain so many times had become part of him. He wielded death and despair on the wings of shining, surging power, and they died.

They all died. The men burned and the vampire flamed into ash on the floor.

And it was good.

But Tiernan, his Tiernan, his true mate. She still lay silent and unmoving, unseeing eyes staring up at the ceiling, the beginning of a smile on her pale, dead face.

He pressed his lips to hers and tried to breathe for her, in and out, over and over, but her lifeless form never responded, though her skin was still warm. He tried, desperate for some response—any response—but it was futile. He straightened at last, the final, dreadful acceptance claiming him.

She was gone.

"It wasn't my fault," a voice came, sniveling from the corner. "Damn Smitty for quitting, I need him here now. It wasn't my fault."

Litton.

"You will die for this," Brennan said, but he didn't recognize his own voice. The lightning had swallowed him up, eaten his soul, and the power surged through him until he had a voice filled with thunder and gale-force winds.

He was no longer Brennan, but a storm-chased tsunami, and he would wreak destruction like the world had never known.

"Who else?" he demanded.

"What?" Litton edged away from him, but Brennan pointed a finger and the lightning surged. The computers and machines near Litton exploded, raining shrapnel on and around the monster who had killed Tiernan.

Litton fell to the floor, bleeding and crying out, but Brennan had no pity. The lightning had consumed pity; eaten it whole and regurgitated vengeance and death.

"Who else knows how to use these machines? Who else knows the science of enthrallment?" Brennan asked. Though he would die soon, in only minutes if the gods were merciful, he would fulfill Tiernan's wishes as his final gift to her. He would avenge her, and Susannah, and the baby, and possibly in some way redeem himself for the baby he had not been able to save.

"Nobody," Litton said. "I didn't let anyone else know all

of my secrets. They would steal them." Triumphant glee lit up the monster's face. "So you can't kill me. You need me, if you want to know how this all works." Litton's tone turned shrill and wheedling. "We can work together. All the power can be yours."

Brennan smiled, a bleak and terrible smile, and Litton flinched, cowering in the corner. "You mistake my intent entirely," Brennan said. "No one should have this knowledge. Now I will face Tiernan in the next world, content in the knowledge that this hideous experiment died with you."

Litton screamed and tried to crawl away, and Brennan knew a moment's pity, Tiernan's words ringing in his ears. Enough death. Enough killing. Litton would be brought to justice and suffer long years in prison. Needing only to get to Tiernan, to hold her one last time, he turned away and crossed to the chair. He gently touched her face, which was still warm, but so very pale. "I will always love you, *mi amara*, through this life and beyond," he whispered.

The first gunshot hit the chair. The second smashed into the back of his leg.

As he fell, he spun on his good leg and threw the power— all the power, every ounce of the power—at Litton, who stood against the far wall, the gun from the fallen guard clutched in his shaking hands.

It was Brennan's turn to call the lightning.

When the smoke cleared, nothing but a blackened pile of smoldering bone remained.

Brennan returned to Tiernan, limping now, blood running freely down his leg. The bullet had missed bone and artery and had gone clear through flesh, but if he left it untreated and unbound, surely it would be enough to kill him.

He prayed it would be enough to kill him.

He ripped the restraints off of Tiernan's wrists and pulled her gently, so carefully, into his arms. Everything he'd ever wished for lay like ash in his arms and heart and mind. He resolved to carry her out of that miserable place of pain and death, find a way back to the park, and sit with her in the cool peace of the forest until his blood left his body in sufficient quantities to allow him to join her.

He stood, turning toward the door, and took the first step toward freedom, prepared to blast his way out, through guards, through scientists, even through the vampires.

The last thing he expected was the vampire who walked through the door.

Chapter 41

"Daniel?" Brennan stared at the vampire who'd suddenly appeared like a hallucination to his overwrought mind. The vampire who had allied with the Atlanteans over and over again, who had saved Quinn's life although at the price of a blood bond, here he was and Brennan's mind could not make sense of it.

"Brennan, we don't have much time," Daniel began, but then he looked—really looked—at Tiernan, and he froze. "No. No, not again."

"She is dead, and the one who brought us here and murdered her lies dead as well," Brennan said, barely managing to speak through the pain that swamped his mind and drained the breath from his lungs. "I will be next."

A female entered the room, another vampire, and she scanned the equipment, then trained her gaze on Tiernan. "How long?" she asked, her voice urgent. "How long since she died?"

"A few minutes, perhaps. Long enough for my heart to die with her. Now, get out of my way or by all the gods, I will destroy you, too, Daniel, no matter what help you have been to me and mine in the past."

The woman pushed past Daniel and blurred with preternatural vampire speed across the floor to Brennan, so fast Brennan didn't have time to move before she was there, staring down at Tiernan and touching her skin.

"We might be able to resuscitate her," she said, and at first the words had no meaning, they were just sounds, but then a great, dark hope lit Brennan's world and he staggered back as though she'd struck him.

"What? How? Vampires have no healing magic," he said, sanity and rationality returning to crush hope.

"No, we have something better," she said, pointing to the as yet undamaged machines that had been behind Brennan, near the chair. "Modern life-saving equipment. Put her back in that chair."

He didn't move. Couldn't move. Could only stand there, holding the body of his woman, not daring to hope.

"The machines, Brennan. They have machines to make her heart start again. I know how to use them."

Daniel leapt across the room to Brennan. "Let Deirdre help, Brennan. Please, let her try." He gently but quickly steered Brennan around and back to the chair.

Brennan hesitated still; no matter that he had some measure of trust for Daniel, he did not know the other vampire and, most of all, to put Tiernan back in the chair that had tortured and killed her felt like the worst kind of blasphemy.

"Please," Deirdre said, looking up at him with eyes that were so familiar, and something clicked in Brennan's mind.

"Deirdre? Erin's sister?"

She nodded, fathomless pain in the dark depths of her deep blue eyes, and she even smiled a little. "Yes. Please let me help this one, as you and your Atlanteans helped my sister."

She put one hand under Tiernan's head and helped Brennan guide her back onto the hated chair, and then Deirdre ripped Tiernan's shirt open and put pads on her chest that were attached to wires and a machine—a different machine, not the same, not the helmet—and she yelled, "Clear," but Brennan didn't know what that meant and he didn't move.

Daniel yanked Brennan back and away from Tiernan, but he didn't have time to protest before Deirdre made the machine bring another kind of lightning, and Tiernan's body jumped in the chair and then fell back, still silent and unmoving.

Brennan roared out his anguish from hope extinguished, and he stumbled back, would have fallen, but Daniel caught his arm in a strong grip.

"It didn't work," Brennan said, unnecessarily, as they could all see that it had not brought his Tiernan back, but Deirdre ignored him and adjusted dials on the machine and again yelled out the word.

"Clear!"

This time Tiernan's body jumped higher, but the result was the same: no life, no heartbeat, no Tiernan. But Brennan looked at the machine and then at Tiernan and he knew what to do.

"I can do it," he said. "I can call the lightning. Put the machine on me."

"What?" Deirdre said. "No, you don't understand, this only works when the heart has already stopped."

"I understand," Brennan said, ripping off his own shirt. "Put the pads on me. Surge the power through me."

Deirdre was shaking her head, but Daniel stopped her. "He has power, Deirdre. Look at that." He pointed to the corner, to what was left of Litton, and around the room at the destroyed equipment. "Do it."

She stared around the room and then shrugged, rapidly removed the pads from Tiernan's chest, and attached them to Brennan's back. Brennan put his hands carefully, so carefully, on Tiernan's chest.

"Do it now," he told Deirdre, and then he smiled down at the woman he loved with every ounce of his being. "One way or another, we will be together."

"Clear!" Deirdre cried out, and then Brennan called the lightning.

The power surged into him and through him stronger than ever before, and he poured it through his hands into Tiernan, into her heart and blood and soul. He shouted her name as the power surged, but it wasn't enough, wasn't enough.

Wasn't enough.

The power fizzled and stopped, and Brennan took a deep, shuddering breath and then turned his own dead gaze to Deirdre. "Again."

"But it will kill you—"

"Now." The command hung in the air, resonating with the measure of power of a Warrior of Poseidon.

Deirdre cried out the word again, like a talisman. "Clear!"

Brennan called the lightning.

Pain scorched through him with the power, leaving a trail of sizzling agony in its wake. The energy burned through him from his back, through his bloodstream, and to his own heart, and then down his arms to his hands and into Tiernan's heart.

He called the lightning, and screamed her name through the pain that threatened to incinerate him. Screamed her name and pledged his vow: "Poseidon, channel this power through me to save my woman and I freely give my life for hers."

He staggered and nearly fell, his wounded leg screaming out as the jagged holes from the gunshot were seared shut, the flesh burned and melted to instant scarring from the heat and fury of the lightning. The power surged through him, biting with its jagged teeth, eating everything he was and consuming it as fuel for the lightning that then poured into Tiernan's body, filling her organs and blood and bone with the power.

This time, the lightning conquered death itself.

Tiernan arched up off the table, crying out, but then she opened her eyes and smiled.

He fell then, against the chair, but she held up her arms to him and he fell forward into his life, into the future, into hope. He kissed her and she tasted of the power and, together, they swallowed the lightning.

They dove, as one, into the soul-meld, and this time they were together, in Atlantis, dancing in the moonlit night, and the future belonged to them, forever and ever. He kissed her, and he tasted eternity.

A sound brought him back. Behind him, Daniel cleared his throat, and Brennan's conscious mind clicked back into place. "We're not out of danger yet," he told Tiernan. "We have to run."

"As long as I'm with you," she said, and then her gaze shifted, and she stared at something behind Brennan and to his right. Confusion played over her expressive features and her brows drew together.

Daniel stepped up, next to Brennan, and smiled at Tiernan. Brennan opened his mouth to explain, but Tiernan spoke first.

"Devon? What are you doing here?"

Chapter 42

Tiernan stared at the vampire, wondering what possibly could have happened when she was . . . when she was . . .

Dead.

She had been dead. Her mind rejected the fact, but her soul knew the truth, and some things were far more important than Devon and his intrigues.

"I was dead," she whispered to Brennan. "I saw Susannah, and the baby. They were so happy, and loved, and they shared that joy with me, but I felt something was missing."

She sat up and put her hands on his solemn face. "Someone was missing. You were missing."

"I was ready to follow you," he said fiercely, resting his forehead on hers. "I planned to fulfill your mission, and avenge your friend, and then follow you into death and past its dark shores."

"Corelia was there, too. She sent me back," Tiernan said, the memory glowing in her eyes. "She said to tell you that she is in a place beyond the need of vengeance, and that you should forgive yourself. That your entire life has been a quest for redemption, and you should be at peace with yourself now."

"If I am truly redeemed, you are my reward," he said, gathering her into his arms again.

"While this is touching, we need to get out of here. Now." Tiernan didn't recognize the voice and looked up to find a woman standing near Devon and almost dancing with impatience. No, not quite a woman. A female vampire.

"Deirdre is right," Devon said. "Back-from-death reunion later, running now. Jones had followers, and they're going to be very unhappy with me. Not to mention all the vamps who want your billions, Brennan."

Devon pointed to the black pile of ash on the floor where the vampire had been. "I'm guessing that's Smith, which means I now have two blood prides and two sets of followers out for my head. We need to go, and we need to go now."

"Daniel," Brennan said. "We must destroy this equipment first, so that it can never be used to harm another living being."

Devon hesitated, then nodded. Tiernan held up a hand. "Wait. Why is he calling you Daniel?"

Devon laughed. "That's my name. I've also been Drakos, D'Artagnan, Demetrios, and, among many, many other names, Devon. Call me Daniel, please. It's less confusing."

"We'll call you a dead man, if we don't hurry," Deirdre said, grabbing Devon-turned-Daniel's arm. "We have to get out of here now. I won't be captured. Ever, ever again."

The searing pain and overwhelming terror in Deirdre's voice and eyes jolted Tiernan into action. She was surprised to find herself filled with energy, as if she'd just eaten a full meal and slept for eight hours, instead of having been dead, held captive, and tortured for who knew how long. Whatever Brennan had done had given her a massive jolt and power boost.

She jumped into action, going to examine the computer consoles and other machinery, but it took only a few seconds for her to realize she had no idea how to destroy any of it. Unlike in the films, there was no giant red button labeled

"SELF DESTRUCT." "I don't know how to do it," she had to admit.

A tray of medical instruments caught her eye and she grabbed a couple of them. Just in case. "I don't know how," she repeated. "I'm sorry."

"I do," Brennan said. He gestured for them to move aside, and he raised his hands into the air. Power crackled through the room, sucking the moisture and oxygen out of the air, and it swirled and surged around Brennan and then funneled down and into his body.

She gasped and took a step forward, but Daniel/Devon, whoever he was, caught her around the waist and held her back. "He'd fry you," Daniel said. "Just wait."

An icy, silvery blue light like the aura of a lightning god surrounded Brennan, and he smiled. "For Tiernan, and for Susannah, and for Atlantis," he said, and then he sliced his hands through the air and shoved the power across the room and into the machines. For an instant nothing happened except they lit up with an unearthly blue light.

"Now we duck," Daniel said in her ear, and he yanked her down, and as they hit the floor, the room exploded.

Tiernan pulled her head away from Daniel's restraining arm just in time to see Brennan standing, legs braced and arms out, bent forward into the shield of light he'd created that protected them from the results of the blast. After several seconds, when the debris from the explosion had all fallen back down to the floor and lay burning, Brennan turned around.

Tiernan ran to him and jumped into his arms, and he kissed her so hard and so deeply that she tasted the lightning. Her own world exploded around her, pulling her further and further into his soul. This time, it was a place she wanted to be.

Finally, Brennan lifted his head and took a deep breath. "Now we run."

Chapter 43

Brennan lifted Tiernan into his arms and started running, following Daniel and Deirdre as they led the way through the maze of corridors to safety. Normally he never could have kept up with vampire speed, unless he'd been soaring as mist, but the lightning still infused his body. He raced along the corridors and took sharp turns without slowing, laughing as the power gave his feet wings of pure, shimmering electricity.

Minutes later, Daniel stopped so suddenly that Deirdre nearly ran into him and, behind them both, Brennan skidded to a stop.

"I hear something loud," Daniel said, looking grim. "The shit, as the expression goes, is about to hit the fan."

Brennan carefully lowered Tiernan to her feet. "Stay behind me," he said, and she nodded. He took a step forward, then stopped and spun around.

"I love you," he told her. "You need to know that, before we take one more step. Not because of the curse or the soul-meld or anything else except the goodness of your heart and the enormity of your courage. You are my soul and my life, *mi amara*, and I will love you until the end of this life and beyond. Can you ever love me?"

She simply stood there and blinked, and his heart teetered on the precipice of despair, but then she laughed, and warmth that had nothing at all to do with the lightning spread throughout his body. "Brennan. I left *heaven* for you. I may not be poetic, but you have to know how much I love you, too."

He kissed her again, quickly, then turned to face whatever lay in wait.

Daniel flashed away, moving in a blur, but was back seconds later. "I was right. Jones had plenty of followers. They heard the explosion; they never wanted me for Primator, anyway, and they are very eager to get their hands on you and your billions."

"Primator?" Tiernan said, and Brennan could hear the professional curiosity in her voice.

"Later," Daniel promised, and Tiernan nodded.

They started forward, but then Deirdre stopped Brennan with a cold, pale hand on his wrist. "Atlantean, I want to know about my sister. Is she well?"

He nodded. "Erin is very well, and she is happy. She brings great joy to our prince, Vengeance, brother to the high prince."

"And her magic?" Her eyes were huge, pleading with him for something—reassurance, perhaps? He was glad to give it.

"She has discovered power beyond any she knew before. As a gem singer, she is a great healer and beloved by our people," he told her. "Erin's magic helped save the lives of the princess and her unborn child. Prince Aidan lives because of your sacrifice and her magic."

A single bloodred tear rolled down her face from each eye, and then she nodded. "I would like to see her again."

"Can we discuss family reunions later?" Daniel demanded impatiently. "We've got bad guys dead ahead."

Tiernan snorted. "Or dead guys bad ahead."

Daniel groaned. "You come back from the dead, and that's all you've got? Bad puns?"

"Laugh in the face of danger," she said, holding up two long, shiny blades. "Scalpels," she said, to Brennan's unspoken question. "Thought they might come in handy, since I don't have fangs or lightning bolts."

Pride swept over Brennan. His little warrior. Even death itself could not stop her.

"Showtime," she said, and the first wave of vampires rounded the corner.

One vampire, ancient judging by the look of his long, yellowed fangs, led the pack. "Well, Devon. We were wondering where you were. Who are your friends?"

Devon narrowed his eyes, the only signal Brennan expected to get, and pushed Deirdre behind him. "How serendipitous that you should appear now. We were just on the way to inform you all that Jones and Smith killed each other in a struggle for power, and in the course of their fight, they blew up the lab. We're leaving and suggest you do the same."

Another vamp hissed at them and jumped to the wall, clinging to it and hanging like a spider. "Why would we do that? Your word alone? Where is proof?"

The vampire in the front whipped his head to the side. "Silence, fool. Of course Devon is telling us the truth." He returned his red, glowing gaze to Devon, ignoring Brennan completely. "You must be hungry, though, after your . . . ordeal . . . with Mr. Jones."

He snapped his fingers, and another vamp dragged a human woman forward. "You know what to do," the vamp told her.

The woman was shaking like a sapling tree caught in a hurricane, but she took a tiny step forward and pasted a sick-looking smile on her face. After looking back once at the vampire, she walked closer to Devon. "I'm a gift to you, as proof that my master will follow you anywhere."

Brennan hesitated, caught between his need to protect the woman and his reluctance to get Tiernan killed over some nuance of vampire politics.

Tiernan herself solved that problem for him.

"She's lying," she said clearly. "Huge lie. That vampire has no intention to follow you or anybody else, Daniel."

"Good enough for me," Brennan said and, one more time, he called the lightning.

The vampire's look of surprise remained on his face while his head rolled across the floor.

If Brennan had thought killing their leader would stop them, he'd been very wrong. The death acted like a trigger, and they all exploded toward Brennan and his small group like a deadly swarm, clinging to walls, floor, and even the ceiling, all with fangs bared and promises of death in their eyes.

Brennan welcomed the berserker rage and pulled every ounce of available energy into his body, feeling his hair lift away from his head and float in the air, driven by the electrical charge his body was generating. They came at him— they came at *Tiernan*—and he called the lightning.

It came once more to his command, but there was a cost. His body was not made to channel the power of the gods, and Atlantean flesh could not carry pure, sizzling, electrical energy at this rate for this long.

He felt something rip and tear inside him, and he stumbled, but he threw the power at the first wave of vampires and they burst into flames, incinerated in seconds, and the second wave fell back, hissing and shouting insults and epithets.

"Can you keep doing that?" Daniel asked. "Also, don't send any of it my way, if you don't mind."

"Daniel!" Deirdre shrieked, and they all turned to see that another wave was coming from behind them. They'd be trapped.

"Oh, this is not good," Tiernan said, holding her scalpels

up in the air. "I have no plans to die twice in one day, so let's kick some vampire ass." She threw an apologetic glance at Daniel and Deirdre. "No offense."

Deirdre smiled, and for a moment, some of the anguish on her face seemed to lighten. "None taken," she said.

And then the vampires charged, and the battle was on.

Chapter 44

Alaric soared down to the ground to meet Quinn, Alexios, and the shifters and rebels. It had taken far longer than he'd expected, and Brennan was still blocked by some extremely unusual interference, but they'd finally found it, though it was unmarked.

The heavy guard at the access road had been their first indication.

Quinn hopped out of the vehicle, and it took everything in Alaric not to spirit her away from there. Protect her from any fight.

She pulled a deadly looking gun from her pocket and held it at the ready. "Are you sure? It looks like a warehouse."

"This is it. Litton's institute. We found Wesley and made him talk," one of Lucas's Pack members said, grinning at the memory.

It wasn't a very pleasant grin.

With no warning, a psychic blast smashed Alaric so hard his head rocked back on his neck. It was Brennan, and he was sending a mental communication more powerful than any the warrior had ever been able to send before.

Protect Tiernan.

Brennan's abilities struck Alaric as very different and very, very wrong. He headed for the building, without waiting to see if anyone followed him. "We go now."

Before he even reached the door, it slammed open and human men with guns streamed out shooting. Alaric heard screaming behind him, but it wasn't Quinn, he knew her voice, and he did not have time to stop for anyone else. He channeled Poseidon's pure, blue-green power in the form of small spheres, and he fired at the men in a steady stream, blowing the resistance apart. The men scattered, still shooting, but the rebels had guns, too, and the shifters had fangs and claws, so Alaric kept going.

He hit the door at a dead run. "Brennan," he shouted. "I'm coming."

Chapter 45

Brennan called the lightning again and seared flame through the second wave of vampires, but the power flickered and went out, leaving a hollowness in his stomach like the charred earth of a battleground. Something deep in his skull—something vital—twisted and snapped when he tried again to reach for the unfamiliar power. He fell forward, but Tiernan darted in front of him and caught him by throwing her body under his and taking his weight on her back. She stumbled and then steadied, and he gained his own balance and was able to stand.

"It's gone. The power—I can't call the lightning," he said.

"Then call the water. Isn't that your real power?" Tiernan said, slashing out with her scalpels at a vampire who dared to come too close.

Daniel and Deirdre fought like wild animals, feral and single-minded in their fury. They tore through the oncoming swarm two at a time, Daniel facing one vanguard and Deirdre the other. But without Brennan's lightning bolts, it wasn't going to be enough.

Not nearly enough.

"Call the water," Tiernan insisted. "Do the ice spears."

Brennan did just that, but for the first time in more than two thousand years, neither power nor water came easily to his hand. Perhaps the lightning had ruined him. Killed the magic.

"Now would be a good time for some help," Daniel yelled, and then he went down, buried under a half dozen vampires.

"Brennan," Tiernan cried out. "Help!"

She pointed up and he saw a vampire crawling on the ceiling toward them, hanging like a bloated spider but faster than any spider had ever moved. Before Brennan could react, the repulsive creature leapt down through the air and grabbed Tiernan, then threw her across the corridor so hard that she smashed into the opposite wall with an audible crack.

She screamed and held up her arm, which dangled in an unnatural way, clearly broken. Slumping back against the wall, cradling her wounded arm, she slid down until she was sitting on the floor staring up at Brennan, her face strained with the pain.

Tiernan's pain blasted through the barrier in Brennan's mind, and he called the water again. "For Atlantis!" he roared, and this time the water came. He created spears of ice and arrows of pure, shining water, and it came to his call and followed his command, shooting through the corridors in swirls and ribbons like a deadly ballet; dancers pirouetting on blades of death.

The vampire who had harmed Tiernan was the first to die.

When Brennan lowered his hands and finally released the water, there was no one left standing. The corridors in both directions were littered with piles of disintegrating vampires, and he saw the backs of several more who were fleeing the battle, having evidently decided they did not care to face the true death just yet.

He ran to Tiernan and carefully lifted her in his arms. Her face was white with pain, but she gritted her teeth and didn't cry out.

"Daniel?" she said and he looked around, prepared to regret having destroyed his ally, but knowing he would have sacrificed far more for Tiernan.

"I'm here," Daniel said from behind them, his voice cracking. "But Deirdre isn't doing very well."

Brennan turned around, carefully so as not to jostle Tiernan. "Did I—"

"No," Deirdre, who was lying on the ground with a stake in her chest, said. "No. It was one of them. He was going to stake Daniel."

Daniel, covered with wounds himself, pulled Deirdre into his arms, anguish in his eyes. "She did it for me. She stepped between the stake and my back."

Daniel looked down at Deirdre, bloodred tears streaming down his face. "Not for me. You should not have done this for me. You were still too weak from the torture to survive this trauma."

Deirdre smiled a little, then gasped and doubled over. Daniel cried out, but she wasn't dead. Not yet. But Brennan could tell from the way she looked that it wouldn't be long.

"You saved me once, now I return the favor," Deirdre told Daniel. "You can still accomplish so much good. I am broken and more than ready to rest." She looked up at Brennan. "Please give my love to my sister, and tell her I died with a prayer in my heart for her."

Then she grasped the stake and, before Daniel could stop her, pushed down until it angled into her heart and shoved it farther into her chest with one powerful movement.

"No," Tiernan cried, but it was too late, and they watched, unable to look away, as Deirdre dissolved into pale, silvery ash in Daniel's arms, and even that faded and vanished before their eyes.

"No," someone cried out, but it wasn't Tiernan this time. Brennan jerked his head to the right to see what new danger was approaching, but it was Quinn, running down the corridor toward them, keeping pace with Alaric, who juggled spheres of blue-green power.

Quinn stopped and fell to her knees beside Daniel. "No," she said again.

But it was too late.

Daniel threw his head back and screamed a long, wild, feral cry and Quinn flinched back. Alaric reached for her, but stopped himself before he touched her shoulder, instead turning to Brennan.

"We're here to rescue you," Alaric said, raising an eyebrow and scanning the area.

"Great timing," Tiernan managed to say.

Alaric's lips moved a fraction, which for him was almost a smile. "Perhaps I could at least assist with that?" He pointed to her broken arm.

Before she could answer, he released the power spheres he'd been holding and let them roll down her arm, where they re-formed, coalescing into a sleeve of pure light.

Tiernan made a contented humming sound deep in her throat, her head falling back while the magic did its work, and then the light winked out. She held out her arm and cautiously stretched it and bent it and then looked up, her eyes wide, and smiled at Alaric.

"Thank you very much. That was hurting a bit," she said.

Alaric inclined his head. "Think nothing of it."

Tiernan took Brennan's hand. "Okay, I won't. After Brennan brought me back from the dead, fixing a broken arm seems kind of ordinary."

Alaric trained a piercing stare on Brennan. "I will need to hear more of this."

"Fine. Later. Let's get out of here," Tiernan said. She knelt down by Daniel. "I'm so very sorry for your loss, Daniel. She saved us. She was very brave."

Daniel stared blindly at her, not seeing Tiernan or anything else, Brennan suspected. "She was mine to protect, and I failed her."

"No," Brennan said. "She made her choice, and she died a hero."

Quinn put a hand on Daniel's arm. "We need to go."

"Yes, please," Tiernan said. "Can we *please* get out of here? I can't die or face death one more time down in these miserable tunnels."

Daniel nodded and stood up, leaning on Quinn. His nostrils flared when he came close to her, and his face hardened, taking on a predatory cast for a split second, but then he pulled away from her, shaking his head. Brennan noticed that Alaric tensed, like he was ready to lunge at the vampire, and didn't relax at all even when Daniel backed away from Quinn. They started down the corridor in the direction from which Alaric and Quinn had come, and met no more resistance along the way.

"Lucas is rounding up the rest of the scientists in the conference room upstairs," Quinn said.

"I will remove their memories of anything to do with this horrible procedure," Daniel said.

"You've been going by the name Devon?" Quinn asked. Evidently the rebels knew quite a bit about what had been happening here, as usual.

"Yes. I was here for the same reason you are. Enthralling shifters and humans is wrong. Categorically wrong. I'm not going to let power-mad vampires take over the world and turn everyone on the planet into a sheep."

"Will you still be Primator?" Tiernan asked.

"I must. Nothing less will be enough to succeed."

"If you take their memories, will that damage their minds?" Brennan asked, suddenly flashing back to his time in that godsdamned chair.

"It might."

They were silent then, climbing the stairs that led back to the fresh air and the light, each contemplating what moral ground he or she was willing to offer up for the greater good, Brennan suspected. Or, at least, he was.

"I have no problem with that," Tiernan finally said, breaking the silence. "But not for Susannah, who's in a place beyond vengeance. For all the people who might have been caught and experimented on in the future. Let's make sure they never have to suffer this ordeal."

"Agreed," Brennan said, wrapping his arm around Tiernan's waist as they crossed the lobby to the door. "For the future."

A high, keening shriek was his only warning before a heavy weight dropped on his back and he realized it was a vampire screaming in his ear. The vampire reared back, fangs glistening, and struck . . . but didn't connect with Brennan's flesh.

Instead, the vampire's head slid slowly to one side and fell off its neck. Its body followed, collapsing to the floor, and leaving a clear line of sight to Smitty, who stood there with a short sword in his hand, the blade bloody.

"You!" Tiernan said.

Smitty's dead stare lightened for a fraction of a second, admitting an ounce of human emotion, as he glanced at Tiernan. But then he returned his gaze to Brennan, and it was as icy cold as ever. "Just stopped by for my final paycheck. Couldn't stomach any more. Now we're even."

He wiped his blade on the back of the vamp's shirt and then crossed the floor to Tiernan. He stopped and lifted a hand, almost touching her hair. "I'm sorry," he said, so quietly Brennan almost didn't hear it, and then he headed toward the door.

"Brennan?" Alaric said, but Tiernan shook her head.

"We've had enough killing," she said. "And he was almost kind, in his own, murderous way."

"She spared your life, but know this. If I see you again, I will kill you," Brennan said.

Smitty paused but didn't turn around. He simply nodded, resumed walking, and left the building. When they walked through the door only a few seconds behind him, he was already gone.

Chapter 46

Brennan walked out into the daylight and praised the gods that they had made it out alive. He pulled Tiernan closer to him, realizing that he wouldn't be willing to let her out of his sight for a long time, if ever. Not until he could feel safe again, after losing her.

"That might take years," he murmured, and she glanced up at him, puzzled, but he just smiled and kissed the top of her head.

Lucas, who'd been leaning against the front of a shiny black vehicle, walked over to them. "You're alive," he said, grinning. "Thank the goddess. Honey was going to kill me if I let something happen to you."

Brennan smiled, feeling joy—simple, grateful, joy—slowly wash over him. "I thank you for the rescue," he said, raising an eyebrow. "Perhaps next time you can remain in your vehicle and listen to music on the radio."

"Hey! I took care of the goons out here on patrol," Lucas protested. "I wasn't slacking off."

Tiernan smiled. "Thank you. Thank you all. I'm feeling

pretty great right now for a woman who was dead recently." She turned her face up to the sunshine and closed her eyes, snuggling closer to Brennan, who enjoyed the feeling very much. "Maybe next time we can have a nice beach vacation?"

Lucas laughed. "Your boyfriend has some nice underwater property." But then the shifter's face turned grim. "We lost one of ours and two of the rebels to the gunfire. Quinn's people and mine are heading down into the tunnels with Alexios for a search-and-destroy mission. We need to make sure every bit of that mind-control equipment is demolished."

"We got a good start on it," Brennan said.

"Take those damn chairs apart piece by piece and burn them, is all I ask," Tiernan said, shuddering against him. "No one should ever have to endure that again."

"We'll handle the cleanup," Lucas said. "You go. Heal. Rest. But come back in a week for the boys' naming ceremony."

"We will," Brennan promised. He and Lucas clasped arms, and Lucas pounded him on the back, and then the shifter bounded over to the institute and disappeared inside.

"Where is Daniel? Oh, wait," Tiernan said, looking up again. "Sunshine."

"He will stay and help in the tunnels," Alaric said from behind them, making Tiernan jump.

"I hate when you do that," she muttered.

He smiled a little. "I know. In any event, Daniel will stay and help. His exact words were 'the third time is a charm.' His undercover days are over, since he is too well-known now. He was also voted Primator, or so he claims, and I choose not to look into that claim too closely."

Alaric's eyes glowed hotter, and Brennan turned to follow his gaze. Quinn was coming out of the front door of the institute, and her face was white and strained. She crossed to where they were standing.

"Daniel said good-bye," she said. "He's going to work openly with us and with you from here on out."

Suddenly Tiernan made a small, startled noise and slipped out of Brennan's grasp, falling to the ground. She looked up from where she was sprawled in a clumsy sitting pose, her face comically surprised.

"I think all that energy you gave me when you brought me back to life just vanished with a thud," she said. "My legs turned to rubber."

"Brought her back to life?" Quinn said, her eyes widening. "What?"

"Long story. I'll tell you later, when you finally come to Atlantis to meet your nephew," Brennan told her, bending and scooping Tiernan up off the ground. "Alaric?"

"Already done," Alaric said, pointing to the shimmering portal forming in the air. "Rest well, both of you. Job very well-done."

Tiernan smiled. "You, too. Nice rescue," she mumbled, her eyelids drooping.

"I'm taking my woman home," Brennan said, feeling the power of it fill him with peace. As he stepped through the portal, Tiernan whispered into his ear.

"Yes, take me home, please."

Brennan was never sure, later, that it had actually happened, but at the moment he stepped into the portal with his sleepy mate in his arms, he could have sworn he heard the portal speak to him.

It said: "About time."

~~~~~

Brennan pushed the damp hair back from Tiernan's face, inhaling her clean, sweet scent. She'd insisted on a very long, hot shower when they'd reached his rooms, after the brief but very painful task of telling Conlan about Deirdre. The prince had promised to give Erin the news when she and Ven returned.

Brennan had needed to hold Tiernan up in the shower; she was too exhausted to stand. Not that he was complaining. But even though his body had responded to her as usual, he'd ignored his straining cock and simply helped her wash the stain and stench of the days of captivity from her lovely body. He, too, had scrubbed frantically, not stopping until she spoke his name and looked up at him, understanding in her dark eyes.

"It won't work. We can never wash away the memories," she said.

"I would give much if I could remove the memories of that horror from your mind," he said, lifting her into his arms and holding her close.

She put her arms around his neck and kissed his cheek. "No. I need to keep those memories, for always. Especially Susannah. That one moment pays for all the rest."

He kissed her, deeply, showing her without words how much she meant to him. "And this moment?"

"And especially this moment." She suddenly yawned hugely, her eyes drooping shut, and put her head down on his shoulder. "Can we sleep now?"

"We can." He lifted her out of the shower and carefully dried her hair and body while she stood, slumped with exhaustion. He quickly dried himself and then carried her to his bed. She burrowed under the covers, but he stood there for a moment, looking down at her, thanking all the gods— yes, even Poseidon—that she was finally home where she belonged.

Safe.

And his.

She patted the bed next to her and he climbed in, pulling her close, wrapping his arms around her, sinking into the peace and joy of knowing she was with him.

She stirred suddenly, twisting her head to stare into his eyes. "Brennan, you can't fall asleep. Remember what happened before? Wait—how did you remember me after they took me away?"

He realized he hadn't told her any of it. Turning onto his side so that he faced her, he related what had happened in the cell. His memories returning, when she'd died.

A dawning realization spread across her face. "My soul had definitely fully gone," she said, when he'd finished.

"The terms of the curse—we met them. Of course! Poseidon didn't have modern defibrillator equipment around when he threw in that part."

"Exactly. Since that part of the curse was fulfilled and my memories fully returned, I must assume that the rest is broken, as well."

"But what if we're wrong?"

He shook his head and then kissed her, a slow, lingering brush against her soft lips. "We cannot think that way. I am unable to stay awake nonstop for the rest of my life, and I refuse to believe that I have found you and carried you back from death itself, only to lose you each dawn when I awake."

She smiled but still looked worried. "I hope you're right. I think we're going to find out soon, since I can't stay awake a single second more."

As she curled up against him and her breathing immediately slowed and lengthened into the steady rhythm of slumber, he offered up a silent prayer.

Please, Poseidon, please may it be so.

And then Tiernan's warm, sleeping body seduced his own deep into the same respite and refuge.

～～～

Tiernan woke up and lay still for a moment, reveling in the warmth of the hard chest underneath her cheek. The sunlight flooded the room from the large windows, and she felt like she rested in a circle of peace that had embraced her and would hold her close for as long as she needed sanctuary.

She touched Brennan's chest with her fingertips, drew circles around the muscles of his abdomen, and lightly stroked—just a tease—the erection tenting up the sheet.

He tensed underneath her touch, and she smiled up at him. "You're awake."

He blinked sleepily a few times, those gorgeous green eyes filled with contentment. "I am awake. How did you sleep?"

"Wonderfully. You?" She stretched luxuriously, enjoying the delicious feeling. Most of her bruises and cuts and aches had been improved enormously by whatever Alaric had done to heal her arm yesterday. Apparently the healing power didn't confine itself to only one body part.

"I slept very well," Brennan said, lifting his hand to cup her breast. Her body instantly responded, and she turned toward him, twining her leg between his.

"I only have one question," he said, his forehead furrowing. "Who exactly are you?"

Chapter 47

Brennan couldn't hold back the grin when she froze, stiffening in his arms. "I find that I love making jokes, Tiernan Butler, *mi amara*."

Her mouth fell open, and then she sat up and yanked his pillow out from under his head and smacked him in the face with it. "Oh, you . . . you . . . *man*."

He shouted with laughter, then pounced on her and rolled her underneath him. "I want to wake up looking at your lovely face every day for the rest of my life."

He kissed her, claiming her mouth until she was breathless. She wrapped her arms around his neck, returning his kisses enthusiastically, but when he stopped she mock-growled at him.

"I'm not so sure I'm going to put up with your version of humor for that long," she said, laughing. "You scared me to death."

He instantly sobered. "I am so sorry. I had no intention—"

"It's okay," she said, grinning. "I promise to get you back."

"The curse is finally broken," he said, in little more than a whisper, somehow afraid Poseidon would hear and change his mind.

"Are you sure? Forever?"

"I have no way to know. We will have to live our lives, one day at a time, and discover the truth upon each wakening."

She turned in his arms and smiled up at him, inviting him, and he slowly, carefully, entered her body with his own, taking his time as they moved together, rocking in a bliss deeper than lust, deeper than want or hunger. Waves of warmth and contentment washed over him, and the look on her face mirrored his own. He whispered her name when they drifted over the edge of the abyss together, promising never, ever to leave her side.

Chapter 48

Two days later, the palace gardens, Atlantis

Tiernan wandered through the most beautiful garden she'd ever seen outside of a dream, and laughed out loud with joy. A pair of peacocks tilted their heads in identical motions at the sound and then strolled off, intent on important peacock business, no doubt. Birds she didn't recognize sang songs that seemed to be especially for her. She was walking in a miniature paradise, and much of the reason the world was so perfect was currently sprawled on a bench, basking in the magically created sunlight.

"You are a lazy man," she said, stopping to brush the silky hair away from his forehead.

Brennan opened one eye. "If you hadn't wearied me to the point of exhaustion with your insatiable sexual demands, I might have energy to join you while you explore the gardens."

In spite of the fact that this man had had his hands, his mouth, or both, on every inch of her body over the past couple of days, a hot blush rose into her cheeks. "Hush. Somebody might hear you."

"No one will disturb us here," he said, opening the other eye and smiling at her. "They know better."

"Well, get up and walk around with me, then. I want to see everything."

He groaned and made a show of heaving himself up off the bench, but he was still smiling. Warmth and desire and happiness swirled through her in an effervescent mixture until she thought her head might pop like a champagne cork.

He held out his hand, and she took it and pulled him down one of the paths, toward the intriguing sounds of bells and water. "What's down here?"

"One of many, many fountains. This one is an idyllic representation of Poseidon at play," he said. A shadow crossed his face, but only for an instant.

She slowed her steps, suddenly reluctant to face a reminder of the curse they were still afraid might come back someday. "Maybe we should go another way."

"It's only a fountain. We can't be afraid of our own shadows. It's lovely, besides. You should see it." Brennan pulled her gently forward, and they stepped into a clearing. The fountain was enormous; her first impression was that Poseidon was big enough to drown the entire world.

But then reason replaced fancy, and the statue was once again only a statue, made of marble and stone. Poseidon reclined on his side, surrounded by several nymphs who held various delicacies out to him.

"Looks like a pretty hedonistic guy," she observed. "Doesn't quite seem fair that he'd punish you for youthful indiscretions."

Brennan's smile faded. "He is a god, capricious but all-powerful. He does what he will with his warriors."

Tiernan suddenly shivered, and goose bumps climbed up her arms. "My mom would say that a goose walked over my grave," she said, trying to laugh.

"Oh, no," Brennan said.

"It's just a saying—an old wives' tale thing. It doesn't mean—" She stopped talking and her mouth fell open as she realized why Brennan had said *oh, no.*

The statue was no longer merely a statue. Its marble eyes rolled in their sockets and its head turned until the statue was staring at Brennan and Tiernan.

Brennan knelt instantly.

The statue opened its mouth, and Tiernan stumbled backward in shock, losing her balance. Brennan caught her arm and pulled her down to kneel beside him.

SHE IS NOT DEAD. DID YOU BELIEVE YOU COULD FOOL A GOD? the statue thundered, as it ripped its marble body free of the base of the fountain and stood, looming over them. Beside it, the nymphs came to life and began to dance.

"Oh, this is so far down the rabbit hole," Tiernan murmured, as reality fractured right in front of her eyes.

"She did die, my lord, and her soul had flown, fulfilling the terms of the curse," Brennan said, his voice ringing out pure and strong. "I humbly submit that you accept my deepest, most sincere apologies for my transgressions and sins."

DO YOU DESERVE FORGIVENESS? Poseidon, for it couldn't be anybody else, roared.

Tiernan's eyes narrowed. "Wait just a minute, sir. Don't you think he has suffered enough? Two thousand years? Really? For something that was at least as much her fault as his?"

Poseidon raised a marble arm and pointed at her. *YOU DARE TO QUESTION A GOD?*

The sense of power gathering in the air strengthened, and she had a moment to wonder if he was going to hurl a lightning bolt or his trident or one of the nymphs at her. A marble nymph could probably do a lot of damage.

Brennan leapt up and threw himself in front of Tiernan. "My life for hers. My existence is nothing without her, so if you must punish me, do so by taking my life, my lord."

Poseidon grabbed marble grapes from a marble plate and hurled them at Brennan. *DO YOU GIVE ME COMMANDS, WARRIOR?*

Brennan stood, unflinching, as the grapes whizzed past, missing his head by inches, and hit the tree behind them so hard that they burrowed into the trunk.

"I apologize for my insolence, my lord, but I repeat my request. Spare this woman, please."

Tiernan jumped up and stood next to Brennan, planting her fists on her hips and trying to ignore the pounding of her heart in her chest. "He has served you and protected humanity for longer than anybody else. This is so unfair. We fulfilled the curse. I died. Isn't that enough for you?"

Poseidon leaned down, far down, until his enormous head was almost on a level with hers, intimidating the heck out of her, but the expression on his marble features seemed to be more amused than angry.

WILL YOU STAND FOR HIM AND WITH HIM, FOR ALL THE DAYS OF YOUR LIFE?

It sounded like a vow. Tiernan didn't hesitate for even a heartbeat. "Yes, for as long as I live, even though my life is nothing but a drop in your ocean compared to his."

Poseidon turned his marble head from her to Brennan and then back, then he straightened to the statue's full height and pointed his trident at her. A bolt of pure shimmering silver light streamed out of the tip of the trident and smashed into her, knocking her into the ground and shattering her with pain worse than anything she'd ever felt in her life. She screamed, writhing on the ground, and Brennan pulled her into his arms, tears streaming down his face.

"No," he shouted. "Not her. Me. Take me."

But Poseidon merely smiled and, finally, after what felt like years to Tiernan, lowered his trident. The pain vanished instantly, and Tiernan raised her head to look around, her vision blurred by tears.

She tested her various limbs, grateful to find them whole and in working order. "I'm okay," she said, reassuring Brennan. "It doesn't hurt anymore."

Poseidon slammed the shaft of the trident against the stone base of the fountain three times.

SO BE IT. JUSTICE DECREES THAT BRENNAN SHOULD KNOW JOY FOR AS LONG AS HE HAS BEEN DEPRIVED OF IT.

The sea god flashed a bizarre smile filled with shiny marble teeth.

OF COURSE, IF YOU ARE LIKE MOST OF YOUR FAIR SEX, YOU WILL SOON CAUSE HIM TO WISH THAT ETERNITY WERE MUCH SHORTER.

Tiernan laughed. She couldn't help it. A god had just fried her with his mythical trident and then cracked a lame joke. Talk about down the rabbit hole.

Poseidon nodded.

YOU WILL DO, HUMAN. I ADMIRE YOUR COUR-AGE, AND IT SAYS MUCH, TO BE ADMIRED BY A GOD. YOUR CHILDREN, TOO, WILL BECOME PART OF THE PROPHECY.

Brennan's arms tightened around Tiernan. "Children?"

NOT YET. SOME YEARS FROM NOW, WHEN YOUR SONS ARE NEEDED.

"Sons?" Tiernan repeated. "How many sons?"

TWINS, I THINK. PERHAPS TRIPLETS. STRAPPING BOYS.

Tiernan swallowed, hard. "But—"

I HAVE NO TIME FOR THIS. Poseidon pointed a finger at Brennan. *DO NOT MAKE ME REGRET MY GENEROSITY.*

Brennan bowed deeply. "My lord, I am yours, and I thank you with everything that I am."

OF COURSE YOU DO. DON'T SCREW THIS UP.

Tiernan's mouth dropped open at the sound of slang coming from an ancient god, but before she could find any words, Poseidon and the nymphs were gone in a burst of fireworks and cascading water.

Silently, she and Brennan stared at the fountain, empty now of statues and all but a few drops of water.

"I . . . I . . ." Tiernan stopped, unable to think of what to say. "We're going to have a hard time explaining this to Conlan and the gang." She pointed at the fountain-less fountain.

Brennan sighed. "Unfortunately, this sort of thing happens around here a lot more than you might think."

Tiernan suddenly lost interest in the fountain. "I'm going to have twins? Or triplets?" Her legs lost their strength, and she collapsed down on the edge of the empty fountain.

"Perhaps we could begin at the beginning," Brennan said, kneeling before her. "Tiernan Butler, will you wed me and live out the rest of eternity as my bride and the mother of my children?"

She stared at him, stunned.

He took her hand and smiled at her, but his eyebrows drew together. "Tiernan, your silence is worrying me more than I care to admit right now."

She laughed and threw herself at him, knocking him over into the grass. "Yes, yes, a thousand times yes."

She kissed every inch of his face, lingering on his lips, and then she sat up, straddling him, and pulled her shirt over her head. "Just how private is this garden?"

Brennan's dangerously sexy smile spread across his face. "Private enough."

Epilogue

Yellowstone National Park, Wolf Pack Ceremonial Grounds, five days later

Brennan looked at the circle of people ringing the fire. Shifters, humans, and Atlanteans. Even a vampire. He nodded to Daniel, who kept back and a little apart from the rest.

Conlan and Riley held little Prince Aidan. Near them, Alexios and Grace stood in a place of honor, each of them holding one of Lucas and Honey's twins. Ven and Erin huddled together on Tiernan's far side. Erin was in deep mourning for the loss of her sister, but had insisted on attending the naming ceremony, saying they all needed to see hope and life, instead of just death and battle. Apparently whatever mission Conlan had sent them on in Europe had not gone well.

They had all attended Deirdre's memorial service the day before, and Erin's grief was still very fresh. It was part of the great circle of life, death, and love. Brennan had experienced so much of the first two but never had dared hope for the third over the course of his millennia-long life. He pulled Tiernan closer, yet again silently giving thanks for the gift of her presence in his life.

Lucas stepped forward, holding his mate's hand, and everyone quieted. "We thank you for sharing our joy during this sacred ceremony of naming, a tradition in our Pack since the beginning of recorded history."

Honey raised their joined hands. "As we pledged our lives to each other, we pledge our lives and our sons' lives to this alliance between our peoples and to the quest to bring all of us together in harmony, for now and forever."

Lucas nodded at Tiernan. "Your newspaper series about Litton and his schemes with the vampires has placed enormous pressure on Washington to take action. Already, many members of the Primus have been forced to resign."

Next, he nodded at Daniel. "Your accession to Primator gives us great hope."

Daniel bowed elegantly. "I will do my best not to let you down."

Grace and Alexios handed the babies to Lucas and Honey, who held them up in the air.

"I name you Lucas Alexios and Nathan Brennan," Lucas proclaimed, his voice ringing clear and loud. "May you be spokes in the wheel of peace that rules our planet for centuries to come."

Brennan met Alexios's stunned gaze across the fire.

Did you know? he sent on the mental pathway.

Alexios shook his head. He hadn't known, either.

Brennan bowed, his heart full. "I am honored beyond the telling of it. May the waters of your ancestors bless and nourish your boys for every day of their lives and every step of their paths, both as human and as wolf."

Alexios bowed and uttered a similar sentiment, but Brennan didn't hear it, because Tiernan whispered in his ear, "Nice job, Uncle Brennan."

He grinned. "Uncle now, father soon. Should we start thinking of names? Lots and lots of names?"

"Let me at least finish my series of articles before we think about babies," she said, looking a little pale.

"*Mi amara*, you'll probably get a Pulitzer for this," he said, knowing she had always dreamed of the prestigious prize.

"Maybe," she said, shrugging. "It doesn't matter as much to me anymore. Dying gives a girl a different perspective on life." As everyone around the fire cheered for the babies, Tiernan pulled Brennan's face down to hers and kissed him thoroughly. "I have all I need right here."

Brennan thought his heart might burst from his chest, it was filled with so much joy. He pulled her into his arms, rejoicing in the wonder of standing shoulder to shoulder with a circle of allies and friends.

The babies chose that moment to wake up and start crying for milk, and everyone laughed, but then a large rustling shook the underbrush back away from the clearing and all the shifters tensed. Seconds later, an enormous tiger leapt from between the trees and strolled up to the fire, transforming as he walked.

"Man, I love this place," Jack said, now fully human and fully dressed. "Startled the hell out of some buffalo, though."

"Bison," Tiernan and Brennan said in unison.

Everybody laughed again.

Suddenly, a shimmering spiral of green and golden light appeared in the center of the fire, and it resolved itself into a man. A Fae prince to be precise. Rhys na Garanwyn, high prince of the High Court Seelie Fae. "I am here, you can proceed," he drawled, impossibly arrogant as always.

He bowed to Lucas and Honey, and then again, deeper, to Conlan and Riley.

Lucas smiled. "Be welcome, Prince of the Fae. The future of our world will depend upon cooperation between all men and women of like mind, regardless of race or species. We will do all within our power to ensure that our children will grow up in that world."

"As will we for our son," Conlan declared.

"We, too, for our child," Alexios said, one hand on Grace's belly.

Everyone spontaneously cheered, and there, by the fire, for that little time, they all had hope that battle and war would soon be done and peace would, finally, reign.

"Our triplets, as well," Brennan murmured to Tiernan, under cover of the cheering. She smiled, content to keep that prediction safely between the two of them for a while longer.

Several of Lucas's Pack members poured champagne for everyone and they all raised their glasses. Brennan offered the first toast. "To the shining hope of the next generation, as the wheel of time turns and peace again rules the world. May we live to see it."

They all drank to that, and to many other toasts, and then the gathering broke up into small groups of conversation. Brennan steered Tiernan away from the fire and found a quiet corner among the trees in the moonlight.

"A future together in a better world that we will help create," she said. "No matter what it takes."

"We have each other," Brennan replied. "There is nothing more that I need to face eternity."

"We have each other," she agreed.

He grinned and put a hand on her belly. "And the triplets," he reminded her.

She put her arms around his neck and smiled that sexy smile, full of feminine intrigue and mystery. "Shut up and kiss me."

So he did.

Turn the page for
a special preview of the next book
in the Warriors of Poseidon series

ATLANTIS BETRAYED

By Alyssa Day

Present day: London, England

Jack the Ripper must have been a vampire.

Christophe sat on the tiny ledge underneath the minute hand on Big Ben's western face—twenty-five past midnight—thinking random thoughts and surveying the city that had always been like a second home to him. The clock tower was arguably London's most recognizable landmark, and something about perching on it, nearly three hundred feet off the ground, made Christophe feel like the master of all he surveyed. He sat with his back against the familiar gilt lettering, DOMINE SALVAM FAC REGINAM NOSTRAM VICTORIAM PRIMAM, and wondered if Queen Victoria the First had been honored to have each of the four clock faces proclaim that her people called out to their god to keep her safe.

A bitter laugh escaped him at the idea that Poseidon would ever worry about keeping *him* safe. Centuries of fighting had taught Christophe the bloody and painful lesson that the sea god didn't care much about keeping his Atlantean warriors anything but honed for battle. Throwing them to the wolves and the other shifters, sure. Using them as cannon fodder against the vampires, no problem. Eleven thousand years after the original pact, the current members of the elite Atlantean fighting force were still fulfilling their sacred duty to protect humanity.

Humanity should protect its own damn self.

Not that it could, or had ever been able to, against the dark and ugly that crawled out of the night. Since the monsters revealed themselves to humans more than a decade ago, the stupid humans had done more and more to offer themselves up on the proverbial silver platter, like the sheep the vamps called them. Christophe had suggested a few times that the warriors change their mission from protecting humans to rounding them up, stuffing apples in their mouths, and then jamming sticks up their asses.

Human-kabobs. Simple, easy, and everybody goes home happy.

The high prince wasn't exactly down with the idea. Christophe "wasn't a team player." "Had a chip on his shoulder." Insert social worker psychobabble here. Conlan's new human wife had the prince by the balls and Princess Riley was all about kindness and understanding.

Which sucked.

Christophe would have preferred that Conlan just haul off and punch him in the face, like the prince used to do in the old days when somebody pissed him off. It would have been far less painful.

"Less painful than smelling your stench, for example," he said to the vampire who was floating up the side of the tower, probably trying to surprise him.

"Interesting place to hang out, mate." The vamp levitated up until he was eye level with Christophe. "Got a death wish?"

Christophe scanned the vamp, his gaze raking it from spiky blue hair to steel-toed boots. He blamed London's punk rock scene.

"You threatening me?"

The vamp shrugged. "Just pointing out that you're pretty far up for a breakable human."

Christophe bared his teeth in what passed for a smile with him these days, and the vamp flinched a little. "Not human. Not breakable."

Holding his hands up in a placating gesture, Punker Boy floated back and away from him. "Got no beef with you. Just surprised to see somebody in my spot."

"You're Queen Victoria, then?"

The vampire laughed and, surprisingly, seemed to be genuinely amused. "Know your Latin, do you?"

It was Christophe's turn to shrug. "I get by." But then an inconvenient twinge of duty nagged at him, and he sighed. "You planning to kill any humanity tonight?"

"Any humanity?" The vamp floated closer, his eyebrows drawing together as he studied Christophe. "What are you talking about?"

Christophe dropped his daggers from their arm sheaths into his hands and balanced them, not taking his gaze from the vamp. "Duty, sacred oath, blah blah blah. If you're planning to kill any humans, I need to end you."

"I'd be stupid to say yes, then, wouldn't I?" The vamp's voice held genuine curiosity, and not a little wariness.

"Stupid. Vampire." Christophe shrugged again. "Yeah, those words have gone together a time or two."

"No."

"No?"

The vamp eyed the daggers. "No, I'm not planning to kill anybody tonight. Or ever, for that matter. Who needs all the trauma, with synth blood and donors?"

Christophe judged the vamp to be sincere enough. He considered killing him anyway, just for something to do, but didn't really feel like chasing his daggers all the way down after they'd sliced the vamp's head off. Especially since his night wasn't over—he still had to go steal one of the crown jewels from the Tower of London.

He slid the blades into their sheaths and shot a considering stare at the bloodsucker. "So. Here's a question. Was Jack the Ripper a vampire?"

~~~~~

Campbell's Hunt Manor, an hour outside of London

Fiona Campbell pulled the scarlet leggings up over her legs and then fastened her belt into place. So important to have the right accessories these days, although no fashion magazine would ever feature her handworked leather tool belt on its up-and-coming-trends page. A memory flashed into her mind, though, as her fingers checked the snap on one tiny pocket that held her backup switchblade, and she laughed. Her assistant, Madeleine, had rushed into Fiona's office just last week, waving a glossy magazine in the air. *Vogue UK* had done a spread on the new color for spring: bright crimson red.

The Scarlet Ninja was setting fashion trends.

"Sorry, Dad," she murmured, glancing out the window into the uncharacteristically clear night sky. Spring weather was wet, wet, and more wet, but she'd planned this little outing for the one night this week that the meteorologists had promised to be dry. So unpleasant to plan impossible heists in the pouring rain, after all.

The expected knock came and she heaved a sigh. "I'm not decent, Hopkins, please go away."

The door opened and the man who was the nearest thing to a grandfather she'd ever had walked in, carrying a tray. "I prefer indecency in both women and foreign films. Chocolate?"

Fiona sighed again and tried not to grit her teeth at the sight of his perfectly combed silver hair and his perfectly proper black suit. It was after midnight, for Heaven's sake. "I don't have time for chocolate. And I'm not a little girl anymore, whom you must coddle out of her nightmares. You should be in bed, wearing your lovely pajamas that

Madeleine gave you for your birthday. You look like a butler, Hopkins."

"I am a butler, Lady Fiona," he responded, exactly as he had a billion or so times since they'd started this verbal dance more than twenty years ago when her father died. "I was your father's butler, may he rest in peace, and before that your grandfather's butler, may God rot his vicious soul."

"You're not supposed to speak ill of the dead."

"I said far worse when he was still alive," he said dryly, raising one silver eyebrow. He whipped the cover off the silver pot of chocolate and the aroma teased her senses. "Furthermore, should you ever catch me wearing silk pajamas decorated with tiny barnyard animals, please feel free to commit me to a home for the senile."

"They're sheep, Hopkins." She clamped her lips together to keep the laugh from escaping. "You know, for counting sheep? It's a sort of joke. Also, when will you drop the 'Lady' and start calling me Fiona?"

"Undoubtedly at the same time I begin wearing the barnyard animal night clothes." He poured the rich chocolate into a delicate china cup and handed it to her.

Fiona took the chocolate. It was just easier to go along on the little things. "She means well."

"Faint praise, indeed," he pointed out. His brilliantly blue eyes sparkled with amusement, though, and she wasn't fooled. She'd caught him bringing chocolate to Madeleine just that morning.

"Down to business, Lady Fiona. Do you have your untraceable phone?"

"Always."

"Is it charged? When you broke into the British Museum—"

"How long are you going to hold that against me? I came out of that with an entire collection of jade figurines, including Tlaloc." She pulled out the top drawer of the Louis XIV bureau until the faint depression in the wood bottom of the drawer was in sight. A muffled click signaled the opening of the hidden compartment, and she removed one of her scarlet hooded masks and a single glossy silver card.

"Yes, Tlaloc. The rain god. The wettest autumn in recorded history after you brought that home, if I recall. Thank you *so* much. We certainly needed more rain on our property," Hopkins managed to say with a straight face. "A clean handkerchief?"

She froze, slowly turning her head to stare at him. "A clean handkerchief? Are you actually making a joke, Hopkins?"

He carefully folded her unused cloth napkin, its white linen folds as spotless as the gloves he still insisted on wearing, before he looked up and met her gaze. "I never joke. If an employer of mine is planning to steal one of the most famous gems in history from the Tower of London itself—which is, mind you, absolutely burglar-proof—then by queen and country she *will* have a clean handkerchief."

Fiona stared at the spots of color flaming on his cheekbones and realized she'd been a fool. She'd spent all of her time worrying about the logistics of the job and no time at all concerned with the people who cared about her. She dropped her mask and the card on the table next to the chocolate and walked over to him.

"I'm not stealing anything tonight. This is just an exploratory expedition, you daft old man. Now, give me a hug."

She thought for a moment that he was actually going to refuse, but finally he sighed and embraced her, patting her back as he'd done when she was a child restless with the burdens of position and, later, tragedy.

He quickly released her and handed her the mask, which she tucked into her belt, and then the card.

"Do you really want to leave your calling card before you take the Siren? They'll throw everything they have to prevent you coming back, after you made Scotland Yard look like fools the last time."

She shrugged, glancing down at the silver-gilt card with

the tiny figure of a scarlet ninja embossed in its exact center. "It's only sporting, isn't it?"

"Sporting might get you killed. Or sent to prison for a very long time."

"Not tonight. This is just a scouting trip." She shouldered her small pack and grinned up at him.

"After all, how dangerous can it be?"